W9-AYP-680

DISCARD

INNOCENT BLOOD

INNOCENT BLOOD

Graham Masterton

This first world edition published in Great Britain 2005 by
SEVERN HOUSE PUBLISHERS LTD of
9–15 High Street, Sutton, Surrey SM1 1DF.
This first world edition published in the USA 2005 by
SEVERN HOUSE PUBLISHERS INC of
595 Madison Avenue, New York, N.Y. 10022.

British Library Cataloguing in Publication Data

Masterton, Graham
    Innocent blood
    1.   Motion picture industry - California - Los Angeles - Fiction
    2.   Hollywood (Los Angeles, Calif.) - Fiction
    3.   Horror tales
    I.   Title
    823.9'14 [F]

    ISBN 0-7278-6189-1 (cased)
    ISBN 0-7278-9136-7 (paper)

Typeset by Palimpsest Book Production Ltd.,
Polmont, Stirlingshire, Scotland.
Printed and bound in Great Britain by
MPG Books Ltd., Bodmin, Cornwall.

Wednesday, September 22, 8:34 A.M.

As usual, the school gateway was jammed with mothers awkwardly trying to maneuver their oversized SUVs in and out, so Lynn steered her Explorer over to the opposite side of the street and parked it with two wheels mounted on the grass.

'Remember it's your dance class today,' she told Kathy, turning around in her seat. 'That means no dawdling after school, OK?'

'I don't *feel* good,' Kathy protested, flopping in her seat.

'Nonsense. I've never seen you look healthier. Just because you have a math test.'

'I think I'm going to barf. I *know* I'm going to barf. I can feel all of those mushed-up pancakes in my tummy, and they don't *like* it down there.'

Lynn snapped her seat-belt buckle back into place. 'OK, then. If you feel so bad, I'll just have to take you back home to bed and cancel your dance class.'

'Not my dance class! That's not till three thirty! I'll be better by then!'

'No, I'll have to cancel it. You can't jeté with a tummy full of mutinous pancakes.'

'But I want to be an actress like you. Why do I have to learn math? You don't have to know math to be an actress, do you?'

'You don't think so? Supposing you're an actress and you make squillions and squillions of dollars like Julia Roberts and your agent takes three and a quarter percent more than he's supposed to? How are you going to know?'

1

'Because *all* agents take more than they're supposed to. Agents are chiselers and shysters and they all work for Satan.'

'Oh for goodness' sake! Who told you that?'

'You did.'

'Come on,' said Lynn, unbuckling her seat belt again. 'Let's get you into school before Ms Redmond gives you another demerit for being late.'

Kathy climbed out and tugged on her beret. She was a small girl for ten years old, with blonde braids and a pale, elfin face like her mother's. Her eyes were that same luminous green as her mother's, too, like pieces of a glass bottle found on the seashore. Her legs were so skinny that she kept having to pull up her long white socks.

'What do you want to do after your dance class? We could go to De Lunghi's for spaghetti if you like.'

'So long as Gene doesn't have to come with us.'

'I thought you *liked* Gene.'

'I don't like his nose. He looks like an anteater.'

'He does not. You're just being obnoxious.'

'He does too. Every time he has soup the end of his nose dips right into it.'

They crossed Franklin Avenue to the school gates. The Cedars private elementary school didn't look like a school at all: although it had no religious affiliations, it shared the First Methodist Church building, with its tall square tower and its gray stone walls, and several of the classrooms, even though they were large and airy, had stained-glass windows, with scenes of Christ surrounded by little children.

'You won't forget to bring home your hockey kit, will you?' asked Lynn. But at that moment Kathy caught sight of her friend Terra, and waved, and jumped, and immediately skipped off. Terra's mother, Sidne, came up to Lynn and the two of them watched their daughters run through the school gates and into the yard, where thirty or forty other children were jumping and screaming and tearing around in circles.

'Some tummy ache,' said Lynn.

'Oh, the math test,' smiled Sidne. 'Terra said she had leprosy.'

'*Leprosy?*'

2

'That's right. On the spur of the moment, it was the only illness she could think of. At least it shows she's reading her Bible.'

'They really kill you sometimes, don't they? I love Terra's braids.'

'Janie did them. I don't know how she has the patience.'

They walked back to Sidne's car together. 'Did you hear from George Lowenstein?' Lynn asked her.

'No, nothing. If you want to know the truth, I think he's looking for somebody younger.'

'But you'd be *perfect* as Corinne, you know you would!'

'I don't know. Maybe. I used to wonder when I would have to stop playing wayward daughters and start to play harassed mothers, and maybe it's now. I think I'll go to Miska's and have a massage and a pedicure. And then I'll go to Freddie's and order a treble strawberry sundae with extra cream.'

'I'd join you, believe me, if we didn't have a read-through.'

Lynn said goodbye to Sidne and crossed the street. A short, crop-haired man with a neck like a stovepipe and a maroon polyester shirt was waiting beside her Explorer. His face was the same maroon as his shirt, and beaded with sweat.

'What the fuck do you call this?' he demanded.

'What the fuck do I call what?' Lynn didn't want to show that she was the slightest bit afraid of him.

'What, you're blind? Where's your goddamned guide dog? You parked on the goddamned grass, for Christ's sake.'

'Well, I'm sorry, but there was no parking space anyplace else.'

'Oh, and you think that's some kind of excuse? If there was no parking space anyplace else you should've gone around the block again until there *was*. You're all the same, you women. You think you can *do* whatever you damn well like and *say* whatever you damn well like and *park* wherever you damn well like and you don't give squat for nobody else.'

Lynn opened the Explorer's door and climbed into the driver's seat, but the man clung on to the door to prevent her from closing it.

'Listen, lady, I don't even have to take care of this piece of grass, but I do, because it's outside of my house and I'm proud of my house, and then somebody like you comes along and drives their goddamned vehicle all over it. How would you like it if I came around to your house and drove my goddamned vehicle all over *your* goddamned grass?'

'I think you'd better take your hands off my door,' said Lynn.

'And what if I don't?'

'I'll call for the school security guard, that's what.' All the same, her heart was thumping wildly. The man had a large maroon wart on the left side of his nose and she couldn't stop looking at it and she was convinced that he *knew* she was looking at it.

He turned his head around for a moment, as if he were looking for somebody, and wiped the sweat from his forehead with the back of his hand. Then he turned back to Lynn and said, 'OK. I'll tell you what *I'm* going to do. I'm going to curse you for this. I'm going to wish on you the shittiest day that you ever experienced in your entire life.'

He took his hands off the door. Lynn immediately slammed it and locked it. He stood beside the Explorer, not saying anything more, but he lifted his finger and pointed it at her as if to say, *you mark my words, lady, you're going to remember this day for ever.*

Wednesday, September 22, 8:43 A.M.

Ann Redmond looked out of the window of her study and frowned. A group of children had gathered around the bench on the far side of the schoolyard, ten or twelve of them at least, and she was experienced enough in grade school crowd patterns to see at once that they were *huddling*.

Huddling was what children did when there was something exciting to look at and they didn't want the teachers to see what it was. As far as Ms Redmond was concerned, they might just as well have raised a placard announcing WE ARE BEING NAUGHTY. She took off her half-glasses, marched out of her study, and went out on to the front steps where Lilian Bushmeyer, the physical education teacher, was sitting on the wall and supervising the schoolyard by reading a dog-eared copy of *The Bridges of Madison County*.

4

'Over there, Ms Bushmeyer,' she said curtly, nodding her head.

Lilian Bushmeyer shaded her eyes and peered across the asphalt. After a while she shook her head and said, 'I don't see anything.'

'Conspiratorial body language,' said Ms Redmond impatiently. 'Go and see what they're up to.'

Lilian Bushmeyer reluctantly put down her book and plodded across in her Birkenstocks to see what all the fuss was about. As she came closer, she could hear the children giggling and squealing, and then suddenly there was a flustered '*Shh! Shh! It's Bush Baby. Put it away!*' Some of the children broke away from the huddle, leaving a small knot of girls right in the middle. Lilian Bushmeyer walked right up to them and held out her hand.

'What?' asked Jade Peller. She had just turned eleven, and she was taller and more mature than most of the girls in the sixth grade. She had long black hair, a thin pale face, and she always dressed in black, with silver bangles around her wrists. Her father was Oliver Peller, who had written music for Wes Craven and John Carpenter.

'Whatever it is, give it to me,' said Lilian Bushmeyer.

'It's nothing.'

'Well it's obviously a very interesting nothing. Hand it over.'

'It's only a stupid *game*, Ms Bushmeyer,' complained Helen Fairfax. She was plump and pink-cheeked but she had a mass of curly blonde hair and it was obvious that once she had lost her puppy fat she was going to grow up as stunning as her mother, Juliana. Her father, Greg, was one of Hollywood's most talked-about independent producers and had recently bankrolled the stalker movie, *Breather*.

Lilian Bushmeyer waited patiently, her hand still held out. Maybe she hadn't yet developed Ms Redmond's radar for subversive crowd formations, but she knew how to deal with the spoiled children of minor celebrities. You had to act resolutely unimpressed, which Lilian Bushmeyer genuinely was.

At last, Jade produced a crown-shaped piece of paper from

5

behind her back, and handed it over. It was nothing more than one of those fortune-telling devices, with the paper folded into triangles, and a fortune written on each of them. Except that the fortunes on this device were much stronger than the usual 'you will be lucky in love' or 'you will be rich and famous' or 'you will go to jail.'

One of them read 'you will suck Mr Lomax's cock.' Another said 'you will lose both your legs in an auto accident.' A third predicted 'you will get pregnant at thirteen.'

'Like Helen said, it's only a game,' Jade protested as Lilian Bushmeyer opened each triangle in turn. The last prediction was 'you will die before your next birthday.'

When she had finished, Lilian Bushmeyer looked at the children one after the other. It was obvious that three or four of them were really embarrassed and ashamed, and it seemed that the boys went pinker than the girls.

'Do you want me to show this to Ms Redmond?' she asked.

'Sure,' said Jade. 'Might give her a thrill.'

'No!' gasped David Ritter. 'She'll *kill* us. I know my mom will kill me. My stepmom will kill me, too.'

Lilian Bushmeyer said, 'I know that you probably didn't mean any real harm, but you know what this is? It's tasteless, and there's little enough taste left in this world without you young people making things worse. Supposing one of you *did* lose your legs, or *did* get pregnant, or *did* get sexually abused? How would you feel then?'

'I'd feel like my fortune-telling really works.' Jade grinned.

'So which one did *you* pick?' Lilian Bushmeyer asked her.

'Die before my next birthday.'

'And do you want that to happen, just to prove you right?'

'I don't care. Like, what's death? It's only like not being born.'

Wednesday, September 22, 9:03 A.M.

Ms Redmond stood up in assembly and the sun shone on her glasses so that she looked as if she were blind.

'As usual, October brings our first great event of the year – the all-school camp-out. This year we will all be going to

6

Silverwood Lake in the beautiful San Bernardino Mountains. Over the weekend, students and parents will get to know one another by camp-fire singing and storytelling, pot-luck dinners, hiking, swimming and picnics. This is a wonderful way for new families to join the Cedars community. At the end of October, we will be holding our first fund-raising event, which this year is going to be a Latin fiesta.'

'*Arriba! Arriba!*' called out Tony Perlman, the geography teacher, and then looked deeply embarrassed.

Wednesday, September 22, 9:06 A.M.

A tractor-trailer had jackknifed right across the off-ramp from the Hollywood Freeway, causing a southbound tailback of glittering cars as far as Ventura Boulevard. Frank shifted the Buick into neutral and pressed down the parking brake.

'I'm going to be *late*,' Danny protested.

'Sorry, champ, there's nothing I can do. I'm going to be late, too, and I have a script meeting.'

'I'm *paint* monitor, I'm supposed to put out the *paints*.'

'Don't worry, I'll tell your teacher what happened.'

Danny frowned furiously out of the window, as if the traffic could be willed to get moving just by glaring at it. But they had to sit and wait for over twenty minutes while highway patrolmen stood around in their mirror sunglasses and chatted to each other and yawned, and drivers climbed out of their automobiles to use their cellphones and stretch their legs, and one woman even took a folding chair out of the back of her station wagon and sat reading the paper as if she were sitting in her own back yard.

'I bet Susan Capelli is putting out the paints,' said Danny, as if he were suffering the greatest personal tragedy since Hamlet.

'You can do it next time, can't you?'

'You have to be *reliable* when you're a monitor.'

Frank shook his head and said nothing. Danny always amused him because he was so serious about everything. He may have been a tufty-haired eight-year-old kid with freckles and a snubby nose and scabs on his knees, but he had the

7

mind of a forty-eight-year-old man. He said he wanted to be a real-estate developer when he grew up, building low-cost housing in some of Hollywood's most expensive enclaves, so that poor people and rich people could learn to get along. Like, for an eight-year-old, how serious was *that*?

'Is it Ms Pulaski I have to talk to?' Frank asked him.

'You don't have to. I can tell her myself.'

Another five minutes passed before a huge green and silver tow truck came grinding up the hard shoulder, and after a further ten minutes of gesticulating between the police and the tow truck guys, the tractor-trailer was finally chained up and dragged clear of the off-ramp.

'*Stupid* truck,' said Danny venomously, as they drove past it and down the off-ramp.

'It was an accident, Danny, that's all. Accidents happen.'

'Not if people were more reliable.'

Traffic was slow all the way along Hollywood Boulevard, and Danny gave a theatrical groan at every red signal, but eventually they reached La Brea and turned right toward Franklin Avenue.

Frank said, 'Remind me what time you finish school today. You don't have drama rehearsals, do you?'

Danny had been picked to play Abraham Lincoln in the school play, *Heroes and Heroines of America*. He had been bitterly disappointed that he hadn't been given the part of John Wilkes Booth, since John Wilkes Booth got to fire a gun and jump off the stage.

'That's tomorrow,' Danny replied.

Frank parked the car outside the school and Danny scrambled out. 'See you later then, champ. Have a good day.'

Danny ran toward the school gates, swinging his X-Men satchel like a propeller. Frank turned around to check the back seat and saw that, in his hurry, Danny had left his sandwiches behind. Danny suffered from a nut allergy, so he always had to take a home-prepared lunch.

Frank climbed out of the car and shouted, 'Danny! Hey, Danny! You forgot your . . .' He held up his Tupperware box.

Danny skidded to a stop, hesitated, and then began to run

back. As he did so, Frank saw a white van drive through the school gates and stop by Mr Lomax's little glass booth.

Wednesday, September 22, 9:32 A.M.

Kathy had changed into her field hockey kit and joined the shuffling, giggling line at the changing-room door. Eventually Ms Bushmeyer appeared, wearing her cerise and white tracksuit, with her whistle around her neck on a lanyard.

'All right, girls, an orderly line, please! No pushing and shoving!'

'Amanda pulled my braids.'

'I did not! I was nowhere near you!'

They left the church building by the side entrance, still arguing. Kathy and Terra walked on either side of Lilian Bushmeyer. They liked talking to Ms Bushmeyer because she was always telling them that she dreamed about a handsome man with thick black hair and shining white teeth, who would come striding through the school gates one morning, walk straight into assembly, and lift her clean off her feet in front of everybody. Then he would fly her off to a Caribbean island where they would lie on the dazzling white sands all day and drink cocktails out of half coconuts.

'Did you ever have a boyfriend, Ms Bushmeyer?'

'Of course I did. His name was Clark.'

'You mean like Superman?'

Lilian Bushmeyer pushed her frizzy hair into her sweatband. 'Not exactly, Kathy. He sold carpets.'

They were nearly halfway across the parking lot on their way to the playing fields when they saw the white van, too.

Wednesday, September 22, 9:34 A.M.

It was an ordinary white panel van. It had to stop because the school gates were always locked after nine A.M., for the sake of security. There were too many students at The Cedars whose parents may not have been Hollywood A-list, but who were certainly wealthy and well known and who could have been potential targets for kidnap.

9

The van driver tooted his horn and Mr Lomax came out of his booth. Mr Lomax was very tall and loopy, like a basketball player, and he wore a beige uniform with a peaked cap. Lilian Bushmeyer couldn't stop herself from thinking about the 'Mr Lomax' prediction in Jade Peller's fortune-teller, and – to her own embarrassment – found herself blushing. She turned to the chattering crocodile behind her and called out, 'Come along, girls, we don't have all day!'

Mr Lomax opened the gates and the van drove into the parking lot toward them. Lilian Bushmeyer noticed how slowly it was being driven, as if she were watching it in a dream.

'Keep well out of the way, girls!'

The van was almost alongside them now. Lilian Bushmeyer looked at the driver and for some reason he was smiling at her, really smiling, as if today was the happiest day of his whole life. He was unshaven and he was wearing a black woolly hat. There was a woman sitting next to him, wearing dark glasses, but she wasn't smiling at all.

Wednesday, September 22, 9:35 A.M.

Lilian Bushmeyer felt a strange compression in her ears, but she didn't hear anything. The van exploded only ten feet away, blowing off her legs and arms and sending her torso flying through the high stained-glass window of the Zeigler Memorial Library, where nine students were just beginning a class in creative writing. Six of them were killed instantly.

The field hockey team were strewn across the parking lot, so violently torn apart that it looked as if they had been attacked by wild animals.

The van itself was blown into a wild sculptural question mark of twisted paneling. An orange fireball rolled out of it, up into the blue morning sky, and the bang echoed around the canyons like a frightening shout.

Wednesday, September 22, 9:35 A.M.

Even though the van had blown up nearly two hundred feet away, the force of the blast was so powerful that Frank had

10

been hurled against the passenger door of a parked Toyota, denting it into the shape of his body. Danny was thrown face-first on to the sidewalk. The Cedars had completely disappeared behind a huge cloud of black smoke and dust. Leaves had been stripped from the yucca trees all the way along the street and sent whirling up into the air.

Now, through the fog, fragments of metal – nuts, bolts, a windshield wiper, a length of exhaust pipe – began to rain down all around them, clanging and tinkling like a chorus of badly tuned bells. Frank was hit on the shoulder by a tire iron, and then by a stinging shower of ball bearings. He tossed aside Danny's sandwich box, grabbed hold of his arm and hoisted him to his feet. Danny's nose and knees were scratched, but apart from that he seemed to be unhurt.

'Are you OK?' Frank shouted, still deafened.

'My back hurts.'

'What?'

'My back hurts!'

Frank turned him around and around but he couldn't see any sign of injury. No blood, no rips in his jacket. 'Come on,' he said, 'let's get out of here.' He took hold of Danny's hand and pulled him along the street as fast as he could run until they reached their car. He wrenched open the door, bundled Danny into the back seat, and then seized his cellphone.

'Emergency? You're going to have to send everything you've got – fire, police, ambulance, everything. A bomb's gone off at The Cedars school on Franklin Avenue . . . That's right . . . No, no. It's a bomb for sure. People have been killed, I've seen them. Children. I don't know how many.'

'Can you give me your name, sir?'

'Frank. Frank Bell. I was just taking my son to school and *bang*! There were children killed. They're lying all over the parking lot. It's just terrible.'

'OK, sir, please try to stay calm. Are you at a safe distance from the school now?'

'Yes, yes I am, I think. Me and my son.'

'Stay well away until the emergency services arrive. There could be a secondary device. Warn others to stay away, too.'

11

'A secondary device? You mean *another* bomb?'

'Just stay well away, sir, but make yourself known to the police when they reach you.'

'Got you, yes.'

Danny was white. 'Was that a bomb? Was that really a bomb?'

Frank nodded. He was shaking so much that he could hardly speak. 'How do you feel now? Does your back still hurt?'

Danny grimaced and nodded. 'My knees are bleeding.'

Frank reached into the glovebox and found him a Kleenex. He looked back toward The Cedars and saw a thick cloud of gray dust rolling out of the school parking lot and across the street. People were staggering out of it with their hands held out in front of them, like zombies.

'Listen,' he said, 'I have to go back to help. You stay here and call Mommy. Tell her what's happened; tell her we're both OK.'

Danny said, 'You have blood on your face.'

'What?' He touched his forehead and it felt wet. He pulled down his sun visor to look at himself in the mirror. There was a small cut just below his hairline and the blood was sliding down toward his nose. He tugged out another Kleenex and dabbed at it, staring at himself as he did so. Apart from that single minor injury, he looked completely normal. Thin-faced, pale, bespectacled. How could he look so normal when he had just witnessed a bomb going off, and all those children killed?

'Call Mommy, OK?' he said, handing Danny his cellphone. 'She's going to see this on TV and I want her to know that we're safe.'

Wednesday, September 22, 9:41 A.M.

Frank jogged back toward the school. The dust was settling now and gradually the outline of the church building was reappearing. It looked from the street as if the entire front of the library had been demolished, as well as half of the front portico, and every single window was broken. Teachers and children were emerging from the side entrance, most of them bloodied and smothered in dust, all of them walking in a strange hypnotized shuffle, like hermits let out of a cave. Some of them were screaming a high, monotonous scream.

Several people were already sitting on the sidewalk, their faces scorched, their clothing ripped, their eyes staring in shock. A middle-aged woman came limping toward him, holding up her left arm. She wore a brown floral dress and her ginger hair was sticking up in the air as if she had been electrocuted. She had no left hand, only a stump with a white bone sticking out.

'I'm all right,' she reassured him as she approached. 'Don't worry about me. See to the children.'

'Here, sit down,' he told her, and eased her on to the grass with her back against the wheel of a parked car. He yanked off his red and yellow necktie and twisted it around her forearm, knotting it tight. 'Just stay here, ma'am; you're going to be OK. The paramedics will be here in a couple of minutes.'

'It doesn't hurt, you know,' she said, looking at her wrist and turning it this way and that, as if it were quite a novelty. 'It doesn't hurt in the slightest.'

The wrought-iron school gates were still standing but they had been strangely twisted, as if he was looking at them through rippling water. Beside the gates, Mr Lomax's security booth was leaning at an angle, and all the glass had been blown out of the windows. Mr Lomax himself was sitting on his revolving chair, his beige uniform in black tatters, like crow's feathers. There was a large black lump by his left eye, and as Frank moved cautiously closer he realized that it was the head of a claw hammer. The shaft of the hammer had penetrated Mr Lomax's eye socket and it was only the hammer head that had prevented it from going clean through his skull and out the other side.

Frank stood by the security booth, breathless, swimmy-headed, feeling completely helpless. Teachers and children were still milling around outside the side entrance, and he desperately wanted to do something to help them, but he couldn't think what. As for the children lying in the parking lot, they were beyond anything but burial – and prayers.

'Oh shit,' he said. 'Oh shit.' He turned away and his eyes suddenly became crowded with tears.

A girl appeared, close beside him. Her cropped brown hair was ashen with dust, and her jeans and her buttermilk-colored blouse were finely spattered with blood. She was wearing only one sandal.

'Are you OK?' she asked him. She reached out and gently touched his shoulder as if she were trying to make sure that he was real.

'What?' he said, frowning at her. He was still half deaf.

She leaned closer, holding his shoulder more firmly. 'Are you OK?' she asked him. 'You're not hurt, are you?' She had a husky voice, like a heavy smoker.

'I have this ringing in my ears. But otherwise, no, I'm fine.'

'It was a bomb,' she said.

'I know. But I don't know what to do. I called 911 but they said I had to keep away.' He cleared his throat and wiped his eyes with his fingers, leaving wet gray smears down his cheeks. 'Something about a . . . secondary something. Device, bomb.'

'You didn't have a child here, did you?' she asked him.

'My son, he goes here. But we were held up in traffic. Otherwise . . . Jesus. But all those other kids. Oh, God. All those other kids . . .'

'I've lost somebody,' the girl told him. She said it in such a flat tone of voice that he blinked and focused on her more closely. Her irises were rinsed-out blue, almost colorless, and he had the strangest feeling that he had seen her before. More than that – that he actually *knew* her.

'I'm so sorry. Not your child, I hope?'

'No, not a child. Somebody closer than that.'

He looked around. He could hear sirens whooping and racing toward them in the warm morning air. 'Listen, why don't you sit down?' he suggested.

'I'm OK. I just wanted to make sure that *you* were OK.'

'Sure, I'm OK.'

Around the devastated school an unnatural quiet had descended. The yucca leaves were rustling down; the dust was settling. The children had stopped screaming and,

14

although some of them were still sobbing, they were very muted, as if they were afraid to make too much noise.

Wednesday, September 22, 9:44 A.M.

A police car slewed to a halt in front of the school, quickly followed by another, and another. Then two fire trucks came up the street, their lights flashing and their horns blaring like enraged elephants. Next came an ambulance, and two more squad cars, and another ambulance, and another fire truck, and three TV vans. In the space of a few minutes, Franklin Avenue was crowded with emergency vehicles and police and firemen running out hoses.

A police officer with a gingery sweeping-brush moustache came up to Frank and said, 'Did you witness this, sir?'

'I was taking my boy to school . . . We were late.'

'But you saw what happened?'

'There was a white panel van . . . it just exploded. I came back to help but I didn't know what to do.'

'OK, listen. Right now we have to get this situation under control, but we'll need to speak to you later. Give me your name and address and telephone number and somebody will be in touch with you later today.'

Frank reached into his billfold and took out his business card. 'This young lady saw what happened, too.'

The police officer looked around him, left, then right, and then he shrugged in bafflement. Frank turned, and was just in time to see the girl disappearing around the corner of Gardner Street.

'She . . . er . . . she left. She's probably even more shocked than I am.'

'That's OK, sir. Now, if you can leave the area and let the emergency people get on with what they have to do.'

'Of course, yes. Absolutely.'

Frank took one more look across at the school. Paramedics were already stepping through the litter of the fallen children, kneeling down now and again to check if any of them were still alive. The clock in the church steeple chimed the three-quarter hour. Usually this provoked a flutter of California

15

quail, but this time there were none. They had all been frightened far away by the bomb blast.

Frank walked back to his car and climbed in. Danny was still sitting in the back seat, although he looked very pale. Delayed shock, thought Frank. *He* was suffering from shock, too, to the point where he found it difficult to make his lips speak any sense.

'Danny? Did you manage to talk to Mom?'

Danny didn't answer but simply stared at him. He had the strangest expression on his face, as if he were smiling at a private joke.

'Danny? Are you feeling OK?'

Still Danny didn't answer. Frank twisted round in his seat and said, 'Come on, champ. I'll take you home and you can go to bed for the rest of the day.' Danny continued to stare at him. 'Danny? Quit fooling around, Danny, this is too damn serious.'

He climbed out of the car again and opened Danny's door. He reached out for Danny's shoulder and as he did so the boy fell sideways on to the seat. The back of his blazer was soaked dark with blood.

Oh, God, no. Oh, God, not Danny. Frank lifted Danny up and cupped his face in both hands. He was still warm. But his eyes were unfocused and his mouth was hanging open and he wasn't breathing.

Frank felt as if his heart had dropped ten thousand feet. He scooped his hands under Danny's legs and lifted him awkwardly out of the car. There was blood everywhere, all over his shorts, all over his thighs, even on his sneakers.

'Paramedic!' he screamed, running back along the sidewalk with Danny lolling in his arms. 'For Christ's sake, get me a paramedic!'

Wednesday, September 22, 6:47 P.M.

At the hospital, the young medical examiner came out to the waiting area where Frank and Margot were sitting beside a parched yucca and a black youth with an interminable sniff. The medical examiner was soft-spoken, evasive, with

16

hairy hands that crawled around his knees like two tame tarantulas.

'I've examined Danny and I've discovered what happened. An ordinary woodworking nail penetrated his middle back between his fifth and sixth ribs. It was traveling at considerable velocity, almost as fast as a bullet. If it had gone right through him, back to front, his chances of survival would have been very much higher. But, unfortunately, it struck his sternum – his breastbone – and was deflected back into his abdomen. It entered his liver at an oblique angle, causing considerable trauma.'

Margot covered her mouth with her hand and her eyes filled up with tears.

Frank said, 'I want you to be honest with me, doctor.'

'Of course.'

'If I had realized that Danny was so badly injured . . . I mean, if I had taken him to the hospital immediately he was injured . . . do you think they could have saved him?'

The medical examiner glanced uneasily at Margot, and then turned back to Frank.

'In my opinion, yes. But that's only my opinion.'

One

He sat on the couch in front of the television and watched the bombing on the news, again and again. Margot had taken a wicker chair to the conservatory window and sat staring out at the red and yellow swing set in the yard. He didn't know whether she was listening to the television or not, or whether she was even aware that he was still sitting there. She was smoking for the first time in four and a half years. Very occasionally, she coughed.

'Hollywood and the world were devastated this morning when a terrorist bomb exploded in the grounds of one of the city's most exclusive elementary schools, killing at least seventeen students and three faculty members and seriously injuring very many more.

'A suicide bomber drove the device into the school's front yard in a white panel van, detonating it only ten feet away from a line of children who were on their way to play sports in a nearby field. Some of the children have yet to be formally identified.

'Among the dead and injured were the sons and daughters of some of Hollywood's best-known celebrities, including the ten-year-old daughter of Lynn Ashbee, who plays Megan White in *May to September*; the nine-year-old daughter of Billy Kretchmer, who plays Jed Summers in *The Fairchild Family*, and the eight-year-old son of scriptwriter Frank Bell, who has penned more than nineteen episodes of the hit comedy series *If Pigs Could Sing*.

'Eye witnesses described the scene as "carnage," with children's bodies strewn all over the schoolyard. The bomb blast was heard seven miles away in Sherman Oaks, and initial estimates suggest that the van contained more than three hundred and fifty pounds of high explosive. It was also packed with scrap metal, including tools, ball bearings, razor-wire and auto parts, in order to make its effect doubly devastating.

'Los Angeles police commissioner, Marvin Campbell, immediately called for the assistance of the Federal Emergency Management Agency from Denton, Texas, as well as FBI explosives experts and anti-terrorist teams. So far no group or individual has claimed responsibility for the outrage, which Commissioner Campbell described as "a sickening act of war against the innocent."'

Eventually, Margot got up from her chair, came across the living room, and switched the television off. She stood and stared at Frank. A woman so small that she was almost like a child, she had a short brown bob, and she was wearing a brick-red artist's smock that was two sizes too big for her, and black leggings. She had a sharp, uptilted nose and the same large brown eyes that had always made Danny look so serious.

'Why did you leave him?' she asked. Her throat sounded dry.

'I told you, Margot, I left him for no time at all. Minutes,

18

seconds, not even that. I didn't realize that he was hurt so bad. There were other people – there was a woman with her hand blown off. Do you think that if I'd had the slightest inkling—?'

'He was your *son*, Frank. He wasn't *other people*. He was dying and you left him alone. He died by himself, don't you understand that? He died and his daddy wasn't even there to hold his hand.'

Frank stood up. 'How do you think *I* feel about that? Do you have any idea? I picked him up off the sidewalk and I checked him to see if he was hurt and I couldn't see anything, nothing at all. Just a scratch on his nose and a couple of scrapes on his knees.'

'Not forgetting the four-inch nail that tore his liver to pieces.'

'Margot, I couldn't see it! There was no blood – his coat wasn't torn. He said his back hurt but I thought that was only from the blast.'

'He said his back hurt and you just *left* him!'

'For Christ's sake, you weren't there, you didn't see it! There were dozens of people who needed help! It was . . . smoke and dust and blood and children screaming and . . . Jesus, Margot. There was no way of knowing that he was hurt so bad.'

Margot was about to say something but changed her mind. She crushed out her cigarette in the Mexican ashtray on top of the television, hesitated for a moment, thinking, and then stalked out of the living room. Frank switched on the television, but all of the network news channels were still reporting the bomb story, and so he switched it off again.

He went over to the patio doors and stared out at the yard. His reflection in the glass looked like a ghost of himself.

At seven thirty-seven that evening the doorbell rang and Frank went to answer it. Two men in suits were standing outside, holding up police badges. One of them was very tall and lugubrious-looking, with wavy gray hair and a large Roman nose, while the other was short, and black, with a pencil moustache.

'Frank Bell? I'm Lieutenant Walter Chessman from the Los Angeles Police Department and this is Detective Stan Booker.

I understand that you were a witness to The Cedars school bombing this morning.'

'That's right.'

'I also understand that your son was a casualty. I want to offer our condolences.'

'That's . . . Thank you.'

'If you don't want to talk to us now I'll quite understand. But I don't think I have to tell you that the sooner we find the bastards who set off that bomb, the better.'

'It's OK. Come on in. To tell you the truth, I think I need to talk to somebody about it. My wife's . . . well, my wife's very distressed about it. She . . .'

Margot appeared from the bedroom. Her eyes were pink and swollen and she was clutching Danny's old brown teddy bear, Mr Rumbles. 'Frank?'

'It's the police. They want to ask me some questions about this morning.'

Margot nodded. 'I see.' She turned to Lieutenant Chessman and said, 'Do you know who did it yet?'

Lieutenant Chessman shook his head. 'Not so far, ma'am.'

'At least *I* know who killed my son.'

'Oh, yes?' Lieutenant Chessman raised one eyebrow.

Frank said, 'Margot, for Christ's sake.'

'There he is,' said Margot, pointing directly at Frank. 'Danny was dying and his own father left him bleeding in the back seat of his car while he went to take care of a whole lot of people he didn't even know. His own father. Behold the man.'

Lieutenant Chessman glanced at Detective Booker and then he looked back at Margot. 'I have to tell you, Mrs Bell, I've been in this game for twenty-seven years and it isn't always easy in such stressful circumstances to make the most appropriate decision.'

'Oh, the most appropriate decision. I see. You don't think that saving the life of your only child is not just an appropriate decision, but a *critical* one?'

'Mrs Bell, I really need to talk to your husband alone. I want to go through his recollections, one by one, and I don't want those recollections distorted by any untoward pressure.'

'Untoward pressure? Oh, you mean guilt.'

'Mrs Bell, I have to find the group or individual who killed all of those children, and the longer it takes to gather all of the information I need, the further away that group or individual is going to be.'

'Yes, of course. Yes. I'm sounding aggrieved, aren't I?'

'Mrs Bell, what you're feeling – it's perfectly understandable. But I haven't come here to blame anybody for anything. I've come here to collect some more facts, that's all.'

'Do you have a child?' Margot challenged him.

'Yes, ma'am. Three daughters, as a matter of fact.'

'And if a bomb went off, would you leave them, even for a minute?'

'I'm sorry, ma'am, that's a hypothetical question that I can't honestly answer.'

'You wouldn't leave them for a second, would you, those girls of yours? You certainly wouldn't let them die.'

Lieutenant Chessman said nothing, but shrugged and took out his notebook.

'You wouldn't let them bleed to death, all alone, would you? Well, *would* you?'

'If you don't mind, ma'am. We're kind of pushed for time.'

Frank sat hunched forward on the couch, his arms wrapped around himself as if he were feeling the cold.

'You saw the van stop outside the school gates?' Lieutenant Chessman asked him.

He nodded. 'I didn't really take any notice of it. It was just a van.'

'It had no distinguishing markings at all?'

'Not that I recall.'

'Did you notice the driver?'

'No. It was too far away. Besides, there was no reason to.'

Lieutenant Chessman made a few quick notes, and then he said, 'In your opinion, how tight was the security at The Cedars? The gates to the parking lot were always closed at nine A.M., or so I'm told. What happened if you wanted to enter the parking lot after that time?'

'You'd have to stop at the security booth and show yourself. Or some ID, if Mr Lomax didn't know you.'

'Do you have any first-hand experience of that?'

'Well, sure, I've been late taking Danny to school a couple of times, and Mr Lomax would always take a look into the car to see who it was. And once there was a delivery truck ahead of me, and Mr Lomax came out of his booth and made quite a performance of checking the driver's ID.'

'Did he come out of his booth this morning?'

'No, he didn't. The van only stopped for a second, and then he waved it through.'

'So what do you conclude from that?'

'I don't know. You're the detective. He must have known the driver by sight.'

'That's a reasonable conclusion, yes.'

The sun was gradually sinking, and it shone into Lieutenant Chessman's eyes. Frank went over to the patio window and angled the blinds. Outside in the yard Danny's swing set was casting a long-legged shadow across the grass, as gaunt as a scaffold.

Lieutenant Chessman came up behind him and laid a hand on his shoulder. 'You're sure you're OK with this?'

Frank said, 'Yes, sure. Yes. Let's get it over with.' He didn't want any sympathy. He felt as if somebody was squeezing his throat and if Lieutenant Chessman gave him any sympathy he wouldn't be able to speak at all.

'Did you see any kind of flash when the bomb went off?' Detective Booker asked him.

'A flash? Yes.'

'How bright was that flash?'

'Not particularly bright. Not much brighter than a camera-flash. But there was a whole lot of smoke.'

'Would you say that was black smoke or gray smoke or brown smoke?'

'I don't know. Dark gray, I guess. What difference does it make?'

'You'd be surprised. Different explosives produce different amounts of smoke. IMI demolition blocks produce a whole lot of black smoke, because they're almost one hundred percent TNT, while your RDX, for example, produces considerably less. Once we've identified the type of explosive, we can start

22

to source it, find out where it was acquired, and who acquired it.'

'Well, there was a lot of smoke. Dark gray smoke, almost black. For a time it was like midnight. I couldn't see the school building at all.'

'The officer who spoke to you at the scene . . . he made a note that you mentioned another witness, a young woman.'

'That's right. She came up to me right after the blast. One of her shoes was blown off but otherwise she seemed OK.'

'You said your son seemed OK, too.'

Frank stared at him. 'Excuse me? What exactly are you trying to imply?'

'I'm sorry, I didn't mean it to come out like that. I was simply trying to suggest that this young woman could have been more seriously injured than she first appeared.'

'She was walking and she was talking and she was articulate, OK?'

'Did you know her?'

'No. No, I didn't.'

'She wasn't a parent at The Cedars or a member of the faculty or anything like that?'

'I have no idea who she was, none at all. She asked me if I was OK, and then she asked me if I had lost anybody in the blast. I said . . .' He pursed his lips, and then he looked away, toward the window.

'I understand,' said Lieutenant Chessman. 'At that time you didn't know that Danny had been hurt.'

'We're just trying to find as many eye witnesses as possible,' put in Detective Booker. 'Like, if you saw this young woman again, do you think you would recognize her?'

Frank pictured the young woman's dusty, short-cropped hair, and her bleached-out blue eyes. She had been almost beautiful in a rather Slavic way. Not the kind of looks that usually attracted him – he had always preferred Audrey Hepburn types like Margot, small and dark and vivacious. But now he came to think about the young woman again, he thought yes, there had been something about her, something both assertive and wounded. Something that would catch you like fish hooks, and cause you a whole lot of trouble to get free.

'She . . . ah . . . well. She just walked off. Shocked, I guess, like everybody else.'

'Did she say anything before she walked off?'

I've lost somebody, too. Not a child. Somebody closer than that. What had she meant by that? *Somebody closer than that.* Who can be closer than your own child?

'She . . . no.'

Detective Booker raised an eyebrow. 'You're absolutely sure about that?'

'Yes.'

That night he watched television until well past midnight and drank three-quarters of a bottle of Stolichnaya. For most of the time he quietly cried, his cheeks glistening in the light of *The X-Files* and *Stargate SG-1*, letting out a thin agonized whine that hurt his chest.

He couldn't bear to watch the news again. The same footage was being repeated over and over – the smoke, the dust, the bloodied bodies in the schoolyard.

At last, exhausted, he switched off the television and made his way to the bedroom, walking like Captain Ahab on the tilting deck of the *Pequod*. He collided with the half-open door and it was only then that he realized how badly he had been bruised when he had been blown into that parked Toyota. He unbuttoned his shirt, pulled down his sleeve and frowned at it, although he was finding it hard to focus. His shoulder was a mass of crimson and purple.

'Oh, God,' he said, closing his eyes. 'Please turn back the clock. Oh, God, please let it be yesterday.'

But when he negotiated his way along the corridor to Danny's room and switched on the light, he found that Danny's bed with its X-Men bedcover was neatly made and empty, and that Danny's Star Wars figures were still crowded on the shelf, as bereaved as he was. Nobody would ever play with them again.

He sat down on the end of Danny's bed. He didn't cry any more because he didn't have any tears left. He didn't want to think about this morning ever again. He wanted to forget that it had ever happened. But even with his eyes open, all he could see was an endless silent re-run of the bomb going off, and Danny sitting in the back of the car, and the expression on the face of the paramedic who had lifted Danny out of his arms.

A few minutes after two A.M. he knew for certain that when dawn came it wasn't going to be yesterday, and so he shuffled along to the bedroom and tried to open the door. It was locked.

'Margot,' he called. There was no reply. 'Margot, could you open the door please.' Still no reply.

He raised his fist, ready to knock, but then he thought, no, I'm too tired and I'm too drunk and she blames me for Danny's death and I can't stand the thought of a screaming, furniture-breaking argument, not tonight. Think of Danny, lying in the morgue. Show some respect.

'Margot, I know you can hear me. I'm showing some respect.'

He paused, and swayed, and held on to the door frame to catch his balance. 'I just want you to know that whatever happens, whatever happens, I never wanted it to happen, not that way. Not Danny. I did . . . I made the wrong decision. I know I made the wrong decision. Nobody . . . nobody loved Danny more than I did. Nobody. And I made the wrong decision. I admit it.'

He pressed his ear to the door, holding his breath, listening, but he couldn't hear anything at all, not even sobbing. After a while he went back to the living room and sat down on one of the white leather couches. The living-room walls were painted pale magnolia but they were hung all around with Margot's paintings – enormous paintings, six feet by seven feet some of them, *Impressions In White I – VII*. She had painted them all on untreated canvas, in white oil paint, and although they were textured with whorls and curls and cross-hatching, that was all they were: white.

'Painting is all about *paint*,' she always said, crossing her legs in the lotus position. 'I want people to forget about form and shape and composition. Form and shape and composition – they're all tricks, to stop people seeing what really *matters*.'

What *matters*, Margot, is our only son lying dead and chilly in the morgue. What *matters* is all those poor children blasted to bits in the schoolyard. But then, if people in this world are capable of acts as hideous as that, maybe nothing matters. Not hoping, not believing, not kindness, not smiling.

When we went to bed on Tuesday night, he thought, little did we know that a dark army of scene-shifters would be busy while we slept, so that when we woke up, without realizing it, we would no longer be living in a world in which we were confident and happy, but a dangerous and heartless replica in which nothing was certain and nobody could ever be trusted ever again.

He stood up and went over to *Impressions In White IV*. He stared at it for a long time. Then he took a thick black marker pen out of the box on the coffee table and drew a huge cartoon face of a boy on it, with tears in both eyes.

Two

She appeared from the bedroom just before seven A.M. It was obvious from her face that she hadn't slept. Frank was sitting at the breakfast counter with a large cup of black coffee. He had made some toast but he had only taken one bite out of it.

'Coffee?' he asked her.

She shook her head. She went to the fridge and took out a carton of cranberry juice.

'There's been some news about the bombing,' he told her. 'Some Arab terrorist group say that it was them.'

She poured out her juice and drank half of it. Still she didn't speak.

'There, look,' he said, nodding toward the caption underneath CNN News. 'Dar Tariki Tariqat, whoever they are. Nobody's heard of them before, but I guess they're connected to Al Qaeda.'

Margot said, 'I saw what you did to my painting.'

'Yes.'

She waited, and waited, but when he continued sipping his coffee and watching the news, she banged her glass of cranberry juice down on the counter in front of him.

'Is that it? "Yes"? Is that all you have to say?'

Frank turned to her and put down his coffee cup. He was trying to be calm but his heart was beating unnaturally fast. 'No, Margot. I could say a whole lot more, but right now I don't think you'd understand. I don't think you'd *want* to understand.'

Margot let out a disbelieving '*hahhh!*'

'What would you like me to do? Apologize?'

'No I damn well wouldn't. You could say a million times and it still couldn't make up for what you've done. You've killed my only son, Frank. Danny's dead and it was you who allowed him to die.'

'I know.'

'"I know"?' she screamed at him. '"I *know*"? You've killed him, and now you've made a mockery out of his death by defacing my work with some grotesque . . .' She had to take another breath to control her fury. 'Do you really hate me that much, Frank? Come on, tell me! My God, I can't believe how much you must hate me!'

Frank closed his eyes for a moment. 'Margot, I don't hate you, I love you, and if I could bring Danny back to life – even if it meant that I had to die instead of him – I would do it, without a second's hesitation.'

'You don't love anybody, Frank.'

'Well, whatever you say, sweetheart. But nothing that either of us says or does can change what's happened. If Danny had arrived at school on time he would have been killed instantly like the rest of the kids. If he had arrived two minutes later he wouldn't have been hurt at all. But he arrived when he did, and by bad fortune he was hit by a nail. If you had been with him, instead of me, you probably wouldn't have realized that he was hurt so bad, either. Or maybe you would. But ifs don't count for anything.'

Margot said nothing for a long time, her nostrils flared,

27

breathing like a runner at the end of a race. Eventually, however, she flapped her right hand toward the living room. 'So why did you deface my painting?'

'I don't think I defaced it, Margot. I think I made it mean something, which it never did before. I think I gave it some humanity.'

He drove to work. When he walked into the office suite at Fox, his secretary, Daphne, stared at him with her mouth open.

'Mr Bell! I didn't expect to see you today! I'm so sorry about Danny! It was such a terrible thing to happen.'

Mo Cohen came out of the conference room wearing a bright-blue shirt with palm trees on it and smoking a cigar. He was balding and big-bellied, with black curly hair like a clown.

'Frank, for Christ's sake.' He came up and hugged him so hard that Frank could hardly breathe. When he let him go, he had tears in his eyes. 'What can I say? Poor little Danny. I can't even believe it's true.'

'No, well, neither can I.'

'What the hell are you doing at work? You should be home, taking care of Margot.'

'I needed to get away for a while, that's all.'

Mo put his arm around Frank's shoulders and squeezed him. Frank winced. 'You OK?' Mo asked him.

'Bruises. Nothing serious.'

'Come inside, take the weight off. You want a cup of coffee? Daphne, my angel, make this man a cup of coffee.'

The conference room was where they worked on the scripts of *If Pigs Could Sing*. It was a large, cream-painted room with three red leather couches and a long table with three PCs on it, as well as heaps of paper and scripts and felt-tip pens, an Emmy with a pink beret hanging on it, and a plaster statuette of three singing pigs. On the walls hung framed TV awards from all over the world, as well as photographs of Frank and Mo and their partner, Lizzie Fries, and all of their guest stars, like Joan Rivers and Will Smith and Rush Limbaugh.

Cream loose-weave drapes were drawn across the windows

28

to hide the view of the parking lot. When they were writing, anything could prove a distraction – even watching Gene Wilder trying to park his BMW. High up on the left-hand wall there was a basketball hoop, and on the floor underneath it lay heaps of crumpled-up pieces of paper. If they couldn't decide if a gag was funny or not, they tossed it up at the hoop, and if they missed, it wasn't funny.

Mo said, 'I would have called you yesterday, as soon as I heard, but . . . you know . . . Lizzie thought you probably needed some space.'

'Well, she was right. I was still in shock yesterday. I'm still in shock today.'

'It's like a nightmare, you know?' Mo said. 'A total fucking nightmare. How can people deliberately kill kids like that?'

'I don't know, Mo. I haven't even gotten round to thinking about what they did it for. It was absolutely the most terrible thing I've ever seen.'

'You shouldn't have come into the office. For Christ's sake, Frank, you're going to need a long, long time to deal with this.'

'No, I'd rather be here. Margot's taken it pretty badly, to tell you the truth. She . . . ah . . . she thinks that I was responsible for Danny dying, and in a way I was.'

Mo sat down next to him and took his cigar out of his mouth. 'How could you be responsible? It was a fucking bomb, for Christ's sake.'

Frank told him. Mo sat and listened to him and then he took hold of his hand, twisting his wedding band around and around in the way that women do. 'It wasn't your fault, Frank. How were you to know? It could have happened to anybody.'

'Maybe. But it didn't happen to anybody. It happened to Danny, and it happened to me.'

Commissioner Marvin Campbell appeared on the wide-screen television in the far corner of the room. Frank picked up the remote control and turned up the sound.

' . . . with a coded password. This came from a group calling themselves Dar Tariki Tariqat, which in Arabic means "in the darkness, the path." They gave us no reason for the bombing and made no demands of any kind. We are working on the possibility that they may be associated with Al Qaeda or other terrorist organizations, but as yet we have found no evidence one way or the other.'

Then it was back to the anchorwoman, Barbra Cole. 'Eight-year-old Heidi Martinez, the daughter of *Philly 500* star James Martinez and folk singer Kelly Gooding, died early this morning from injuries she received in the blast. This brings the total of student fatalities to twenty-one, while five faculty members were killed, including principal Ann Redmond.

'FBI explosives experts calculate that the bomb was made out of approximately two hundred and fifty pounds of TNT, a favorite with terrorist groups because it is so easily obtainable and not easily traced.

'Examination of the van in which the device was driven into the grounds of The Cedars school has shown that the driver was male and that he was carrying a female passenger. In the words of forensic specialists, however, both driver and passenger were "vaporized" by the blast and identification is likely to prove extremely difficult.

'Police Commissioner Marvin Campbell received a telephone call shortly after five A.M. from a man who claimed to represent a group called Dar Tariki Tariqat. He said that Dar Tariki Tariqat were responsible for the bombing but gave no further details about their aims, their origins or their affiliations – if any.

'Police are urgently seeking more witnesses to the bombing, and they want to speak to anybody who might have seen a white Ford E-series panel van parked in any unusual locations during the past few days, or anybody who might have had a white Ford panel van recently stolen. Also any dealers who might have sold such a vehicle.'

Lieutenant Chessman appeared on the screen, looking red-faced and hot. 'Basically we need to hear from anybody in the demolition or quarrying businesses who has a large quantity of TNT unaccounted for. Detonators, too. Apart from that, we'd like to talk to any auto wreckers who might have sold two engine blocks – one from a four-point-eight-liter Northstar engine and one from a one-point-six-liter Honda V-Tec engine. These blocks were carried inside the van on either side of the bomb and when they were blown apart they caused appalling VO injury . . .' He hesitated, as if somebody were talking to him, and then he said, 'Oh, sorry, VO – that's vital organ.'

Frank pressed the mute button. Mo said, 'Terrible, appalling. They must be fucking animals, these people. Worse than animals. Did you ever hear of them? Kon-Tiki Paraquat or whatever? *I* never heard of them.'

Frank shook his head. 'I just hope they find them, that's all. And find them guilty. And gas them.'

Mo gave him a quick, disturbed look. He had never heard Frank talk like that before. Daphne came in with a cup of coffee. She was a tall black girl with beaded cornrows and big yellow-tinted glasses and lips that were, in Mo's words, 'like two red satin cushions just begging to be sat on.' Frank had not employed her just because she was efficient and incredibly good-natured, considering how cantankerous they could all be when a deadline was pressing and they couldn't think of anything remotely funny. Today, however, she couldn't stop weeping.

'I keep seeing little Danny. I don't know how you can bear it.'

'Well,' said Frank, 'I don't think I can.'

'Oh God,' she said. 'I hope he's at peace.'

'I think so, Daphne. Thanks.'

'What are you going to do now?' Mo asked him, after Daphne had left the room. 'You'll have to go home sooner or later.'

'I don't know. I'm not sure that our marriage is going to be able to survive a thing like this.'

'Of course it will. Margot's in shock, that's all, just like you are. She needs somebody to blame for what happened and you're that somebody. You wait till the cops nab these bastards, then she'll see that it wasn't your fault.'

Frank sat staring at the balls of crumpled-up paper all over the floor. He had been thinking about Danny so much that he felt as if somebody had been repeatedly hitting him on the head with a heavy book. He needed to sleep but he knew that he couldn't. He needed to talk to Margot, too, to try to atone for what he had done, but he knew he couldn't do that, either.

'What about next week's show?' he asked Mo. 'Do you think you and Lizzie can wrap it up on your own?'

'For Christ's sake, don't worry about the show, Frank. They'll probably cancel it in any case.'

'They shouldn't. They shouldn't cancel it. We can't let people like that destroy everything we've worked for. That's just what they want.'

'Frank, it's not just *Pigs* that's going to be affected here. What about *Philly 500* and *The Fairchild Family* and *May To September* and *The Kings of Orange County*? What about Ollie Peller? He's halfway through scoring that new John Badham picture. It's going to be total fucking paralysis. Anybody who lost a kid is not going to be able to do any serious work, are they? And everybody else is going to be far too jumpy.'

Frank slowly shook his head. 'They sure know how to pick their targets, don't they? American capitalism on September 11, American popular culture on September 22.'

Mo said, 'My advice to you is go home. You have to face up to this situation with Margot. *You* do and *she* does, both. I'm talking to you as a brother.'

'OK,' said Frank. He looked around the conference room and gave something that was nearly a smile. 'I can't think of any good gags, anyhow.'

Three

He didn't go home. He was too sick at heart and he knew that Margot wasn't yet ready to talk to him. He called her from his cellphone but she didn't pick up. Either she didn't want to hear from him, or she was out seeing her friend Ruth in Coldwater Canyon.

The smog had cleared and it was a warm, clear morning.

He had the impression that there were more police cars around than usual, and he saw two police helicopters in the time it took him to drive from The Avenue of the Stars to the San Diego Freeway. He didn't switch on his car radio, though. There was only one topic of conversation on every waveband.

He reached the ocean. The water was glittering like smashed mirrors, and gulls were wheeling and screaming over the beach. He parked his car and walked along the promenade toward the municipal pier.

An old man approached him. He was wearing a long-billed baseball cap and a saggy gray T-shirt and saggy orange shorts. The veins in his legs looked like a street map of Laurel Canyon, a mass of wriggly blue roads. One of his eyes was totally white.

'Lost?' He grinned, showing four mahogany-colored teeth.

Frank shook his head and carried on walking, but the old man limped along beside him. 'I can always tell when someone's lost. They have that look about them.'

'Really? What look is that?'

'That lost look.'

'Well, let me put your mind at rest. I'm not lost. In fact I know exactly where I'm going and I really don't need anybody to help me. Particularly you.'

'You're misunderstanding my meaning. When I say "lost," I don't mean geographically lost. I mean lost in the sense that you don't know what the hell you're going to do next.'

Frank stopped, reached into his shirt pocket and gave the old man a ten-dollar bill. The old man took it and flapped it from side to side. 'What's this for?'

'Philosophical services rendered. Now will you push off and leave me alone?'

The old man pulled his mouth down in an exaggerated expression of dismay. 'I'm not a panhandler, if that's what you're thinking. I can tell when people need guidance, that's all. I can see when they've reached an impasse.'

'Well, that's a very great gift. Now, if you'll just . . .' He made a toddling gesture with his fingers.

The old man stayed where he was, so Frank carried on walking toward the pier. He had only gone a few paces, however, when the old man called out, 'It wasn't your fault, Frank!'

Frank felt a fizzing sensation in his scalp, as if he had touched a bare electric wire. He turned around and stared at the old man. '*What?*'

'You heard me. It wasn't your fault.'

'How do you know my name?' Frank demanded, walking back to him.

'That's a gift, too. See that girl on the roller-skates there? Her name's Helena. Go ask her if you don't believe me. See that fellow with the dog? Guy.'

'This is a scam. Get the hell out of here before I call a cop.'

'No scam, Frank. It wasn't your fault, and that's the top and bottom of it. What you have to do now is forgive yourself, and move on.'

'So why should you care?'

The old man took out a filthy crumpled handkerchief and blew his nose. 'I care because I care because I care. What's the point of having a God-granted gift if you never share it with anyone?'

'All right, you know my name, or else you've guessed it, or you've seen me on TV. What does that prove?'

'I know more than your name, Frank. I know what's going to happen to you. I know the reason you're here, even if you don't. You'll cross the road and you'll never come back.'

Frank waited for the old man to explain what he meant, but he simply stood there smiling at him with his four brown teeth and a look in his one good eye that was almost triumphant. After more than a minute, Frank turned, hesitated, and then he walked away. The old man continued to smile at him until he disappeared amongst the crowds.

Frank leaned on the pier railing and closed his eyes and let the ocean breeze blow into his face. He could hear slowly moving traffic and the *slurr-chunk!* of skateboards and

34

people talking and laughing. He could hear the Pacific, and the monotonous clanking of yachts. He could hear the gulls.

Inside his head, soundlessly, The Cedars was still blowing up, black smoke growing up into the air like fir trees, bits of metal and bits of brick falling all around him. And Danny's blood-streaked arm, waggling from side to side as he ran along the street, silently screaming for help.

You'll cross the road and you'll never come back.

'Hey!' said a woman's voice, very close to him.

He opened his eyes and blinked. A young woman was leaning against the rail just two or three feet away, although the ocean was sparkling so brightly behind her that he could see little more than a silhouette. The silhouette wore a wide-brimmed straw hat and a sleeveless white cotton dress.

'I'm afraid I don't know your name,' she told him.

He thought, *that makes a change. Everybody else around here seems to know it.*

'Don't you remember me?' she said. 'We met yesterday. When the school was bombed.'

He shaded his eyes with his hand. It was the young woman with one sandal. She was wearing brass-rimmed sunglasses with very tiny oval lenses, and a white ribbon around her neck.

'Well, this is one heck of a coincidence,' he said. 'What are you doing here?'

'I guess the same as you. Trying to clear my head.'

'You weren't hurt, were you?'

'No, it didn't hurt. How about you?'

'My . . . uh . . . my son died. I lost my son.'

'Oh my God, I'm so sorry.' She reached out and touched his forearm. 'You must be absolutely torn apart.'

'He was hit by a flying nail. I didn't even realize. You and I, we were talking, and all the time he was bleeding to death in the back of my car.'

'That's tragic. I don't know what to say to you.'

'Don't worry, my wife does.'

'She doesn't *blame* you, does she?'

'Blame me? The way she talks, you'd think I planted that bomb myself.' He looked around. A suntanned young

35

man in a blue and yellow T-shirt was standing not far away, eating an ice-cream cone. 'Are you alone?' he asked. 'Or is that . . .?'

She turned, and frowned, and then she shook her head. The young man lifted his ice cream to her in salute. 'No,' she said, 'I'm all by myself.'

'Maybe I can buy you a coffee, or a drink.'

'All right,' she nodded. 'A drink. I think I'd like that.'

They crossed Palisades Beach Road together, and halfway across she took hold of his hand, as if they were already friends. A woman in a soiled floral-print dress was standing on the opposite side of the road with a shopping cart piled high with old newspapers and broken lampshades and 7-Up cans. As they crossed she cackled like a chicken and called out, 'Young love! Don't it make you want to throw up!' But the young woman still didn't let go of his hand.

Frank took her into Ziggy's, a light and airy bar with a blond wood floor and shiny stainless-steel chairs. On the wall behind the counter hung a strange painting of six women with blue faces, their eyes closed, their hair waving in the wind.

'I'm Frank,' said Frank, holding out his hand.

'Hello, Frank. You can call me Astrid.'

'What does that mean? Isn't Astrid your real name?'

'What's in a name, Frank?'

Frank resisted the temptation to quote Shakespeare. *That which we call a rose, by any other name would smell as sweet.*

'They do a great strawberry daiquiri here,' he told her.

'OK. Strawberry daiquiri it is.'

'You said you lost somebody close to you.'

Astrid took off her hat and placed it on the table, with her sunglasses neatly folded in the brim. 'I . . . ah . . . don't really want to talk about it, Frank, not today. Today I came out to think about something else.'

'Yes, I'm sorry. Did you see the news? It looks like some Arab terrorist group is supposed to have done it.'

'Maybe.'

'Jesus, though. I can't imagine how *anybody* could blow

36

up innocent children like that. I mean, what kind of demonic thought process was going on in their heads when they decided to do it?'

Astrid looked at him with those pale, pale eyes. 'Everybody's fair game, Frank, to people like that. All they think about is showing the world how aggrieved they are. They don't care who suffers. They don't care who dies.'

The server came over in shiny blue hot pants and Frank asked for a strawberry daiquiri and a Scotch. 'By the way, the police want to interview as many eye witnesses as they can find. I have their number if you want to go talk to them.'

'I don't think so. I didn't see anything.'

'Come on, you were right there beside me. You must have seen *something*. Maybe you think that it wasn't particularly important, but you never know. It might give the cops that one small piece of sky that's going to finish the jigsaw.'

Astrid said, 'The truth is, Frank, I wasn't supposed to be there. I was supposed to be someplace else.'

'Oh. Oh, right, I understand. But couldn't you make an anonymous phone call?'

'I didn't see anything, Frank. Nothing at all.'

There was a long silence between them. Eventually Frank nodded toward the painting of the six blue-faced women and said, 'What do you think *that's* all about?'

'It's about women and their mystery. If you look at the faces for long enough, the eyes appear to open.'

'I didn't know that, and I've been coming to this place since day one.'

'That's because you've never looked at it for long enough. Look at me, Frank. Go on, really look at me. Who do you see?'

'Um . . . I don't exactly know what you're asking.'

'I'm asking you to *see* me, that's all. Describe what you see.'

'I see . . . What do I see? A young woman of maybe twenty-three, twenty-four years. Brown hair, blue eyes. Maybe a Swedish or a Polish mother, judging by your cheekbones. Sure of herself, independent. Lives on her own, maybe with a white cat.'

Astrid laughed. 'Sorry, no white cat. But what else do you see?'

'I don't know. I don't know you well enough. What do you do for a living?'

'A living? Nothing. Not now. But I used to pretend to be somebody else.'

'You used to *what*? I don't think you and I are talking on the same wavelength.'

'Oh, yes we are. Or we could, if you really wanted to. Tell me about you.'

'There isn't much to tell. Frank Bell, very distantly related to Alexander Graham Bell. Very, *very* distantly. Thirty-four and one half years old.'

'That's it? No career?'

'Oh, you want my whole life story? OK . . . my father used to run a hotel in Ojai so he expected me to run it after he retired.'

'But you didn't?'

'No way. I hated the hotel business. Hotel guests behave like swine. They steal everything, they break everything, and you should see what they do to the mattresses. So I took a job as a bartender, and then I cleaned swimming pools, and then I took dance lessons, and then I appeared as an extra in three episodes of *Star Trek Voyager*, wearing a red jumpsuit and a false nose and pretending to drink Aldebaran whiskey in Ten Forward.

'While I was waiting around the *Star Trek* set I wrote a TV pilot about two Mid-Western farm boys who always wanted to be famous rock stars. I sold it to Fox, made a success of it, end of story.'

'*If Pigs Could Sing*,' smiled Astrid.

'That's the one.'

'I *love* that show. I really adore it. Dusty and Henry, they're so kind of gentle and goofy, and I just *love* their grandpa. What's that song he always used to sing? The one about the limp?'

'"The Girl With The Left-Footed Limp." It went to number ninety-seven in the Hot One Hundred. And straight back out again the next morning.'

38

Astrid reached across the table and took hold of both of Frank's hands. On her wedding-band finger she wore an emerald ring. If the emerald was real, thought Frank, it must be worth nearly ten thousand dollars. She looked as if she were about to say something but then she didn't.

'What?' he asked her as their drinks arrived.

'I was just thinking that you won't feel like writing that kind of stuff anymore, after losing Danny.'

'Not just yet, maybe. But nothing is ever really funny unless it really, really hurts.'

Afterwards, they walked along the beach together. Frank looked out at the ocean and said, 'I think this has done me some good.'

'Me too.'

A young boy turned cartwheels all around them, just like Danny used to. Frank watched him as he ran laughing into the surf, and then he turned to see that Astrid was watching him, too.

'You're crying,' she said, and he hadn't even realized.

They walked a little further and then Frank checked his watch. It was almost two thirty. 'I guess I'd better be getting back. I have a wife to face, funeral arrangements to think about.'

'Do you want to see me again?'

The wind blew his hair into his eyes. He was trying to read her expression, but he couldn't. 'Of course I want to see you again.'

'Tomorrow? Is that too soon?'

'No! Well, no – tomorrow would be fine. Where do you want to meet? Do you live around here?'

'I used to, but not now. We can meet wherever you like.'

'I live in Burbank, but let's think. Do you know the Garden restaurant, on Sunset? A couple of blocks west of the Chateau Marmont.'

'No, but I'm sure I can find it.'

'OK then, the Garden at twelve o'clock, how's that?'

'Good,' she said. Then, 'Sing it for me.'

'What?'

'"The Girl With The Left-Footed Limp." Sing it for me.'

Frank shook his head. 'Not today. Maybe one day. But not today.'

Four

When he arrived home, Ruth's red Jeep was parked in the driveway. Margot and Ruth were sitting together in the conservatory, drinking green Chinese tea and smoking cigarettes. Ruth was wearing a black dress, which made her look even more like Morticia than usual, and Margot was wearing a white cotton pajama suit. They both looked up at him with undisguised disgust.

'So where were you?' Margot demanded.

'Out, that's all. I went to the beach.'

'Oh, you went to the beach. How nice for you. The hospital called and asked which funeral home we wanted Danny taken to.'

'Funeral home?'

'Yes, Frank. He's dead, remember?'

Frank covered his mouth with his hand. This was going to be harder than he had ever imagined. At last he took his hand away. 'Which . . . um . . . what did you say?'

'I said Kennedy and Lester's, on Olive. They handled my grandfather's funeral.'

'Good, yes. That's fine.'

'I called Kennedy and Lester's and John Lester said they're going to arrange it all. We can go see Danny tomorrow afternoon.'

'OK. OK, good.'

He didn't know what else to say. It was no use asking Margot how she was feeling because it was obvious how she was feeling. Looking around, he saw that she had taken down the painting that he had scrawled on, and replaced it with another *Impression In White*. He had no idea how many *Impressions In White* she had painted, because he could never

40

tell one from the other. All he knew is that every time he came home she was standing in front of her easel, surrounded by dozens of squeezed-out tubes of titanium white. It looked like the massacre of the maggots.

'Are you staying for a while, Ruth?' he asked.

'So long as Margot needs me,' Ruth challenged him.

'Well, that's good. I'd say she needs you a whole lot just at the moment, considering the circumstances. I'm just going to . . .' He hesitated, because he didn't know what he was going to do or where he was going to go. 'Make a few phone calls,' he added lamely.

He couldn't sleep that night. He tried watching television in his study but on the first channel he flicked on to they were showing *Boys' Town* and on the next one *Batman Forever*, which had been one of Danny's favorites.

He went into the kitchen and opened the icebox. There were two pork chops on a plate, covered with Saran Wrap. He took them out and looked at them but then he put them back again. They were left over from the last meal that they had eaten together, on Tuesday evening.

Back in his study, he picked up the book he was reading, whenever he had the time, which wasn't very often. It was called *The Process* by Brion Gysin, about a black Fulbright student who goes to Morocco to discover the Sahara Desert and smoke copious pipes of *kif*.

'The silky surreptitious silence of the Sahara starts in Ghardaia, where every soft footfall is shod in sand. Men speak softly, knowing that they will be heard. Everything crackles with static electricity as if one were shuffling over a great rug. Everyone in the Sahara is very aware, tuned into the great humming silence through which drones the sound of an approaching diesel from hours away.'

But after ten minutes he found that he couldn't focus any more, so he placed an *I Ching* stick in the book to mark his place, and closed it. Dawn found him in the conservatory, his forehead pressed against the cold patio window, staring at nothing.

*　　*　　*

41

He made two mugs of strong coffee and took one in to Margot. She was lying in an Indian rope-trick of sheets, either sleeping or pretending to sleep.

'Margot.'

He stood over her and at last she opened her eyes, blinking against the seven o'clock sunlight.

'I brought you some coffee.'

'I don't want any. I don't want anything from you.'

'Margot, we ought to talk about this.'

'I don't want to talk about it. I don't have anything to say. You let Danny die and that's all there is to it.'

He stayed there for a few moments more. Then he said, 'I'm going to see Gerald Marquette. I should be back around three. Then we can go visit Danny.'

'Don't worry about it, I'll go on my own.'

He went back into the kitchen and poured the coffee down the sink.

He was an hour too early for his meeting with Astrid so he drove to Franklin Avenue. Outside The Cedars, the street was still cordoned off by fluttering police tapes, and at least seven squad cars were parked on the sidewalk, as well as two station wagons from the Coroner's Department and a dark green armored van. FBI, probably.

Frank left his car on the corner of Sierra Bonita Avenue and walked the rest of the way. As he approached the school, he saw scores of investigators in Tyvek suits and respirators, crawling all over the wreckage like white ants. Three backhoe diggers had been brought in, and two of them were nudging down the front wall of the Memorial Library, while the third was demolishing the portico. There was a pall of fine gray dust over everything, and Frank's shoes crunched on the concrete as he came nearer.

Lieutenant Chessman was standing just behind the police lines with his hands thrust into the pockets of a sagging green linen coat. Detective Booker was there, too, in his shirt-sleeves, talking to a tall young man with black wavy hair, a black polo neck and an expensive gray sport coat. The young man glanced over at Frank as he approached, and gave the briefest of frowns, as if he recognized him. Frank thought he looked rather saturnine, like the Devil on his weekend off.

'Mr Bell,' said Lieutenant Chessman, lifting one hand in acknowledgement. 'What brings you here?'

'I don't know exactly. I guess I had to take another look at it, just to convince myself that it really happened.'

'Well, be my guest.' He lifted the tape and Frank ducked underneath. 'We've recovered all the bodies so far, and everybody's been identified and accounted for. Now we're looking for shrapnel. Pieces of van, and any other junk that those bastards were carrying.'

'You still don't know who they are – this terrorist group?'

Lieutenant Chessman took out a Rolaid and popped it into his mouth. 'So far, we don't have any leads at all. The FBI tell us that they've never heard of them before, and neither have the CIA. Apparently there was a broadcast yesterday evening on the Al Jazeera network, and they specifically denied that Dar Tariki Tariqat has any connection with Al Qaeda.'

Frank bit his lip and wondered if he ought to tell Lieutenant Chessman that he had met Astrid. After all, if she could help the police to find out who had killed Danny and all those other children . . .

But Astrid had sworn to him that she hadn't seen anything, and told him in confidence that she wasn't supposed to be here on Franklin Avenue at all. He didn't want to betray her trust before he had even had a chance to get to know her.

Lieutenant Chessman said, 'Usually, you know, you get a buzz of information when something like this happens. We have some pretty good contacts in the Muslim community, Algerians and Iranians and all those guys. But this time, stony silence.'

'You haven't found out who was driving the van?'

Lieutenant Chessman shook his head. 'They were atomized, both of them. The only way we could tell that they were a man and a woman was because we found one of the guy's Nikes about a hundred and fifty feet away, and because there was an intra-uterine device melted into the door of the glovebox.'

43

At that moment, the saturnine young man in the gray coat made his excuses to Detective Booker and came over to join them. Frank could tell by the way he walked that he was very fit. His shoulders were broad and his pecs bulged under his sweater. He had a long straight nose like a Greek statue, and dark, deeply buried eyes. Frank disliked him even before he opened his mouth. Too damn handsome, too damn self-possessed.

He held out his hand. 'I think we may have met before,' he said in a distinctly British accent.

'I don't think so.'

'Nevile Strange. Maybe you've heard of me.'

'Sorry.'

Lieutenant Chessman said, 'Nevile is what you might call a psychic detective. We call him in from time to time when we're not making much headway with good old-fashioned procedure. You remember last January, when the Dikstrom girl was kidnapped?'

'Sure, I remember.'

'Nevile told us that her little bead bracelet had fallen down the crack in the rear seat of the suspect's station wagon. Sure enough, when we searched the vehicle again, there it was.'

'Really.'

'You don't sound terribly impressed,' Nevile said and smiled at him.

'Well, no. I'm afraid I don't believe in the world beyond.'

'I can't say that I do, either,' Lieutenant Chessman put in. 'But Nevile has a terrific record of helping us with some very intractable cases. Whether you believe in it or not, seven times out of ten, he gets it right.'

'Let me show you what I'm doing here,' Nevile suggested. 'Frank, is it? Detective Booker was telling me you lost your little boy.'

Frank looked at Lieutenant Chessman and Lieutenant Chessman pulled a face as if to say, *why not?*

Nevile walked off between the distorted school gates. When he reached the shattered security booth he turned and waited, like a parent waiting for a laggardly child. Frank hesitated and then reluctantly followed him.

As they crossed the parking lot, Nevile said, 'Everybody has the potential to be psychic, you know. It's a skill, not a gift. But some people have it more than others.'

'Oh, yes?'

'Me, I've been blessed with psychic perception all my life, ever since I was a snotty-nosed kid in South London. My parents just accepted it – for instance, if ever my mother lost her purse, she'd come to ask me where it was and I'd say, "under the couch" or "you left it at Mrs So-and-so's house." I never thought that there was anything amazing about it.

'Then one day, when I was about ten, my best friend, Robert, was knocked down by a hit-and-run driver, right outside his house, and killed. There were no witnesses and nobody came forward to admit it. I went to the spot where he had died, and while I was standing there, Robert appeared, just the way he was before the car hit him.

'I couldn't see him directly, not face-on, but I could see him out of the corner of my eye, as if he was standing just behind me, and a little way off to one side. It was then that I heard the car coming, and I stepped back on to the pavement. The car drove past me, *whoooosh*, maybe forty or fifty miles an hour. It almost hit me, but I didn't feel any slipstream, nothing at all. The only thing was, I saw Robert rolling over and over on the road, arms and legs flapping like a scarecrow, and I knew that I had seen him being killed.

'The car was a gray Hillman Minx, and the last three numbers on its license plate were seven-six-six. I went back home and told my father what I'd seen, and my father took me to the police station. Of course the police were highly skeptical, but they checked it out all the same. They found the car in Brighton, about a week later. It still had a clump of Robert's scalp sticking to the front grille.'

They had reached the area in front of the school where the bomb had exploded. The bodies and the pieces of bodies had been removed, but all of the rest of the debris had been left where it was, so that the forensic team could catalog every scrap of it, from shredded T-shirts to charred sports bags. Most of them were on their hands and knees, carefully picking

45

up the fragments of twenty-three lost lives and dropping them into polythene evidence bags.

Frank breathed in the stench of detonated explosive and scorched metal and brick-dust. The clatter from the diggers was so loud that Nevile had to shout.

'When somebody is violently killed, they leave what I like to call a *psychic imprint* on their physical surroundings. When my friend Robert was killed, the trauma of those moments was imprinted on the highway, almost like a series of high-speed photographs. What I can do – because I have very developed mental awareness – is I can develop those photographs in my mind's eye, so that I can see the event happening all over again.'

'So . . . what can you see here?'

Nevile looked down at a chalk outline on the blistered tarmac. 'A little girl with blonde curls died here. Her first name was Amy and her second name had something to do with ships. She was laughing when the blast hit her. She had her head thrown back and her eyes closed. And then – bang. Now . . . now she's thinking . . .'

'*Now?*'

'She's dead, Frank, in the physical sense. But now she's worried about her pet hamster, who's going to take care of it.'

'Her pet *hamster?*' Frank didn't know whether to laugh or to walk away.

'What?' said Nevile. 'You think I'm being cynical? What do *you* think a little girl would be worrying about, if she knew that she could never go back home?'

One of the forensic investigators came waddling toward them in her white Tyvek suit, her short red hair sticking up like rooster feathers. She took off her face mask and wiped the perspiration from her freckled forehead with the back of her hand. 'So they brought *you* in, Nevile,' she said. 'They must be desperate.'

Nevile turned to Frank and grinned. 'Lorraine's a non-believer, like you. If you can't touch it, feel it, eat it, or see it under a microscope, Lorraine won't admit it exists. How about dinner, Lorraine? I could put you in touch with your

46

dead grandmother and find out what she did with that cultured-pearl necklace you always wanted so badly.'

'How the *hell* do you know about that?'

'Because I can read your mind. And because I met your sister about three days ago at the Roeg Gallery and she asked me if there was any chance of my tracing it for you.'

'You fake.'

'All right,' said Nevile. 'If I'm such a fake, tell me who was killed right here.'

Lorraine lifted up the clipboard that was dangling from her belt and leafed through it until she found a diagram of all of the dead and injured. 'Amy Cutter, aged eight and a half. She was Pam Cutter's daughter – you know, the actress who plays Kirsty Harris in *Time Of Our Life*.'

Nevile looked at Frank as if to say, *there you are, what did I tell you?'*

Frank said, 'OK, I'm about three-tenths impressed. Why don't you take a look at the van, see if you can't work out who the killers were.'

'Well . . . I've already done that. That was Lieutenant Chessman's first priority.'

'And?'

'There's very little in the van in the way of psychic imprints. Maybe it was something to do with the bomb going off only two or three feet away from them. They were atomized in a millionth of a second, so their spirits didn't have the time to make an impression on their immediate surroundings. The man left a very faint resonance, the driver. I'd guess that he was a loner, quite a disturbed kind of individual, with some very odd beliefs about forces from outer space. His name could have been David but he was usually known as something else, something Arabic like Hassan.'

'Is that all? No hint of where he came from or why he did it?'

'I'm working on it, but that's all I'm getting so far.'

'How about the woman?'

'Hardly a whisper. Not even a name or a part of a name. All I can pick up is a taste of vinegar.'

'*What?*'

'I can taste things, and smell them, as well as see them in my head. It's called eidetics. If I taste salt in my mouth, it's usually something to do with bells ringing. If I taste copper, like a mouthful of pennies, it's anxiety. Vinegar, that's vengeance. The taste of vinegar means that this lady was very, very sour about something, and she wanted to get her own back.'

'Well, I guess that could be a clue, couldn't it? There couldn't have been many women who felt so sore about The Cedars that they wanted to blow it up.'

'That's what I suggested to Lieutenant Chessman. He's initiated a search through the school records, to see if anybody was aggrieved enough to do something like this. She could have been a parent, or somebody whose child was refused entry, or maybe a former pupil with some kind of imagined grudge.'

'It could have been political. Some nut who has a fanatical objection to private education.'

They walked back to the gates together. Frank said to Nevile, 'How come you thought that you knew me? Have we ever met before, and I just don't remember it?'

'I don't think so. But there's something about you . . . some aura . . . I saw it as you came walking along the street.'

Nevile stopped and looked into his eyes so seriously that Frank began to wonder if he were gay, and that this was one of his come-on lines. He was even more concerned when Nevile said, 'Give me your hand – your left hand.'

Frank did what he was told. Nevile held it for a while, and to Frank's discomfort he closed his eyes and began to rub his knuckles with the ball of his thumb.

After a while, however, he opened his eyes again and said, '*Now* I know what it is. You have a spiritual companion. That means you have somebody's spiritual presence very close to you, somebody who needs your help. It's as though you're all charged up with psychic energy, like static electricity.'

As if one were shuffling over a great rug.

Frank's mouth felt dry. 'Do you think it could be Danny?'

'Danny? Your son? Very possibly, although I can't see very clearly *who* it is.'

48

'I don't believe in this. Danny's dead.'

'I don't know what to tell you, Frank. If you don't believe it, that's it, there's an end to it. But I can sense a spirit and I can sense that spirit's need. I can also sense *your* need. You think you were responsible for Danny's death, don't you, and you can't think how to make amends.'

'Did Detective Booker tell you that?'

'He didn't have to, Frank. You're wearing your pain like a placard.'

They walked a little further until they reached the gates. Then Frank said, 'I guess you can understand that this is causing me some very big problems with my wife.'

'Well, naturally.'

'Like . . . what it amounts to . . . our marriage has run into a concrete block at a hundred miles an hour. It's over, as far as Margot's concerned. She suffered complications when she was pregnant with Danny. He nearly died, and when he was born the doctors told her that she could never have any more children. So, Danny was her only chance at natural mother-hood, and I'm supposed to have killed him.'

'I'm really very sorry.'

Frank turned his head away, almost as if he were talking to somebody standing on his left. 'What I was thinking was . . . I know what I said a moment ago about not believing in the world beyond and everything . . . but I was wondering if you could come round and somehow show Margot that Danny's still with us. I don't know – do you ever do that kind of thing?'

'You're talking about psychic communication. What some people might call a séance.'

'I guess so. I mean, is it possible for you to talk to Danny, to find out what he's feeling now?'

'It depends if he wants to or not. We don't talk to the spirits, remember. They talk to us.'

'I admit that I'm skeptical. But I'm prepared to give it a chance.'

'So what do you need to know about Danny? Do you need to know that he forgives you for letting him die?'

Frank took a deep, steadying breath. 'Maybe.'

'And you think that if Danny forgives you, then Margot might find a way to forgive you, too?'

Frank exhaled like a man stepping chest-deep into cold water.

'All right,' said Nevile. 'I'll give it a try, if you really want me to. I'm afraid I don't do it for nothing. Five hundred and fifty dollars, plus expenses.'

'That's OK, that's fine.'

'Give me your number and I'll call you tomorrow, when I've finished with Lieutenant Chessman. And by the way, you don't have to worry.'

Frank, handing his business card over, said, 'Worry? Worry about what?'

'I'm single, unattached, and always looking for the perfect partner. But I'm not gay, and so that perfect partner won't be you.'

Five

Before he left The Cedars, Frank walked over to have a word with Lieutenant Chessman.

'That was very interesting,' he said.

'Don't tell me he's converted you already.'

'Well, let's put it this way. I didn't much care for the guy when I first saw him, but there's a whole lot more to him than meets the eye.'

'He's very good, no question. One of the best in the world. He came over to California about ten years ago, to help with the Santa Monica Strangler investigation, and he's been here ever since. I wouldn't say that I know how he does it, but he does it, and that's good enough for me.'

Detective Booker said, 'You should meet my grandma. She can tell your fortune out of chicken's guts and broken mirrors.'

'You don't mind if I take a rain check on that?' said Lieutenant Chessman. 'By the way, Mr Bell, I've just heard from headquarters. Charles Lasser has offered a five million dollar reward for information that leads to the arrest and conviction of all members of Dar Tariki Tariqat. That could help us.'

'Charles Lasser? Star-TV?'

'The very man.'

'And he's offering a five million reward? What's the catch? He hates every other TV network with a passion, and they hate him.'

'It's probably nothing more than a PR stunt. But who cares? If it encourages just one more witness to come forward and give evidence, then it's worth it.'

'I guess so,' said Frank. 'Talking of witnesses . . .'

'Yes?'

It was seven minutes of twelve. Astrid was probably waiting for him already. He could picture that faded, faraway look of hers, and the sun shining in her hair.

'If you need me to make any more statements, you know. Or look through mugshots . . .'

Lieutenant Chessman clapped him on the back. 'Thanks for the offer, Mr Bell. I'll let you know.'

As it turned out, Astrid wasn't waiting for him, so he settled at his table next to the fountain, under the shade of a large green parasol, and ordered a vodka-tonic. It was a hot afternoon but there was a steady breeze flowing through the gardens, and the bougainvillea trembled all around him. He saw several people he recognized at other tables: Yvette Kane, the agent, Laszlo Wittenski, the TV director, and Gordon Thurman from *People* magazine. He was sure that they had seen him, too, but he guessed that they didn't want to think about blown-apart children while they sipped their Chardonnay spritzers and toyed with their *chèvre* and green chili calzone. Real blown-apart children were too real. No latex involved. No stunt persons. No clever trickery with Maya digital software. The bombing at The Cedars had been met in Hollywood with an unexpected variety of emotions – anger, hysteria, bewilderment – but after the initial shock had worn off, most people had been irritated more than

51

grief-stricken. (*We* control the tears and the tragedy and the big explosions around here . . . how dare these Arab terrorists upstage us?)

Frank heard laughter, but then he heard Yvette Kane say, '*Ssh.*'

After ten minutes, Astrid came down the stone steps into the garden, wearing a pale blue straw hat and a pale blue cotton dress with an off-the-shoulder top. He stood up, and they kissed, and she smelled of Flowers. Light, fragrant, tempting. 'What's wrong?' she asked him. 'I haven't kept you waiting too long, have I?'

'No, no. You're fine. I've had a strange morning, that's all.'

'Strange in what way?'

He told her about Nevile Strange and his 'psychic imprints,' and what he had said about Amy Cutter, and about *him*, too. Astrid listened, but for some reason she didn't appear to be particularly interested, and she kept twiddling her fork and looking around the gardens as if she expected to see somebody she knew.

'What do you think?' he asked her. 'I never believed in this stuff before – séances and spirits and getting in touch with your long-dead relatives. But he seemed to be convinced that Danny was still with me, and if Danny still wants to be with me, that must mean that he doesn't blame me for what happened, right?'

'Strange was sure that it was Danny?'

'Who else could it be? I don't know anybody else who's died, not for years. "A spiritual companion," that's what he said – a spirit who's very close to me and also depends on me. It has to be Danny.'

Astrid tugged her off-the-shoulder dress a little further off her shoulder, so that she was showing more of her cleavage. She had very full breasts, with a pattern of moles across them like a star map, and from the way they moved Frank could see that she wasn't wearing a bra. The Mexican waiter in the tight black pants brought her a tequila sunrise and gave Frank a conspiratorial wink.

'So what are you going to do?' Astrid asked him, sipping

her drink and looking up at him with those bleached-out eyes. 'You're not really going to hold a séance, are you?'

'I don't see why not. If I can prove to Margot that Danny forgives me . . .'

'Do you really think that will make any difference?'

'What do you mean? Of course it will.'

'I mean that if Margot really loved you *she* would have forgiven you, without any need for Danny's ghost to tell her.'

'So you're saying that she doesn't really love me? You don't even know her.'

'Why would I want to?'

'Because she's pretty and she's intelligent and unlike most women she has a mind of her own.'

'And how would you know what most women are like? You're thirty-four, you had a child of eight.'

Frank sat back in his chair and drummed his fingers on the table. 'What is this? You're, like, what? You're questioning my marriage?'

Astrid laughed, and took hold of his hand. 'I know what you need, Frank, and it's not forgiveness. You killed Danny, but you didn't do it because you wanted to. You want to be able to talk to somebody and tell them how bad you feel, and you want to be able to scream at God, and tell Him how unfair everything is. Well, you and me both. Life's a shit, Frank, and the trouble is that most of the time, it's mostly our own fault.'

Frank ordered *matata*, spinach and clams in peanut butter sauce, while Astrid asked for a tuna and vegetable salad. They shared a very cold bottle of Arniston Bay Sauvignon between them.

Frank wiped his mouth with his napkin. 'So, you know, tell me something about yourself.'

'Do you think I need to?'

'You don't need to, but I'm interested. I just want to get some idea of who you are.'

'I was born and raised in Oxnard. My father was a TV producer and my mother was a dancer. I always wanted to be a doctor, taking care of sick children in Africa.'

'But you never were a doctor, and you never went to Africa?'

'No. Not exactly.'

'Are your parents still alive?'

'Are yours?'

'Well, OK, they spend most of their days playing bridge, but they're not physically dead yet, if that's what you mean.'

They said almost nothing for the rest of their lunch, but looked at each other as they ate, guardedly. Now and then Astrid gave him a small, secretive smile, as if she knew something that he didn't. Frank didn't know what to make of her. She seemed interested in him but he couldn't really work out why.

Most of the people that Frank knew left the Garden early. For them, it was back-to-the-office or back-to-the-studio time. One or two of them came over and shook his hand and gave him their condolences. Yvette Kane gave Frank a kiss on both cheeks and there were genuine tears in her eyes. 'I'm so sorry, Frank. It was such a shock.'

'Thanks, Yvette.'

'How's Margot taking it?'

'Not very well, I'm afraid.'

'Give her my love, won't you?' said Yvette. She was just about to leave when she stopped and looked at Astrid again. 'I'm sorry – do I know you?'

Astrid put on her sunglasses and turned around. 'I don't think so.'

'I'm sure we've met before. Didn't I see you at Hugo Mason's birthday party?'

Frank said, 'Astrid and I didn't meet till Wednesday. She was there when the bomb went off.'

'Astrid,' Yvette repeated. 'It's so weird, could have sworn that I've met you before.'

'No,' said Astrid emphatically, and turned her back. Yvette looked at Frank and gave him a mystified shrug.

Matt Fielding came over next and clasped Frank's hand between both of his, like a meaty sandwich, but all the same he couldn't keep his eyes away from Astrid's cleavage. 'What can I say?' he kept saying. 'What can I say?'

'Appreciate it, Matt,' said Frank. 'Really appreciate it.'

'This is . . .?' asked Matt, nodding at Astrid.

'Oh, I'm sorry. Astrid, this is Matt Fielding. Matt, this is Astrid.'

Matt abandoned Frank's hand and took hold of Astrid's, and gave her knuckles a rubbery kiss. 'I'm charmed.'

With her other hand, Astrid pointed to her hairline.

'Excuse me?' Matt frowned at her.

She jabbed at her hairline even more emphatically.

'Sorry, I don't know what . . .?'

'Hairpiece. Your hairpiece. It's slipping a little to the left.'

'My what is what?' He stared at her as if she had blasphemed in seven languages.

After Matt had left, Frank smacked his forehead with the heel of his hand. 'Do you have any idea who that *is*?'

'I don't care who it is. He was trying to see all the way down to my navel.'

'Matt Fielding is the head of development at Universal. If there's one word that nobody in the greater Los Angeles area ever says to Matt Fielding, it's "hairpiece."'

'I think I was very polite. I could have said "rug."'

When they left the restaurant, he looked up and down Sunset and said, 'Where did you leave your car?'

'I didn't. A friend of mine gave me a ride.'

'In that case I'd better drive you home.'

She thought about that for a while, cupping her hand over the crown of her hat to keep it from blowing away in the breeze. Then she said, 'All right. Do you know Venice at all? Palms Boulevard, off Lincoln.'

Frank checked his watch. Ten after two. He took out his cellphone and called Margot.

'Margot? Gerald was caught up in a partners' meeting so I'm running maybe thirty minutes late. I'll be back around four.'

'All right,' she said. Her voice had no expression at all.

'Margot . . .' There were so many things he wanted to say to her. That he was sorry. That Nevile Strange could show her that Danny forgave him. That he wished it were still Tuesday morning, and that he and Danny were still stuck in traffic on the Hollywood Freeway. Instead he ended the call.

'I'm not finding this easy,' he told Astrid as they drove westward on Santa Monica.

'Of course it isn't easy. You've lost your son.'

'No, I don't mean Margot. I mean you and me.'

'Is there any special reason it has to be easy?'

'I guess not. But I'm finding it very hard to get to know you. I'm beginning to ask myself why you wanted to meet me at all.'

'I wanted to meet you because we both went through that experience together, that bomb.'

'And why else?'

'I wanted to meet you because . . . well, we're kind of kindred spirits.'

'Kindred spirits, huh?'

She said nothing, but leaned her head back against the head rest and half closed her eyes, as if she were focusing on something in the very far distance.

He turned off Lincoln Boulevard into Palms, and she directed him to draw up in front of a peeling pink apartment building with dark green wooden shutters and a red-tiled veranda. 'This is it,' she said. 'Do you want to come up for a drink?'

He checked his watch again. 'OK. So long as I'm out of here by three thirty.' He locked his car and followed her up the steps and wondered why he didn't feel guilty. He felt, instead, an unexpected sense of freedom, as if a load had been taken off his mind.

Astrid unlocked the front door and they stepped into a Mexican-tiled hallway with an oak side table that was scattered with junk mail, and a large gilt mirror with business cards tucked into the frame. She led him up the stairs to the second floor and opened the door on the left-hand side – apartment number three. It was sunny and bright, with a shiny wood floor and plain calico couches with Navajo rugs draped over them. On the wall hung a lithograph of a naked young man, completely green, with the most supercilious look on his face that Frank had ever seen.

'You live here alone?' Frank asked her.

'No.'

He peeked into one of the bedrooms. There was a queen-sized bed with a carved oak bedhead, loosely strewn with a red and yellow throw. Astrid walked through to the second bedroom, where the bed was immaculately tidy with a brown and white cover and three white pillows on it.

'Who do you share with?'

'Carla, she's a flight attendant. She's in Europe this weekend. Frankfurt, Rome, Madrid. Do you want a cup of coffee? Or another glass of wine?'

She was standing in the middle of the room and he walked up behind her and laced his arms around her waist. Her perfume, and the warmth of her shoulder, and the criss-cross elasticized smocking of her dress engulfed his senses.

'Who did *you* lose?' he asked her. 'Are you ever going to tell me?'

She twisted around and kissed him directly on the lips. 'I might. But not yet.'

'You said it was somebody closer than a child. I'm . . . intrigued. I didn't know anybody who was closer to me than Danny, except for Margot. Who could be closer?'

'You can't think?'

'No,' he said. She kissed him again, and touched his cheek with her fingertips, in the same way that she had touched him when she first met him, as if she wanted to make sure that he was real.

Six

Danny's hair was shiny with hair tonic and combed with a center parting, like a child movie star from the 1940s. His cheeks were florid and his eyebrows were unnaturally dark brown. He wore a white shirt and a bow tie, and his hands were demurely clasped in front of his well-pressed black shorts.

John Lester Junior was a small man with rimless glasses

and small polished shoes and a dyed chestnut pompadour. He stood next to the non-denominational stained-glass window so that one side of his face was yellow and the other green.

'I'm sure you'll want some moments alone,' he said.

Frank nodded, and John Lester Junior stepped neatly backward out of the chapel of rest, closing the double doors behind him without a sound. He'd make a good butler, thought Frank.

Margot stayed where she was, about eight feet away from the casket, her hands hanging by her sides, as if all the strength had drained out of them.

Frank cleared his throat. 'He doesn't look too much like Danny, does he?' Margot didn't answer. Frank stepped closer to the casket and looked down at the small, utterly still figure that used to be their son. After a while he said, 'Look, he has scratches on his knees.'

What he actually meant was, *he isn't a waxwork after all; he's the real Danny.* For some reason, he had to be sure.

After a long, long silence, Margot approached the casket, too. She reached out and touched Danny's lips with her fingertips. Then she bent forward and kissed him. Her tears dropped on to his sugar-pink cheeks, so that it looked as if he had been crying, too.

As they drove home, Frank said, 'I have to ask you something. If you don't want to do it, you only have to say so. I know that it was all my fault that Danny died, but I think that he forgives me, and I want you to hear it directly from him.'

Margot very slowly turned her head and stared at him. 'Excuse me? What are you talking about, "directly from him"?'

'This morning I went to The Cedars before I met George. Lieutenant Chessman introduced me to this . . . psychic detective. He's supposed to be famous. He helps the police to look for children who go missing. He has this . . . talent, I guess you'd call it. He can see things happening after they've happened, even when there were no witnesses, and he can sense things that are going to happen, before they actually do.'

'What has this to do with Danny forgiving you?'

Frank took a right turn toward their house. 'This psychic, he can contact the dead.'

'What?'

'He can communicate with people who have . . . what do they call it? . . . *passed over*. He seems pretty sure that he can communicate with Danny.'

'And that's what you want us to do? Communicate with Danny, disturb him even when he's dead, so that you can feel better about killing him?'

Frank swung into the driveway and stopped the car an inch short of the garage doors. 'Yes,' he said. 'That's exactly what I want us to do.'

Frank spent the evening in his study, trying to finish the next episode of *Pigs*. Fourteen-year-old Dusty and twelve-year-old Henry were lying in bunk beds in their grandpa's house, where their parents had been forced to move after their own house had been blown away by a tornado.

HENRY: You know what Randy Bennett said today about Ellie-Jane Kuhne?

DUSTY: What, that she'll let you take a look at her hooters?

HENRY (sniffing loudly): That's right. (beat) How much does she charge?

DUSTY: Fifty cents, that's what I heard.

HENRY (sorting through a handful of sticky pennies): I have twenty-six cents. Do you think she'll let me take a look at just one?

DUSTY: What's the point of looking at a single hooter?

HENRY (after a moment's thought): I don't know. It's better than no hooter at all.

DUSTY (kind of admits that Henry has a point): Well, I have eleven cents. Maybe if we club together she'll let us take a look at a hooter and a half.

Frank sat back and stared at the screen. He couldn't decide if any of this was remotely funny or not. He had intended to show it to Mo and Liz at Wednesday morning's script meeting, but Wednesday morning seemed so long ago that maybe people's sense of humor had changed. Maybe they would think this was tragedy now, instead of comedy. He was still staring at it when Margot came in.

'Lynn called me.'

'Oh, yes?'

'I told her that we went to see Danny today at the funeral home, but of course Lynn can't even do that. Kathy was standing right next to the van when it blew up and there was almost nothing left of her.

Frank waited for what she was going to say next.

'The thing is . . . I mentioned this psychic detective of yours, and that you'd asked me if we could arrange a séance . . .' Another pause. 'Lynn said that if we *did* . . .'

'Go on.'

'If we did, she would very, very much like to come. She badly needs to talk to Kathy. She doesn't even have a body to bury.'

Frank said nothing for a moment, but then he leaned forward and pressed the delete button on his keyboard. 'OK. I'll arrange it.'

Police Commissioner Marvin Campbell appeared on the news at six o'clock that evening.

'About an hour ago we received a further coded telephone call from Dar Tariki Tariqat – the terrorist group who claim to be responsible for Wednesday's bombing at The Cedars elementary school in Hollywood.

'They warned us that they are planning further explosions aimed at the motion picture and television industries. Specifically, they state that "the corruption of religious and political thought throughout the world by the godless moguls of American entertainment amounts to cultural imperialism of the most oppressive nature. We are committed to smashing them and all their Satanic works."'

Commissioner Campbell was asked what he took this threat to mean.

'I think the meaning is pretty clear. These fanatics believe that American movies and television are an evil influence in countries where women have to cover their faces and risk being stoned to death for adultery. They think that *Sex and the City* is an insult to Allah and that freedom of expression is a blasphemy.'

How serious did he estimate the threat to be?

'One hundred and ten percent serious. Anybody who has no qualms about murdering innocent children will certainly be capable of committing atrocities that are similar or even worse.'

So what was he going to do to protect the entertainment industry?

'We're going to be vigilant. We're not closing anything down. No studios, no theme parks, no guided tours. Entertainment is this city's lifeblood and we're not going to allow a bunch of psychopaths to cut off our blood supply. Security at all major studios will be intensified, both by police presence and by private security officers. There will be some delays and some inconveniences, especially at public attractions such as Disneyland, Knott's Berry Farm and all the various studio tours. But we are absolutely determined that a whole city's way of life will not be undermined by a rabid minority.'

Were they any closer to finding out who Dar Tariki Tariqat actually were, and making any arrests?

'We have a number of promising leads that we're working on right now, so I can't say too much about this. But I'll have to admit that we're still no nearer to discovering exactly who these people are, or if they're affiliated to any known terror organization such as Al Qaeda.'

You've already brought in Nevile Strange, the well-known psychic detective. Is this an early admission that you don't think you're going to be able to solve this case by conventional police procedure?

'Not at all. The Los Angeles Police Department has the most experienced detectives and forensic specialists working round the clock and I have every confidence that they are going to hunt these terrorists down and bring them to justice. Mr Strange is a respected investigator with unusual but internationally acknowledged abilities, and I simply think I would have been failing in my duty if I hadn't availed myself of

61

every possible assistance, no matter how unconventional it might be.'

Frank stayed up until well past two A.M., listening to all of their favorite songs on his headphones so that he wouldn't keep Margot awake. 'We Have All the Time in the World' by Louis Armstrong; 'Easy' by The Commodores; 'Days Like These' by Van Morrison. He had poured himself a large Stolichnaya but he didn't even sip it. He didn't feel like drinking anymore.

Eventually he took off the headphones, unbuttoned his shirt, and went through to his study so that he could sleep on the couch. Margot hadn't told him that he wasn't welcome back in the bedroom, but he couldn't face the thought of lying next to her all night when she felt so bitter toward him.

He was pulling off his socks when the phone rang.

'Frank?'

'Who is this?'

'Who do you think it is?'

'Astrid? Do you have any idea what time it is?'

'Of course I do. I just wanted to tell you that I've been thinking about you.'

'I've been thinking about you, too.'

There was a long pause. It was so quiet in the house that he could hear Astrid breathing on the other end of the phone.

Eventually, she said, 'I wanted to know when I could see you again.'

'Tomorrow, if you like. I mean today. Maybe sometime in the afternoon. How does three o'clock sound?'

'Three o'clock sounds perfect. You can come round to my apartment if you like.'

'OK.' He didn't know what else to say.

Astrid hesitated, and then she said, 'You're worried, aren't you, because you can't work out who I am. Well, you needn't worry, because it doesn't matter.'

'How can you say that? Of course it matters. Finding out who you are – that's part of the whole process of getting to know you, sharing things. All I know about you so far is that your father was a television producer and your mother was a dancer and that you wanted to be a doctor in Africa.'

'You don't even know that. I lied.'

'You *lied*? What did you do that for?'

'Because you wanted to know all about me and I didn't want to disappoint you. But I want you to like what you *see*, not what you *know*. You *do* like what you see, don't you, Frank?'

'Of course I do. I'm not entirely sure where I stand, that's all.'

'I'll see you at three o'clock. Sleep well.'

Saturday, September 25, 10:09 A.M.

Matty was already beginning to think that bringing the North Hollywood cub scout pack on a weekend outing to Universal Studios had been a very reckless idea. It was little more than an hour since the turnstiles had opened and yet the lines of hot and impatient sightseers were winding all the way back to the parking lot. Three police cars were parked close to the entrance, and everybody who passed through the turnstiles was being frisked by police and security guards and having their bags looked into. One or two were being taken aside and questioned more closely.

The Silber brothers had already gone missing twice, and so Matty had been forced to send Irene Wallach to find them, which meant that he had been left in sole charge of eighteen overexcited small boys, most of whom seemed to be desperate to go to the bathroom every three minutes.

Even more trying, with Irene Wallach rounding up the strays, Kevin Millfield had decided to attach himself to Matty and engage him in one of his long, lugubrious conversations. Matty was sure that Kevin was going to grow up to be a professional prophet of doom, or at the very least a loss adjuster.

Kevin had tufty brown hair and very large ears that shone red in the sunlight. Matty didn't think that he had ever seen him smile. As a cub scout, he was conscientious and thoughtful but completely incompetent at everything from tying knots

63

to making an impromptu spit-roaster. His father owned Millfield's Sensible Shoe Stores on Magnolia.

'I can understand why all the major studios have tours,' he was saying, in his mournful monotone. 'They can make a profit out of all of their old movie sets – which are only a lot of junk, after all – and at the same time they can advertise their up-and-coming movies. But I do think that it spoils the illusion, finding out what goes on behind the scenes. Don't you, Mr Doggett?'

'Don't I what, Kevin?'

'Don't you think that these tours make it hard to believe in movies anymore?'

'Well, no, Kevin, not really. I think they're very interesting, and very educational. Did you see where Joey Mendez disappeared to?'

'I wouldn't go to see a magic act if the magician explained how he managed to saw a lady in half and put her back together again. I mean, what would be the point? Don't you think so, Mr Doggett?'

Matty caught sight of Joey Mendez and blew his whistle and furiously beckoned him to get back into line. 'Where have you been? You're supposed to stay with the group. What did I tell you? Stay with the group!'

'I saw the Terminator over there, sir. Like, the real-life Terminator. I had to go say *hasta la vista*, baby.'

'You stay with the group, OK, or else the only person who's going to get terminated is you.'

'He wasn't the *real* Terminator,' Kevin told Joey pedantically. 'He was only an actor.'

'Oh, he was only an actor?' said Matty. 'So what do you think Arnold Schwarzenegger used to do for a living?'

After more than twenty minutes they finally reached the pay booths and Matty bought their group ticket. He had to squeeze, gasping, to get through the turnstile, because of the size of his belly.

A security officer immediately approached him and said, 'Have to search you, sir. Sorry.'

'That's OK. The only thing I'm smuggling under this shirt is a lifetime addiction to chicken-fried steak.'

'These your boys?' the security guard asked him as he patted Matty's red and orange Hawaiian paunch.

'Cubs from the Eighteenth Scout Troop. Don't worry, they'll only take about twenty minutes to wreck the place, then they'll leave.'

The security guard grinned at him and slapped him on the back. 'Have a good day, sir, and thank you for your co-operation.'

The cub scouts whooped and jumped and ran off to claim their seats on the tram. Irene Wallach came across, all spindly arms and spindly legs, with buck teeth and wiry black hair and sunglasses with white upswept frames. 'This is the bit I like the best,' she confessed, linking arms. 'We can sit down and relax and we don't have to worry about losing them.'

'I'm getting too old for this,' said Matty, heaving himself up into the second to back bench of the first tram car. The bench behind them immediately filled up with giggling Japanese girls and a young man in a Desert Storm shirt and mirror sunglasses who was almost twice Matty's size.

'Have we decided on a date for Chula Vista yet?' asked Irene. She was wearing a loose pink blouse and Matty was disconcerted to see her left breast, as pale and as flat as a flapjack, with a raisin for a nipple.

'Oh, you mean the cook-out? Ray suggested November twenty-third.'

'I think we ought to concentrate on ethnic food. You know, something healthy, like stir fry, or tacos. Stay away from hot dogs and cheeseburgers and all those saturated fats.'

'You're not trying to make a point, are you?'

'Oh, for goodness' sake, Matty! We all love you the way you are!'

'I know. A roly-poly figure of fun. Don't you know why fat men laugh? It's the only thing they can do to stop themselves from crying.'

The tram jerked and began to move. A tour guide with bouncy blonde hair and improbably white teeth picked up the microphone and said, 'Welcome to Universal Studios, ladies and gentlemen and children! Today we're going to take you

65

on a trip into the magical world of the movies – a ride that you'll never, ever forget!'

Kevin turned around to Matty and said, 'We won't forget it because we'll never be able to go to the movies again and think that they're true.'

'Kevin, for Pete's sake, stop being so pessimistic. Besides, didn't you tell me you'd been on this tour once before?'

'That's how I know how disappointed we're all going to be.'

Saturday, September 25, 10:32 A.M.

As the tram slowly descended the slope toward the lake where Jaws would appear, Kevin said, dolefully, 'This is the lake where the great white shark comes out of the water and sprays everybody except that it's only rubber and nobody ever gets hurt.'

'Thanks, Kevin,' said Matty. 'That's very reassuring. That's also spoiled the surprise for everybody else.'

But the big young man sitting right behind Matty suddenly let out a whoop, clapped his hands, and shouted, 'Woweee! Ain't this something!'

Matty turned around and frowned at him, but the young man clapped his hands again, and stamped his feet on the floor of the tram. The Japanese girls who were sitting beside him looked alarmed, and edged themselves as far away him as they could.

'This is the ride to glory!' the young man yelled. 'This train don't take no backsliders, this train! This is where we get to see God, in all His majesty! Yes, sir! This is going to be a ride to remember, all right!'

He stood up in his seat, his belly almost knocking Matty's cap off, and began to sway from side to side, clapping his hands with every sway, and letting out whoop after whoop.

The guide said, 'Sir – you at the back of the car – yes, you sir. Will you sit down, please? No standing is permitted while the tram is in motion. That's a city ordinance.'

The young man whooped again. 'We're coming to the Kingdom! We're coming to the Kingdom! This train don't take no unholy, this train!'

66

'Sit down, sir! You'll have to sit down!'

But now the young man leaned over Matty and grinned at the cub scout pack. 'Do you boys know where you're headed? Do you have *any* idea? You're headed for the Promised Land, that's where you're headed, and ain't you the lucky ones!'

The driver brought the tram to a stop, right next to Amityville Lake. On schedule – as part of the *Jaws* display, the fishing pier was dragged away from its moorings, into the center of the lake, and a row of oil drums bounced across the surface as if they were being pulled by the great white shark. But the driver climbed out of his seat and came back toward the end of the car, and at the same time the guide picked up her radio-telephone and called for security.

'Sir, I want you to step down out of the tram,' said the driver. He was over sixty years old, with gray hair, a gray moustache and a stoop. The young man looked down at him and let out another whoop.

'This is destiny, old man. This is the force of nature. Ain't nothing on this earth can stand up against the force of nature.'

Matty turned around in his seat. 'Listen, you asshole. Get off the tram and stop upsetting all of these kids.'

The young man stared at him but all Matty could see in his mirror sunglasses was his own crimson face. Out on the lake, the row of oil drums began to bounce even faster toward the shoreline, but hardly anybody on the tram was watching.

'You want to say hello to your maker?' the young man asked Matty.

Matty stood up so that the two of them were standing belly to belly. 'Do you think I'm scared of you?' Matty challenged him. 'I served in the Gulf, and I saw scarier camels than you.'

'Oh, really?' the young man retorted, but this time his tone was quieter and much more reasonable. 'So how scary do you think *this* is?'

He lifted his fist and opened his fingers just a little and

67

just for an instant, but it was enough for Matty to see the switch device that he was holding in the palm of his hand and the thin wire than ran down his arm and into the sleeve of his camouflage shirt.

'You wouldn't,' said Matty.

But now the driver climbed up on to the boarding step and said, 'Come on, sir. Until you get off, this tram's going nowhere.'

The young man ignored him. 'See this beer gut of mine?' he asked Matty, even more softly. 'What do you think it's really made of? Fat? *Wrong*! It's C4 – plasticized RDX.'

Matty turned to Irene Wallach. 'Irene, get all the kids off the tram, now.'

'What?' she frowned.

'Get all the kids off the tram and do it now. Please.'

'Unh-unh,' said the young man in the mirror sunglasses, shaking his head. 'Nobody's getting off. You're all coming with me.'

Matty shouted, 'No!' and made a lunge for the wire that ran down the young man's arm, trying to wrench it free. At the same time, Jaws reared out of the lake in a blast of compressed air, its eyes staring and its teeth bared. With the exception of Kevin, all the children screamed.

Saturday, September 25, 10:34 A.M.

The blast was heard five miles away in every direction – a dull, emphatic thud. The front car of the tram was blown apart so violently that there was nothing left of it but a blackened chassis and a surreal arrangement of twisted seats. Most of the second car was burned out, and hundreds of windows were broken, all over the lot.

Jaws, the great white shark, was wrecked even more comprehensively than it had been in the movie. All of the latex was blasted away from its frame, leaving a smoking, grinning skeleton.

But the human litter was so terrible that when the first police and security officers arrived at the scene, they couldn't understand what they were looking at. As a *Times* reporter was later to write, 'They looked not like cubs, but like cherubs, shot down by anti-aircraft fire.'

Seven

Frank rang the doorbell. Through the intercom, Astrid said, 'Hold on,' and then she pressed the buzzer so that he could let himself in. He walked across the Mexican-tiled hallway and climbed the stairs. She was waiting for him outside apartment three, wearing a very short white muslin dress and bare feet, with silver rings on her toes. She was looking pale and fretful, as if she had taken too many pills.

'There's been another bomb,' she told him.

'I know. I actually heard it. I was out in the yard, putting out the trash. Then *bamm!* like somebody slamming a door.'

'They said on the news that nineteen people were killed. Eleven cub scouts. They showed pictures. God, it's so terrible.'

'Hey, you're shaking.'

'I'm *upset*, Frank. I'm so upset. All those little boys.'

Frank closed the door behind them and laid his hands on her shoulders. 'I know. As soon as I heard about it, I thought about all of their parents. Nobody should have to suffer like this. Not for the sake of some crazy idea about religion or politics or whatever.'

'Do you think the same people could have done it?'

'Those Arabs? Who knows. But who else could it be? The cops are pretty sure that it was a suicide bombing and Western terrorists don't go in for blowing themselves up, do they? And you heard what they said yesterday about wrecking the entertainment industry.'

'Do you want a drink?' Astrid asked him.

He nodded. She went to the white wicker table on the opposite side of the room and poured out two long-stemmed glasses of Shiraz Cabernet. He could see her face in the mirror on the wall, and he was surprised how different she looked, in

69

reflection. Perhaps it was the lack of symmetry that made her face so striking.

She brought him his wine. 'They said that all of the studios are going to suspend their tours. And they're closing down Disneyland.'

'A little too late for that, don't you think?' said Frank. 'The next time they'll probably hit someplace totally different, like a TV studio, right in the middle of a game show or something.'

'Eleven children killed,' said Astrid. 'And what's it all for?'

The French windows were open. Astrid stepped outside on to the narrow tiled balcony and Frank followed her. Below them was a small shadowy yard with a stone fountain, overgrown with orange blossom. A warm ocean breeze blew across the rooftops and stirred her muslin dress, so that now and again Frank could see the curve of her bare bottom and her hip. 'That's the way to kill people,' she said, almost as if she were quoting somebody. 'Kill their children.'

'They'll catch them, especially after this.'

'You really think so?'

'Half of the LAPD is out looking for them, as well as the FBI.'

'Yes, but who are they looking for?'

Frank shook his head, as if an insect had tried to fly into his ear. She spoke in riddles sometimes. 'Did you really lie to me about your father and mother?' he asked her.

'Maybe I did, maybe I didn't.'

'You're teasing me.'

'No, I'm not. I'm simply asking you to use your eyes.' She leaned on the railing for a while, sipping her wine. Then she suggested, 'Let's go inside.'

He took off his shoes and they sat on the couch together, cross-legged, facing each other. He lifted his glass to her and said, '*Salut*, whoever you are.' A curved reflection from her red wine danced on her lips, making it look as if she was smiling when she wasn't.

'How's your wife?' she asked.

'No different. We went to the funeral home yesterday and saw Danny. That didn't improve matters.'

70

'What did he look like – Danny?'

'What did he *look* like?'

'I'm sorry . . . I was just curious. I never saw anybody dead before.'

Frank thought about it and then shrugged. 'He looked like Danny but he wasn't Danny, if you know what I mean. I saw my grandfather when he was laid out and I can remember thinking, *why am I here, why am I saying goodbye to this . . . storefront dummy*? My grandfather's body was there but I knew my grandfather wasn't. He was long gone.'

'You're right. A body without a spirit, it's like an hourglass with no sand in it. It's meaningless.'

He finished his wine and put down his glass. 'Talking of spirits, I've arranged for Nevile Strange to come around to our house tomorrow and hold a séance.'

'You're kidding me.' She peered at him more closely and then she said, 'You're *not* kidding me.'

'He thinks he can get in touch with Danny – and one of Danny's school friends, too.'

'Whoo! Doesn't your wife object?'

'She did at first, but then her friend called her and they got to talking about it, and I guess her friend won her round. Lynn Ashbee, poor woman. There was nothing left of her daughter but her feet, still in their shoes. What kind of a world are we living in when we have nothing left to bury but our children's feet?'

'A very heartless world, Frank. Even more heartless than you know.'

They watched the television news. The latest casualty figures from Universal Studios were fifteen children killed, and seven adults. Over a hundred people of all ages had been seriously injured, and the damage to property had already run into hundreds of thousands of dollars. Not to mention the indefinite closure of Universal City to the public, and almost every other major attraction in Los Angeles.

An FBI press officer said, 'Early tests have led us to speculate that the suicide bomber fashioned himself a corset or a false abdomen out of malleable plastic explosive to avoid detection at the gates. Yes, there was a dog there trained to sniff out explosives but in this case the bomber somehow managed to elude it. The explosive bears strong similarities to C4 – cyclotrimethylenetrinitramine – which has a less pungent odor than many other explosives.'

Frank switched off the television. 'Shit. This is serious. It's coming to the point where we're not going to feel safe anywhere.'

Astrid leaned forward and touched his forehead, and then the tip of his nose, and then his lips. 'Do you think you're safe with me?' she asked him.

He grasped her wrist to stop her from touching him anymore. 'Any reason why I shouldn't be?'

'Because I think that you and I should think of becoming lovers.'

He looked at her narrowly, still holding her wrist, trying to read those stone-washed denim eyes. 'I lost my only son less than three days ago. You lost somebody too, although you won't tell me who it is. I don't think I'm ready for this yet, even if you are.'

'Meaning that you might be, given enough time?'

When he arrived home he found that Margot was preparing dinner for them both. She said, 'Hi,' and busied herself laying the kitchen table. He stood and watched her. Maybe this was her way of telling him that she might, in time, be able to forgive him. She was making wide noodles with fragments of poached salmon and Pacific Rim pesto, which he detested, but of course he had never told her that he detested it.

She had washed and brushed her hair and put on makeup and she was wearing her white silk Saks Fifth Avenue sweater with baggy sleeves and oatmeal-colored slacks. He recognized her perfume, too. Flowers, the same perfume that Astrid wore.

'There's some wine in the fridge,' she told him.

'Thanks.'

'How was your meeting with Joe?'

'Oh, fine,' he lied. 'They're going to give me as long as I want.'

He poured himself a glass of cold Sauvignon and sat down

at the kitchen table. Along the top three shelves of the white oak hutch stood rows of white plates and white milk jugs that Margot had thrown herself, at pottery class. Next to the hutch hung a painting of a red-haired woman covering her face with her hands. It was titled *Blind Witness*.

'What time is Nevile Strange coming tomorrow?' asked Margot as she spooned out pasta.

'He said he'd try to get here by one o'clock. Hey – that's enough for me, thanks. Really.'

She served herself and then she sat down. He wound some pasta around his fork but he didn't lift it up. Instead he found himself staring at Margot with an unexpected feeling of resentment. All right, she was talking to him. All right, she might be ready to forgive him. But he wasn't sure if he *wanted* to be forgiven – not if it was going to be like this.

She glanced up at him with those big dark Audrey Hepburn eyes. 'Is it OK? Your pasta?'

'Sure, it's . . .' He waved a reassuring forkful at her.

'Lynn will probably be here about twelve.'

'OK, good.'

'She's going to bring a photograph of Kathy, like you said.'

He lowered his fork again. This wasn't going to work. He felt so badly bruised, not just physically but mentally. Their life could never be the same, not after losing Danny. When he looked at Margot, he had the same feeling as watching a home video of a summer day that could never be relived. What had he read in *The Process*? 'You will never pass this way again in a lifetime, effendi.'

'You're not eating.'

He frowned down at his plate.

'You ought to eat something, Frank.'

He couldn't speak. After a while, she stood up and took his plate away. He heard her in the laundry room, scraping it into the trash. She came back and stood close to him. 'If you want to come to bed tonight, Frank . . .'

He cleared his throat. 'Sure, I'll just . . . watch a little television, you know.'

She stayed where she was. From the way she was fidgeting he could tell that she had something to tell him. 'Frank

. . . I do know that you didn't let Danny die on purpose. What I said to you – the way I blamed you – well, you have to understand how I felt.'

He nodded, still looking down at the place where his plate had been.

'I've been thinking about tomorrow, and if I can hear that Danny's at peace . . . that's all I care about.'

Frank nodded again.

Margot tore off a sheet of kitchen towel and blew her nose. She stood beside him for another minute or so, but he felt too bruised even to raise his head. Eventually she left him in the kitchen and went to the bedroom. When he passed the bedroom door on his way to his study, he saw that she had left it a half-inch ajar.

He crept into the bedroom a few minutes after two A.M., wearing his pajamas, which he never normally wore. He stood still for a long moment, trying to decide if Margot was asleep or not. Eventually, so tired that he felt dizzy, he eased himself under the covers beside her, turning his back to her, as hers was turned to him.

He lay there, unable to sleep, until six fifteen. Then he climbed out of bed as carefully as he had climbed in, and went into the kitchen to make himself a cup of coffee.

While the coffee perked, he switched on the television. Charles Lasser was being interviewed on the early-morning news. A huge, bulky man, with shiny dyed-black hair and a head that looked like a half-finished sculpture by Rodin, with a massive brow and a hooked nose.

'So you've doubled your reward to ten million dollars, Mr Lasser?'

'That's right. And if necessary I'll go on increasing it, until these scum are caught.'

'Some people in the entertainment industry are suggesting that this is nothing more than another Charles Lasser publicity stunt . . . and that you're using these outrages as a vehicle to promote Star-TV.'

'Of course they're saying that. They're jealous and they're mean-spirited. But they can think whatever they like and they

74

can say whatever they like. I didn't get where I am today by being Mr Nice Guy, I'll admit that, and I know that many people in the television business resent me for being an upstart – and not only that, a highly successful upstart.

'But in times of crisis, we should forget about personal ill-feeling and work together for our common protection. This is just such a time of crisis, and that's why I've increased my reward. Not a single more innocent life must be lost. Not one more child must be injured. I want to see every member of Dar Tariki Tariqat arrested, tried, and sent to Death Row.'

Eight

Nevile Strange arrived nearly an hour late. He was driving a black Mercedes saloon, which was at least fifteen years old but very highly waxed. The day was strangely overcast, a dull lavender color, and there were distant grumbles of thunder from the San Gabriel mountains. Nevile climbed out of his car wearing a black suit and a black shirt, relieved only by a red poppy in his buttonhole.

'Sorry, Frank. They wanted me to take a look at the crime scene at Universal Studios.'

'Bad, huh?'

Nevile looked at him and nodded and the expression in his eyes told it all.

'Did you pick up anything?' Frank asked him. 'Any of those . . . psychic imprints?'

'A great deal of shock. A great deal of pain. It was a little too soon to make sense of it all.'

'You're sure you want to go through with this séance today? We could always postpone it.'

Nevile shook his head. 'No . . . it'll do me good to focus on something else. There were so many voices . . . so much chaos.'

Frank led Nevile up the driveway and showed him into the

house. As he stepped into the wide, oak-boarded hallway, he stopped and looked around, almost as if he could smell something unusual.

'Everything OK?'

'Oh, yes. Everything's fine.' But he stayed where he was, turning his head this way and that, and keeping one finger raised, as if he were listening.

'Danny was your only child?' he said at last. 'That's what you told me, wasn't it?'

'That's right.'

'Odd,' said Nevile.

'Odd in what way?'

'I can distinctly feel another departed presence here, apart from Danny's.'

'What kind of a presence?'

'It's hard to say, exactly. A very elusive presence. One that's trying to stay out of sight, psychically speaking. I don't know if it's a man or a woman, or a child. Maybe a child, the way it's playing hide-and-go-seek.'

'The couple who lived here before us – their daughter died when she was eighteen months.'

'Well, maybe it's her. Little children can be very mischievous spirits.'

Frank showed him through to the living room. Lynn was already there, sitting on the couch, shoeless, talking to Margot. On the white coffee table in front of them, on either side of a tall vase of lilies, stood two framed photographs, one of Kathy and one of Danny, both of them smiling. Kathy was missing her two front teeth.

'Nevile, this is my wife, Margot, and this is Lynn Ashbee. How about a drink? I guess you could use one.'

'A Pernod if you have one, Frank, or a Ricard. There's something about the taste of aniseed that clears the perceptions.'

'Nevile was over at Universal City,' Frank explained. 'The police wanted him to see what kind of psychic vibrations he could pick up.'

'Oh my God,' said Lynn. She was looking very pallid, almost gray, with no makeup and her hair scraped back in a ponytail. A light green turtleneck did nothing to give her any color. 'Oh my God, it must be dreadful.'

'Yes,' said Nevile. 'Yes, it is.'

'They still have no idea who these people are, these terrorists?' asked Margot. She was dressed all in white, a loose silk top with a Chinese collar and flowing silk pants.

Nevile said, 'Not yet. The official line is that they're some kind of offshoot of Al Qaeda, but it's impossible to say. They gave me the bomber's sunglasses to hold, or what was left of them, and I must say they gave me a very confusing message.'

'His *sunglasses* gave you a message?' asked Margot.

'That's right. When something really stressful happens to you, your personal possessions often absorb your psychic resonance. Your sunglasses, your jewelry, your combs, your shoes – even your clothes. I've been able to locate missing people through a purse, or a wristwatch, or a piece of torn dress material. I suppose you could say that I'm rather like a bloodhound. Let me sniff the psychic scent and I can follow it.'

'And these sunglasses?'

'I don't know. I sensed anger, and frustration, but a lack of self-confidence, too. Strangely enough – considering these people are supposed to be Arabs – I felt a fervent Christian evangelism, too – almost fanatical.'

'Maybe he'd converted. People do, don't they?'

Frank brought Nevile a glass of Ricard. 'Please, sit down.'

Nevile took a sip of his drink and then sat down. Lynn said, 'Can I just ask you one question?'

'Of course. You're going to ask me if Kathy will be aware that you're trying to get in touch with her.'

'Yes . . . well, yes. How did you know that?'

Nevile smiled at her, reached across the coffee table and held her hand. 'First of all you have to understand that everybody has the potential to do what I do. You do, Lynn, and you do, Margot, and Frank, you do too. Psychic sensitivity is nothing special, it's a mental ability that we're all born with, but not many of us ever develop it to its full potential.'

'You mean that if I practiced enough, I could get in touch with Kathy any time I wanted?'

'Yes, pretty much. Of course there are times when it's easier to communicate with spirits than others, and there are some places where you can get better reception than others – especially places that Kathy was familiar with, like her own bedroom.'

Margot said, 'I have to admit that I'm more than a little scared.'

Nevile turned around and took hold of her hand, too. 'There's no need to be frightened. Danny may have passed over, but he's still Danny. The only scary spirits are the spirits of people who were scary when they were alive.'

Frank said, 'I can ask Danny questions? He'll be able to hear me?'

'It depends. He passed over only very recently, and passing over is always a tremendous shock. It can take days or weeks for a spirit to understand that he or she is no longer living in the physical world. Some spirits go on for years and still can't accept that they're dead.'

'All right, then,' said Frank. 'What do we have to do?'

'You don't have to hold hands. You don't have to close your eyes, although some people find that it helps them to concentrate. All you have to do is think about Danny and Kathy, and imagine them the way they were the very last time you saw them. That's a very potent emotional image. Look at their photographs, and try to believe that they're still with us, not in the flesh, maybe, but in our minds.'

Lynn said, 'How will we know when you've gotten in touch?'

'It can happen in all kinds of different ways. Sometimes the spirits are very subtle, and contact us through signs and hints and coded suggestions. For instance you might suddenly become aware of a smell that reminds you of a time you spent together, and at the same time the radio will be playing their favorite song.

'Other times, though, they can speak quite clearly, so that you can hear their voices. And, very occasionally, they become visible. Only very rarely, however. It takes a very high degree of psychic sensitivity to be able to see somebody who has passed over.'

'You mean they actually *appear*?' asked Frank. 'Like ghosts?'

'Not exactly. Not like the popular concept of ghosts. More like the way I saw my friend Robert, kind of an action replay.'

'All right,' said Frank. 'Are we ready to do this?'

They sat in silence for nearly five minutes while Nevile clasped his hands together and seemed to be focusing very far away. Lynn kept twisting the end of the green silk scarf that she was wearing as a belt, while Margot sat in the lotus position with her head tilted back, breathing as if she had taken lessons in Zen meditation. Frank had been hopeful about this séance to begin with, but now that Nevile was actually here, he found himself growing increasingly skeptical, and wondering what Margot's reaction would be if nothing happened.

He stared at Danny's laughing face in the photograph and tried to remember what he was like when he was happy and alive, but the photograph was blotted out by the picture in his mind's eye of Danny sitting in the back seat of his car, staring at him, dead.

Nevile suddenly sat up straight and cleared his throat. 'Kathy . . . your mother's looking for you. Can you hear me, Kathy?'

Lynn couldn't stop herself from letting out a whimper, and covered her mouth with her hand.

'Kathy . . . do you know where you are? Do you know what happened to you?'

There was a long pause, and then Nevile nodded, and nodded again, one finger lifted close to his ear as if he were listening to somebody.

'Kathy, your mother's here and she wants to talk to you. Your mother wants you to know that she loves you and misses you and that you're not forgotten.'

'Can you hear her?' said Lynn. 'Is that Kathy? Can you really hear her?'

'She's close,' Nevile reassured her. 'Please try to be patient.'

He sat in silence for another two or three minutes, and then he said, 'Kathy? Are you going to talk to your mother,

79

sweetheart? Your mother would really like to know that you're here.'

Again he looked as if he were listening. Frank couldn't help thinking, *I hope this isn't starting to look like a scam. Anybody can pretend that they're talking to a spirit. Even I could do it. And so far we haven't seen any evidence at all that he's really talking to anyone at all.*

'What did you say, Kathy?' said Nevile. 'You don't know what happened? There was an accident, sweetheart, that's what happened. You and some of your friends got hurt. You passed over to the place where people go when they die.'

He listened some more, and then he said to Lynn, 'She doesn't really understand. She wants to know why she can't come back.'

Lynn's eyes were filled with tears. 'Tell her I love her. Please, tell her I'll always love her.'

Frank said, 'You're sure that it's Kathy you're talking to? I mean, I'm not being critical or anything, but there must be thousands of spirits out there – how do you get to talk to the one you want?'

'Oh, spirits aren't difficult to find. Kathy's spirit is very close to her mother, just like Danny's is close to you and Margot. Spirits never leave the ones they love. They never leave the ones they hate, either. It works both ways.'

There was yet another pause, then Nevile nodded and said, 'Yes,' twice. He turned to Lynn and said, 'Kathy says that she loves you too and she can't wait to come home.'

'Is it really her?' asked Lynn. 'You're not telling me this just to make me feel better? Please tell me it's really her.'

'Kathy,' said Nevile, 'your mother wants to hear your voice. Do you think that you can talk to your mother?'

Nothing. It was now almost three P.M. and Frank was seriously beginning to wish that he hadn't invited Nevile over. *If Margot can find it in her heart to forgive me, then I can probably forgive myself too, given time, and I don't need to hear from some smooth-talking British psychic that Danny doesn't bear me any ill-will, either,* he thought.

'Kathy,' said Nevile, in a coaxing voice. 'Come on now, sweetheart, talk to your mother.'

80

Again, nothing. Lynn had stopped crying now and glanced at Frank as if she, too, was having her doubts.

But then Nevile took hold of Lynn's hand and said, 'She thinks it was your fault.'

'What was my fault?'

'You didn't want her to go to dance class, so you sent her to this other place.'

Lynn slowly opened her mouth. 'How did you know that? How do you know about the dance class?'

'She also says you punished her for being rude about Gene's nose.'

'Oh my God.'

'She says she's sorry and can she come back now.'

'Oh, no. Oh my God. Oh, no. My baby!' Lynn was biting her knuckles and the tears were streaming down her cheeks.

Nevile gripped her hand very tight. 'She's here, Lynn. Tell her you love her. Tell her what happened was an accident, it wasn't her fault.'

Lynn took a deep, wrenching breath, and cried out, 'Kathy, I didn't . . .' But she was too choked up to say any more. Margot put her arm around her and held her tight, while Nevile continued to grip her hand and also to stare at her, as if he were willing her to hear what he could hear.

He *can* hear her, thought Frank. He must be able to hear her. He half rose in his chair, reaching out for Margot, and it was then that he glimpsed something out of the corner of his eye – a blur, a movement – and he turned toward the patio windows. He felt his scalp tingle and tighten and his hairs stood on end, one by one, all frizzling out slowly in a fuzzy electric halo that came down around his ears.

Standing on the patio was Danny, in his school clothes, with his X-Men bag on his shoulder. He was deathly white, and he was staring in the same expressionless way as he was when Frank had found him dead in the back of the car. His image blurred and flickered, and for a split second it disappeared altogether, but then it came back again, and it was still staring at him.

Nevile turned around, too. 'Jesus!' he cried.

Margot let out a sound that would have been a scream if

81

she had had any air in her lungs. Instead it was a high, wavering gasp.

'It's Danny,' Frank heard himself saying, as if he were somebody else.

'Stay still,' Nevile warned him. 'Don't go any nearer. He's shocked enough already, we don't want to scare him.'

'But we have to let him in,' begged Margot.

'It's his spirit, Margot. It's his resonance. It's not his physical self. If he wanted to come inside, he could, and he would.'

'Danny,' Margot pleaded. 'Danny, can you talk to me? Oh, Danny, I love you so much!'

Danny continued to stare, but he didn't speak. Frank said, 'Danny, can you hear me? I didn't know that you were hurt. If only I'd known . . .'

'Your mom and dad love you, Danny,' put in Nevile. 'Why don't you tell them that you love them, too?'

Almost a minute went past with Danny's image staring at them, unmoving.

'Danny,' said Nevile, 'do you understand what's happened to you? Do you know where you are?'

It was then that they heard a thin, muffled voice, which seemed closer than the image on the patio. *'He didn't care.'*

'Who didn't care?'

'My dad. I was dying and he didn't care.'

'Danny,' said Frank, 'I swear to God that I didn't know you were hurt so bad. I swear it.'

'I was dying and I called you and I called you but you didn't hear me and you didn't come back.'

'Danny . . .' Frank started, but it was all he could do not to choke.

'You want me to forgive you but you didn't care and I will never forgive you, ever. I hope you see my dead face every day until you die, and when you die I hope you go to hell.'

'Danny, for Christ's sake . . .'

'For nobody's sake, Dad. For nobody's sake but your own. You took my whole life away from me because you didn't care, and not caring is the greatest sin of all.'

Frank took a step toward the windows. Margot snatched at his sleeve and said, 'No, Frank,' but he pried himself free and carried on, until he was close enough to touch the glass. Danny stayed where he was, out on the patio, white-faced, staring.

Nevile said, 'Careful, Frank. He's totally traumatized by what happened to him. You don't want to make things worse.'

'How can I make things worse? I let him die and he won't forgive me.'

'Not yet. But give him a little time.'

'Time? What time? I took all his time away from him.'

'Frank . . .' Nevile cautioned him, but Frank took hold of the door handle and unlocked it. 'Frank, maybe you don't want to do that.'

Frank rolled the door to one side. And there, out on the patio, was nothing at all. Nothing but the breeze, and the gloomy afternoon light, and the pungent smell of eucalyptus.

'Danny, I didn't know,' Frank whispered. Thunder rumbled over the San Gabriel Mountains. 'I'm so sorry, Danny. I didn't know.'

He turned back into the living room. Margot was standing on the opposite side of the room with her back turned. Nevile was sitting next to Lynn, holding both of her hands.

'What do I do now?' Frank asked.

Nine

'Danny *will* forgive you, you know, given time,' said Nevile.

Frank finished writing his check on the roof of Nevile's Mercedes, signed it, and handed it over. 'I can't say you didn't earn it.'

'I don't know, Frank. I still have the feeling that something wasn't quite right. Of course I've had visual manifestations before, but this is the first time that anybody else has been able to see them.'

'Well, maybe we ought to try it again, when Danny's been

83

laid to rest. You know, maybe he might have learned to accept it.'

'When's the funeral?'

'Wednesday morning, at Oak Lawn. You're welcome to come if you want to.'

'Maybe I will. Thanks. And thanks for the . . . um . . .' He held up the still-drying check.

He drove off, and Frank watched him go. As he turned back to the house, he saw Margot and Lynn coming out. Lynn had her handkerchief pressed to her mouth, and Margot gave Frank a look that meant, *don't even come near us, OK?*

'I'm taking Lynn home,' she said, 'and then I'm going to see my parents.'

'All right. What time do you think you'll be back?'

'I don't know. Maybe I'll stay overnight. There's some left-over pasta in the fridge if you're hungry.'

'Margot . . .'

'There's nothing to say, Frank. I can hardly believe what happened today, but it did, and I need some time to think about it.'

'You heard what Nevile said. Danny's traumatized. He doesn't know what he's saying.'

'He's *dead*, Frank, and he *still* doesn't forgive you. Doesn't that tell you something?'

Frank didn't know what to say to that. He stood on the porch while Margot backed her car down the driveway, turned in the street with a protesting squeal of tires, and drove off toward Hollywood Way without looking back at him once.

He was about to go back into the house when a gray Ford Taurus appeared around the corner and parked right outside. Lieutenant Chessman climbed out, followed by Detective Booker.

'Mr Bell! Glad I caught you at home!'

'Hi, there, Lieutenant. What can I do for you today?'

Lieutenant Chessman came up the driveway and took his notebook out of his coat pocket. 'I hope I'm not interrupting anything, but I still have one or two loose ends to tie up, and I was hoping that maybe I could jog your memory a little more.'

'Lieutenant, I told you everything I saw.'

'You did, yes. But I'm still having difficulty locating this woman you say you met immediately after the explosion. I've identified and talked to every other eye witness, and pinpointed their exact whereabouts immediately prior to the explosion, and also immediately after. But this one woman remains a mystery – Ms X. I don't know who she is, or what she was doing there, or what she might have seen.'

'I'm sorry,' said Frank. 'I don't see how I can help you. I asked her if she was OK, and she asked me if *I* was OK, and that was about all we said to each other. I gave my address to one of the officers at the scene, and when I turned around she was gone.'

'Was there anything memorable about her? Anything at all?'

'She was about five-four, mid-twenties I guess. Short hair.'

'What was she wearing?'

'Just a plain, ordinary dress. Yellow, or cream, as I recall.'

'And one shoe? Did you notice what kind of shoe?'

'A sandal, I think. One of those strappy things. Brown.'

'OK. And that's all you remember? She wasn't wearing any distinctive jewelry? She didn't say anything that struck you as odd?'

'No, sorry.'

Lieutenant Chessman laid a hand on his shoulder. 'Very well, Mr Bell. Thank you for your time. If possible, I'd like you to try to think back to that morning, and visualize that young woman, and if anything at all comes to mind – and I really mean *anything* – please give me a call.'

'She's not a suspect, is she?'

'Oh, no. This is just for the sake of completeness. In investigations like this, we're very great sticklers for completeness.'

When Lieutenant Chessman had left, Frank went back into the house. He stepped out on to the patio and looked around, but of course there was no trace at all that Danny had been here. Danny, or his psychic imprint, or his ghost, or whatever it had been. The skies over the mountains were beginning to clear, and suddenly the sun appeared, but Frank shivered.

He had the nagging suspicion that something was happening in his life that he didn't fully understand. He felt almost like a cheated husband who comes home early and finds an unfamiliar set of car keys on the table in the hall, or answers the telephone only to have the caller hang up. Everybody seemed to know more than he did. Why was Lieutenant Chessman so intent on finding Astrid? What was it that Nevile thought 'wasn't quite right?' Why wouldn't Astrid tell him who she really was?

He could have told Lieutenant Chessman that he was seeing Astrid. *Should* have told him. But Astrid's identity was the only thing that he knew that nobody else appeared to know, and although he didn't know why, he wanted to keep it to himself, for the time being at least.

The phone rang. It was Mo.

'How's it going, old buddy?'

'About as crappy as it gets.'

'Did you hear the news? Those Dar Tariki lunatics have demanded that all TV shows with any kind of immoral content have to be taken off the air, otherwise they're going to stage the biggest act of terrorism since September 11.'

'They've demanded *what*? This is insane. What the hell do they mean by "immoral content"? Just about every TV show has some kind of immoral content. Soaps, cop shows, everything. How can you show good defeating evil if you can't show evil?'

'Nevertheless, old buddy, that's the ultimatum.'

'So how has the network taken it?'

'Think "headless chicken."'

Frank drove to Sherman Oaks to see his sister Carol, who lived with her husband, Smitty, and their three children in a large, scruffy house on the corner of Stone Canyon Avenue. The front lawn was always strewn with scooters and Action Man toys and Smitty's lime-green '68 Plymouth Barracuda was always jacked up in the driveway, in varying degrees of dismemberment.

He walked in to find Carol in her saucepan-cluttered kitchen, trying to make *estofado*. She was a hopeless cook, which was one of the reasons why Frank didn't visit very often. The last time he had come round to dinner she had cooked chicken breasts in chili cream and he had spent the next day crouched on the toilet with his teeth chattering, praying for death. How Smitty and the kids had survived for so long he couldn't imagine.

'You look like shit,' Carol told him, slicing up green and red capsicums. She was a big woman, three years older than him, with the same brown eyes, but a very much rounder face, and a pudgier nose, and wild brown curls that looked as if she chopped them into shape herself.

'I think this has finished us off,' he said. 'Margot and me. I think it's *kaput*sville.'

'Hey – you're still in shock, both of you.'

'All of us.'

'*All* of you?'

'Me and Margot and Danny, too. We held a séance today. You've heard of this British guy, Nevile Strange, the psychic detective? The one who's been helping out with the investigation into these bombings?'

'You held a *séance*? For Christ's sake, Frank. I didn't think you believed in any of that crap.'

'I don't. I *didn't*. Not until today. I saw Danny, sis. I actually saw him, and I heard his voice, too.'

Smitty came into the kitchen. He was about two inches shorter than Carol, with thinning blond hair that stuck vertically up in the air, bright blue eyes and a permanently surprised face. He was wearing a T-shirt that read PROFANITY IS THE LAST RESORT OF THE INARTICULATE. He hijacked a slice of red pepper from the chopping board and crunched it between his highly irregular teeth.

'Did I hear séance?'

Frank said, 'That's right. I met this guy Nevile Strange when he was looking around The Cedars. He said he could get in touch with people who had passed over, so I asked him if we could talk to Danny. I guess I wanted to hear Danny forgive me. Well, that isn't strictly true. I wanted *Margot* to hear Danny forgive me'

'What's to forgive?' Smitty protested. 'A bomb went off, for chrissakes. Besides, these séances, what a phony!'

87

'I don't think this one was phony.'

'Oh yeah? My old lady went to a séance after my old man kicked the bucket. This medium told her that my old man was waiting for her in heaven so that they could dance the night away just like they always did. Total baloney, of course, because my old man lost both his feet at Inch'on. Stupid palooka stood too close to a tank.'

Carol flapped her hand at Smitty in irritable dismissal. 'You really *saw* Danny?' she asked Frank.

'Standing in the back yard. As clear as I can see you now. We all saw him.'

'You're serious?' asked Smitty, crunching another slice of pepper.

'He said it was all my fault that he was dead and that he wanted to see me in hell.'

Smitty emphatically shook his head. 'Nah, you don't want to take any notice of that. You didn't see nothing. That was a . . . what . . . an optical delusion. That's what these mediums do. They delude you. Optically. And financially. You didn't *pay* this guy, did you?'

They sat in the swing in the back yard in the last warm light of the day, drinking beer and eating pretzels. Carol's three boys were rolling around on the crabgrass, playing space ninjas.

Carol said, 'You won't lose Margot, believe me. But she's always been kind of private, hasn't she? She needs some time to work things out inside of her head.'

'I guess you're right. But I feel like something's gone out of our marriage. Something we can never get back.'

'That's life, Frank. We're always losing things we can never get back.'

He looked at Carol and he knew what she was saying. When she was nineteen she had married her high-school sweetheart, Nick Vereno, and she had been so happy that she had blossomed like her family had never seen her before. For seven months, she had almost looked pretty. But then Nick didn't come home one night, and a week later he told her he had met somebody else. A twenty-eight-year-old exotic dancer with surgically enhanced breasts and a two-year-old kid in tow. Carol's happiness had been switched off like the lights in an empty house, when you leave it for the very last time.

Smitty swigged Coors and said, 'You know what you ought to do, Frank? You ought to insist that this Strange guy does it again. Just to prove that what you saw was genuine. I'll bet you a lobster dinner that he can't.'

'Talking of dinner,' said Frank, 'can I smell something burning?'

'God damn it,' said Carol. 'I forgot you're supposed to keep on adding stock.'

She hurried inside. Smitty, unperturbed, carried on swinging on the swing and drinking his beer. 'Maybe you and Margot could use a break,' he suggested.

'A break?'

'Well, if your relationship had been in really good shape, it seems to me that she wouldn't have blamed you for what happened to Danny. Maybe you both need to step back and take a look at what's wrong. There's marriage, you know, and then there's something else. Carol was married to Nick and I know that she still carries this eternal flame for him because he was handsome and charming and everything she thought she ever wanted. But what we have together, Carol and me, is such a closeness that you can't say where one of us ends and the other begins.'

He finished his can and crumpled it up, and tossed it into the trashcan. 'No disrespect to Margot, but she's always been kind of serious, you know, whereas you're always the guy who can't keep a straight face for more than five minutes.' He sniffed. 'Take my advice, Frank. Don't force it. Give yourself some space. She's trying to glue herself back together again and you should do the same, with whatever adhesive you can lay your hands on.'

Frank and Smitty drank so many cans of Coors between them that Frank spent the night on the couch. At two thirty-three A.M. one of the family's golden retrievers came up to him and licked his face, and he woke up shouting '*eeaurrghh!*' in disgust. The dog wagged his tail and kept running to the door and back again to tell him that he wanted to go for a walk.

He shuffled to the kitchen door and let the dog out into the yard. The moon was so bright that it could have been daylight. He stood there and thought about all the words of advice that had been given to him since Danny died. It was almost as if everybody else in the world had been discussing what he should do next, behind his back. The old man with the long-billed baseball cap; Nevile Strange; Lieutenant Chessman, and Smitty.

Give yourself some space. Cross the road and never come back.

Carol came up behind him and linked arms with him. 'Are you all right?'

'I don't know. I don't think so.'

The next morning, after a breakfast of charred bacon and fried eggs with broken yolks, he kissed Carol and shook hands with Smitty and gave five dollars to each of the boys and then he drove home. Margot's Jeep was already parked in the driveway. He let himself into the house and found Margot standing in the middle of the living room with her arms folded, like a schoolteacher impatiently waiting for an explanation.

'Hi,' he said. 'Are you OK?'

'Do I *look* OK?'

He tried to focus on her through his hangover. 'I'm not sure,' he said slowly. 'You tell me.'

'Well, *no*, as a matter of fact, I'm not OK. In fact I'm devastated. I don't know what you're trying to do to me, Frank. I always thought you were cynical. I thought that was par for the course for comedy writers. But I never realized that you were cruel.'

He couldn't understand what she meant. Not until he stepped into living room and she waved her arms at the walls all around her. Her eyes were blurry with tears.

Every one of her *Impressions In White* had been defaced with red aerosol. One of them had been marked with a swastika, another had the word BITCH scrawled across it. A third had a crude vagina sprayed on to it, and yet another said FORGIVE?? The used aerosol can had been dropped on to the white leather couch, leaving splatters and smears.

'Christ – who did this?'

Margot stared at him in disbelief. 'Who *did* this? You're asking *me* who *did* this?'

'Hey, you don't think that it was me?'

'Who else, Frank? Nobody else has a key, nobody else knows the alarm code. Nobody else knows how much my paintings mean to me. Nobody else despises them like you do, and nobody else thinks that I'm a Nazi and a bitch because I blame you for what happened to Danny.'

Frank opened and closed his mouth and simply couldn't think what to say to her.

'I want you out of here, Frank. I don't care where the hell you go. You can come to the funeral but after that I don't want to see you. Not until we've sorted this out.'

'Margot, I swear to God I didn't do this! I wasn't even here last night. I went to Carol's.'

She stood still for a moment, with one hand on top of her head, as if she were making one of the most important decisions of her life.

'Margot . . . can you really see me doing something like this? Sure, I got angry with you the other night, but that was frustration more than anything else. I need you, Margot, and you need me. We have to talk all of this out.'

'No,' she said. 'No, we don't. All you want to do is hurt me, because I won't forget what you did to Danny. I could have *forgiven* you, yes. I started to forgive you. But that isn't enough for you, is it? You want me to pretend that it never happened at all.'

'Margot . . .'

'I'm going out, Frank. I'll be back around three. When I come back, I don't want to find you here. Please.'

She walked out and left Frank standing in the middle of the living room, with the red-smeared paintings on every side. He felt as if he had woken up this morning in a parallel universe. He had stayed round at Carol and Smitty's last night, hadn't he? The dog had licked his face and he had stood in the moonlit yard. Or maybe he hadn't. Maybe he had driven around here and spray-painted Margot's *Impressions In White.*

He approached the painting with the swastika on it, and touched it. The red paint was still slightly tacky, so it couldn't have been sprayed more than three or four hours ago. He knew for an absolute certainty that he hadn't done it. He *couldn't* have done it.

But if it wasn't him, who had?

Ten

'Joe says they're not going to cancel under any circumstances but one more bomb and I think they're going to cancel,' Mo said.

'This is insane. What are they going to do? Put on endless repeats of *Rebecca of Sunnybrook Farm?*'

'Frank, everybody's running scared. What's going to happen if they let off a bomb right in the middle of *Wheel of Fortune?* What if they blow up the new *Mission Impossible* movie and kill Tom Cruise? The insurance companies are pulling out of movies and television like Napoleon pulling out of Moscow.'

Lizzie Fries lit another More and blew smoke out of her nostrils. 'Maybe we could introduce a sympathetic Taliban character and have all our women dress in burkas.'

'In Iowa?'

'It was only a suggestion,' said Lizzie. She was sixty-two and skeletally thin, with a puffball of dyed orange hair and a face with striking bone structure but lizard-like skin. She always wore pant suits and frilly blouses, and enormous dangly earrings. In her twenties she had been a comedienne and a singer, and even Lucille Ball had said she was going to be the next Lucille Ball. But drink and pills and four failed marriages had destroyed her looks, even though they had never diluted her corrosive sense of humor.

'So what's the score?' asked Frank. 'Is there any point in

us finishing the next script? If they're going to cancel, we might as well go play some golf.'

'You shouldn't even *be* here,' Mo told him. 'Lizzie and I can manage. We'll send you the first draft by email and you can tear it to shreds in the privacy of your own home.'

'I wish. Margot's thrown me out.'

'She's *what?*'

'She's thrown me out.' Frank explained about the séance and *Impressions In White.*

Lizzie waved aside a cloud of smoke. 'Are you *sure* you didn't deface those paintings? Me, I can't tell you how often I wake up in the night with an insatiable urge to paint swastikas and vaginas all over the wall.'

'It wasn't me, Lizzie. I don't know who the hell it could have been, but it wasn't me.'

'What about this séance?' asked Mo. 'I got to tell you, Frank, it sounds to me like you're very close to cracking up. Why don't you stay with Naomi and me for a while, just until you've got your head back together?'

'Oh God, just what he needs,' said Lizzie. 'Chicken soup and old Zero Mostel jokes.'

'Thanks for the offer,' said Frank. 'I think I need to spend some time on my own.'

'You're not going to do anything stupid?'

'What, like sit in the bath and drop a hairdryer in it? No, Mo, I'm not going to do anything stupid. I just need to rearrange my head.'

He drove to Venice. On the car radio, the chief executive of NBC was repeating his determination not to be intimidated by terrorists.

'The very first amendment to the American Constitution guarantees freedom of expression and a free media. We at NBC value this freedom beyond the price of gold or rubies. We are not going to allow a maniac minority to destroy the legacy that our founding fathers handed down to us.

'On the other hand, we are taking every precaution to protect our employees and our property. Everybody who enters an NBC office or studio for whatever reason will be thoroughly searched, and if this causes delay and disruption – well, I'm afraid that's the price we have to pay for vigilance.'

Newscaster Will Chase said, 'In spite of these redoubtable words, a wave of blind panic continues to sweep through Hollywood. Extra police and deputies have been brought in to guard all major TV networks and movie studios, including Fox, Universal, Sony, Warner Brothers, MGM/Pathé and Disney at Burbank.

'Fashionable restaurants and nightspots frequented by movie and TV celebrities are reporting that business has fallen off overnight. At the Beverly Hills Hotel, the Polo Lounge was described today as a "mausoleum," and Rodeo Drive as a "ghost town." Personal protection companies are reporting a desperate shortage of bodyguards and security experts available for hire, and Armet, the Florida-based company which produces "discreetly bomb-proofed" cars and SUVs, say they have been inundated with inquiries from Hollywood's rich, famous and scared.

'There is no question about it, the TV and movie industry is living in fear, and nobody doubts that there will be another bomb outrage very soon. The only questions are *when*, and *where*.'

Frank parked outside Astrid's apartment building. He sat behind the wheel for a few minutes, trying to decide if he was doing the right thing.

He was still sitting there when the old man in the long-billed baseball cap suddenly appeared around the corner, wearing a sagging pair of maroon jogging pants and a faded yellow T-shirt. The old man hesitated for a moment, looking screwy eyed from right to left. He licked his finger and lifted it up as if he were testing which way the wind was blowing. Then he came loping over to Frank's car and tapped on the window.

'How's it going, Frank?'

'Not too good.'

'Shouldn't lose your nerve, Frank. No good never came of losing your nerve.'

'I haven't lost my nerve. I can't decide what to do next, that's all.'

'Maybe it ain't your decision.'

'Oh, really? Then whose decision is it?'

'Fate, karma, call it whatever you like. Sometimes we're destined to play a part in history and we don't even know it. In which case all we can do is put one foot in front of the other and keep on following that road and see where it takes us.'

'I'm burying my only son on Wednesday.'

The old man laid his hand on the roof of the car. He wore a silver ring on every finger and his nails were blackened and broken. He smelled, too – of urine and alcohol.

'There's a reason for everything, Frank. It's not always a reason we can understand, or a reason we approve of. But there's a reason all the same.'

'So what do you think I should do next?' Frank asked him. He was being bitter, but at the same time he really wanted to hear what the old man had to say.

'You don't have any choice, Frank. You crossed the road. There's no turning back now.'

Frank knew that he was right. He couldn't go back. Yesterday was closed for business. He sat staring at the Buick emblem on his steering wheel and he could almost feel life's rug being dragged out from under him.

After more than a minute of silence, the old man coughed and spat. 'That's a ten spot.'

'What is?'

'Spiritual guidance. Warnings I give for nothing – especially dire warnings; that's my philanthropic duty. But I'm sorry. Spiritual guidance I have to make a nominal charge for.'

Frank opened his billfold and gave him a twenty. The old man grinned and showed his four mahogany teeth. 'You're a generous man, Frank. Your generosity will pay you back one day. Not this year. Maybe not next year, neither. But one day, when you least expect it.'

He went hobbling off along the sidewalk and disappeared around the next corner. Frank told himself that his appearance had been nothing more than a coincidence. After all, he must spend all day panhandling up and down the coast, annoying people. And what kind of spiritual guidance was 'put one foot in front of the other'? You could get better advice out of a fortune cookie.

Frank climbed out of the car, went across to Astrid's door and rang the bell. There was no answer so he waited a minute and then rang it again.

'Who is it?' said a voice over the intercom.

'It's Frank. I've come to see Astrid.'

'Astrid? There's no Astrid here.'

'Is this apartment three?'

'That's right, apartment three.'

'You must be Carla. I've come to see the girl you share with. I think she must have given me a different name.'

'There's nobody here but me.'

'You mean she's out? Can I leave her a message?'

'I mean nobody *lives* here but me.'

'Excuse me? There has to be. I visited her yesterday afternoon.'

'You must have made a mistake. Maybe another apartment. Nobody lives here but me.'

'Listen – please. She has short brown hair and blue eyes. She wears rings on her toes.'

The intercom clicked off. Frank pressed the bell again, and then again, and then again, but Carla wouldn't answer. He stepped back and tried to look up to the second story, but the dark green shutters were all closed. Eventually he climbed back into his car.

What the hell is happening here? I know I didn't make a mistake. Not unless Astrid didn't really share the apartment at all. Maybe she found out that Carla was away in Europe for a few days, and crashed in it without asking.

The trouble was, he had no way of contacting Astrid now. He didn't know her telephone number. He didn't even know her surname. It suddenly occurred to him that he might never see her again.

He drove back to Hollywood, to the Sunset Marquis Hotel on Alta Loma Road, a short, steeply sloping street that climbed from Holloway Drive to Sunset.

'How long will you be you staying with us, Mr Bell?' the

96

receptionist asked him. She had tightly braided blonde hair and unnervingly wide-apart eyes.

'I'm not sure. At least a week. Maybe the rest of my life. It all depends on . . . you know . . . fate.'

'Fate,' the receptionist repeated. She didn't seem at all mystified. A lot of rock stars stayed at the Sunset Marquis.

His second-story room was sunny and painted yellow, with splashy floral prints on the wall. He opened all the windows so that the warm midday breeze could blow in, and then he took a can of beer out of the icebox and sat in one of the big stripy armchairs and closed his eyes.

Shouldn't lose your nerve, Frank. No good ever came of losing your nerve.

He was woken by a quiet rapping at the door. For a split second he didn't know where he was, and he thought that it was Margot rapping on the door of his study.

'What time is it?' he asked. But of course it wasn't Margot, and he was still here, in his room at the Sunset Marquis.

The rapping was repeated. He heaved himself out of his chair and went to answer it.

'Yes?'

'Room service.'

He opened the door. It was Astrid. She stepped straight past him into the room and did a twirl.

'Hey! Nice place! She said that I would probably find you here.'

'Who did?'

'Your secretary.'

'My secretary? You called my office?'

'I went round to your home first but your wife said that you'd packed your bags and moved out.'

'You saw Margot?' Or rather, he thought, Margot saw *you*, with your tight white T-shirt and your tan leather mini-skirt and your tan leather ankle boots with the high spiky heels.

Astrid laughed. 'Oh, yes, I saw Margot all right. What *happened* between you two?' She put on Margot's snappy don't-talk-to-me-like-that tone. '"I don't know where Frank is and quite frankly, my dear, I don't *give* a damn." Or words to that effect.'

'We had another row. It's the shock, I guess, and the grief. It's a goddamned mess. It's going to take us a long time to get over losing Danny.'

Astrid looked in the icebox. 'You don't mind if I help myself to a glass of wine?'

'Sure, I'll do it.' He took out a bottle of Chilean rosé, pulled out the cork, and poured her a glass.

She lifted it up and said, 'Mud in your eye.' For the first time he noticed that she had a sprinkling of light-brown freckles across the bridge of her nose. She looked into his eyes while she was drinking as if she could tell exactly what was thinking.

'I was looking for you,' he told her. 'I went to Carla's place first.'

'I thought you might.'

'So why did you make out that you live there when you don't?'

'I *did* live there. It's just that I don't live there now.'

'I see. So where have you moved to?'

'Does it matter?'

'No, I suppose it doesn't. Maybe I'm just being old-fashioned.'

She sat down on the couch. Her leather skirt was so short that he could see a triangle of purple lace thong. 'You're not old-fashioned, Frank. Not at all. You have wings but you've never learned how to *fly*. You were successful too young, you were married too young, you became a daddy too young. All that responsibility. All that weight. You've never had the chance to be *you*.'

'Well, that's not so easy. How can I be me when I don't even know who I am?'

She reached out and traced a circle around the dimple on his chin, around and around. 'I think it's time you found out, don't you?'

'It's Danny's funeral on Wednesday. Maybe when that's over . . .'

'He's gone, Frank. I know how much you loved him, but

you have to start thinking about what you're going to do next. *You.*'

'Yes, I understand that. The trouble is . . .' He felt exhausted and confused and he was finding it very hard to swallow. They drank their drinks in silence for a while. Then Frank said, 'We held the séance.'

'Oh, yes? I was going to ask you about that.'

'It worked. He did it. Nevile Strange. He actually put us in touch.'

'You talked to Danny's spirit?'

'Much more than that. We *saw* Danny, actually saw him, standing outside the window. We all did. Margot, Nevile, me, Margot's friend.'

'That's unbelievable. You're sure it wasn't a trick?'

'If it was, I can't think how the hell it was done. But the worst part about it was that Danny told me that he couldn't forgive me.'

Astrid carried on stroking his cheek, and then she ran her fingers into his hair. 'You shouldn't take it to heart. Nevile Strange is probably a fraud, in any case.'

'Astrid, I saw Danny with my own eyes.'

'You *thought* you did. But maybe he was only a projection, something like that. I mean, he might have *looked* as if he was standing outside the window, but supposing Nevile Strange was shining an image on to the glass?'

'It was Danny. Where was he going to get hold of an image of Danny?'

'He probably didn't. But you wanted the image to be Danny so you believed that it was.'

'No, I don't buy that. It couldn't have been a projection. Besides, he didn't have any equipment with him, not even a briefcase.'

'Maybe he set it up beforehand, outside in the yard. Maybe he *hypnotized* you.'

Frank got up and popped open another can of beer. 'I know what I saw, Astrid.'

'And Danny didn't forgive you?'

'No.'

'So why do you think that Danny didn't forgive you?'

'Because I left him in the back seat of my car, didn't I? Bleeding to death. He called me and called me but I didn't come.'

'Maybe Danny's spirit wouldn't forgive you because that was a sure-fire way for Nevile Strange to persuade you to go back for another séance?'

He slowly shook his head. 'I thought *I* was cynical.'

'I'm not being cynical, Frank. I'm being realistic. Before you lost Danny, did you believe that dead people could come back and talk to you? Did you believe in spirits?'

'No, I didn't.'

'You believed that when people died, that was it, that was the end of them?'

'That's right.'

'But now you've changed your mind, just like so many other people change their minds when they lose somebody they love.'

'I know what I saw, Astrid. I know what I heard.'

'If you say so. But Nevile Strange is a very clever man. He knows how to play on people's expectations. Even the police. Do you really believe that people leave a psychic resonance in their sunglasses?'

'I'm very tired, Astrid.'

She knelt up on the couch and took his can of beer away from him. 'You should rest,' she said, and she started to unbutton his shirt.

'Hey,' he said.

She paused for a moment and stared at him. 'You need this, Frank. You need somebody to take care of you. For once in your life, stop trying to be responsible for everything that goes on around you.'

He could have told her to stop. He could have told her to go and leave him alone. But somehow he couldn't find the strength, or the will. When she carried on unbuttoning his shirt, he didn't resist. He just lay back and watched her eyes, as if they would explain why she wanted him so much. But her eyes were as pale blue as ever, as empty as a windy sky, and they gave away nothing at all.

She unbuckled his Gucci belt and tugged out his shirt tails.

She smoothed her hands over his bare chest, rolling his nipples between finger and thumb. 'I love skinny men,' she said. 'All those ribs. They feel like Jesus.'

She lifted him up off the cushion and pulled his shirt over his head. Then she kissed him on the forehead, three times. 'I anoint thee. I anoint thee. I anoint thee.'

She twisted around, lifted up his legs one after the other, and took off his bright red socks. 'You know what red socks mean? They mean you're going to travel to hell and back.'

'I didn't know that.'

'That's because you've never been there.'

Next she drew down his zipper and began to work his pants down over his hips. Under his white Calvin Klein shorts he was stiffening already, but she ignored it until she had taken his pants off completely and bundled them over the back of the couch. Then she sat next to him, and gently laid her hand on his erection. She looked at him and he looked at her.

'You're not used to this, are you?'

'No.'

'It's about time you allowed other people to take charge of you, once in a while. You can trust them, you know.'

'What do you want from me?'

'If I told you, you wouldn't understand.'

'Try me.'

She leaned forward and kissed him on the tip of the nose, and then on the lips. 'First of all, I want you to enjoy being with me.'

'Then what?'

'That'll do for now.'

Without explaining herself any further, she pulled down his shorts, so that his cock rose up into the air, steadily beating in time with his pulse. She took hold of it in her left hand and squeezed it hard, so that the glans turned dark purple and the opening gaped.

'Eve was tempted by an apple,' she said, smiling. 'But I prefer plums.' She stuck out her tongue and licked him all around, until his glans gleamed with her saliva. She lifted her head and stared at him, and there was still a trail of saliva connecting the tip of her tongue to his cock.

Then she ran her tongue all the way down his shaft until she reached his tight, wrinkled balls. She lifted each of them up in turn, and took them between her lips, and gently sucked them. Frank slid his fingers into her hair, but she gave an impatient little shake of her head to indicate that it was *her* turn first, and that all he was supposed to do was lie back and enjoy it.

She slid her tongue upward again, then opened her mouth wide and swallowed his cock so deeply that he thought it was going to choke her. She sucked him up and down, the tip of her tongue pattering, and he closed his eyes. *God, what's happening to me? In the midst of all this grief and unhappiness, bliss.*

And it wasn't just the erotic feelings that she was giving him. It was her closeness, and her flowery smell, and the fact that she was caring for him. He had never cried during love-making before, but now the tears were sliding from his eyes as he became overwhelmed with emotion. She gave him a last lingering suck, and then she sat up, still holding his cock in her left hand, her lips shining and her face bright.

'You're crying,' she said, triumphantly. 'I knew that you would.'

With her right hand, she wrestled off her T-shirt, revealing a lacy purple bra. 'I'll let you do that,' she said hoarsely. He reached behind her to unfasten it and her big round breasts fell out of the cups with a deliciously complicated double sway. The areolas around her nipples were as wide as fallen rose petals, and the same faded pink color, edged with brown.

He tried to hold her breasts in his hands, but she pushed him away. Instead she leaned over him, so that her nipples just brushed his chest, and swung them from side to side, until they crinkled and stood up.

Every time he tried to raise his hands to touch her, she forced them back down. He felt a rising frustration, but at the same time he was growing more and more aroused. His heart was pumping so hard that he could hear the blood rushing in his ears, and he was actually trembling.

Astrid pulled down the zipper of her leather mini-skirt and let it drop down on to the carpet. Now she was wearing nothing but her thong and her ankle boots. 'Come on,' she said. 'You can take this off, too.'

She climbed back on to the couch and sat astride him so that the thong was right in front of his face. He hesitated, but she waited for him, looking down at him, steadily breathing.

He looked back up at her. 'I don't know whether I can do this.'

'Then don't,' she said, but she didn't move.

He took hold of her waistband. Her stomach was rising and falling and he could feel her radiated warmth against his forehead. He knew that whatever he decided to do now, it would change everything. His life would never be the same again.

'There's no turning back, Frank,' Astrid told him.

He rolled down the thin elastic and pulled down her thong. She'd had a Brazilian-wax and was completely hairless, like a ripe pink fruit. Her lips were slightly parted and he could see that she was already glistening wet.

Again he tried to touch her but again she snatched his wrists and levered his arms away. 'Now, then. I want absolute submission.'

'I'm not used to this.'

'Exactly.'

She took hold of his cock and angled it between her legs. All the time he was looking at her, trying to understand why she was doing this, but she gave nothing away. She waited for a very long moment, her lips enclosing his glans, but only just, her head back, staring at the ceiling. Then she slowly sat down, so that Frank sank into her, as deep as it was possible to go, and she let out an *aahhhhhhhh* of satisfaction.

When he woke up again it was already growing dark. The sky was the color of royal-blue ink, the cicadas were chirruping, and he could hear people splashing and laughing in the pool below. He sat up in bed and pulled at his cheeks to stretch his dehydrated skin.

'Astrid?'

She appeared in the bedroom doorway wearing a white fluffy hotel bathrobe and holding a glass of wine. Her hair was sticking up at the back and she was smiling.

'You're awake, then?'

'I don't think I've slept so good in days.'

She sat down on the bed beside him and ran her hand through his hair. 'You needed it. You've been needing something like this for a long time.'

'I guess I ought to feel guilty.'

Her robe had fallen open so that he could see the curved underside of her breast. She gave him a lingering kiss on the lips. 'So do you?'

He thought about it, and he suddenly began to understand that he could tell her the truth. It had been a long time since he had been able to do that with Margot. He had never lied to Margot about anything serious, like how much he loved her. But he had told her again and again how impressed he was by her paintings, and how much he liked her friends (particularly that wiry-haired busybody Helen Mitchell, and her catarrhal husband, Byron) and how delicious he found her pasta with salmon and Pacific pesto. And somehow all of those small, inconsequential untruths had crept up year by year like ivy over a fairytale window and stifled their life together.

'No,' he said. 'I'm sad, but I don't feel guilty.'

'Sad?'

'Sad for Danny. Sad for Margot. But it's like breaking a piece of precious china, isn't it? No use trying to stick it back together again. Best to remember it the way it was, when it was perfect.'

'Do you want me to stay tonight?'

He reached into her open bathrobe and caressed her bare shoulder. This time she didn't try to twist herself away.

'What do you think?' he asked her.

Astrid did things for him that night that he had fantasized about but never had the nerve to try, not with Margot. She seemed to have no inhibitions at all, and an endlessly burning sexual hunger. Each time he turned over and tried to sleep, her hand crept over his hip and started to pull at his cock yet again, and her tongue paddled in his ear. 'Not *tired* yet, are you?' she breathed.

104

Sometime shortly after midnight she was kneeling astride his face, her back arched, gripping the bedposts while he licked her and her juice coursed down his chin. At two in the morning she wriggled her finger into his anus while she bit the skin of his scrotum until it bled. At four thirty he was taking her, doggy fashion, grunting, on the bedside rug. At a quarter after six, when the sky was already light, she climbed on top of him again and made love to him in dreamy slow motion.

She woke him again just after eight, lying heavily on top of him and nuzzling his neck.

'Not again, Astrid,' he begged her. 'I'm bushed.'

'Don't worry, you poor old man, I have to go. I'll see you again tonight.'

He tried to turn his head around. 'How can I get in touch with you?'

She kissed him once, twice, three times, then she climbed off him. 'You can't. I'll get in touch with you.'

'Astrid . . .' he said as she hooked up her bra.

'You'll have to trust me, Frank.'

'Look, I'm not asking for commitment. I'm just asking where I can phone you, in case something comes up.'

'*Ohhh*,' she teased, sitting down next to him and squeezing the sheet in between his legs. 'In case something comes up, huh?'

He kissed her. 'You're extraordinary, do you know that?'

'I'm no different from any other girl, Frank. It's just that you've forgotten what girls are really like . . . That's if you ever knew.'

Frank watched her as she finished dressing and brushed her hair. 'You make me feel . . . totally different.'

'I know.' She gave him the gentlest of kisses on the forehead, then left him. After she had gone, he lay back on the bed and stared at the swirling plaster patterns on the ceiling, thinking of *The Process*.

Of course the sands of Present Time are running out beneath our feet. And why not? The Great Conundrum, 'What are we here for?' is all that ever held us here in the first place. Fear.

105

'What are we here for?' But the Riddle of the Ages has actually been out in the street since the First Step in Space. We are here to go!

Tuesday, September 28, 3:27 P.M.

'How's it going, people?' Garry Sherman breezed into the so-called 'hospitality suite' at Panorama-TV with a makeup towel still tied around his neck. His hair was as black as crows' feathers; his suit was sapphire blue and his face was orange.

His three guests were sitting around a small Formica-topped table eating sandwiches and barbecued chicken legs and drinking wine out of plastic cups.

'You're all *way* too polite,' Garry grinned. 'You haven't started throwing food at each other yet.'

'Actually, we've been getting along like a house on fire,' drawled Jean Lassiter. She was a handsome fiftyish woman with silvery bouffant hair. She was wearing a salmon-pink suit and strappy silver shoes.

'That's not what I want to hear,' said Garry in mock disgust. 'I want aggression! I want tantrums! I want overweening egos!'

'Oh, I think you'll get plenty of contention,' said Dr Fortensky. 'Just because we're all nice people doesn't mean we don't have very strong differences of opinion.' Dr Fortensky had a bald, suntanned dome of a head and the kind of huge yellow-tinted designer glasses that had been popular in the mid-1980s.

'That's right,' put in Sara Velman. 'So far we haven't even been able to agree what sexual domination actually *is*. Is it handcuffing your lover to the bedpost and whipping him with wet spaghetti, or is it making him iron his own shirts?' Sara Velman had glossy brunette hair, fashionably chopped, and a highly groomed assertiveness that came from being the Vassar-educated only daughter of a very wealthy family.

'Give me the handcuffs and wet spaghetti every time,' said Garry.

106

A bespectacled young studio assistant opened the door and said, 'Two minutes, Mr Sherman.'

Garry went to the mirror on the opposite side of the room, jutted out his chin, and closely inspected each of his profiles in turn. 'OK, I'm going to introduce you to our studio audience one after the other. I'm going to say a few highly flattering words about your respective books, at which time your book covers will appear on the screen. I'm going to ask each of you in turn what you think about today's subject: Women on Top. After that, I'm going to invite you to rip each other to shreds, and I don't care how outspoken you are or how riled up you get, short of getting out of your seat and socking each other on the nose. This isn't the Jerry Springer show – besides, my budget doesn't run to bodyguards.

'Halfway through we go into a short commercial break and then we open up the floor to questions from the audience, some of which will be dumb and some of which will be stupefyingly dumb. See if you can coax the audience to come up with some personal anecdotes about sexual domination . . . you know the kind of thing – I make my husband fry pork chops in the nude.'

'What's wrong with frying pork chops in the nude?' asked Dr Fortensky.

'Nothing,' said Jean Lassiter, 'so long as you wear a little frilly apron.'

'What did I tell you?' said Sara Velman. 'All men secretly want to be women. Under every business suit is a metaphorical garter belt.'

'OK, then,' said Gary Sherman, smacking his hands together. 'Let's get out there and shake our tambourines.'

He led the way along a corridor stacked with folding chairs and pieces of studio backdrop. At last they came out into the studio itself, under hot and dazzling lights. An audience of over a hundred people were sitting waiting for them, and when Garry walked over to his big white leather chair, there were whoops and whistles and a clatter of applause.

Studio assistants led Garry's three guests up on to a raised

107

platform, where three white chairs were positioned, with white side tables and glasses of water. The audience stared at them as if they were human exhibits on *The Planet of the Apes*.

'Why do we do this? We must be mad,' Sara said.

Jean flapped her hand dismissively. 'We do it to sell books, dear. Can you think of a better reason?'

'Who cares about books?' said Dr Fortensky. 'They give us warm white wine and curled-up Kraft cheese sandwiches and our plane fare home. What more could anybody ask for?'

'Quiet, please,' said the producer, raising his arm.

Tuesday, September 28, 3:41 P.M.

Outside Studio V, where *The Garry Sherman Show* was being recorded, Bill Dunphy and Joan Napela were sitting on an Italianate garden bench made of fiberglass painted to look like stone. Bill had tilted his cap over his eyes but Joan had taken her sunglasses off so that she could refresh her tan. She had been on night duty for the past three weeks and thought that she was starting to look yellow.

The lot was almost deserted, except for two stage hands outside Studio III, moving pieces of Greek columns and lengths of scaffolding with a forklift truck. Now that the studio tours had been suspended, the whole Panorama TV complex was eerily quiet. Bill and Joan had only had cause to challenge one visitor today, and he had turned out to be a plumber who had been called to unblock the executive toilets, and got lost in costumes.

'Three weeks, two days, five hours and forty-one minutes,' Bill announced.

'Since when?'

'Since I gave up smoking.'

'That's very *good*, Bill! You should be proud of yourself.'

'I don't have time to be proud of myself. I'm too busy feeling like something the dog sicked up.'

Joan sat up straight and put on her sunglasses. 'You'll get over it. One day you'll go to bed and you'll realize that you've not even thought about smoking all day.'

'I'll be dead from overeating by then. I've put on seven

pounds already, and all I can think of is cheeseburgers. I'm thinking of cheeseburgers right now, as a matter of fact. *Triple* cheeseburgers, with extra cheese, and a basket of fried pickles on the side.'

Bill had worked for Studio Security for over eleven years. Back at home, he had photographs all over the living-room walls. Bill and Warren Beatty; Bill and Meryl Streep. Bill and Leonardo DiCaprio. He was an ex-traffic cop, a big dog-faced man with a scar down his left cheek. He looked as if he would tear your arms off just for looking at him funny, but in reality he was shy, soft spoken and careful in his ways. His hobby was collecting the tiniest moths.

Joan was small and wiry, with a big nose and frizzy blonde hair. Her alcoholic husband Carl had left her eighteen months ago with two children under five to take care of, and for a time she had held down two jobs – one behind the deli counter at Ralph's and the other as an office cleaner. But then her best friend's husband had told her that Studio Security were looking for recruits, male or female, big or little, white or black, and she had astonished herself by being accepted. She didn't know that she had impressed Studio Security's personnel manager by the fact that she never stopped talking. People would stop causing trouble just to shut her up.

'You should try acupuncture,' she suggested. 'My friend Lena lost seventeen pounds with acupuncture. Mind you, she lost her husband as well. He said that if he had wanted a human skeleton he would have married Calista Flockhart. Now there's the inflated male ego for you. He looked like an orangutan in a plaid sport coat.'

'Acupuncture, that's when they stick needles in you? I can't stand needles. Brrr.'

'Well, maybe you should try hypnotism. Or aversion therapy.'

'What's aversion therapy?'

'What they would do is, they would make you eat triple cheeseburgers all day, every day, so that you never want to *look* at another triple cheeseburger, ever again.'

Bill shook his head. 'Sounds great. Wouldn't work on me. But I sure wouldn't mind trying it.'

As they talked, a dark blue Mack truck came around the corner of Studio IV, and drove slowly toward them.

Tuesday, September 28, 3:47 P.M.

In the studio, the audience were screaming with laughter. Sara Velman had said that women were sexually excited by hurting their lovers, and so Garry had invited her to prove it by hurting him. She had strutted over to his seat and climbed on to his lap. Now she was twisting his ears and pulling his hair.

'Hey, be careful with the hair, all right? This cost me nearly fourteen hundred dollars!'

One tall ginger-freckled woman put up her hand and said, 'I love to bite my husband. I give him love bites all over, especially on his tush.'

'Well, biting your partner is an indication of possessiveness, rather than domination,' said Dr Fortensky. 'You want your husband physically marked so that any other woman will know that he belongs to you. It's like branding a steer.'

Garry said, 'No, I think it's simpler than that. I think it's an indication that she's not getting nearly enough to eat.'

'Hurting your lover isn't necessarily an act of sexual domination,' put in Jean Lassiter. 'In my experience, many men are highly aroused by being bitten or scratched or whipped. They *want* to be hurt. So you have to ask yourself, who is really doing the dominating here? The biter or the bitten?'

'The scratcher or the scratchee?' Garry added. 'The whipper or the whipped?'

Sara Velman suddenly lunged her head forward and nipped at Garry's neck.

'Ow! No!' he protested, kicking his feet. 'Get off! Honest injun! Honest injun!'

Tuesday, September 28, 3:49 P.M.

The dark blue truck turned right and parked very close to the studio wall. Its side panels were painted with reels of film,

110

and in each frame of film there was chicken or salad or pasta or lobsters. Underneath, in white lettering, it read: A MOVIEBLE FEAST, CATERING SPECIALISTS FOR THE ENTERTAINMENT INDUSTRY.

Joan picked up her clipboard and ran her finger down it. 'Here it is. Sixteen hundred hours, catering supplies.'

'I'll check it out,' said Bill, rousing himself off the mock-stone bench. 'Maybe they can spare us a couple of subs.'

He straightened his cap and walked around the corner. The truck was stationary and its doors were still closed but its engine was running. Bill walked up to the cab and gave the driver a wave. The driver waved back. He was a swarthy-looking guy with dark glasses and a black beard. Sitting next to him was a suntanned girl, around eighteen or nineteen years old, wearing a sleeveless T-shirt and a red head scarf. She waved, too.

'You delivering to *The Garry Sherman Show*?' Bill shouted.

The driver cupped his hand to his ear to show that he couldn't hear.

Bill made a twisting gesture with his right hand to tell the driver that he should cut his engine. 'Switch your engine off! I have to check your ID!'

But the driver kept the engine running, and both he and the girl went on staring at Bill through the windshield and smiling that same vacant smile. Bill did the twisting gesture again but the driver simply shrugged.

'Sir! Will you please switch your engine off and get out of the vehicle?'

Still no response. Although he was always easy-going, Bill was beginning to get irritated.

'Joan!' he called. 'Come around here! I think I got me a couple of zombies!'

Joan came around the corner and said, 'What?'

'These two are just sitting there. Won't kill the engine, won't get out.'

Joan climbed on to the step below the passenger door and tapped on the window with her wedding ring. 'Excuse me, sir, miss – security. Will you switch off your engine, please, and climb down out of the cab?'

111

They didn't even turn to look at her. She tried the door handle but it was locked.

'What the hell do they think they're playing at?' Bill demanded.

Joan climbed down from the step and unhooked her r/t. 'Gate? Hi, Kevin, this is Joan. We have a catering truck down here at Studio V. A Movieble Feast. That's right. They checked out OK, did they? That's fine, but they've parked their vehicle around the back of the studio building and they're not making any attempt to get out of it and make their delivery.' She nodded, and nodded again, and then said, 'Repeat that, please.'

'What is it?' asked Bill.

Joan clipped her radio back in her pocket. 'We have to get the hell out of here,' she said.

'What?'

'We have to go into the studio and evacuate it right now, and move everybody as far away as possible.'

Bill stared up at the truck driver and his passenger. The driver gave him another wave, and although there was a diagonal reflection of clouds across the windshield, he thought he could see the girl laughing. 'You start the evacuation,' he said. 'I'll deal with these two clowns.'

'Bill, they specifically said to get the hell out.'

'Do like I told you, Joan. I was a cop for twenty-eight years and I never let nobody get away with nothing.'

Bill unfastened his holster and pulled out his .38. Joan hesitated, but he pushed her shoulder and said, 'Go! OK? Get those people out of there!'

Joan ran off around the corner. Bill lifted up his revolver in both hands and cocked it. 'OK! Do you understand this? *Comprende*? I'm asking you to switch off the engine and get out of the truck. I'm asking you nicely.'

Tuesday, September 28, 3:52 P.M.

Joan pushed her way through the swing doors and into the carpet-tiled reception area, which was lined with blown-up photographs of Garry Sherman and Lauren Baker and Whitney

112

De Lano. The receptionist was painting her fingernails and chatting to a friend on the phone.

Joan went up to the counter and snapped, 'Put me through to the producer! Now!'

'Say what? I can't do that, we're right in the middle of a show.'

'It's an emergency; do it now.'

'Emergency? What kind of emergency? Mr Kasabian will *kill* me!'

'Just do it, will you? Or else *everybody's* going to get killed!'

Flapping one nail-polished hand, the receptionist did as she was told and handed over the phone.

'Mr Kasabian?' said Joan. 'This is Joan Napela from Studio Security. Yes, Studio Security. I'm sorry, Mr Kasabian, but we have a security situation directly outside the studio and we have to evacuate everybody immediately. Yes, sir, everybody. No, sir, I can't tell you the exact nature of the situation but we have been advised to clear the building as quickly as we can.'

She listened for a moment, and then she said, 'Yes, sir. Thank you, sir. I'll come into the studio right now and help to usher people out. If you can try to reassure them that there isn't any cause for alarm.'

As she handed the phone back, the receptionist stared at her wide-eyed. 'What is it? What's happening?'

'Possible bomb,' Joan told her. 'Just get out of here.'

'Oh my God!' cried the receptionist, and started to gather up her nail polish and her combs and her magazines.

'I said *bomb*,' said Joan in disbelief.

She crossed the reception area and pushed open the double doors to the studio. The main lights had just been switched on, and Milo Kasabian was halfway through making his announcement.

'If you would all please make your way to the exit doors on either side of the podium, as quickly and as quietly as you can. Once you're outside, follow the directions given to you by our security staff. Don't be alarmed, this is only a precautionary measure.'

Garry Sherman was standing up and waving to his

113

audience to come down out of their seats. 'I knew it! I knew they'd interrupt us once we started talking dirty! That's right, everybody, head for the doors! No need to panic, they're only doing it because we're steaming up their monitors!'

The audience started to file down to the floor of the studio, jostling and laughing. Joan stood by the doors and beckoned them to hurry.

'What's up?' asked an elderly man in a bright-pink polo shirt.

'Probably a false alarm,' said Joan. 'But once you're out of the studio, turn right, OK, and keep on walking as fast as you can.'

'Do we still get pizza?'

'Sure, you still get pizza. Now get going.'

Joan unhooked her radio and said, 'Bill? We've made a good start on clearing the studio. How's it going with our friends out there?'

'They're still not responding. Schaefer's on his way down here, and he's called the bomb squad, too.'

'Bill, why don't you back off and let the police deal with this?'

'I *am* the police.'

'You were, Bill. Not anymore. This isn't worth the risk. Come and help me get these people out of here.'

'Don't you worry; I can handle a couple of pointy-headed specimens like these two.'

'Bill? Bill, are you listening to me? Back off – you don't know what the hell they're planning to do!'

There was no reply. Joan kept on tugging at people's sleeves as they shuffled past her, trying to hustle them out of the studio. But Garry had told them that there was no need to panic, and panicking they weren't. Some of them said, 'Hey, relax,' when she caught hold of them, and others were even waiting by the doorway so that their friends could catch up with them.

'They'll still serve us pizza?' asked a large black woman in a spotted turquoise dress. 'I only come here for the pizza.'

Joan was about to say, 'Yes, you'll still get your pizza, but for God's sake get moving.' But then the world split open with the most devastating bang that she had ever heard. She

114

was hurled backward through the open doors, colliding with ten or eleven other people, hitting the reception desk at a sharp angle and breaking her neck. More people were thrown out of the studio on top of her, heaps of them – *thud, thud, thud, thud* – most of them legless or armless or headless.

The explosion blew away the entire back wall of the studio, bringing down the roof. Dozens of people were buried as masonry fell like thunder and scaffolding jangled like the bells of hell. Garry Sherman half-turned away from the blast with his left arm lifted. His arm was ripped out of its socket and the flesh on the left side of his face was blasted off, right to the cheekbone. One middle-aged woman was jammed between the side of Garry Sherman's podium and the low wall that led to the exit, so that she was shielded from the bouncing lumps of cinder block. But as she tried to climb to her feet, a DeSisti studio light fell from its rigging and dropped on top of her – over fifty pounds of metal at sixty degrees. She lay on her back with this monster in her arms, crushed and burning, and she screamed for nearly five minutes without stopping.

Her screams were joined by scores of others, as well as sobbing and moaning and coughing. Studio V was open to the sky now, but it seemed like twilight because of the dust and the thick black smoke. It was almost unrecognizable as a television studio. There were mountains of rubble everywhere, as well as tiers of collapsed seats and twisted scaffolding. Bodies lay everywhere – bodies and pieces of bodies, some of them barbecue black and others red raw. And everything twinkled and glittered, because all of this carnage was strewn with shattered glass.

Eleven

Wednesday was gray and chilly. The wind had a nasty saw-toothed edge to it and rain was forecast for later in the day. More than sixty guests came to St Luke's for

Danny's funeral service, including Frank's father and mother; Margot's mother; Carol and Smitty; Mo and Sherma; Lizzie Fries and her partner, Walford; Joe Peruggio, their executive producer, and his wife, Sharleen; Rick and Lynn Ashbee, as well as Frank's agent Nero Tabori and most of the cast of *Pigs*. Frank and Margot sat together but they didn't touch each other or exchange more than two or three words, even though Frank could feel the pew shaking as Margot sobbed. She wore a black hat with a black veil. Frank couldn't help thinking that she looked like a grieving widow in a Charles Addams cartoon.

Reverend Trent climbed into the pulpit, thirtyish but pinkly bald, with circular glasses, so that he looked like the boy at school who always went home in tears.

'We have all shed tears for young Daniel today, but none grieves as sorely as Christ, our Lord, who always weeps when one of his little ones falls asleep and never re-awakens.

'We saw only the early morning of Daniel's life, and we shall never know what he could have become if he had reached his noonday hour. But I can tell you this: he would have shined as brightly as the sun high above, and the world will be a dimmer place without him.'

Before he finished, Reverend Trent said a prayer for the hundred and six victims of the bomb that had demolished Studio V at Panorama-TV, and condemned Dar Tariki Tariqat. 'A group of people are terrorizing our community – a group who have acted without pity and without remorse. They are slaughtering our friends and our loved ones without discrimination. They took young Daniel away from us, and his schoolmates, and his teachers, and yesterday they took away over a hundred more innocent lives.

'We pray for the souls of all of those lost, that they may find eternal peace and happiness in Heaven. In spite of our anger, we also pray for all of those misguided people who have conspired in these terrible outrages, that they may look into the mirror and see how evil they have become, and what misery and anguish they have caused, and repent.'

He hesitated, and then he said, much more quietly, 'I hold out very little hope, however, that they will.'

116

There was an even longer pause, as if he were trying to make up his mind if he really ought to say any more. But eventually he lifted his head and took off his glasses, his lower lip trembling with passion. 'If it were possible for us to ask the Lord our God to act on our behalf as a vengeful God, and to show no mercy to those who have broken his Commandments, then I have to confess that I, for one, would ask Him now.'

They stood under the overcast sky and Danny's casket was lowered in the ground. Frank threw a handful of crumbly soil on to the lid, and then Margot did the same.

'So that's that, then,' she said.

He looked at her, but the smokescreen of her veil made it impossible for him to see the subtleties of her expression. Did she mean that this was the end of their life as parents, as Danny's dad and mom – or that this was the end of their marriage altogether? He didn't know how to ask her, and he wasn't sure that he wanted to.

Without another word, Margot walked off and linked arms with Ruth. Frank was left alone by the graveside. He stared down at the casket and thought of what Francis Bacon had written: 'Men fear death as children fear to go in the dark.' Now Danny was in the dark, forever. Frank knew that Danny hadn't forgiven him, but he prayed that he wasn't afraid.

Somebody came and stood close beside him. When he turned around, Frank saw that it was Nevile Strange, wearing a black shirt and a black necktie and a very long black over-coat, and carrying a black Homburg hat.

'Very moving service,' said Nevile.

'Yes.'

'I like a clergyman who can show some genuine Old Testament wrath once in a while. Nothing like an occasional smite to keep the sinners shaking in their shoes.'

Frank took a last look down at Danny's casket, and then he turned away. 'We're having a few drinks back at the house. Are you going to join us?'

Nevile replaced his hat. 'Actually, I need to talk to you, but this may not be the time for it.'

'Why not? Things can't get very much worse than they are already.'

'Oh, you mean the séance. That was one of the things I wanted to talk to you about. It didn't turn out to be very helpful, did it? Not as far as your marriage is concerned.'

'Not only the séance.' Frank told him about the graffiti that had been smeared over Margot's paintings. 'I even began to believe that maybe I *did* do it, that I drove back home from my sister's house and ruined her paintings in my sleep.'

Nevile laid his hand on Frank's shoulder. 'It wasn't you, Frank; that's for certain.'

'Oh, no? If I didn't, who did?'

'Well . . . there's a remote possibility that Margot did it herself, so that she could blame you for it, as a way of conceptualizing her anger toward you. But personally I very much doubt it. I suspect that there are other forces involved here.'

'When you say "other forces," you mean what? Like, spirits?'

Nevile shrugged. 'We can always discuss this another time.'

'Nevile, I know what I saw on the patio, but the more I think about it, the more I wonder if it really *was* Danny. A friend of mine . . . well, you may think this is offensive, but a friend of mine even suggested that you rigged it somehow – that it wasn't really a spiritual manifestation at all, but some kind of optical illusion.'

'And what do you think about that?'

'If it *was* an optical illusion, I don't see how you could have found the time to set it up, to be honest. Or *why*. My friend said you might have done it for the money – you know, to induce me to pay for more séances. But I can't believe you would go to those lengths just for five hundred bucks.'

Nevile smiled. 'Your friend is perfectly entitled to have doubts, Frank, especially about this particular séance. This was the very first time that anyone apart from myself was actually able to *see* a spirit, as well as hear it. So believe me, I think it could have been a fake, too. Not a fake in the sense that your friend obviously means – not a con-trick with lights and mirrors. But a spiritual impersonation. Another spirit, pretending to be Danny.'

118

'When you first walked into the house, you sensed another presence, didn't you? That little girl, maybe.'

'That's true, but she was only eighteen months old, wasn't she, when she died? Far too young to stage an elaborate deception like this. Children who pass over, you see, they never grow older. In fact nobody who passes over grows older.'

They had reached Nevile's shiny old Mercedes, which was already speckled with rain. 'No,' said Nevile, as he took out his keys, 'I think we're talking about an adult spirit here. It was the way Danny spoke, mostly. He said something like, "You didn't care . . . you took away my whole life because you didn't care . . . and not caring is the greatest sin of all."'

'That's right.'

'Don't tell me Danny ever spoke like that. I didn't know him, Frank, but he was only eight years old, wasn't he? I don't think I've heard *any* eight-year-olds speak like that.'

Frank thought about it. 'I guess you're right. It didn't hit me before. I couldn't think about anything else except how much Danny hated me, and was never going to forgive me.'

'Mull it over, Frank. It could be very important. If it wasn't Danny, then we should try to find out who he was, and why he went to such lengths to deceive you.'

Margot approached them. She had lifted her veil and draped it over her hat. Her eyes were reddened but her lips were thin and tight and she wore no lipstick.

'I've asked Nevile back to the house,' Frank told her.

'I suppose I can't stop you.'

'I've asked him as our guest, Margot.'

'All right. So long as he doesn't conjure up Danny's ghost again. I don't think our friends would find it very amusing.'

'Margot, we just buried him.'

'Exactly,' she said, and walked away.

Nevile watched her go, and then he said, 'Listen, I think it would be more diplomatic if I didn't come. Let me meet you later. Where are you staying?'

Frank lay on his bed at the Sunset Marquis with a cold bottle of Molson, watching the television news. Outside his window, three girls were screaming and laughing as their boyfriends threw them into the pool. It was late afternoon already, over twenty-four hours since all of those people had been killed at Panorama-TV, and soon it would be Thursday, and then Friday, and then a week.

It was already a week since Danny had died, but he would always be stuck at Wednesday, September 12, like a small boy who has missed the bus home, gradually receding out of sight, and one day, out of mind.

On the news, the anchorwoman was saying '. . . killing one hundred and six people and seriously injuring a further seventy-three, including TV personality Garry Sherman, who lost an arm and was badly disfigured by the blast.

'However it was confirmed less than an hour ago that the FBI anti-terrorist task force has positively identified the truck driver. He was named as Richard Haze Abbott, twenty-seven years old, an unemployed construction worker from Simi Valley.'

A blurry color photograph appeared on the screen of a grinning young man with a red baseball cap and a sunburned nose, with his arms around a black and white mongrel. Frank narrowed his eyes to focus on him. He certainly didn't *look* like an Arab terrorist. More like one of those spotty kids who flipped burgers at MacDonald's.

'If you recognize Richard Abbott, or ever knew him, or have seen or talked to him recently, FBI agents and police would very much like to hear from you. The numbers are—'

The phone rang. Even before he answered it he knew it was Astrid. Maybe he was starting to develop that psychic sense that Nevile had talked about.

'Frank? Are you OK?'

'Sure, I'm fine.'

'The funeral – it must have been terrible for you.'

'Well, it was. But it's all over now, and I guess it helped.'

'How did Margot take it?'

'Margot and me, we're not really talking at the moment.'

'I'm sorry. You really need someone to talk to at a time like this.'

'I suppose I'm lucky, then. I have you.'

'Do you want me to come round tonight? I won't if you'd rather be alone.'

'No, no. I'd like that. Come around ten thirty, we'll have a couple of drinks together.'

'Frank . . .'

'What is it?'

'Nothing. I'll tell you later.'

'Tell me now.'

'No, forget I ever said anything. I'll see you later.'

Frank turned back to the TV. At a media conference in Sacramento, the Governor of California, Gene Krupnik, had declared a state of emergency in the greater Los Angeles area, and was calling out the National Guard to set up security cordons around all the major studios. A bomb threat had been received by Sony and they had evacuated their lot 'until further notice.' Production on seven daytime soaps had been suspended and two new series – the gung-ho military drama *Desert Force* and the dark supernatural thriller *Exorcists* – had both been canceled, and the cancellation of other shows was 'imminent.'

The Governor said, 'There are no two ways about it. War has been declared on America's broadcasting industry, which means that war has been declared on our freedom of speech, which we hold more dear than life itself. Well, I can tell you this: violence will be met by determination. Terrorism will be met by steadfastness. We refuse to flinch. Whatever it takes, we are going to prevail.'

The news channel immediately switched to pictures of the San Diego and the Pomona Freeways, which were jammed solid with SUVs trying to escape from the city.

Nevile arrived just after six and Frank took him to the Alligator Bar on Sunset. They sat in the shadows in a semicircular booth, with the lights of Los Angeles glittering below them. The bar was conspicuously empty. It was a favorite haunt of some of Hollywood's older celebrities, TV stars of the seventies and eighties, but not tonight. The pianist played a desultory version of the theme tune to *Hill Street Blues*, and kept stopping every now and then for a drink and a chat with one of the hostesses.

Nevile had changed into a dark gray three-piece suit with a cream shirt and a red silk necktie. 'I agreed to be guest of honor at a new art exhibition,' he explained. '"Visions of the World Beyond."'

'Where's that?'

'Rodeo Drive, the Kleban Gallery, nine o'clock. Don't ask. I know just what it's going to be like and I'm beginning to regret it already. Most American artists seem to think that the "world beyond" looks like one of those episodes of *Star Trek* when Kirk and the crew go on shore leave. You know, all Greek pillars and orange skies and girls walking around in lime-green mini-dresses.'

'You're quite a cynic, for a psychic.'

'Not at all. I'm just a realist. The world beyond looks exactly like the world of the living, except that everybody's in stasis – the same as they were the day they passed over, for ever. If you die angry, you stay angry. Let that be a warning to you.'

'Tell me about Danny. Or this spirit that pretended he was Danny.'

Nevile sipped his Tom Collins. 'When I spoke to Lynn Ashbee's little girl, Kathy, there was no question at all that it was her. Young Kathy was shocked, and she was very faint, and she didn't really understand what had happened to her, especially since she had suffered such massive physical trauma. The way you die has an enormous effect on you. If you pass over peacefully, your spirit adapts to death much more easily; you're ready for it, you can accept it. But if it's *wham!* – the way it was with Kathy and all of those other school-children – it can take you a long time before you adjust. Months, or even years.'

'Did you *see* Kathy?'

'I saw a dancing light, like a will o' the wisp, and only for a few seconds. That's all I would have expected to see, so soon after such a violent death. That's why Danny's appearance was such a surprise to me. Danny may not have passed over instantaneously, like Kathy and her classmates, but all

122

the same he wasn't really expecting to die, was he?

'Yet there he was, and his image was almost as clear as if he were still alive. Not only that, he wasn't bewildered or confused. Quite the opposite. He was full of resentment, and he was able to articulate that resentment very clearly. That's why I'm ninety percent convinced that it wasn't Danny, but another spirit trying to pass itself off as Danny.'

'Can spirits do that? I mean, take on the shape of other spirits?'

'Of course. A person's spirit has no physical substance. It's nothing but a highly charged collection of all the electrical impulses that made up their personality when they were alive. A spirit makes itself seen and heard by stimulating the synapses in your brain, so that you *think* you can see it and you *think* you can hear it, even though it's invisible and it's not making a sound. Why do you think there are no authenticated tapes of spirit voices, and no video recordings of ghosts – even though people swear that they've heard their dead mothers talking to them, and seen their dead lovers standing over their beds? What you saw outside the window was very vivid, but it was nothing more than a picture from your own memory.'

'So how come *you* saw it, too?'

'Because whoever this spirit is, it was able to conjure up Danny's image in my brain, too, and Margot's, and Lynn's, so that we all witnessed what was more or less the same manifestation.'

Frank finished his vodka and beckoned the hostess for another one. 'What I want to know is, why would another spirit do that?'

'I'm not at all sure. But spirits often make attempts to influence us, so that we can take care of unfinished business for them.'

'What do you mean?'

'Well, there are some things that spirits can do for themselves. If a man never got the chance to tell a woman that he loved her before he died, he might whisper it to her, inside her mind, or evoke a song or a smell that reminds her of him. He might even be able to appear to her, or give her the feeling

123

that he was touching her. But spirits can't hurt anybody. They can't take revenge – not with their own hands, anyway.'

'Really?'

'Absolutely. That's why people shouldn't ever be scared by ghosts. Spirits can sometimes make a room feel chilly, or make the lights appear to go dim, but that's not because it *really* goes colder or darker; they're just affecting our perception. They can move objects, sometimes, that's elementary psychokinesis. But they certainly can't strangle you or stab you or push you off a building. That's because they can't make your brain act against your own self-preservation. What they *can* do, however, is try to persuade some other living person to get their revenge by proxy.'

'What do you mean by that?'

'I've done quite a lot of research into it – and there are several recorded instances where people have been killed and this seems to be the only plausible explanation. The most recent case I heard of was in New York two or three years ago when Antonio "Horseface" Agnelli was shot dead by one of his closest friends, George D'Auria.

'In his defense, D'Auria said that he had met one of Horseface's cousins, Bruno, in a restaurant in Brooklyn and that Cousin Bruno had tipped him off that Horseface had been having a passionate affair with his wife.

'However it turned out at the Grand Jury hearing that Bruno had been expelled from the Agnelli family in 1994, and that his body had been found in 1997 in a burned-out car in Queens. So we have to ask ourselves, who did George D'Auria meet in that restaurant, if anybody? The manager and the waiter swore blind that he had eaten alone.'

The pianist started to play an even more careless interpretation of the theme from *The Love Boat*. Frank said, 'I still don't understand why a spirit should have appeared to me as Danny, and told me that he didn't forgive me.'

'Quite honestly, Frank, I don't either. But it stirred up serious trouble for you, didn't it, between you and Margot? And that graffiti all over her paintings – that must have been the last straw, as far as she was concerned.'

'You think a *spirit* could have spoiled her paintings?'

124

'I suppose it's possible. As I say, spirits can't hurt you directly, but many of them are capable of moving things, like pictures, or even furniture, and some spirits can fling things around.'

Frank said, 'I have a very bad feeling about this. I feel like I'm being led somewhere, but I don't know where.'

'Well, there's only one way to find out. We ought to try another communication session – another séance. And before you say no, this one will be free of charge. I've been commissioned to write a new book about psychic detection and this will make a terrific chapter all on its own. It's an extremely unusual case, Frank. It really is.'

'OK . . . if you think it might help.'

'More than anything else, I think it's a sensible precaution. I don't want to be alarmist, but it seems to me as if this spirit is intent on doing you some serious mischief.'

Twelve

Astrid knocked on his door just after eleven. As soon as he let her in she clung to him and held him tight, without saying anything. A young musician with a beaky nose and curly, shoulder-length hair came out of the room next door and winked at him. 'Looks like you're all right there, mate.'

Frank said, 'I'm OK, Astrid. Really, I'm OK.' He disentangled himself from her arms and closed the door.

'I couldn't stop thinking about you all day.' She looked different – her hair was different, slicked back with gel, and she was wearing a white silk Spanish-style blouse and tight black satin pants, flared at the ankle.

'I'm OK. The funeral was good for me.'

'It didn't upset you too much?'

He shook his head. 'We sang some of Danny's favorite hymns and some of his friends said a few words about him and everybody cried. And it was good. It wasn't closure. Closure's going to take a long, long time. But at least it gave me the chance to say goodbye to him. And sorry.'

'I don't know why you had to say sorry.'

'Because Danny still blames me, that's why. Even if it wasn't really my fault.'

He went into the kitchen area and poured them both a vodka and tonic, with a slice of lime. Astrid sat cross-legged on the couch. 'Nothing on television,' she complained. 'Nothing but bombs, bombs, bombs.'

'Well, it's getting serious,' said Frank. 'The whole industry's in a state of total paralysis. They haven't put *Pigs* on hold yet, but Mo reckons they're going to make an announcement in the morning. Did you see that Hallmark have canceled *Beltway*? Disappointing ratings, that's the excuse they gave. Actually it was doing pretty good. The only trouble was, the chief villain is a treacherous, lecherous, Middle-Eastern diplomat.'

'I don't want to talk about the bombing. It scares me.'

'I think it scares everybody, and with damn good reason.'

'It's never going to be the same again, is it? Hollywood?'

He nodded. She was right, Hollywood had been changed forever. Not just the town itself, but the whole self-image of America that Hollywood had reflected in a million movies and television series. This wasn't a fictitious threat from giant ants in the desert, or aliens with mile-long mother ships. This was a real threat that really killed people you knew, and it was everywhere and anywhere. You couldn't escape it by walking out of the movie theater or switching it off.

You could never mow your lawn again, or invite your family around for Thanksgiving, or drive along the coast with the sun in your eyes, in the absolute certainty that because you were in America, you were safe. Dar Tariki Tariqat had murdered much more than people. They had murdered certainty, and left its blood running into the gutters.

Frank had ordered pepperoni pizza and they ate it, very messily, in bed.

'What are you going to do about Margot?' asked Astrid, sucking her fingers.

'I don't know what I can do. Give her some time to cool off, I guess.'

'Do you think she will? Cool off, I mean.'

'I don't know.' He didn't actually say that he didn't care, either, but he nearly did, and he surprised himself because he meant it. If he *had* cared, he wouldn't be sitting in bed with Astrid on the night of their only child's funeral. But, he thought to himself, I'm the last person in the world that Margot wants to console her. Just like she said, she might be able to forgive me one day, but she could never forget, and how could she bear to stay married to me, if she was always going to blame me for Danny's death?

He looked at Astrid's profile, limned by the light from the TV screen – her hooded eyes and sharp cheekbones and her sensual, slightly parted lips. He looked at her feet, her long toes with silver rings on every one of them. There was something elvish about her, a magical quality, as if she came from Middle Earth. He didn't know if this relationship would develop into anything, but there was a strange sparkle about it that he had never known with Margot.

'You were going to tell me something,' he said.

'Was I? What?'

'I don't know. You started to tell me on the phone but then you said you'd leave it till later.'

'Oh, yes. I was going to ask you if you wanted to come away with me this weekend.'

'Where did you have in mind?'

'I have a friend who has a cottage in Rancho Santa Fe. It's only an hour's drive.'

'And we could do what?'

'Swim. Talk. Eat too many strawberries.'

'Well . . . I probably won't have any writing to do.'

'Is that a yes?'

'Yes, OK. It's a yes.'

'Good. You can sing me "The Girl With the Left-Footed Limp."'

He tried to read her eyes. They were sparkling and alive,

127

but he couldn't decide if they were lit up with pleasure, or with something else altogether – the secret delight of a woman who has got exactly what she wants.

They slept in each other's arms, restlessly, all tangled up, but they didn't make love. In the small hours of the morning, when it was just beginning to grow light, Frank was woken up by somebody talking. At first he thought there was somebody in the living room, but then he realized that it was Astrid.

'Believe it . . . in your head. It's the only path. Dark . . . I know it is. Dark! Can't you hear the fountain? Go through the garden and never come back.'

After a while she turned her back to him and started to breathe very deeply, as if she were trying to calm herself down. The sky outside grew lighter and lighter, and at last the sun came in, and lit up the bed. She opened her eyes and smiled at him.

'I was dreaming,' she said.

Frank didn't realize that he had overshot the entrance to Nevile's house until he passed the Earth Mother Juice Stand by the side of the road. If you pass the Earth Mother Juice Stand, Nevile had told him, you've gone two hundred yards too far. He twisted around in his seat and backed his car up all the way.

The driveway to Nevile's house sloped steeply downhill between two dark yew hedges. He followed it around a tight left-hand curve until he reached a wide shingled area in front of the house, where a skinny teenager in a splashy Hawaiian shirt was waxing Nevile's Mercedes. Frank didn't have to ask if Nevile was home. The house was walled almost entirely in glass, so that Frank could see right through the living room to the deck at the rear, where Nevile was pacing up and down with his cellphone.

He went to the front door and pushed the bell. A dumpy Mexican woman in a flowery apron stopped chopping red capsicums in the kitchen and came waddling along the shiny hardwood hallway.

'Yes?' she said, as if she were surprised to see anybody standing outside.

'Frank Bell. Nevile's expecting me.'

'Hokay. You come inside.'

She showed him into the living room, which was furnished with low couches upholstered in natural linen and chrome-plated Italian chairs. A tall bronze statue of a naked woman stood in one corner, her hands covering her eyes. On the opposite wall hung an abstract painting of a scarlet triangle and a black square. It was titled *Doubt*.

Nevile saw Frank through the window and beckoned him out on to the deck. The back of the house was built up on pilings and it commanded a precipitous view of Laurel Canyon, with trees and rooftops and bright-blue swimming-pools, and the hazy city sprawling in the distance. Nevile gestured to Frank to sit down.

'*Yes*,' he snapped, into his cellphone. 'That's all it's giving me. I've tried, believe me, but you wouldn't want me to *fabricate* evidence, would you? Even psychic evidence.' He dropped the cellphone into the pocket of his blue-black Armani shirt. 'Lieutenant Chessman again,' he said to Frank. 'He gave me what was left of the driver's seat from the catering truck, the one they used to bomb *The Garry Sherman Show*. He wants to know if I got any feedback from it.'

'And did you?'

'A couple of flashes, but they didn't make any particular sense. One was somebody shouting; it sounded like an angry father telling off a child. The other was more like a dream . . . walking between two rows of cypress trees, with a full moon shining overhead.'

'So what do you make out of that?'

'Absolutely bugger all, so far. Both flashes obviously represent highly significant moments in the driver's life, otherwise they wouldn't have left such a strong resonance in his seat. It's also likely that they're both connected with his decision to act as a suicide bomber. But how, and why . . . well, your guess is as good as mine.'

'You still don't have any idea who these terrorists are?'

'Not really. I get a strong feeling that there's a religious

129

motive behind it, although it's impossible to say *which* religion. I also get the feeling that Dar Tariki Tariqat has a very powerful and charismatic leader behind it – somebody that these suicide bombers desperately wanted to impress. In almost every fragment I've picked up, there's an extraordinary sensation of *pride*. That's something I've never sensed at a crime scene before, even when the British Army had me sorting through bomb debris in Northern Ireland.'

Frank pulled a face. 'Whoever they are, they've certainly done what they set out to do. Almost every new TV series is on hold, and three major movies have been closed down altogether.'

'Why don't you come inside?' said Nevile. 'Let's see if Danny can't give us some answers.'

Nevile showed him into his study. One wall was lined with reference books and leather-bound encyclopedias and files on the paranormal; another was clustered with photographs of Nevile with various famous people – Uri Geller, Elton John, Shirley Maclaine, Henry Kissinger. There was no desk, only a large, low table in the center of the room, made out of a solid square of highly polished black marble.

'This is my pride and joy, this table. I had it shipped over from Delphi, where the oracle Pythia lived. You've heard of the Oracle of Delphi?'

'Sure.'

'The story is that she could tell the future by getting high on bay leaves. But I think there's much more convincing evidence that she was a psychic. She was capable of giving accurate predictions of what was going to happen in the near future, but only in flashes and riddles, the same way that things come to me, and any other psychic detective. For instance, she foresaw that "wooden walls will save Athens from Persia," and what happened? The Greek fleet defeated the invasion fleet of King Xerxes of Persia at the battle of Salamis, 480 BC. And she predicted dozens of other famous events.'

Frank said, 'There's one thing I wanted to ask you, before we started. If another spirit's pretending to be Danny, how are we going to get in touch with the *real* Danny?'

'I think he'll make himself known, if he's recovered. It's my belief that he must have been just as shocked as Kathy Ashbee and all the other children, and so the last time I tried to contact him, his spirit was still very weak. The other spirit was much more mature and consequently much stronger and so it was able to drown him out. It jammed his signal, as it were. But I'm hoping very much that Danny is going to be able to talk to us, this time.'

'OK, then. I understand. Let's get on with it.'

Nevile sat up straight in his black leather armchair and focused on the wall just above Frank's head. Frank sat up straight, too, although Nevile hadn't asked him to.

There was a long, long silence. It was so quiet that Frank could hear Nevile breathing. After three or four moments, a clock chimed eleven. Outside the house, in the sunlight, the teenager in the Hawaiian shirt was giving a last brisk polish to the Mercedes' front bumpers.

'Is that you, Danny?' asked Nevile suddenly. 'I want to talk to Danny.'

Frank sat up even straighter, right on the edge of his chair. He looked at Nevile, trying to catch his attention, but Nevile's eyes were still focused on the wall above his head.

'I want to talk to Danny,' Nevile repeated. 'Nobody else.'

It was all Frank could do to stay in his seat. 'Nevile,' he demanded, 'is somebody there?'

Nevile glanced at him quickly and nodded.

'Is it Danny? Please, God, let it be Danny.'

There was another silence. Nevile slowly lowered his head, so that he was staring down at the shiny oak floor, and he nodded, and nodded again, as if he were listening.

Eventually, he said, 'All right, if you're really Danny, why don't you give me a sign? Better yet, why don't you show yourself?

Frank waited, his heart beating – *thumpp, thumpp, thumpp* – as slowly as a funeral drum.

Nevile nodded again and then he looked up. 'He says you should forget about him and make a new life for yourself.'

'*What*? How can I forget about him?'

'He says that you have to look forward, not back.'

'How do I know that it's really him?'

'He says he forgives you, he knows that it wasn't really your fault. He was angry before because he didn't realize that he was dead.'

'Yes, but how do I know that it's really *him*, and not this other spirit pretending to be him?'

Nevile covered his eyes with one hand, and didn't say a word for more than a minute. At last he said, 'Mr Rumbles. Does that mean anything to you?'

'What?'

'Mr Rumbles, his teddy bear. He says that you called it Mr Rumbles because you blamed it for your stomach rumbling when you were reading him a bedtime story. *Green Eggs and Ham*, that's what you were reading him.'

Frank opened his mouth and closed it again. It *was* Danny. It had to be Danny. What other spirit could have known that? And Danny had said that he was forgiven. Unexpectedly, his eyes filled up with tears.

'Danny! Danny, can you hear me, it's Daddy!'

Nevile listened again, and then said, 'Yes, he can hear you. He loves you. He just wants you to be happy. He says you should make a new life.'

'Danny, I'm not going to forget you. Not ever.'

'He says you should follow your heart. You've already met the person you're going to spend the rest of your life with.'

Frank frowned at him. 'I don't understand. How does he know about that?'

'Because he's with you, wherever you go, and he always will be.'

'Danny – who do you mean? Who are you talking about?'

Another pause. 'He says her name begins with A. A is for aardvark.'

'Who do you mean, Danny? Who are you talking about?'

Nevile waited, and waited. 'No answer. I think he may have gone. Either that, or he's too tired to talk to us anymore. It's very exhausting, getting in touch with people who have passed over; and *they* find it very exhausting, too.'

Frank said, 'You're sure he's gone?' He looked around the

room, half expecting to see Danny standing in one of the corners, or out on the deck.

'I think so. I can't hear anything, and I can't feel any resonance.'

Frank pulled out a crumpled tissue and blew his nose. 'I don't know what to say. That *was* Danny, wasn't it? I mean, he knew what his teddy bear was called, and why.'

'I wouldn't take that as conclusive proof, Frank. But it does seem very likely that it was him.'

'God, I wish I could have heard him myself. But he forgives me, and that's what I care about most.'

Nevile stood up and laid his hand on Frank's shoulder. 'I'm pleased about that. I'm really very pleased. But . . . I don't know. There was one thing that didn't quite ring true.'

Frank looked up at him and frowned.

'It's nothing much,' said Nevile. 'I just wonder why he was so enthusiastic about your starting a new life.'

'Maybe he knows that Margot and I have reached the end of the road. I mean, if Margot can't accept that I didn't kill Danny on purpose—'

'I don't know. It seems to me that most eight-year-old boys would want their parents to stay together, no matter what.'

'I guess he realizes that we're never going to be happy.'

'Hmm. That's rather a grown-up assessment for an eight-year-old boy – particularly an eight-year-old boy who's just been killed . . . But how about a drink? I've got some rather good Riesling if you like that kind of thing.'

'No, thanks. I think I'd better be going. I have to get back to the studio to find out what's happening with *Pigs*.'

'*Is* there a woman in your life beginning with A?'

Frank hesitated for a moment, and then said, 'Yes.'

'I hope you don't think I'm being inquisitive. But when I come to write this up for my book, I'd like to be able to say if Danny hit the mark or not.'

'Her name's Astrid. I met her at The Cedars after the bomb went off. She's very attractive, and I guess we get along pretty good, although I think it's way too soon to think about spending the rest of my life with her.'

'Of course.'

'For one thing, she's very secretive about her background. I don't know where she lives or what she does for a living. I've never met any of her friends. For all I know, her name isn't Astrid at all.'

'That's unusual. Not unheard of, I suppose, especially if she's married. But unusual.'

'I know. But she's a very good listener, and she seems to understand how I feel, and as far as I'm concerned that's all that matters for now.' He stood up and took hold of Nevile's hand. 'I want to thank you for this. You've taken a load off my mind. Really.'

'We should do it again. Perhaps we can find out more.'

Nevile opened the study door and Frank went into the hallway. As he did so, Danny stepped out of the living room, right in front of him, even though the walls were all glass and Frank hadn't seen him waiting for him.

Frank heard himself saying, 'Oh my God!'

Danny looked as solid as if he were still alive, except that his hair was wildly tousled and his face was deathly white. He was wearing a gray check shirt and khaki shorts and gray worn-out sneakers with no socks – clothes that Frank didn't recognize. His shirt and his shorts were blotchy with dried blood, and there was dried blood on his left ear, as well as bruises on his forehead and briar scratches on his legs. His eyes were wide open but they stared at him like glass eyes in a stuffed animal, expressionless.

Frank felt as if his skin were shrinking. 'Danny?' he said hoarsely. He took a step forward, but Nevile grabbed hold of his arm.

'Frank – don't!'

'You see him too?'

'Yes, but it isn't Danny. Believe me, Frank, Danny wouldn't have the strength to do this.'

'Danny?' Frank repeated. 'Danny, what the hell happened to you? Did somebody hurt you?'

He tried to pry Nevile's fingers free from his arm, but now Nevile caught him around the waist as well, trying to pull him back. 'Don't, Frank! He could be dangerous!'

'That's *Danny*, Nevile! Look at him! That's Danny!'

134

'For God's sake, he *can't* be!'

'Danny, who did this to you? Who hurt you? Let me go, Nevile. For Christ's sake, let me go. I have to know who's hurt him.'

Danny said nothing but continued to stare. Frank wrestled himself free from Nevile and took two or three steps toward him, holding out his hands.

'Frank, will you listen to me – *don't!*'

Frank went down on one knee. 'Danny, don't you know me? It's Daddy. Who hurt you, Danny? Let me help you.'

Danny's eyes turned toward him. They didn't look like Danny's, but there was something about them that Frank recognized, as if somebody familiar were watching him through the cut-out eyes of a Danny mask. 'Daddy,' he whispered.

'What?'

'*Daddy* hurt me.'

'I don't understand. I never beat up on you, not like this.'

'*Daddy* hurt me.'

'Danny, come here, let's get you cleaned up.'

Nevile said, 'He's a spirit, Frank. You can't clean him up. You can't even touch him. He isn't there.'

Frank turned around. 'What the hell do you mean, he isn't here? I can see him and I can hear him and he's been hurt, and that's good enough for me.'

'Frank—'

But as Frank turned back again, Danny let out a scream of terror and hurtled against the wall. Then he was flung across the hallway, hitting his head and his shoulder against the leg of the side table. A glass vase toppled off the table and smashed on the floor. Danny slid feet-first toward the front door, as if he were being dragged by his ankles.

Frank tried to grab his hands and pull him back. He felt a sharp slice across his knuckles but there was nothing there. No hands, no Danny. Danny had vanished, instantly, in the same way that he had appeared. Frank stood up, shaking, confused, blood dripping from his elbow. He had cut himself on a curved piece of broken glass vase.

'What happened? Where is he?'

'I told you, Frank. You could see him but he wasn't there.'

'He knocked the vase off the table! If he wasn't there, how could he knock the vase off the table?'

'Psychokinetic energy, that's all, like a poltergeist. Here, come into the kitchen. Let's take a look at that cut.'

'He was there, Nevile. He was right there in front of me.'

'I know. I saw him too. But he was only in our minds.'

The dumpy cook stared disapprovingly as Nevile held Frank's knuckles under cold running water. Then Nevile tore off a sheet of paper towel for him, so that he could dry his hand and stem the bleeding.

'There – it's not serious. You'll live.'

'That looked so much like Danny . . . I just can't get my head round it.'

'I know, Frank, but it wasn't him. I think it was probably the same spirit we saw on your patio.'

'But why? What does it want?'

'I imagine it's trying to tell you something, trying to explain something to you, but God alone knows what. Spirits are like the Oracle of Delphi. They have a frustrating habit of speaking in riddles, and suggestions, and hints.'

They went out on to the deck and Frank sat down, still trembling. Nevile opened the bottle of wine and handed him a glass. 'Unless you'd rather have a brandy?'

'No, this is fine.'

Nevile sat opposite him, and held his glass of wine up to the sunlight. 'Beautiful color, isn't it? Pure gold.'

'What do I do now?' Frank asked him.

'Under normal circumstances I'd say forget it, leave well enough alone.'

'But these aren't normal circumstances, are they?'

'No. And I think that your first instinct was right. You're being led somewhere, for some reason. It may be nothing more than a prank. Some dead people have a very strange sense of humor. But I don't think this is being done for fun. We need to find out what this spirit is trying to say to you, and urgently.'

136

Thirteen

On the six o'clock television news, anchorwoman Chris Chan announced that the LAPD Anti-Terrorism Unit had released further information about Richard Haze Abbott, the driver of the Movieble Feast catering truck.

'Abbott was a student at Simi Valley High School but was excluded from classes at the age of sixteen for disruptive behavior. Between 1994 and 1996 he took a number of casual jobs, including painting and decorating, roofing, and taxi-driving, but he was unable to hold down any job for longer than a few weeks. According to several of his past employers, he was "argumentative", "insubordinate", and "downright weird." In October of 1996 Abbott joined a commune of thirty-five people based in the mountains near Escondido, in San Diego County. The members of this commune called themselves the Air Traffic Controllers because they believed it was their mission in life to guide alien spacecraft to land on Earth.

'During this time Abbott was arrested for a number of minor offenses including petty theft and vandalism. In 1998 he was sentenced to three years' imprisonment at Vista Detention Facility for drug trafficking and carrying a concealed weapon. In jail he came under the influence of a well-known Islamic agitator, Ibn Athir, who was serving five years for passport forgery. Athir persuaded Abbott to convert to Islam. On his release Abbott joined a splinter group of Islamic activists calling themselves the Sons and Daughters of Iblis – SADI for short.

'A police raid on SADI's headquarters in Reseda in August of 2002 revealed explosive materials, firearms and a large quantity of subversive literature. A warrant was issued for Abbott's arrest, but it was believed that he managed to cross the border into Mexico and he was never apprehended.'

The next shot was of Richard Abbott's mother outside the family home in Simi Valley – a fat, plain woman with greasy hair and a soiled pink T-shirt. 'Richie was a bright boy all right, but his father used to beat seven kinds of bleep out of him for no reason that I could ever tell, and he was bullied at school, too. I'd say that he was always unhappy, all his life, and what he's done – this bombing – well, I can't say that I was surprised. Richie was always saying that one day he was going to get his own back. He used to say people who treat you like you're nothing, they don't deserve nothing. They don't even deserve to live nor breathe.'

Chris Chan said, 'Today, police and FBI admit that they are still no closer to identifying the leaders of Dar Tariki Tariqat, although they have discovered that the explosives used in the *Garry Sherman Show* bombing were stolen from the Raymond granite quarry in Madera County more than a year ago. Police Commissioner Marvin Campbell said that this was a clear indication of a "cold, calculated, well-thought-out campaign of terror."'

Campbell was shown on screen, looking harassed. 'We shouldn't make the mistake of thinking that these crimes were perpetrated by amateurs or crazed fanatics. These people know exactly what they're doing, they've been planning this for a long, long time and so far they're still one step ahead of us. All I can do is repeat my earlier warnings that everybody in Los Angeles, particularly those involved with the entertainment industry, must be extra vigilant. If in any doubt, call nine-one-one.'

'Meanwhile, Charles Lasser, the owner of Star-TV, announced that Star is determined to defy Dar Tariki Tariqat by running all of its normal schedules, including its steamy daytime serial *Paradise Grove* and the *Karen Mulcahy Show*, in which guests are encouraged to confess their most outrageous sexual fantasies in front of their partners. Not to mention *Star World News*, which was famously described by *Newsweek* magazine as "slightly to the right of Newt Gingrich, and straight on till morning."'

Charles Lasser was seen climbing out of his chauffeur-driven Rolls Royce. 'The day I change one second of Star-

TV's scheduled programs because I'm afraid of some wild-eyed lunatics in nightgowns, that's the day I'm going to lock myself in my office with a bottle of whiskey and shoot myself.'

Charles Lasser's determination not to be intimidated by the terrorists had trebled his audience overnight, so he claimed, and boosted Star-TV's advertising revenues by more than seventeen percent. 'But I'm not doing this to make money – every extra penny of profit is going into my reward fund. I want to see these sons of bitches stamped out and I don't care if it takes a hundred million dollars to do it.'

A news reporter asked him if he wasn't recklessly endangering his employees and his studio audiences.

'None of my employees is obliged to show up for work during the current crisis if he or she feels that the risk is unacceptable. Nobody who makes this choice will be penalized in any way, and they will be welcome back at Star-TV once the crisis is over. Members of the public who come to our studios to take part in live TV shows or other entertainments will have to sign a waiver absolving Star-TV from any claim for death or injury. But our security is second to none, and the choice to be part of a studio audience is entirely theirs.'

Frank said to Astrid, 'Isn't that generous? Even if you're too chicken shit to show up for work, Charlie Lasser will still welcome you back with open arms once the bombing's stopped. Notice how he doesn't promise that you'll get your old job back. Vice president in charge of international syndication before the bombing; toilet attendant afterward.'

'Have you ever met him?' asked Astrid. She was snuggled up close to him, wearing nothing but a pink candy-stripe blouse.

'Charles Lasser? Only once, at some TV award ceremony. He's *big,* that's all I remember. I mean, he looks pretty big on the screen, but when you meet him in real life, he's a *giant.* He made me feel like Stuart Little.'

'I think he really has something. I don't know – charisma.'

'That's because he's very large, and very wealthy, and he's a bully, and all women are irresistibly drawn to large, wealthy bullies.'

'You're not a large, wealthy bully, and I'm irresistibly drawn to you.'

'That's because I make you laugh, which is what men do to attract women if they're too weak and shy to be bullies.'

'You make me cry, too. That episode of *Pigs* when Henry gets upset because of all the patches in his pants. That was so sad.'

Frank smiled at the memory of it, and quoted the voice-over. '"Our pants had so many patches in the seats that they were more patch than pant. Personally I couldn't understand why my father's pride meant that we had to walk to school with what looked like traditional American quilts sewn on to our otherwise gray-flannel asses, but I guess the experience taught me why pride is one of the seven deadly sins, because no man's pride is worth two small brothers staying in a hot, empty classroom during recess, silently crayoning, because they can't take any more taunts about their chintz and brocade behinds."'

'Oh, it's so sad,' said Astrid. 'Poor Dusty. Poor Henry.'

'Life is sad, period,' Frank told her, and kissed her on the forehead.

When they went to bed that night Astrid's love-making was ravenous. To begin with, she made him feel like a Viking, freshly waded out of the surf, eager to have any woman he came across. But as the night wore on, he began to feel increasingly scratched and bruised, and exhausted, and desperate for a few hours' sleep. But she wanted him to take her in every way that he had ever imagined, and in some that he hadn't, and when she reached her climaxes she made noises that he had never heard a woman make before, hissing and crowing and screaming.

She clawed him and slapped him and bit him, and they rolled together on the sweaty, knotted sheets, over and over, until Frank lost any sense of where he was or who he was or what he was doing.

When morning came, he opened his eyes to find himself looking at her feet. He raised himself up on one elbow. She was sleeping face-down, her hair sticking up in spikes. He looked at her for a long, long time, his eyes following the curves of her back, and he thought that he had never seen a woman so magical. Her skin was so silky; the back of her neck was so beautifully hollowed. He loved the smell of her, too – stale juices and faded flowers. He noticed for the first time that she had a tiny tattoo on her left hip, a figure that looked like a hunchbacked goat, wrapped in a cloak.

He eased himself out of bed and went across to draw back the drapes. She stirred and blinked at him. 'What time is it?'

'Five after eight. You're not in a hurry, are you?'

'No.'

'I thought maybe we could have breakfast at Charlie's. They do corned-beef hash to kill your mother for.'

'My mother?'

'Figure of speech. I don't mean literally.'

'My *mother*,' she repeated, in that hoarse, smoky voice, as if she couldn't remember that she had ever had a mother.

'Listen, forget I mentioned it. How about a shower?'

She sat up and stretched, her back arched, her skinny arms spread stiffly behind her like wings. 'I have so much to do today.'

'Like what? I thought you might like to come to the office. I could introduce you to Mo and Lizzie.'

'It's a little too soon for that, don't you think?'

He sat down beside her and kissed her. 'Not at all. Mo and Lizzie are both men of the world, particularly Lizzie. But you still have time for breakfast, don't you?'

'No. I think I'd better go.'

'So . . . what? I'm going to see you this evening?'

She looked into his eyes as if she were trying to penetrate the darkness inside his head. 'It depends.'

'On what?'

'On this and that. On whether I'm busy.'

'Well, OK. But why don't you give me a number, so that I can call you?'

'I told you before. I don't have a number.'

'You must at least have a cellphone.'

She shook her head.

141

'Jesus, everybody on the planet has a cellphone, apart from one or two stone-deaf bushmen in the Kalahari.'

She stood up and walked naked to the bathroom. Frank followed her. She sat unselfconsciously on the toilet but she still looked at him with that odd, unfocused stare.

'I don't understand,' he said. 'How can you not have a phone number?'

'I like to stay out of touch.'

'Even with me?'

She flushed the toilet and went to the basin, splashing water on her face and wetting her hair. Frank came up to her and touched the drips on her eyelashes and the tip of her nose. 'Nevile did another séance for me.'

'Oh, yes?'

'He contacted Danny. I'm pretty sure it was Danny this time. The real Danny.'

Astrid dried her face and went through to the bedroom. She took out a comb and started to slick back her hair. Again Frank followed her.

'Danny said that I had already met the person I was going to spend the rest of my life with. He said her name began with an A.'

'And?'

'Well, Astrid begins with an A, doesn't it?'

'*Pff!* You really believe this stuff? What did I tell you before? Nevile's nothing more than a hustler. If he wasn't running around playing psychic detective, he'd be out on the boardwalk running a shell game.'

'I don't think so. He knew what Danny's teddy bear was called, and why.'

Astrid found her sapphire-blue thong under the bed and stepped into it. 'That was his proof, was it?'

'It was proof enough for me.'

'Frank, *I* know what Danny's teddy bear was called, too, and so does everybody else in the United States. They featured him on NBC News. "Today, a lonesome teddy bear pines for the boy who used to cuddle him."'

'Really? I never saw that.'

'It was Wednesday, when you were burying him.'

She fastened her bra and put on her candy-stripe blouse. Frank did up the buttons for her. 'All the same, I believe that Nevile got through to Danny. And Danny said that my new life started here and now, with this woman whose name begins with an A.'

Astrid slowly shook her head. 'You think I'm part of your new life? Frank, you don't know me at all.'

'It's not for want of trying, is it? But come on, Astrid. You won't even tell me your surname, or where you live!'

She found her purse and took out her mascara. 'Knowing a person's name and address doesn't mean you know them.'

'Maybe it doesn't, but it's a start.'

She turned to him and kissed him, a very light but lingering kiss, the tip of her tongue touching his front teeth. 'You were wonderful last night,' she told him. 'I had a fantasy that I was the Queen of Sheba and you were my slave.'

'It felt like it, believe me. In fact I felt like several slaves.'

'Look,' she said, and turned him around so that he could see his back in the dressing-table mirror. His shoulders and his buttocks were criss-crossed with scarlet scratches. 'You like me hurting you, don't you? You know what I'm going to do to you next time? I'm going to bite you so hard that you scream.' Her eyes widened as she kissed him again. 'See you,' she said. She opened the door, and then she was gone, her pink mules slip-slapping down the stairs. Frank stood in the middle of the living room, his arms by his sides, and for the first time in years he felt as if he had lost control of his life. It was like that winter three years ago when he had been driving to Portland, Oregon, and his rental car had skidded on an icy curve. He had frantically twisted the steering wheel from side to side, but he had seen the black rocks sliding toward him, and all he could do was brace himself for the impact.

He waited by the phone but Astrid didn't call that evening, so shortly after eight o'clock he drove over to Burbank to see Margot. They were still husband and wife, after all, and he was beginning to feel guilty about leaving her to cope with her grief on her own.

Margot answered the door but Ruth was close behind her, dressed in some extraordinary hand-woven poncho with fraying edges, embroidered with a sun symbol, and baggy brown cotton pants. Margot was wearing denim dungarees and no makeup. Her face was as pale as a scrubbed potato.

'Was there something you wanted?' she asked him.

'I thought we could talk.'

'I thought you said everything you had to say when you defaced my paintings.'

'You still believe that I did it?'

'Do you care what I believe?'

Frank looked at Ruth and Ruth looked back at him with her usual slitty-eyed hostility. 'Margot needs time to repair her emotional value system.'

'Oh. I didn't know it was broken.'

'Of course it's broken, Frank. Margot's entire concept of conjugal weights and balances is in total disorder.'

Frank frowned at Margot as if he couldn't quite remember who she was. In fact, he was trying to see in her face the reason why he had married her, and why they had conceived Danny together, and why they had stayed together for so long. But all he could see was the mole on her upper lip.

'Is this true?' he asked her. 'Your *entire* concept of conjugal weights and balances?'

'How can you make fun of me after what's just happened?'

'I'm not making fun of you, Margot. I'm making fun of a world that turns real feelings into meaningless jargon. I'm trying to tell you how sorry I am. But I'm also trying to tell you that we can't turn the clock back. Either we're going to share this grief together, and struggle on, and see what we can make of this marriage, or else we're going to say that we've been holed below the waterline, and abandon ship, and then it's every man for himself. Or woman,' he added, before Rachel could say it.

Margot didn't answer at first. Ruth came forward and took hold of her hand, giving Frank a smug proprietorial look, as if to say, *you've lost her now; she's mine. We're sisters together, look at our hideous clothes and our tied-back hair*

144

and our unplucked eyebrows. We don't need to look attractive to men because we don't need men.

'Frank,' said Margot, 'I know what you're saying, I know how sorry you are. But I really need much more time.'

'All right,' Frank agreed. 'I'm prepared to be generous. How much do you want? Two weeks, a month? A year, maybe? How about a decade?'

Then they finally looked at each other and they both knew that it was over.

Frank said, 'I'll have my horologist get in touch with your horologist, OK?'

When he returned to the Sunset Marquis, he called Nevile.

'Signor Strange, he leave town,' said his maid.

'Do you know when he's going to be back? This is Frank Bell. I needed to talk to him urgently.'

'He no say. Maybe you try his cell-a-phone.'

'OK, thanks.'

He dialed Nevile's cellphone number but the phone was switched off. It was late now, after all – well past 11:30 P.M. He left a message and that was all he could do. For some reason he was beginning to feel panicky, as if something bad was going to happen, even though he couldn't think what it was. He had been very disturbed by Danny's appearance in Nevile's hallway, all bruised and bleeding. What did it mean? Had Danny been trying to show him that he had been indifferent as a father, neglectful to the point of cruelty? He had always been pretty strict, he admitted that, sometimes too strict. But he thought that he had always been fair, and caring.

Maybe the bruises had been a metaphor for something else. After all, if Nevile had been right, then it hadn't been Danny at all, but a much more powerful spirit masquerading as Danny. But if it was a much more powerful spirit, why had it allowed itself to be flung across the hallway, and then dragged away?

He stared at himself in the mirror. His hair was wild and there were dark circles under his eyes. 'Portrait of a lunatic,' he decided.

145

He was sitting on his balcony, his legs propped up on the railings, when he thought he heard a bang toward the northeast. Other people must have heard it, too, because they stopped splashing and laughing around the pool, and stood still, listening.

'Hear that?' said the musician with the long hair and the beaky noise. 'That was a bloody bomb, that was.'

Frank went inside and switched on the television. He flicked through the channels until he found CNN, then waited. After less than five minutes, a newsflash came up on the screen.

'Reports are coming in of a massive explosion at Walt Disney Studios on Buena Vista Road in Burbank. Eye witnesses are saying that "scores" of people have been killed and injured, and that over half of the main administrative block has been demolished.'

He stayed in front of the television for the rest of the afternoon. Gradually it emerged that a car bomb had killed forty-five Disney staff and that more than a hundred had been maimed by blast and shrapnel. Offices had collapsed and fires were still raging through the building, destroying millions of dollars worth of irreplaceable artwork and cells. Only three of the Seven Dwarf figures, which held up the roof, remained intact.

Police Commissioner Campbell appeared on the screen. 'Los Angeles has again lost precious lives. The whole world has lost its innocence.'

Fourteen

Two hours after the Disney bomb went off, Frank's producer, Peter Brodsky, called him.

'Now they've bombed *Disney*? Jesus.'

146

'They're not going to stop, Peter. They're not going to stop until there's no Hollywood left.'

They shared a moment's silence, but then Peter said, 'I thought you'd better be the first to know. *Pigs* has been canceled until further notice.'

'Well, I can't say that we haven't been expecting it.'

'You know that it's absolutely no reflection on you or the show. We have to think about the safety of everybody involved in it, that's all. Just as soon as they've caught these goddamned terrorists—'

'Peter, I totally understand.'

'You're OK, are you, Frank? Marcia was wondering if you'd like to come over for brunch on Sunday morning.'

'Well, that's very thoughtful of her, please say thanks. The thing is, though, I'm going down to Rancho Santa Fe to spend the weekend with some friends.'

'Good, good. So long as you're not alone.'

He called Nevile again, but he was still away. He left a message on his voicemail asking him to call back as soon as he could.

'I'm feeling spooked . . . I don't exactly know why. This bomb at Disney hasn't made me feel any better, either.'

Mayor Joseph Lindsay was being interviewed outside the archway of Disney Studios. Behind him, Alameda Avenue was still crowded with fire trucks and ambulances, their red lights flashing. The mayor was saying, 'I think I speak for everybody in the city of Los Angeles when I say that Disney cartoons were a precious part of my growing-up. When somebody attacks the Disney studio, they're attacking not only my freedom of speech as an adult, they're attacking my childhood, too. They're attacking my memories and my values. They're attacking my cultural heritage.'

Part bored, part edgy, Frank drove round to see Mo, who lived in a split-level house on Lincoln Boulevard in Santa Monica. Mo was obviously hosting a party because there were cars parked all the way along the street and colored lights in the trees outside. Mo came to the door in a voluminous

147

gold kaftan, drunk, with a large glass of whiskey in his hand.

'Frank! In the nick of time! Look here, everybody! The ship may be sinking fast but the captain's on the bridge!'

'Sorry, Mo. If I'd known you had guests . . .'

Mo flung his arm around him. 'Baloney. It's the end of the world as we know it, Frank. It's Armageddon. Everybody's welcome.'

The hallway and the living room were crowded with people, most of them shouting and arguing, while almost unheard, a gingery-headed man who looked like an overweight Art Garfunkel, played Irving Berlin favorites on the piano. Mo's wife, Naomi, was in the kitchen serving up tuna knishes and challah sticks and barbecued chicken legs, assisted by seven or eight of her friends who all knew more about serving up food than she did.

'You should never serve barbecue chicken on a paper napkin,' he heard one say. 'It sticks – you want your guests spitting out bits of tissue?'

Mo found Frank a very cold Coors out of the fridge. 'This is my mother's seventy-ninth birthday party. I guess I should have invited you, but then I thought, no, I like Frank too much to have him meet my family. Look at them. The Cohens. I've seen hyenas with Alzheimer's behaving better than this.'

Frank was introduced to the birthday girl, a withered woman in a red silk gown, with a mahogany suntan and diamond-encrusted claws. 'Mo's told me so much about you. I imagined you taller.'

'Well, I expect you were sitting down at the time.'

Mo breathed whiskey in Frank's ear. 'She doesn't understand humor. Only discomfiture. The last thing that made her laugh was Naomi's kugels.'

Frank was introduced to several other Cohens, one of whom owned a local Oldsmobile dealership, another who played cello for the Santa Monica Symphonia, another who was big in tomatoes. Each of them paused for long enough in their arguments to say to Frank, 'You lost your boy, didn't you? What can I say?'

He and Mo ended up on the veranda, by the light of a

guttering torch. 'Strange times, you know, Frank,' said Mo. 'One day you think you know exactly what the world is all about; you think you got all of your parameters fixed. You got steady work, you live in a nice place, you got your family all around you. Then God comes along and says, "Excuse me, may I remind you that you're stuck by your feet by an invisible force to a ball of unstable rock which is hurtling around in a total vacuum, and that you're obliged to share this ball of unstable rock with millions of demented people, many of whom don't use deodorant, and some of whom would like nothing better than to pocket all of your possessions, torture your pets and blow your head off. Not only that, everything that makes this situation bearable, like cheeseburgers and whiskey and reasonably priced cigars, is going to shorten your life, and in any case you're going to die anyhow, half-blind, half-deaf, in wet pajamas, in Pasadena."'

Frank swallowed beer and wiped his mouth with his hand. 'I guess that's one way of looking at it.'

He told Mo about the séance. Mo was beginning to sober up now, and he listened and nodded and occasionally patted his sweaty face with a balled-up tissue.

'You're sure this wasn't your imagination working over-time? After all – what – it's only been ten days now since Danny died. Don't kid me that *you're* not traumatized, too.'

'I saw him, Mo. Or whatever spirit it is that's pretending to be him. I just don't understand what it's all about.'

'Not everything in this life has to have a logical explana-tion, Frank. Look at my family. *Quod erat demonstrandum.*'

'I never hit Danny, though, Mo. I never bruised him, I never made him bleed.'

'Of course you didn't. But look at it this way. Maybe this spirit is using Danny to get your attention.'

'What?'

'Your folks never had much money, right, and when you were a kid you didn't have any confidence, and you kept doing things like the time when you were trying to impress that girl and you sneezed that huge green booger on to the back of her hand. But if you personally went on television and whined about your miserable childhood – *you*, Frank Bell – who would want to know?'

'I don't follow you.'

'Poor old hard-done-by Frank Bell! *Nobody* would want to know, would they? But in *Pigs* you've invented Dusty and Henry, and when Dusty and Henry get embarrassed, or upset, or make idiots of themselves, people can identify with them, right? The audience feel *empathy*. "Gee, that was exactly the way I felt, when I was a kid." That's why the show's so goddamned popular.'

'You've lost me, Mo. Maybe you need another drink.'

'No, no, listen! Maybe this spirit is doing the same thing. If he appeared to you like he really is – some dead guy that you've never even met – you wouldn't be interested in his childhood, would you, no matter how much he was knocked around? But he's pretending to be Danny, because you care what happens to Danny, like your audience cares what happens to Dusty and Henry. In spite of yourself, when you see Danny, even though you know that it's not really him, you can't stop yourself from feeling protective.'

Frank thought about that, and then shrugged. 'I guess that's as good a theory as any. But that still doesn't tell me *why*.'

Mo raised his glass. '"Ah, what is man! Wherefore does he why? Whence did he whence? Whither is he withering?" Do you know who said that? Dan Leno. Do you know who Dan Leno was? And don't say Jay Leno's kid brother.'

'I was right. You *do* need another drink.'

They went back into the living room. The arguing was even louder. The pianist was playing 'Isn't it a Lovely Day?' and Mo's mother was singing along in a high, breathless screech.

'My mother,' said Mo proudly. 'She could empty Carnegie Hall in three minutes flat.'

He was woken up at six twenty-five the next morning by the telephone ringing. He picked it up and said, 'Astrid?'

'Mr Walker? This is your six thirty alarm call.'

'You have the wrong room. This is Frank Bell in 105.'

'Oh, I'm sorry, sir! You have a nice day now.'

'You too,' said Frank. He turned over and tried to get back

150

to sleep but the room was already filled with sunlight and outside the gardener was noisily hosing down the pool. He had only drunk three or four beers at Mo's party but he still felt blurry-headed, as if he had a hangover.

He kept thinking about what Mo had said. He could very well be right about this spirit that was masquerading as Danny. But that still didn't answer the question of why, or what it was that the spirit was trying to tell him.

At six fifty-one he got out of bed and spooned some dark roast coffee into the percolator. Then he took a shower, although he turned the water off three or four times and listened, because he thought he heard the phone ringing. This was ridiculous. Here he was, a grown man, a well-known TV writer, a husband and a father, waiting for some girl to call him and tell him how he was going to spending his weekend.

He sat on his balcony drinking coffee and eating a toasted muffin with apricot jelly. He felt unsettled – not only because Astrid hadn't called, and he still couldn't get in touch with Nevile – but because he didn't have any writing to do. This was the first weekend in three years when he hadn't been pushed to finish a new episode of *Pigs*. He had already blocked out a new storyline in which Dusty had at last won the heart of the classroom beauty, Libby Polaski. Ever since episode three, Dusty had harbored fantasies about sitting on the banks of the Thick Silty River with Libby, picking the scabs off her knees and eating them. 'At the age of twelve, that's about as close as you're going to get to oral sex.' But now there was no point in writing any more.

Maybe he could work on a series about a man whose son was killed, and the son's spirit comes back to help him sort out his tangled love life. Half tragedy, half bittersweet comedy.

Maybe Astrid would call.

By noon, nobody had knocked on the door and the phone had remained silent, so he decided to drive to the ocean. It was a warm day but a strong wind was blowing from the west, and the clouds were tumbling over each other in their hurry to get to the mountains.

Frank didn't know if he had expected the old man to be

there or not, but he had been sitting on the beach for less than ten minutes when he appeared, in his duck-billed baseball cap and purple T-shirt, dragging a moth-eaten gray mongrel behind him on a length of string. The old man stopped about twenty feet away and took off his cap and scratched his scalp.

'All on your own?' he said, his eyes narrowed against the wind.

'I was, until now.'

'Well, Frank, we can't always expect other people to do what we want them to do. Sometimes we have to realize that we're not the sun, and that other people, they're not our planets.'

'I took your advice.'

'Oh, yes? And what advice was that?'

'I kept on putting one foot in front of the other, but I still don't know where the hell it's taking me.'

The old man chuckled and sniffed. 'Have patience, Frank. You'll find out where you're going, sooner than you think.'

He was sitting on the edge of the bed on Sunday evening, taking off his socks, when there was a frantic knocking at his door.

'OK, OK! I'm coming!'

He opened the door to find Astrid standing there. Her hair was messed up and she had two crimson bruises under her eyes. She was hugging a dark-blue sweatshirt around herself as if she were cold.

'For Christ's sake,' said Frank. She limped into the room and immediately sat down on the couch. He saw that she was wearing no shoes, and that her left foot was bleeding. He closed the door and sat down beside her, trying to take hold of her hands. 'For Christ's sake, Astrid, what the hell's happened?'

'It doesn't matter. I got into some trouble, is all.'

'Trouble? What kind of trouble? Look at you – you look like you just went the full distance with Mike Tyson!'

'It doesn't matter. Could I have a drink, please?'

He went through to the kitchen and brought her back a glass of Diet Coke.

'A drink, Frank. A proper drink.'

'You think you ought to? Look at the state of you.'

'Frank, you're not my mother.'

He poured her a Jack Daniel's, straight up. She tipped it back in one, coughed, and held out her glass for another.

'So . . . are you going to tell me what happened? I thought we were going to Rancho Santa Fe.'

'I'm sorry about that, Frank. I had to go see somebody.'

'And that somebody beat up on you? Are you going to tell me who it was?'

She took another swallow of whiskey. 'I told you, it doesn't matter. I deserved it.'

'Look,' he said, sitting down beside her again, 'I don't have any right to stick my nose in your private business, but you and I are a little more than friends, aren't we? And when you come back here all covered in bruises, I think I deserve an explanation.'

'I'm sorry about Rancho Santa Fe. I should have called you.'

'What happened? Where did you go?'

She looked at him and he thought that he had never seen anybody looking so sad. 'I'm sorry,' she repeated.

They sat for a long time in silence. Astrid sipped her whiskey and kept her eyes on the television, even though the sound was turned down. Frank kept his eyes on Astrid. A television reporter was standing amongst the shattered remains of Happy, Sneezy, Sleepy and Bashful. The caption read 'Disney Death Toll Reaches 113.'

Fifteen

He pulled open the shower door without warning. Astrid tried to cover herself, but it was no use. She couldn't hide the bruises on her shoulders and her thighs, or the bite-marks on her breasts. She stood there with water coursing down her face, half ashamed and half defiant.

Frank took a long, long look at her, and then he closed the door. He was sitting on the end of the bed waiting for her when she came out of the shower, wrapped in a thick white hotel robe.

'I don't know what to think about this,' Frank told her, and he didn't.

Astrid stood in front of the mirror and toweled her hair. 'What you don't know can't hurt you, can it?'

'That's bullshit. Anything that hurts you hurts me.'

'Frank, we've spent two nights together. It's not as if we're married.'

'Danny said that you were my future. Don't you think that counts for something? It does to me.'

'For God's sake, Frank, Danny didn't tell you anything. It was Nevile Strange and Nevile Strange is a fake.'

'Well, I don't agree. I heard what I heard and I saw what I saw. And if you're *not* my future, why do you keep calling me and coming around to see me and sharing my bed?'

Astrid came up to him and gently tilted his chin up so that they were looking at each other eye to eye. 'I thought you needed somebody. Somebody who understood how much you're hurting. I also thought that you needed to forget about Danny for a few hours, and think about yourself.'

'Right now I'm thinking about you. I don't see how we can sustain any kind of relationship unless I know who you are.'

Astrid smiled and kissed him on the forehead. 'I'm just *me*, Frank. I'm not worth losing any sleep over.'

'I need to know who hurt you. I also need to know *why* they hurt you.'

She kissed him again. She smelled of summers gone by. 'No, you don't.'

They both drank too much Jack Daniel's that evening, and when they went to bed they fell asleep almost at once. But Frank was woken in the middle of the night by Astrid tugging his penis. He mumbled, 'No,' but she pressed her hand over his mouth, and continued to rub him, harder and harder. When he grew stiff, she climbed on top of him and guided him inside her, gasping with pain.

'*Astrid!*' he cried, and tried to push her off him, but she gripped his wrists and held him flat on the bed.

As she approached orgasm, she began to sob and snuffle. Again he tried to roll over, but she screamed at him, 'Don't! Don't!' and she jumped up and down on him faster and faster until she finally went into spasm, her thighs gripping him tight, her perspiration dropping on his face and scalding his eyes.

Afterward she lay with her back to him, quivering, and when he touched her face with his fingertips her cheeks were wet with tears.

'Astrid,' he said, 'you have to tell me who did this to you.'

'I can't.'

'You have to. Whoever he is, he deserves to be in prison.'

'I'm not worth it, Frank. I've never been worth it.'

He sat up and switched on the bedside light. 'How can you say that? You're beautiful.'

'No, I'm not. I'm nothing.'

He didn't know what to say to that. He was too tired and his head was banging and his mouth was all furred up. But he knew one thing for certain. He would find out who had beat up on Astrid, and he would make sure that the bastard got what he deserved, in spades.

The next morning Astrid slept until almost eleven o'clock. The red bruises on her cheekbones had already turned purple and her eyes were almost closed. The first thing Frank did was sit on the bed beside her and hold up his shaving mirror.

'Oh, God,' she said.

'You're still not going to tell me who did it?'

She shook her head.

'All right. If you won't tell me, you won't tell me. That's your privilege. What are you doing today? How about lunch at Captain Hooker's, up the coast? Come on, you can always wear dark glasses.'

'No, I'm busy today.'

'How about this evening?'

'This evening? Well . . . OK.'

'I'll see you round seven, then? That's if you don't change your mind and go off to get another beating.'

'Frank . . .'

'Yes, I know. Not funny. You'd think that I'd be able to come up with a really good gag about it, wouldn't you, a professional humorist like me? "Does your boyfriend beat you up?" – pause – "No, I'm always out of bed first."'

'Frank . . .'

'I care about you, Astrid, even if you don't care about yourself. I can't understand why you don't want to tell me anything about yourself, but if that's the way you want it, I'm prepared to accept it. I'd rather go on seeing you, even if you keep me in the dark. Even if you come back with bruises and bites and you won't say who did them.'

Astrid kissed him. 'You're a rare man, Frank.'

No I'm not, he thought. *I'm a liar.*

He made two mugs of strong coffee and they drank it together in the living room. He didn't really know what to say to her, because he felt so angry and jealous and he didn't want her to know.

'So, what are you doing today?' he asked her, trying to sound offhand. 'Anything interesting?'

'Running a few errands, that's all. Meeting some friends.'

'Well . . . if you're finished before seven, you can call me any time.'

She didn't answer, but put down her half-empty coffee mug, stood up, and came over to kiss him. 'I'll see you this evening, OK?'

'Sure.'

He waited until she had closed the door behind her. He counted to five, slowly. Then he reached under the couch and pulled out his light tan deck shoes. He picked up his blue linen coat, grabbed his cellphone, and went to the door. He opened it quickly but very quietly, and listened. No footsteps on the stairs; no elevator whining. She must have left the hotel by now.

He hurried down the staircase to the lobby. He was just in time to see Astrid outside in the street, climbing into a red

156

and green taxi. He leaned back against the wall, half-concealed by a bushy fig plant, until the taxi had pulled away. The receptionist raised an eyebrow at him but didn't say anything. As soon as the taxi had disappeared, he pushed his way out through the revolving doors. His own car was parked only fifty feet up the hill, its front wheels cramped against the curb. He climbed into it, started the engine, and backed it into the front bumper of the Jeep parked behind him.

Astrid's taxi took a left on Holloway Drive, and then a tight right on to Santa Monica. Frank had to wait at the intersection with Santa Monica, drumming his fingers on the steering wheel, while a long, dawdling procession of traffic crawled past. But by weaving in and out of the west-bound traffic he caught up with the taxi by the time it reached Rodeo Drive. He could see Astrid's head in the rear window, and he prayed that she wouldn't turn around.

Eventually the taxi took a left into the Avenue of the Stars, and then another right, and pulled into the semicircular parking space in front of the Star-TV building, which was new and gleaming-white, built in an S-shaped wave, with a huge revolving star on the roof, made of dazzling steel. Its windows were all tinted black, and its staff called it the 'Limo.'

Frank drew into the curb behind a UPS delivery truck and watched as Astrid climbed out of the taxi. She crossed the white marble sidewalk and disappeared into the Limo's black-tinted revolving doors.

Frank hesitated for a moment, then got out of his car and followed her. There was a chance that she was still in the lobby, waiting for somebody to meet her, or waiting for an elevator, but he would just have to risk it. He pushed his way inside and was instantly met by a penetrating air-conditioned chill. The lobby was clad in white polished marble, three stories high, with water cascading down one wall and a galaxy of stars suspended from the ceiling.

There were black leather couches for visitors, but there was nobody sitting on them except for two scruffy-looking designers with large art portfolios. The elevator bank was off to the left, but the only people waiting to go up were a UPS messenger and a plump secretary with a bag of doughnuts and a cup of Starbucks coffee.

Frank was immediately approached by two security guards in sky-blue uniforms. One was black and looked like Yaphet Kotto's fatter brother. The other was white and thin and blue-chinned, with close-together eyes.

'Do you have an appointment, sir?'

'Uh, yes, as a matter of fact. A friend of mine said that I was to meet her here.'

'Would you like to give me your friend's name, sir?' said one of the guards, lifting up a clipboard.

'Um, Polaski. Libby Polaski.'

The security guard ran his pen down the list. 'Sorry, sir. No Polaski listed here. Can you tell which department she works in?'

'News. She's an editorial assistant. She's only been working here a few weeks. That's what she told me, anyhow.'

The guard flipped over to another page and glared at it as if he were trying to set it on fire with X-ray vision. Eventually he announced, 'No Polaski in the news department, sir.'

'Oh. Well, it looks like I've been taken for a chump, doesn't it? She gave me this whole spiel about her glamorous new career in television news.'

The security guards were not amused. 'I'm sorry, sir, we're going to have to ask you to leave the premises immediately.'

'Sure. I understand. What with all these bombs going off.'

'We'd appreciate if you didn't mention anything like that, sir.'

'OK, sure. Sorry. Sorry to have caused you any trouble.'

Frank left the building and walked back to his car. A motor-cycle cop was standing beside it, writing in his notebook.

'This your vehicle, sir?'

'Yes, it is. I'm sorry. I had to pick something up from Star-TV.'

'You had to pick what up?'

'Well, nothing, as it turns out. The person I was supposed to meet there didn't show.'

'What was the name of this person?'

'Polaski. Libby Polaski.'

'And what were you supposed to pick up?'

'A DVD. I met her at a bar yesterday evening and she promised to lend me a DVD of *Black Wednesday*, the director's cut. But she's not listed as working at Star-TV, so it looks like I've been taken for a mug.'

The cop tucked his notebook into his pocket. 'I'm going to have to agree with you, sir.'

'Oh, yes?'

''Fraid so. You never heard the name Libby Polaski before? Libby Polaski is that little blonde girl in *If Pigs Could Sing*.'

Frank smacked the heel of his hand against his forehead. 'Jesus! You're right! Do I feel stupid or do I feel stupid?'

Sixteen

Frank was driving to see his sister, Carol, when his cell-phone rang. It was Nevile.

'I got your messages, Frank. I'm sorry, something came up and I had to go away for the weekend. How are you feeling now?'

'I'm not sure. Baffled, I guess, more than anything else. Worried.'

'Why don't you come and see me? There's some things that I need to tell you, before we go any further.'

'OK. I'll see you in fifteen minutes.'

It must have been the maid's day off because the teenager in the splashy Hawaiian shirt opened the door for him with a grin like a cheap piano.

'Sir, you are very, very welcome, *señor*.'

Nevile was waiting for him out on the deck, dressed in a charcoal-gray shirt and black pants, with black suspenders, like a priest. He looked pale and distracted and there were dark circles under his eyes.

'Hello, Frank.' He lifted a large cut-crystal tumbler of whiskey. 'Can I get you a drink?'

'A little early for me, thanks.'

Nevile drew out a chair and sat down. 'I owe you an apology – vanishing off the face of the earth without telling you. I didn't mean to leave you in the lurch. I had to go away for a couple of days and have a think, otherwise I wouldn't have been any use to anybody, myself included.'

Frank said nothing, but waited for Nevile to explain himself.

'The thing is, this business with Danny is a lot more complicated than it first appeared. I think it might be a lot more dangerous, too. Quite honestly, we might be better off if we called it a day.'

'Just a minute. On Friday you were telling me that it was absolutely critical that we found out what it was that Danny was trying to tell me.'

'That was on Friday.'

'So it's only Monday. What's different?'

'Well . . . after you left, I decided to try picking up some more psychic resonance from that truck seat that Lieutenant Chessman had given me. You know – the one from the *Garry Sherman Show*.'

'Oh yes?'

'I was in the right mood for it, after that séance. How can I describe it? My psychic antennae were still tingling.'

'So what happened?'

Nevile swallowed whiskey and grimaced. 'To begin with I got nothing more than the same flashes that I had seen before. A man shouting, and then a walk between some cypress trees. They still didn't tell me anything coherent. Nothing that might account for a young man wanting to blow himself up.

'But later that evening, when I was sitting in the library, writing up my notes, my PC started misbehaving. No matter what I typed on the keyboard, it insisted on writing something else. Here,' he said, and handed Frank a print-out. The text started off plainly enough.

Thursday, September 20:
I began my communication session with Frank Bell by attempting to establish contact with Danny's real spirit. *see*

160

my notes p.13* In order to give Danny's spirit a recognizable signal, I made use of Mr Bell's overwhelming need to hear that Danny forgave him.

I channeled and amplified the intensity of Frank's feelings so that Danny might home in on them – rather like the Doppler signal that identifies an airport in thick fog. I had no idea whether Danny was prepared to forgive his father or not. He might very well have wanted to curse him for what he had done, or what he failed to do. But the first priority was to make contact and to verify that I had found the genuine Danny.

At this point, however, the text altered completely.

KiLL the basstuds 4 wat they Dun 2 me all them yRs the basstuds never LET UP never LET UP treet me liK sum kind dOg ONy wors than dog more Lik dogshIt pa alwis ScrEEEmin an ScrREEEMIN never LET UP jus never LET UP alwis HITTin and HITTin an makin me DO THEM THINS makin me DO THEM thins all of them ALL of them pa an his frends an all of them utha Men til I was pUkin sick an noBODY NEVER helpt not doCtus not teecHus noboDY NEVER in the hole wirl But now I goT the chants to kLL the basstuds an here I GO.

Frank read it and then he handed it back to him. 'I don't understand.'

'Automatic writing, twenty-first century style,' said Nevile.

'What's automatic writing?'

'It's when a spirit takes over your consciousness and writes messages from the other side. And this is what's happened here.'

'Who is it, do you know?'

'I think it's Richard Abbott. I can't be one hundred percent certain, but I spent the whole afternoon trying to contact him, through that truck seat, and he was the last person who ever sat in it.'

'And he wrote to you?'

Nevile nodded. 'Automatic writing is one of the most effective ways of contacting people who have passed over. You ask a question, you open your mind, and you allow a spirit to

161

control your hand as you write. Some mediums use a Ouija board, but most of them simply use a pen and a notepad. Anybody can do it. *You* could do it, if you were prepared to sit calmly and quietly for twenty minutes and wait for the words to flow. I wouldn't guarantee that the words would make very much sense, or that you'd necessarily know which spirit was using you to communicate its thoughts, but the chances are that you'd get *something* from beyond. Some mediums even claim that Shakespeare has used them to write whole new plays, or that Beethoven has inspired them to finish off his symphonies.'

'But this spirit wrote to you on your PC.'

'Yes and I've heard more and more cases of that. When you think about it, a spirit would probably find a PC much easier to write with than a pen, because it's electrical, and all the spirit has to do is use its own electrical energy to take control of my keyboard mapping.'

'So Richard Abbott is trying to tell you that he was abused by "pa an his frends an all of them utha Men"?'

'It would appear so, yes.'

Frank thought about that. 'That manifestation of Danny . . . *he* was being abused, too.'

'Yes,' said Nevile, 'and that's a very important clue. But I also think it's taking us somewhere very dark indeed. I may be wrong, but I don't think that the real Danny – *your* Danny – has anything to do with any of these phenomena. Danny's image is simply being used to draw you into this. I won't mince words, Frank. This could be very, very dangerous.'

'Dangerous in what sense? I mean, what are we looking at here?'

'Madness and death, Frank. That's what we're looking at.'

He was still talking to Nevile when Lieutenant Chessman arrived at the house, accompanied by Detective Booker. They came out on to the deck and Lieutenant Chessman stood by the rail and took two or three deep breaths.

'Makes a change from carbon monoxide.'

Nevile said, 'This is what I was telling you about on the phone,' and handed him the 'automatic writing' from his PC.

Lieutenant Chessman read it, moving his lips as he read, and then passed it to Detective Booker.

'Weird. How reliable is this kind of message, in your experience?'

'Unusually reliable, as far as spirit communications go. It's absolutely exhausting for a spirit to put anything down on paper, because it requires such intense concentration and a huge amount of natural energy – kinetic, when they're using pen and paper, but in this instance, electrical. Let me put it this way: very few spirits ever take the trouble to write anything stupid or mischievous. It's too much effort.'

'So what do you make of this? You really think it was written by Richard Abbott?'

'I'd put money on it. I'll make some further tests to confirm it, but remember that his mother said on TV that his father used to beat him.'

'So what's Mr Abbott trying to say?'

'If it *is* him, it's my belief that he's trying to explain to us that he wasn't just whipped, but seriously abused by his father and his father's friends and other men, and that this experience was one of the factors that led him to become a suicide bomber.'

Lieutenant Chessman took out a crumpled handkerchief and wiped his nose. 'Pretty tenuous theory, wouldn't you say? What about the other bombers?'

'I don't know yet. But I did some psychic communication for Mr Bell here, to see if he could contact his son, Danny. We had a spirit visitation – not, in my opinion, from Danny, but from another spirit who used Danny's image as a means of arousing Mr Bell's sympathy. Whoever that spirit was, it appeared as if he had suffered from serious childhood abuse.'

'So where does this take us?'

'I don't know with any certainty. But abused children commonly grow up to be abusers themselves, don't they, and to seek revenge on society in general for destroying their self-esteem. Maybe this is what's happening here.'

'Your father belts you and so you blow up Disney Studios?'

'It's conceivable. Do you have any other ideas?'

*   *   *

163

Before he left, Lieutenant Chessman turned back to Frank. 'By the way, Mr Bell, about your mystery woman.'

'What about her?'

'I have another witness who saw her walking along Gardner Street soon after the explosion at The Cedars. She identified her as wearing jeans and a creamy-colored shirt dress and one sandal, so that she was walking with a limp. She even stopped her and asked her if she was OK.'

'I see.'

'The witness said the woman was aged about twenty-three or twenty-four, with short brown hair. Very pretty, she said, in spite of the fact that she had smudges all over her face. Reminded her of somebody she knew, she said, although she couldn't think who it was.'

'Oh.'

'Just thought that might help to jog your own memory, Mr Bell. Try to think of some TV actresses that she could have looked like.'

Frank thought about Astrid but he shook his head. 'Sorry. I only write TV; I hardly ever watch it.'

While Nevile showed Lieutenant Chessman and Detective Booker to the door, Frank took a look around his library. On a side table he noticed a photograph in a silver frame – a slim, blonde woman, leaning on the parapet of a bridge someplace, wearing a straw hat. She had one hand lifted to prevent the hat from blowing away, and she was laughing.

'Attractive lady,' Frank remarked as Nevile came back in.

Nevile took the photograph away from him and gave it a wistful smile. 'Yes. That was taken on Albert Bridge, in London.' Pause. 'We were supposed to be getting married.'

'I'm sorry,' said Frank. 'I didn't mean to pry.'

'No, no. Don't worry about it. That was all a long time ago. Nine years and three months, to be precise. Her name was Alison. She was a very clever girl, great fun. She wanted to be a QC.'

'What happened?'

'An accident. A boat party, actually, on the Thames, for somebody's birthday. I was invited, too, but I was working with the Sussex Police that day, trying to find two little girls who had gone missing on the South Downs. It was such a fine summer evening that I drove all the way back to town with the top of my car down.

'I was driving through Putney when I heard on the radio that a dredger had collided with a pleasure boat close to Westminster Pier, and that a number of young people had been drowned. Fifty-two, as it turned out, in the end; and Alison was one of them.'

'I'm sorry. Jesus, you must have been devastated.'

'Well, I was. I haven't really got over it, even now. I keep thinking of what she would have been like now, if she had lived. Sometimes I'm driving along the street and I catch a glimpse of her, disappearing into a doorway, or climbing into a taxi. I know it can't really be her, but I can't get her out of my mind.

'In fact, it was two years after Alison drowned that I experienced automatic writing for myself, so that's how I know how reliable it can be.'

'Alison wrote to you?'

Nevile nodded. 'I was sitting by the Thames one August afternoon at Boulter's Lock. It's very peaceful there . . . several miles upstream from the City. I was writing notes for a lecture on psychic detection, but I had drunk one two many glasses of wine over lunch and I started to nod off. My writing hand started to go into a sort of a spasm, rather like a cramp, but not so painful. It circled around and around my notebook, and then it made all kinds of squiggles.

'I suddenly felt that Alison was very close by – that she was leaning over my shoulder. I tried to resist turning around because I knew that she wasn't really there, but in the end I couldn't stop myself.'

'And?'

'I was right. She wasn't there.'

Nevile paused for a moment, smiling wistfully at the memory. Then he hunkered down and opened one of the drawers underneath the bookshelves. 'Here,' he said, 'the very piece of paper.'

Frank took it and tried to read it. All he could make out was *RO smmr AD tom FFG*.

'Incomprehensible if you don't know what you're

165

looking for,' Nevile admitted. 'But most automatic writing is very personal. If you fold the paper in the middle, the letters RO and AD join together to form the word ROAD, and *The Road* by Edwin Muir was one of Alison's favorite poems.

'It's all about passing time. "There is a road that turning always|Cuts off the country of Again." And the verse that Alison was trying to remind me of goes: "There a man on a summer evening|Reclines at ease upon his tomb|And is his mortal effigy|And there within the womb|The cell of doom." See . . . "smmr"is "summer", "tom" is "tomb" and "FFG" for "effigy."'

He took the piece of paper back and returned it to the drawer. 'She was telling me that everybody dies. Even when we're laughing on Albert Bridge, we'll soon be dead. Even after we're dead, though, we still journey on, although only the dead know where.'

Seventeen

On the six o'clock network news, Police Commissioner Marvin Campbell announced that he had received a new coded message from Dar Tariki Tariqat. They had called for a total ban within seventy-two hours on 'all films and television programs that glorify salacious or ungodly behaviors.' The consequence for disobeying this warning would be 'Armageddon for Hollywood . . . Starting at twelve noon precisely on Friday, a series of eleven bombs will be detonated around Los Angeles at twenty-four intervals, with the intention of bringing to their knees all those who disseminate licentiousness and blasphemy.'

Commissioner Campbell said he had no reason to believe that the message was a hoax and that he was treating it with 'the utmost gravity.' At the same time, he tried to reassure the citizens of Los Angeles that public security precautions had never been so stringent. 'Not only that, our anti-terrorist teams are very close to making some significant arrests.'

'You believe that?' asked Smitty, popping open another beer. They were sitting on the porch, watching the dog rolling on his back on the grass.

Frank shook his head. 'Two detectives came around to Nevile Strange's house this afternoon, when I was there. If they're still asking a psychic for answers, they can't have any solid evidence, can they? I'm not saying that Nevile's not a *good* psychic. In fact, I think he's probably the best. It's just that communications from the spirit world are not exactly a substitute for fingerprints and DNA.'

'You know what I think?' said Smitty. 'I think it's the end of the world as we know it.'

Frank drove back to the Sunset Marquis. When he walked into the lobby, he found Margot waiting for him, alone, looking pale and pinched, her hair wound up in a pale mauve turban.

'Frank,' she said, rising to her feet, 'we really need to talk.'

'Sure, OK.' He checked his watch. It was eight minutes of seven. He led her up to his room and opened the door. She walked in and circled around, her eyes flicking from side to side as if she were looking for clues.

'You want a drink?' he asked her. 'I have Chardonnay, Chardonnay or Chardonnay. Or beer.'

'No thanks. I simply think we need to work out what we're going to do next.'

'I don't know. What do you think we ought to do next?'

'Frank, we've been married for nine years. Doesn't that count for anything?'

'Of course it does. But it's no use pretending that nothing's happened.'

'I *can* forgive you for what happened to Danny, I know I can.'

'But not yet?'

'I'm only asking for time, Frank.'

'I know. And I'm not blaming you. If our positions had been reversed – if it had been *you* taking Danny to school

167

when that bomb went off – I would probably be feeling exactly the same way that you're feeling.'

Margot hesitated, then said, 'The reason I came here today . . . well, I just wanted you to know that in spite of everything I still love you. You talked about divorce, but I don't want to think that this is going to be the end of us.'

Frank took a half-empty bottle of white wine out of the fridge and poured himself a large glass. 'I don't know. I'm beginning to wonder if Danny was all that was holding us together. We've been eating at the same table and sleeping in the same bed, but we haven't been talking to each other very much, have we?'

'Was our marriage really so bad?'

'No, it wasn't. Most of it was great. But maybe we were both changing into different people and because of Danny we didn't realize how much.'

'All I want to know is if I made you happy or not.'

'Jesus, Margot. That's like coming up to somebody who's just walked away from a plane crash and asking them if they had a comfortable seat.'

'I need to know what you're thinking, Frank. I need to know what you're intending to do.'

'I don't know *what* I'm going to do. Neither does anybody else in Los Angeles, until they catch these terrorists. The way things are going, we're all going to wind up jobless and bankrupt.'

'I'm not talking about your work. I'm talking about *us*.'

Frank thought about that for a while, while Margot waited. He glanced at her but her expression gave very little away. He went over to the balcony door, slid it open, and stood in the marmalade-colored light of the setting sun. Eventually he turned back to her and said, 'Nevile did another séance for me. He talked to Danny, and Danny said that I should try to start a new life.'

'He talked to Danny and Danny said that?'

'That's right.'

'You don't really believe that Danny would want us to separate, do you?'

Frank didn't have time to answer. The door opened and

Astrid came in, wearing dark glasses, a buckskin jacket and a tight white tube dress.

'Oh! I'm sorry!' she said when she saw Margot.

Margot turned back to Frank. 'I think I might have made a fool of myself.'

'Of course you haven't. This is Astrid, she was at The Cedars, too.'

'We've already met, thank you. I'd better be going.'

'Margot, if you want to talk tomorrow . . .'

'No, Frank. I don't think I do. I obviously came here to ask you a redundant question.'

He felt irritable that evening. It wasn't just Margot; it was Astrid, too. He took her for *pollo a tegame* at Tony Ascari's but she ate hardly anything. She seemed twitchy and upset and she kept looking around the restaurant as if she were expecting to see somebody she didn't want to see.

'This is not to the lady's taste?' asked Marco, the head waiter, when their plates were collected.

'I'm sorry,' said Astrid. 'Just not hungry, I guess.'

'So what's wrong?' Frank asked her. 'You haven't eaten anything and you've hardly said two words since we came here.'

'Nothing's wrong, OK?'

'So what did you do today? Did somebody upset you?'

'I went to Venice and met some friends, that's all.'

'Venice?'

'That's right. We had pizza at Tomato UFO.'

'Oh . . . That accounts for you not being hungry. You should have said.'

He held her hand over the red checkered tablecloth. He couldn't see her eyes because of her dark glasses; all he could see was two swiveling candle flames. But he still found her as arousing as cat's fur stroked backward – not only because of her perfume, not only because of the way she looked, but because she had lied to him. She hadn't gone to Venice to meet friends. She had gone to Star-TV, and why? To meet the man who had beaten her so badly? To be beaten again? To tell him how much she hated him?

* * *

169

That night, when they went to bed, he was even more sexually charged than she was. They struggled and fought, but he gripped her wrists to prevent her from twisting herself free, and then he pushed himself into her, inch by inch, and kept himself there, as deep as he could possibly go.

'That hurts,' she gasped, her hair bedraggled, her cheek slippery with sweat.

'Lies hurt, too.'

'Lies? What lies? What are you talking about?'

'Lies like, "I went to Venice to meet my friends, that's all. And we all had pizza at Tomato UFO."'

'Why should you care?'

'Because I do. Especially when you come back covered with bruises.'

'You don't own me, Frank.'

'I never said that I did. But I don't like to see you being hurt.'

'You mean you don't like to see me being hurt by another man. It's all right if you do it.'

Frank eased himself out of her. Immediately she wrapped the sheet tightly around herself and rolled over to the other side of the bed. 'You shit,' she said, her voice muffled.

He tried to put his arm around her but she slapped him away. In the end he turned his back to her and tried to get some sleep. It took him two or three hours, because the musician with the beaky nose was playing Bruce Springsteen songs at top volume, and somebody was having a party around the pool, and screaming like a horror movie.

In the very dead of night, he was woken by something touching his cheek. He thought it was a mosquito at first – he had heard one mizzling around the room before he fell asleep. He flapped his hand to brush it away, and then he pulled up the sheet so that it covered his face. He didn't want to wake up in the morning covered in bites.

But he had been lying there for only a minute or two longer before the sheet was slowly pulled down again. He opened his eyes, his skin shrinking with alarm. The bedroom was dark, but there was sufficient light for him to see that somebody was standing close beside the bed, looking down at him. A child, with its eyes glittering in the gloom.

'*Daddy hurt me.*'

Jesus, it was Danny. Frank lay there and stared at him, not daring to move.

'*Daddy hurt me.*'

'It wasn't my fault, Danny,' Frank replied. He had to clear his throat because he had been sleeping on his back. 'It was a bomb, Danny. I didn't know that you'd been injured. There was no way for me to tell.'

'*He beat me and then he said he was sorry and then he made me do all those bad things.*'

'Danny, I didn't beat you and I never made you do anything bad. You know that.'

The figure continued to stare at him. As his eyes gradually grew accustomed to the darkness, he could make out of Danny's mop-top haircut and his pale, triangular face. God, he looked so much like Margot.

'*He beat me and he made me do all those bad things. But I loved him. I loved him so much. Afterward he used to cry and say that he was sorry and that he was never going to hurt me again.*'

Frank eased himself up into a sitting position. Beside him, Astrid stayed deeply asleep, breathing softly and evenly as if she were crossing the universe in the cargo ship *Nostromo*. He was frightened, because his dead son had appeared in his bedroom in the middle of the night, but his fear was equaled by his urgent need to know *why*. If he didn't find out why, he felt that something catastrophic was going to happen to him, and everybody around him.

'Danny . . . I didn't beat you, did I? And I never hurt you in any other way?'

'*Daddy hurt me.*'

Frank reached out into the darkness. 'Here . . . take my hand.'

'*Daddy hurt me. He beat me and he made me do all those bad things.*'

'Take my hand,' Frank insisted. Hesitantly, the figure held out its right hand. 'Come on, there's nothing to be scared of.'

Frank leaned forward and took hold of the child's hand,

171

but the instant he touched it he recoiled in horror. It wasn't a child's hand at all. It was soft, but it was a woman's hand, with long fingernails, and a ring.

He sat there staring at the figure, wide eyed, breathing as quickly as if he had been running. 'Who are you?' he demanded. 'You have to tell me who you are.'

'I'm not allowed to.'

'You can tell me. I won't let anybody know that it was you.'

The figure said nothing, but stayed where it was. The first light of dawn was beginning to appear through the drapes, and the figure was slowly becoming clearer. There was no question that it looked like Danny, but it was wearing soiled yellow pajamas with pictures of marching teddy bears all over them. Danny had never worn pajamas like that.

'You're *not* Danny, are you?' asked Frank.

Astrid stirred. 'Don't. Not tonight,' she said. Frank looked across at her, and when he looked back, the figure had vanished.

He sat up for over twenty minutes, waiting to see if it would reappear, but the drapes grew lighter and lighter, and it was obvious that the figure had gone for good.

In a strange way, Frank was reassured that it wasn't Danny. He didn't like to think of Danny wandering around the spirit world, lost and confused and dressed in dirty clothes. But at the same time, he needed to know why it had chosen to appear as Danny, and where the real Danny was, and if he was at peace.

He eased himself out of bed and went into the kitchen for a drink of orange juice, straight out of the carton, so cold that it made his palate ache. It was only then, though, that it occurred to him that Danny had appeared to him without Nevile's assistance. No séance, no deep concentration, nothing. The figure had just materialized of its own accord.

He went back to bed and found Astrid waiting for him with her eyes open. 'What time is it?' she asked him.

'Five after five.'

'Couldn't you sleep?'

He slapped the pillows and settled back under the sheets. 'Bad dream, that's all.'

They lay in silence for a while and then Astrid propped herself up on one elbow and kissed him lightly on the lips. 'I might lie to you, Frank, but I'll never hurt you.'

'What does that mean?'

'Sometimes the truth is much too painful to bear. Sometimes lying is a kindness.'

'So wherever you went yesterday . . . you think it's better if I don't know?'

'Do you still love your Margot?'

'What does that have to do with the price of pork bellies?'

'I just want to know if you're lying to yourself. You can't give me a hard time for lying to you, if you lie to yourself, too.'

Eighteen

When Astrid left the hotel that morning, Frank followed her again. This time her taxi took her along Sunset Boulevard to Beverly Glen, and up into the winding lanes of Bel Air, among the fragrant flowers and the gilded security gates of Hollywood's wealthiest homes. The sky was streaked with mares' tails, as if a change in the weather was coming.

Astrid's taxi stopped outside the gates of a large white *Gone with the Wind*-style house. It was mostly hidden from the road, but Frank could see a lofty pillared portico and a green copper dome with a weather vane on top of it, pointing to the west. The steeply sloping gardens were laid out with flowering rose bushes and fountains made of grinning stone dolphins and bosomy mermaids. The taxi driver spoke into the intercom beside the gates and after a few seconds they swung open electronically and the taxi drove in. Frank cruised slowly past, and then turned his car around and cruised slowly back again. He parked about fifty yards down the road, and waited.

The taxi reappeared only two or three minutes later. Frank climbed out of his car and flagged it down. The taxi driver put down his window. He was pockmarked, with a droopy moustache, and a rosary wrapped around his fist like a knuckle duster.

'Want to do me a favor?' asked Frank. He produced his Fox-TV business card and handed it over. 'Did you ever hear of *The Beverly Hillbillies*?'

'Are you kidding me?'

'Well, we're planning to remake it, with Steve Martin playing Jed and Pamela Anderson as Elly May. I'm looking for locations, see, and this particular house looks like it could just about fill the bill. You don't happen to know who owns it, do you?'

The taxi driver shook his head. 'I can't give you that information, man. That's privileged.'

'You're a taxi driver, for Christ's sake, not a gynaecologist. Look, how about a finder's fee?'

He opened his billfold and held up twenty dollars. It was snatched so fast that he didn't even see where it went.

'Charles Lasser,' said the taxi driver. He started off, but immediately jammed his brakes on. 'You know, Charles *Lasser*?' Then he sped away.

Frank stood outside the gates looking up at the house. So Astrid had gone to visit Charles Lasser, the owner of Star-TV. That really confused him. Why would a girl like her visit a man like him? Could they be lovers? Worse, could Astrid be a prostitute? That would certainly account for her reluctance to tell him anything about herself.

Yet, if she was a prostitute, why did she keep on coming back to *his* bed, every night? Maybe Charles Lasser was the man who was beating her, and she needed somebody to turn to, somebody who was sympathetic and gentle and wouldn't judge her.

Whether she was a prostitute or not, Frank didn't have to ask himself what Astrid might find attractive about an ugly, domineering bully like Charles Lasser. A private Boeing 767, for a start, and a 250-foot yacht, and houses in five different countries. Frank knew the wives and mistresses of too many

174

famous actors and too many heavyweight studio bosses, and he knew how much humiliation they were prepared to take to stay within the glittering circle. As Mo had once put it, 'They would rather eat shit, these ladies, than lose that lifestyle, and I know one who actually has, and dressed herself up in pink silk and pearls to do it.'

Frank drove to the cemetery to visit Danny's grave. He stood beside it for almost fifteen minutes, his hair flapping in the breeze.

'Danny?' he whispered. No answer, of course, only the distant drone of a plane circling around Burbank airport.

'I wish you'd talk to me, Danny. I just want to know that you're not too unhappy; and that you've found yourself some friends. I can't bear to think of you being lonely.'

He was about to leave when he became aware of a young man standing not far away, wearing dark glasses and a worn-out leather jacket. The young man had black spiky hair and he was standing with his arms folded as if he were waiting for somebody. As Frank walked past him, he said, 'You're one of them, aren't you?'

Frank stopped. 'You talking to me?'

'That's right. I said, you're one of them, aren't you? One of the liars.'

'Whatever you say,' Frank replied and carried on walking. He hadn't gone far, though, before he realized that the young man was following him. He stopped again, and the young man stopped, too. He carried on walking and the young man came after him. Eventually Frank turned around and said, 'Listen, I don't know what you're selling, but I'm not interested.'

The young man smiled. 'I'm not selling anything, Frank, not the way you do. I don't sell lies and impossible dreams. I don't sell hope when I know that there isn't any.'

'How do you know my name?'

'What does that matter? You're one of the liars, that's all that counts. You're one of the moneychangers, in the temple of truth, and just like Our Lord we're going to drive you out.'

'Listen,' said Frank, 'I don't know what the hell you're talking about, and frankly I don't want to know. I came here to visit my son's grave and I'd appreciate it if you'd show us some respect – me and him, both.'

'Respect? What respect do you ever show to anybody? You write about joyful families, but where are they, all of these joyful families? You write about love, when there's nothing but deceit. You make people believe in a happy world that doesn't exist, and what greater cruelty could there ever be than that? "Look, folks! Mom and Dad and Thanksgiving dinner! Look, folks! Good overcomes evil, and the bad people go to jail! Oh, we may have to struggle. We may have to shed a few tears. But it's always waiting for us, in the end! The answer to all of our prayers! The Golden City!"'

The young man took off his sunglasses. Both of his eyes were totally bloodshot, like a vampire. 'The trouble is, it's all a mirage, isn't it, Frank? It's all a story, made up in your head. *If Only Pigs Could Sing*, Frank. If only they fucking could.'

Frank took out his cellphone, ready to call the police, but the young man replaced his sunglasses, turned around, and walked briskly away through the cemetery until he had disappeared amongst the headstones.

That night, Astrid came around to see him just after eight o'clock, and they ordered take-out Chinese: prawn balls, shredded beef, chicken with ginger and vegetarian noodles.

'How was your day?' asked Frank, and promptly dropped a prawn ball under the couch.

'Good,' said Astrid.

'Well, that's good,' said Frank, chasing the prawn ball with a spoon.

'How about you?'

'Good.' He sat up straight. He knew that he was going to have to say it.

'Good?' she repeated.

'Well, yes and no. It depends. I found out something interesting.'

'Yes?'

'I found out where you went.'

Astrid stared at him. 'You did *what*?'

'I followed you, OK? You can't blame me. I care about you. I want to know who you are and what you do. I want to know who your friends are.'

She tossed down her chopsticks. 'You *followed* me? You had absolutely no right!'

'I'm sorry, I beg to disagree. You know everything there is to know about me. You know where I was born. You know all about my family. My job. My marriage. My favorite movies. I never hide anything. Why shouldn't I know something about you?'

'Because I don't want you to. Isn't that a good enough reason? Besides, when did I ever ask you anything about yourself? You volunteered it. Now you've ruined everything.'

She stood up, went across to the door and took down her coat. Frank got up, too.

'Yesterday you went to Star-TV and today I followed you to Charles Lasser's house. For Christ's sake, Astrid, you and I are having an affair. We're lovers! Don't you think I have a right to know if you're seeing another man?'

Astrid opened the door but Frank immediately slammed it shut. 'This is insane! I'm committed to you, Astrid! I've crossed the road, and I'm never going back!'

Her cheeks were flushed and it was obvious that she was trying hard to keep her temper under control. 'That still doesn't give you the right to pry into my private business.'

'Particularly your private business with Charles Lasser, Esquire?'

'What I do when I walk out of here is nothing to do with you, Frank. If you can't accept that, then I'll just have to walk out of here for good.'

'What's the matter? You don't trust me?'

'Of course I trust you. But you don't need to know anything more about me than you know already. It's just not necessary.'

Frank looked around the room, almost as if he were expecting to see a more reasonable Astrid still sitting on the

177

couch. Then he looked back at her, and stepped away from the door. 'Go ahead. If you want to leave, be my guest. I thought that you and I had a future together, but it looks like I was deluded.'

'Frank . . . I've told you so many times before. You can't own me. I'm not one of your characters. I'm very fond of you. I think I might even be in love with you. But you'll just have to take that on trust.'

'Are you having an affair with Charles Lasser?'

'I'm not going to answer that.'

'Is Charles Lasser the man who's been beating you?'

'*Frank!*'

He knew by the tone of her voice and the way she was looking at him that if she walked out now he would never see her again, and of course he would never know where to find her. He went back to the couch and sat down, leaving her standing by the door.

When sunlight filled his bedroom the following morning, he woke up to find that Astrid was sleeping face-down, so close beside him that she was breathing on his arm. He thought he had never felt this way about any woman before, and never would again. He stroked the fine golden-brown hairs at the back of her neck, and ran his fingertip down her spine. God, she was magic.

As he lifted the sheet, he saw that she had an angry scarlet circle on her left shoulder. Lifting it further, he saw two more circles, above her hips, and one on each of her buttocks. They all looked sore, and they were still weeping. Jesus. Cigarette burns.

His immediate reaction was to shake her awake and demand to know who had burned her. But then he thought about her standing at the door last night, prepared to walk out on him and never come back. It was obvious that her life was a whole lot more dark and complicated than he could even guess at, and he didn't want to lose her by blundering around like a lovesick Dusty from *Pigs*. How could he save her if she left him? He let the sheet fall softly back, turned over, and pretended that he was asleep.

He knew what he was going to do, however, and nobody in the world was going to stop him.

Later that morning, when Astrid had left, Frank called his old friend John Berenger at Star-TV.

'Sloop, it's Frank. How's it going?'

'Are you kidding me? It's the California Gold Rush all over again, as far as we're concerned. Our daytime ratings have gone into orbit. I don't know how long it's going to be before these Arabs blow Star-TV to kingdom come, but we're making a shitload of money while we're waiting to die.' He hesitated, and then he said, 'Sorry, Frank. Sorry. Me and my big mouth. How have *you* been? That was so sad about Danny. Tragic. *Tragic*. You got our flowers, yes? How's Margot?'

'Actually, Sloop, Margot and I have been taking a break from each other. Losing Danny . . . well, that was a hell of a jolt. We both decided that we needed some individual space.'

'I'm real sorry to hear that, Frank. Kim and me, you know . . . our hearts go out to you.'

'Thanks, Sloop. Listen, you probably know that *Pigs* has been put on ice.'

'I heard, yes. *Pigs* and every other show that's worth a damn.' Three years ago, John Berenger had been head of creative development at Fox, and his boisterous enthusiasm for *Pigs* had helped to make it a hit from the very first episode. He was big and loud and opinionated, although he wasn't anywhere near as big and loud and opinionated as his boss, Charles Lasser.

Frank said, 'Thing is, Sloop, I could use some work right now. I don't need the money, but I'm hopeless at golf and I can't sit here all day with my thumb up my ass.'

'Go write the Great American Novel. Everybody else is.'

'I wish I could, but comedy is all I know.'

'I'm sorry, Frank. I have all the writers I need right now. And there's no telling when those Dar Tariki Tariqat lunatics are going to bomb *us* off the air, too. I mean, Charlie Lasser may be talking tough, but it's only going to take a couple of hundred pounds of TNT and everybody at Star-TV is going to be heading for the hills, leaving a long trail of diarrhoea.'

'Well, I realize that. But I have this great idea for a new comedy series. It's controversial, it's funny, but Islamically speaking, it's politically correct, so it won't upset any would-be terrorists.'

'What's the concept?'

'I'd rather not discuss it over the phone, if that's OK. Maybe we can meet.'

'OK. What's today? How about tomorrow morning, around eleven thirty? If we carry on talking long enough, we may even be able to drag it on through lunch. How do you like salmon with *chermoula*?'

'Mmm-mmmh, I love it! What the hell is *chermoula*?'

Nineteen

Frank was just about to leave his room when the phone rang.

'Mr Bell? It's reception. There's a Mr Strange here to see you.'

He went downstairs and found Nevile waiting for him in the lobby, dressed in a loose black linen suit and very dark glasses. 'Frank! I'm glad I caught you. Something really important has come up.'

'Oh, yes? Concerning what?'

'Listen, this is a hard thing to ask you, but I think we should try to talk to Danny again.'

'I thought we were leaving the Danny thing alone. Don't you remember? Madness and death.'

'Yes, I know, but I received more automatic writing last night, and I'm sure that it's Richard Abbott trying to get through. The things he says . . . well, to my mind it's further evidence that this terror campaign could somehow be connected with child abuse.'

'Have you told the police?'

'Not yet, no. To be quite honest, I think that Lieutenant

Chessman is losing faith in me. His superiors want to find Arabs, and if I can't confirm that it's Arabs, they're not really interested. They don't want to believe that this could be a home-grown protest, like the Murrah Building, only a hundred times worse. But there's a crisis coming, Frank. They're going to set off a whole lot more bombs, and if there's any way that we can stop them, we have to try it.'

'Let's have a drink.'

They sat on the shady veranda of the New World Bar on Sunset, opposite a huge billboard with a grinning 30-foot cutout of George Clooney on it. Frank ordered a beer but Nevile stuck to mineral water.

Frank raised his glass to George Clooney. 'That's some piece of sign-painting,' he said. 'You can even see the hairs up his nose.'

Nevile reached into his inside pocket and handed Frank a print-out. 'I was trying to write a letter to my publishers yesterday afternoon but this is what came up. I just couldn't stop it, couldn't control it.'

DaY is cumin soon yore goin to Be sorre weer goin 2 give you baCk what you give out to Us. Alwiz hurtin us & mistretin us but now its yore turn. Dar Tariki TariQuat is goin to bring you tHe **dark** lik you alwiz made our livs so **dark**. You made us feel lik 0 so thTs what weer goin 2 do to you Make you feel like 0. WE WAS goin thru HELl an all you ever dID was say that lif was happe but lif was NEVER happe lif was hell.'

'You see?' said Nevile. 'I'm ninety-nine percent certain this is coming through from the spirit of Richard Abbott. He says that Dar Tariki Tariqat is going to bring us darkness and a life of hell. But the interesting thing is, he doesn't say a word about blasphemy. He says the reason that Dar Tariki Tariqat want to punish the entertainment industry is because it mocked them with images of happy families while *they* were being hurt and mistreated. "We was going through hell and all you ever did was say that life was happy." Richard Abbott doesn't sound to me like a Palestinian suicide bomber, or anybody with any connections with Al Qaeda, or Hezbollah.'

Frank reread the print-out and handed it back. 'OK, I agree, he doesn't. What *does* he sound like?'

'He sounds to me like a victim of long-term child abuse.'

'What?'

'He sounds bitter, and crushed, and utterly hopeless – all of his humanity beaten out of him. He was happy to die so long as he could get his revenge on the society that destroyed his life. And he wasn't just looking to punish the people who actually beat him and abused him, but *all* of us, especially Hollywood. Everybody who tries to pretend that the world is sunny and bright while so many children are living in darkness.'

'Danny – or whoever it is that's pretending to be Danny – said he was abused, too.'

'That's right. The trouble is, this isn't really enough evidence to take to the police. I don't want to send them off on the wrong track. All I have so far is the uncorroborated ravings of Richard Abbott and Danny's complaints that "Daddy hurt me." I need badly to talk to Danny again, or whoever it is that's pretending to be Danny.'

Frank hesitated for a moment and then he said, 'Danny paid me a visit, the night before last.'

'Really? Just like that? You weren't trying to make contact?'

'It was just after three in the morning. He touched my cheek and woke me up. He looked exactly like Danny, just like he looked before, except that he was wearing some pajamas that I didn't recognize. He told me that his daddy had beaten him and done things to him. Sexual things, I guess. He said that his daddy cried and said he was sorry but still kept on doing it.'

Nevile sipped his water. 'This spirit is trying very, very hard to elicit your sympathy, isn't he?'

'You say "he," but that's the strange part about it. I took hold of his hand and it felt like a woman's hand.'

'You actually *felt* it?'

Frank nodded. 'It was definitely a woman's hand, with rings on.'

Nevile took off his dark glasses and his expression was

182

very grave. 'He didn't ask you to do anything? For instance, he didn't ask you to find his daddy and punish him for what he'd done?'

'No. He wouldn't even tell me who he was. I asked him, but he said that he wasn't allowed to tell me.'

'Well . . . that's not as silly as it sounds. Even when people die, they often go on doing what they were told to do, when they were still alive. Most of the time they don't realize that they're beyond being punished.'

Frank finished his beer. 'I'll tell you something, Nevile. The more I hear what it's like to be dead, the less I feel like dying.'

They drove to the Travel Town railroad museum in Griffith Park. This had always been one of Danny's favorite places, because he could climb on the old locomotives and pretend that he was an engineer, whooping to make the whistle noises. Frank had liked it, too, because he could sit in one of the passenger cars and work on his scripts, while ostensibly spending quality time with his son. This afternoon there were only four or five other visitors, only half visible in the dusty sunlight, but somehow the air seemed to be crowded with memories.

Nevile looked around and said, 'This is good. I can feel some very strong spiritual resonance here.'

Frank said, 'I don't get it. Why did we have to come here? I know Danny loved this place, but this spirit isn't really Danny, is he? Or *she*?'

Nevile smiled. 'No, she isn't. But it's easier for *you* to picture him here, and she relies on your remembered images of him to make him appear.' They sat down on a bench. 'Take your time, Frank. Think about Danny, when you used to bring him here to play. Try to see him, as he was, standing on the footplate, waving to you.'

'Where are you headed, Danny?' Frank asked, under his breath.

'Salt Lake City, Chicago, and beyond. Whooo! Whooo!'

He heard a small boy laughing. He saw a child's legs, running between the railroad cars.

'I'll tell you something, Frank – this place is teeming with memories. I can feel them. I can hear them. All the people who rode on those trains, all the people who came to meet them when they arrived. And *boys*, Frank. All of the boys like Danny who climb up on to those locomotives and dream about being a grown-up.'

Which is something that Danny will never be, Frank thought.

They must have sat on that bench for nearly twenty minutes. The sun moved around so that it was shining through the windows of the nearest passenger car and Frank had to cup his hand over his eyes. He glanced at Nevile, but he was still sitting up straight, his hands clasped together, staring at nothing in particular.

'Anything?' Frank asked him.

'Oh, he's here, all right,' said Nevile matter-of-factly. 'He's here, but he's hiding.'

'Isn't he going to talk to us?'

'Give him time.'

They waited another five minutes, and then Nevile said, 'All right,' and stood up.

'What is it?' Frank asked him.

'He wants to talk to us. He's in that old locomotive over there, beside the tree.'

Frank felt his heart beat quicken. Nevile began to walk across the tracks and Frank followed him. Halfway toward the locomotive he stumbled on the ballast and nearly fell, and he felt almost as if somebody had deliberately tripped him up. Ever since he had met Nevile, he had become increasingly aware that the world around him was jostling with spirits, some of them mean, some of them kindly, but most of them bewildered and lost.

They reached the locomotive and stopped beside the footplate. A plaque said that it was a Central Pacific 4-4-0, dating from the 1860s. It had a huge bell-shaped smokestack and the steps up to its footplate were shiny and worn with age.

'Are you going to go up?' asked Nevile.

'Do you think he's really there?'

'He said he was. I don't have any reason to doubt him.'

Frank took hold of the first rung, but then he hesitated. 'Crazy, isn't it? I think I'm scared.'

'Whatever's up there, Frank – whether it's Danny or not – it's only a spirit. It can't hurt you, you know that.'

'Yes,' said Frank, although he didn't feel much more confident. He climbed up on to the first step, and then the next, and then he was level with the footplate. He was still half dazzled by the sun, so he couldn't see Danny at first. But as his eyes became accustomed to the shadow he saw that Danny was standing in the far corner, his hair sticking up, his face pasty white. He was wearing a man's shirt with faded brown stripes, its sleeves so long that his hands were hidden. He was barefoot.

'Danny?' said Frank, a catch in his throat.

'Is he there?' asked Nevile.

Frank looked down at him and nodded.

'Go on up, Frank, I'll follow you.'

Cautiously, Frank swung himself into the cabin. Danny stared at him but didn't smile, almost as if he didn't know who Frank was. It could have been the fact that it was so shadowy, but it felt distinctly chilly up here.

'Danny?' Frank repeated, trying to sound reassuring. He was only a spirit, and he probably wasn't Danny at all, but he looked like Danny, and there was nothing Frank could do to stop himself from feeling protective toward him.

Nevile climbed up to join him. He looked at Danny intently, moving his head from side to side to examine him from several different angles. 'Fascinating,' he said. 'You'd think he was real, wouldn't you? Look at the shadows on his face. He's not there, but he has shadows on his face.'

'I won't be Danny anymore,' the boy whispered, scarcely moving his lips.

'What?' said Frank. 'Why not?'

'Danny's better now. He's still sleeping, but he's better.'

'You mean that I can talk to him? The real Danny? *My* Danny?'

The spirit nodded distractedly.

'So when will that be?'

185

The boy looked away, as if he were thinking about something else, and didn't answer.

'When?' Frank demanded, but Nevile laid a hand on his shoulder, as if to warn him to be patient.

'Danny,' said Nevile, 'or whoever you are, I need to ask you some questions.'

Danny shook his head. *'I can't answer questions. I'm not allowed to.'*

'I want you to tell me about Dar Tariki Tariqat. I need to know who they are.'

'Daddy hurt me. Every time he hurt me he said sorry but he always did it again. It was the same with all of the others.'

'There were others? How many?'

'I'm not allowed to say.'

Nevile went up very close to him, and leaned over him, so that he could talk very quietly into his ear. 'Did you belong to Dar Tariki Tariqat? You don't have to say it out loud. All you have to do is nod your head.'

Frank watched him and waited, but Danny didn't say anything, and he didn't nod his head, either.

'You're not Danny, are you?' Nevile asked him. 'You're not even a boy. Can you tell me who you really are?'

'No. I'm not allowed to. Daddy hurt me and he did all those things to me.'

Danny paused, and then he slowly swiveled his head toward Nevile, almost as if he were a life-size doll, and he stared at him with eyes that had absolutely no expression at all. *'Daddy said that it was our special secret, for ever and ever.'*

'Listen,' said Nevile, 'I need to know if you were members of Dar Tariki Tariqat. You and all the others.'

'They were hurt too, all of them.'

'Is that why they want to set off those bombs? Is that why they want to kill off all of those television shows?'

'It's a secret.'

'Shit, this is getting us no place,' Frank said, exasperated.

'No, wait a minute,' said Nevile, and then he turned back to Danny. When he spoke, his voice was very soothing, without any inflexion, as if he wasn't asking questions at all. 'The place where you meet the others, that's a good place, isn't it,

186

where all of you feel much better. You can talk to each other, you can tell each other all about the pain that you suffered when you were young. For the first time in your life, you feel as if somebody understands you and how much you hate the world for what it's done to you. The way the world mocked you, when you were desperate for help.'

Danny was staring at him, unblinking. *'Yes,'* he whispered.

'When you were young, you saw all those families on television, didn't you, but you knew that it was all lies, because nobody could be *that* happy, could they? On television, children had fathers who didn't hurt them and frighten them and force them to do horrible things that they didn't want to do. Children could sit at the dinner table without feeling scared all the time, in case they said the wrong thing, and got slapped, or beaten. But you knew that life wasn't like that, didn't you?'

Danny didn't reply, but lifted his right hand and covered his eyes, peering out through the cracks between his fingers.

'But *then*,' said Nevile, so quietly that Frank could hardly hear him. 'Then, when you joined Dar Tariki Tariqat, you weren't alone. You met people who understood exactly how much anger you had inside you – people like you who could never forget and never forgive. You didn't want therapy, did you? You didn't want to *adjust*. Who wants to adjust to a society that can treat children worse than animals?'

Danny covered his face with his left hand, too. *'Yes,'* he said in a muffled voice.

Frank said, 'Nevile – where are you getting this from? Is this true?'

Nevile stood up straight. 'I'm getting it, indirectly, from him. Or *her*, actually. You were right. Our friend here isn't a boy at all.'

'Do you know who she is?'

'She won't tell me, I'm afraid. But it doesn't really matter. She's saying more or less the same thing that Richard Abbott was trying to write on my computer. I don't think that Dar Tariki Tariqat is anything to do with Islamic fundamentalists. "The path through the darkness" isn't about religion at all. It's a group of men and women who were seriously abused

187

in childhood, trying to get their revenge. Whoever founded it may have given it an Arabic name simply to confuse us.'

Frank looked at Danny, who was still hiding his face behind his hands. 'So how are we going to locate these people? How are we going to stop them setting off any more bombs?'

'I'm not really sure. The police and the social services must have thousands of case files on serious child abuse. They can probably cross-check victim support groups, or victims who have formed informal associations with each other through the Internet.'

'*Emeralds,*' Danny whispered.

'Emeralds? What do you mean?'

'*Emeralds, and orange groves. Seven thousand and eleven orange groves.*' With that, he slowly lowered his hands. He wasn't smiling, but somehow he looked as if he were more at peace with himself.

'Danny,' said Frank. 'Danny – what does that mean? Emeralds and orange groves?'

But Danny began to grow fainter. His colors dimmed, and slowly he turned his head away. It was extraordinary to watch, like a fade-out in a movie. In less than fifteen seconds he had disappeared altogether.

'I don't think we'll be seeing him again,' Nevile remarked, when he was gone. 'Or *her*, rather.'

'What about Danny? I mean the *real* Danny?'

'Well, we shouldn't have any trouble in talking to him, once he's fully awake.'

'Will we be able to see him, too?'

'I'm not sure. I doubt it. You have to remember that visual appearances like this are very rare. This spirit only managed to appear because she was very strong and very highly motivated.'

They climbed down from the locomotive and walked back to Nevile's car. The sun was beginning to go down now, and their shadows were like stilt men, with wide flappy pants and tiny heads.

'Emeralds and orange groves,' Frank repeated. 'What do you think she meant by that?'

Nevile opened his car door. 'My guess is that she was trying

188

to answer our question, even though she wasn't allowed to. I told you before, didn't I, that spirits often talk in riddles and metaphors? We're just going to have to work out what she meant.'

Before he climbed into the passenger seat, Frank looked back at the locomotives and passenger cars of Travel Town. He would probably never come here again. The sun suddenly gleamed on the window of a Union Pacific club car, and as it did, Frank thought he saw somebody sitting inside it, a woman with a black mantilla covering her head. The car was too far away for him to be sure, but he thought he recognized her. He turned to Nevile and pointed and said, 'See that woman?' But by the time Nevile had realized where he was pointing, the woman had gone.

'I could have sworn I saw a woman. She was looking straight at me.'

'Trick of the light,' said Nevile. 'Anyway, I think we've seen enough ghosts for one day, don't you?'

Twenty

Astrid didn't call him that evening and didn't come around. He made himself a cheese omelet but he wasn't really hungry and ate only half of it before scraping the rest into the trash. He telephoned some of his friends, including Pete Brodsky, his producer, and Shanii Wallis, who had first introduced him to Margot, all those years ago, at a movie screening in Culver City.

'Shanii, have you heard from Margot?'

'Yes, I did. She called me yesterday afternoon.'

'How did she sound?'

'Very calm. Very together. Very determined, too.'

'Did she mention me?'

'Only a couple of times. She called you an emotional bankrupt. Oh, and a Neanderthal.'

'Hmm. Comforting to know she still cares.'

He watched television until well past midnight – a strange horror movie called *Dark Waters*. It had been filmed in the Ukraine, by the ocean, under a sky the color of bruised plums. Dilapidated buses rolled past, with people staring out of the windows, and they reminded Frank of the woman in the mantilla staring out of the window of the railroad car at Travel Town. The seashore was strewn with acres of dead, silvery fish. When Frank went to bed, he dreamed that he was wading knee deep through slippery mackerel, and that a long way off, a woman with a hoarse voice was repeatedly calling his name.

'Frank! *Frank*!'

The next morning he drove to Star-TV. Although it was almost midday, it was still humid and smoggy, and the air made his eyes water.

John Berenger had left Frank's name at reception, so he was given an identity tag and allowed to go up to the sixteenth floor. The two security guards frisked him thoroughly and continued to watch him beady-eyed as he waited by the elevator bank. The elevator was crowded at first, and Frank was pressed up against a pretty Chinese secretary. She smiled at him nervously, and he gave her a quick smile back, as if they were sharing a private joke.

When the elevator reached the sixteenth floor, the last two Star-TV employees got out, but Frank stayed where he was. He waited until there was nobody in sight and then he pressed the button marked PENTHOUSE. A young man came running along the corridor calling, 'Hey, wait up!' but Frank quickly jabbed the button again and the doors slid shut. He heard the young man call out, 'Thanks for nothing, asshole!'

The elevator rose to the top floor and when the doors opened again, the corridor was carpeted in deep blue and there was a scented, expensive hush. Frank hesitated for a moment and then he stepped out. There were side tables in the corridor, with vases of white lilies on them, and there were oil paintings on the walls. Ahead of him was a pair of white oak doors with gold handles, and a gold Star-TV logo.

190

He opened the doors and found himself in a wide reception area, with white leather seating and coffee tables arranged with magazines. A blonde receptionist in a tight red sweater was sitting behind a triangular glass desk, painting her nails the same color as her sweater. Behind her was another pair of doors, bearing another Star-TV logo, and the name Charles T. Lasser.

'Mr Lasser in?' Frank asked her.

'And *you* are?'

'Frank Bell. I don't have an appointment.'

'In that case, sir, I'm really very sorry. Mr Lasser can't see anybody without an appointment.'

'He can today.' Frank walked around her desk and took hold of the door handles. The receptionist immediately jumped up and tried to stop him, flapping her hands because her nails were still wet.

'Sir, you can't go in there! I'll have to call security!'

Frank said, 'OK, fine. Call security. I only need a minute of Mr Lasser's time.'

He was just about to open the doors when they were opened for him, from the inside. He found himself face to face with a bald black man in a tight gray double-breasted suit. 'What's going on here?' the man demanded. 'Who are you?'

Frank pushed the door open wider and he could see Charles Lasser standing at the far end of a very large office. Lasser was so huge that it looked as if there was something wrong with the perspective in the room. Three men in suits were talking to him, and even though they were standing much nearer to Frank, they appeared to be very much smaller.

The black man pushed Frank firmly back. 'Excuse me, sir, you can't come in here.'

'I have to talk to Mr Lasser.'

'He doesn't have an appointment,' said the receptionist. 'I tried to stop him, but he walked right past me.'

'Call security,' the man told her.

'You don't need to,' said Frank. 'I need one word with Mr Lasser, that's all. Mr Lasser! I need to have a quick word!'

The man took hold of Frank's security badge. 'This says you have an appointment with Mr John Berenger on the sixteenth floor. You've made a mistake here, sir. This is the penthouse.'

'Mr Lasser!' Frank shouted. 'I need to talk to you about Astrid!'

Charles Lasser stopped talking to three men in his office, and peered toward the doors. 'Stanley!' he called, his voice was a thick, volcanic rumble. 'What the fuck is going on?'

'This gentleman's lost, Mr Lasser, sir, that's all.'

'Get rid of him, will you?'

'Yes, sir, Mr Lasser, sir!'

But then Frank wrestled his way past him, and said, 'You beat her, didn't you? You stubbed your cigarettes out on her back! What else did you do to her, you goddamned sadist?'

The black man twisted Frank's arms behind his back and manhandled him back through the doors, but Charles Lasser shouted, '*Wait!*' He came striding across the office and stood over Frank, looking down at him in disbelief.

Charles Lasser had a forehead like an overhanging rock formation, under which his eyes glittered as if they were hiding in caves. His nose was enormous and complicated, with a bony bridge and wide, fleshy nostrils, and his chin was deeply cleft. His thinning hair was dyed intensely black, and combed straight back over his ears.

He was wearing a billowing white shirt with bright green suspenders and a garish green necktie with purple patterns on it. He smelled very strongly of lavender.

'Who the fuck are *you*?' he demanded.

'Frank Bell. You know that comedy show *If Pigs Could Sing*? That's mine. Creator, writer, associate producer.'

'What are you doing here? What's all this crap about cigarette burns?'

'You're asking *me*? I should be asking you, for Christ's sake. Five cigarette burns, all over her back, not to mention multiple bruises and contusions and black eyes! Gives you a thrill, does it, beating up on defenseless girls?'

'I don't know what you're talking about. Stanley, throw him out of here!'

'I'm talking about Astrid, Mr Lasser. Don't tell me your memory's *that* short.'

'I don't know any Astrid, my friend, and if I were you I wouldn't say one single word more about beatings or bruises or cigarette burns, because if you do I will sue you into total poverty.'

Stanley tried to frogmarch Frank away, but Frank jabbed his elbow into his stomach and pushed him back against the door jamb. 'You don't know any Astrid?' he challenged. 'Who are you trying to kid? Brunette, short hair, twenty-four years old, came to see you at your house yesterday morning? Ring any bells?'

Charles Lasser stared at him with those tiny, deeply hidden eyes. He breathed steadily through his mouth but for nearly ten seconds he didn't say anything at all. It seemed to Frank as if he were trying to work something out in his head, something that didn't fit his known perception of the world around him.

'*If Pigs Could Sing*?' he said at last. 'That's Fox, isn't it?'

Frank said, 'I'm warning you, leave her alone. I can't tell her what to do. I can't tell her not to see you again. But if you hurt her once more, just once, then I swear to God I will personally beat the shit out of you, and I will make sure that the cops and the media know why I did it.'

Charles Lasser pointed a finger at him – a big, thick finger with a squared-off nail. 'You listen to me, little man. I don't know who you've been talking to, or where you got all of your lunatic ideas from, but you're treading on very dangerous ground here. My advice to you is to leave this building right now. If you ever repeat this slander to anybody, ever again, I'll have you hunted down like the vermin you are, and exterminated.'

'OK,' said Frank. 'I'm going. But you be warned, Mr Lasser. One more bruise, one more bite, one more cigarette burn, and I'll be coming after you.'

Charles Lasser had already turned his back. The three men in his office took two or three nervous steps away from him, like gazelles when a lion unexpectedly changes direction.

'Now what about this fucking offer?' he growled. 'Where do we stand on the anti-trust laws?'

*   *   *

193

Frank tried to phone John Berenger from his car to tell him that he couldn't make their appointment, but his personal assistant told him, 'Mr Berenger is in a meeting with Mr Lasser right now.' Jesus, *already*? He hoped that Sloop wasn't about to lose his job. Charles Lasser had been known to fire people simply because they smiled at him in a way that he found disrespectful. 'Did I say something funny? Here's something really hilarious: you're sacked.'

He called Lizzie and at her suggestion they met for lunch at Injera, an Ethiopian restaurant on La Brea. Frank's car was parked by the tallest, spindliest black man he had ever encountered, and it seemed that all of the waiters in the restaurant were equally tall and spindly, with knowing smiles that seemed to suggest that they knew something Frank didn't. The walls were covered in red and brown batik and there were copper lamps and carved birds hanging from the ceiling. Lizzie was sitting in a dark corner hidden by a frondy plant. She was wearing a lime-green suit with extravagantly flared pants and a necklace that looked like a string of cherry tomatoes.

'I don't think I ever ate Ethiopian before,' said Frank, settling into his carved wooden chair and picking up the menu.

'It's an acquired taste,' Lizzie told him. 'I have to confess that I haven't acquired it yet, but they let me smoke.'

A waiter came up and Frank ordered a Harar beer. It was sweeter and stronger than domestic beer, but it was served with a dish of hot chilies and pickles and spicy nuts so he barely tasted it. Lizzie stuck with her usual Polish vodka, straight up and straight out of the freezer compartment.

'You've had more than your fair share of romances, haven't you?' Frank remarked.

'Uh-oh. That sounds as if you're looking for advice.'

'Not really. More like clarification.'

'Go on.'

'I was wondering if you've ever had an affair with somebody you knew nothing about. I'm not talking about a one-night stand here, I'm talking about an ongoing relationship that looks as if it could get serious.'

Lizzie took out a Marlboro and lit it. 'I once had an affair with a man who told me that he did all of Marilyn Monroe's lighting. Biff, his name was, can you believe it? Biff Brennan. "Miss Monroe, she doesn't trust anybody else with her lights but me." It turned out that he cleaned her windows.'

Frank shook his head. 'I'm not kidding, Lizzie. After Danny died I met this girl and we started this incredibly intense affair. Intense physically, that is. And mentally, too, as far as she allows it to go. Her first name's Astrid, but she won't tell me her second name, or where she lives, or what she does for a living, or anything about her family. In the beginning it didn't bother me, because I thought that she was just a way of taking my mind off Danny and escaping from Margot and all of those death stares that Margot kept giving me.'

'But now you're really beginning to care about this girl, and so it *does* bother you?'

Frank ran his hand through his hair. 'Badly. More than I ever thought possible.'

The waiter returned. Lizzie ordered *yemisir wat*. 'Red lentil stew. It tastes disgusting but I can't resist the name.' Frank went for *alitcha fit-fit*, a kind of pungent lamb casserole, and *injera* bread to mop it up with.

'Maybe she's married, this girl,' Lizzie suggested, breathing smoke out of her nostrils.

'I'm pretty sure she isn't.' He told her all about Astrid's bruises, and her cigarette burns, and about his visit to Charles Lasser's office. Lizzie crowed with delight when he told her that he had called Charles Lasser a sadist.

'Why didn't you ask me to come along? You're such a killjoy! I have at least a thousand names I'd like to call Charles Lasser. Fundament Features, for a start.'

'I just want him to stop beating up on her. Well, to tell you the truth, I want him to stop seeing her altogether.'

Lizzie coughed and crushed out her cigarette. 'I'm sorry, Frank, but it sounds to me like you're on a hiding to nothing. You're a nice guy, an incredibly nice guy, but from what you've told me, this girl gets off on power and money and men who treat her bad. I used to be like that, when I was younger. My first husband used to smack me around but I always came crawling back. It was lack of confidence, partly, but it was also this ridiculous belief that if a guy hurts you, that means he still cares about you. It had a lot to do with sex, too. Having my hair pulled, that used to give me orgasms. Nowadays, if a guy pulls my hair, the only thing that comes off is my wig.'

'So what do you think I ought to do?'

Lizzie reached across the table with her claw-like hand, encrusted with rings. 'Talking from experience, Frank, I'd enjoy it while it lasts.'

Their food arrived, aromatic and very hot, and because Injera gave their customers no forks, they tore off large pieces of bread to eat it with.

'What do you think?' asked Lizzie with her mouth full. 'Indescribable, isn't it? I can't decide if I love it or hate it.'

They talked about *Pigs* for a while. Frank didn't feel that it was worth their while to write any more, not while the show was suspended, but Lizzie said, 'It's a living thing . . . Dusty and Henry are living, breathing people.' She said they ought to develop a romantic relationship between Dusty and Libby, and that Henry should start taking slide guitar lessons from an old blues picker called Muddy Puddle, who was born the month after Muddy Waters when it wasn't raining so hard.

'I had a friend who received spirit messages from Louis Armstrong,' said Lizzie. 'He used to give her recipes for chicken gumbo.'

'Do you believe in any of that?' asked Frank, cautiously. 'Talking to the spirits, that kind of thing?'

'Certainly I do. My mother died when I was only six, and my father remarried. I didn't like my stepmother at all, even though – when I look back at it – she tried very hard to be kind to me. So every night before I went to sleep I used to have long conversations with my dead mother, telling her what I was doing at school, and how much I wanted her to come back.'

One of the smiling waiters came up to their table and said, 'You finish, sir?'

Frank looked down at his *alitcha fit-fit*. He felt that he had eaten quite a lot of it, but it looked as if there were twice as much in his bowl as when he had started. 'Yes, I have, thanks. Very good. Very filling.' The waiter cleared the table, still smiling. Frank was sorely tempted to ask him what was so goddamned funny.

Lizzie lit another cigarette. 'One day I went to school and I started my period in the middle of a math lesson. My skirt was stained and you can imagine how embarrassed I was. That night I lay in bed and cried and told my mother all about it. I turned over and went to sleep for a while but then I felt somebody touching my shoulder. I opened my eyes and there was my mother, standing over me. I could smell her perfume. I could feel her warmth. She seemed as real to me then . . . well, as you do now.

'She said, "Don't cry, Lizzie. You're a woman now, like me." And then she said, "Look under my dressing table . . . nobody knows that it's there." Then she simply vanished. At first I was sure that I had been dreaming. But the next morning I went into my stepmother's dressing room and looked under the dressing table, and there it was.'

She reached down inside her frilly blouse and produced a pendant. It was a silver mermaid, set with turquoises. 'It was hers,' said Lizzie. 'It had been missing ever since she died, and my father had looked everywhere for it. Only my mother could have known where it was, so to me that was proof that she really *had* come to see me that night, and that I hadn't been dreaming, after all.'

'Have you ever seen her again?'

'Once, at my father's funeral. I might have been mistaken, because she was standing in the shadow of some trees, but I had a very strong feeling that it was her. I've heard her voice, though, several times, especially when I've been stressed or unhappy, which usually happens whenever I get married.' She paused, puffed smoke. 'In other words, every couple of years.'

Frank gave Lizzie a ride back to her cottage off Clearwater Canyon. As he opened the car door for her, she said, 'Remember what I said, Frank. Live for the moment. Enjoy it while you can. Look at me, whenever I met a man I thought, this is the one, this is for ever. But there's no such thing as

197

forever, Frank, and tomorrow never brings what you expect it to bring, so it's not worth making plans.'

'Remind me to call you next time I'm feeling *really* depressed.'

Lizzie gave him a kiss on the cheek, and then another. 'You'll be OK,' she told him. 'I'll do the cards for you tonight, just to make sure.'

'If it's bad news, I don't want to know.'

He climbed back into his car and waved goodbye to her. It was then that his cellphone rang, and it was John Berenger, and he was so angry that he could scarcely speak.

'Do you know how close I came to being canned? I have a family to support, Frank, in case you'd forgotten! I just want to tell you this: don't ever call me again, *ever*, even if you have the greatest idea since *The Simpsons*.'

'John, I'm sorry. I needed to talk to Lasser and I couldn't think of any other way.'

'Why didn't you just send him a poison-pen letter, for Christ's sake, like everybody else?'

Twenty-One

Frank had just taken a shower when he heard a knock at the door. He wrapped a towel around himself and went to open it. It was Astrid, wearing a bright-pink sleeveless dress and bright-pink lipstick to match, and her hair was all frisky with gel.

'Aren't you pleased to see me?' she said. She took off her wraparound sunglasses. Her bruises had faded to yellow and lilac, and her eyes were far less swollen, although she still had a slightly foxy look about her.

'Of course. Come on in.'

She came into the living room and sat down in the last triangle of sunlight. He stood watching her and said nothing at all. 'Well?' she asked him. 'What's happened? Cat got your tongue?'

'No, everything's fine. How about a drink?'

She frowned at him. 'Something's wrong, isn't it? You don't like my hair like this.'

'Your hair's fine.'

'What, then? You don't like my lipstick?'

'Your lipstick's fine, too.'

'Then *what*?'

Frank took a breath. 'I talked to Charles Lasser. I told him to stop beating up on you.'

Astrid slowly covered her mouth with her hand. She didn't speak but her eyes said, *oh, my God.*

Frank said, 'I know you told me to keep out of your life. I know you told me to mind my own business. But so long as you and I are lovers . . . come on, Astrid, you *are* my business. I care for you. I love you. I can't just stand by and let that bastard hit you and burn you and treat you like shit.' There was a very long silence. Eventually, Frank said, 'I *can't*, Astrid, and that's all there is to it. Even if you tell me that you and I are finished.'

'You really told Charles Lasser to stop hitting me?'

Frank nodded.

Astrid stood up, and came over to him, and draped her arms around his shoulders. 'I can't believe it. What did he say?'

'What do you think he said? He told me that he didn't have any idea what I was talking about.'

'He denied it?'

'Are you kidding? He denied that you even existed.'

'So what did you say?'

'I warned him to stay away from you, that's all.'

Astrid scanned his face with those washed-out eyes as if she were trying to commit every detail to memory, as if she might never see him again. 'Do you think you scared him?'

'What? I very much doubt it. But I warned him that if he touches you again, I'll come after him. And, by God, Astrid, I will.'

'So what did he say to that?'

'He said that if I ever mentioned his name again he'd sue my ass off.'

Astrid tugged at the towel around his waist. It loosened and dropped to the floor. She took hold of his penis and rubbed it up and down. 'So long as he doesn't sue your cock off, I don't mind.'

Later, he opened his eyes and found her staring at him, very closely.

'What?' he asked her.

She stroked his eyebrows, and then licked her fingertip and stuck them up into devilish points. 'I think you're *incredibly* brave.'

'I'm not brave. I never have been. But I don't believe in giving in to men like Charles Lasser.'

She started to tweak his hair into points, too. 'I'm making you into a demon.' He caught hold of her hand to stop her, but he scratched his wrist on her ring.

'Hey, that's sharp.'

She spread her fingers so that he could admire it. It sparkled intensely green in the lamplight. 'Emerald,' she said. 'My father gave it to me for my sixteenth birthday.'

'It's real? I wondered about that when I first saw it. He must be pretty generous, your dad.'

'Not really. He never gave a bent cent to anybody without wanting something in return.'

'So what did you give him, in return for that?'

Astrid gave a non-committal shrug. 'Emerald's my birthstone. It's a saint's stone, too.'

'A saint's stone? What does that mean?'

'Twelve saints have their own special jewels, didn't you know that? St Nevile's is sapphire, St Peter's is jasper. Emerald, that's St John the Evangelist. All twelve jewels together were called the Stones of Fire and they used to belong to Lucifer. But Lucifer misbehaved and so God took them away and buried them in the walls of Jerusalem. If you have a whole set of twelve, they say that you can call on the angels to help you.'

'I could use an angel right now.'

She kissed his nose. 'Has it occurred to you, Mr Bell, that you have one already?'

He didn't answer her, but looked her in the eyes. She was so close that he could hardly focus.

After more than a minute, she said, 'What?'

'I know I don't own you. I know that what you do when you walk out of here is entirely your own business, and that it shouldn't concern me. But you and Charles Lasser? I can't get my head round it.'

'I thought Charles Lasser denied that I existed.'

'Somebody hurt you. If it wasn't him, then who was it?'

Astrid said nothing. After a while, she turned over and closed her eyes, and pretended that she was sleeping. Frank watched her, and couldn't help thinking about Charles Lasser, bulky and coarse, with his Neanderthal forehead and his deep-sunken eyes. For the first time in his life, he actually felt like killing somebody. It was a frightening feeling – frightening but surprisingly exciting. He dreamed that he was driving after Charles Lasser in a subterranean parking structure, determined to run him down.

The next morning, on the seven o'clock news, Commissioner Campbell announced that Dar Tariki Tariqat had contacted the police department to express their 'anger, dissatisfaction and sore disappointment.' They were 'outraged' that the major networks were still showing 'profane' television series, in spite of the fact that *The Wild and the Willing* had been replaced by reruns of *Highway to Heaven*, and that most of the daytime soaps had given way to cartoons and wildlife programs. In the media, a certain gallows humor was beginning to emerge. *Los Angeles Times* reporter Walter Makepeace remarked that 'the only distinction between watching early episodes of *The Waltons* and being blown up by 250 lbs of TNT is that watching early episodes of *The Waltons* is a far more prolonged and agonizing way to go.'

Dar Tariki Tariqat said 'it is obvious to us that the entertainment industries have no intention of changing their evil ways or atoning for their blasphemies. Therefore we will start our campaign of bombing as promised on the stroke of twelve noon today. This will be the first of eleven bombs to be detonated once every twenty-four hours, or until we are satisfied

201

that the entertainment industry has seen the wrongfulness of the path which it seems so wickedly determined to follow.'

'Did you hear that?' Frank asked Astrid. 'I don't know where you're going today – OK, OK, and I'm not going to ask. But like they used to say on *Hill Street Blues*, let's be *careful* out there.'

'I'm not going to Star-TV, if that's what you're worried about. Or Charles Lasser's house.'

'Just as well. My feeling is that Star-TV is next on the list.'

He poured out two mugs of coffee and they sat at the kitchen counter together, drinking it, their eyes fixed on each other. Frank wondered what she was thinking, but her expression gave nothing away.

'It is essential that you report any suspicious behavior by any individuals,' said Commissioner Campbell. 'Also, please dial nine-one-one if you're concerned about any vehicles that may be parked in unusual locations, or any vehicles being driven in a manner that for any reason at all attracts your attention. Your calls will be treated with the utmost seriousness, so please, no hoaxers. In the coming hours, many hundreds of lives could depend on your vigilance.'

'It's frightening, isn't it?' said Astrid.

'Yes. But you still won't tell me where you're going today?'

She reached out and touched his hand. 'Don't worry. I'll be safe.'

'Nobody's safe.'

'You don't think so? I'm invulnerable, Frank. Nobody can hurt me.'

At ten twenty A.M., feeling bored, Frank decided to drive over to Fox. Lizzie had given him fresh enthusiasm for *Pigs* when she described Dusty and Henry as 'living, breathing people.' He had roughed out three or four new story lines and he wanted to find out what Mo and Lizzie thought about them. He had decided that the show needed more pathos, more tears. Maybe Dusty's grandma could be told by her doctor that she was suffering from a life-threatening illness. If anything was guaranteed to bring a lump to the audience's throat, it was a young boy's gradual realization that no matter

202

how much he loved her, his grandma wasn't going to live forever.

When he tried to open the office door, he found that he could only push it six inches before it stuck.

'Daphne?' he said, putting his head around it. Daphne was on her hands and knees, surrounded by mountains of files and dog-eared scripts and photographs. 'I'm sorry, Mr Bell! I didn't know you were coming into the office today.'

'I was pining for you, Daphne. I couldn't stay away a minute longer.'

She shifted a stack of folders away from the door. 'I'm sorry about all this mess. Mr Cohen said that since I didn't have anything else to do, I should sort out the filing cabinet.'

Frank squeezed his way in. As he stepped over the heaps of papers, he caught sight of a glossy black and white publicity photograph of the three of them – him and Mo and Lizzie – taken when *Pigs* first went on air. He stooped down to pick it up.

At the same time, Mo came out of the next room, a cigar in his mouth, patting the pockets of his vest in the time-honored gesture of a man looking for a light.

'Look at us,' said Frank. 'I never realized that we used to be so young.'

Mo frowned at the photograph and said, 'I never realized that I used to be so *handsome*.'

'That's me. You're the ugly one standing on the right.'

Mo picked a book of matches from Daphne's desk and lit his cigar. 'So that's it? You came all the way into the office today just to make me feel grotesque? You could have made me feel equally bad by email. Hey, Daphne, who wrote *Forty Years as a Lion-Tamer*?'

'I don't know, Mo. Who wrote *Forty Years as a Lion-Tamer*?'

'Claude Bottom.'

'Is Lizzie in, too?' Frank interrupted.

'Sure . . . we're both dedicated wage slaves; where else did you expect to find us? Actually, Lizzie's come up with a great scenario for Dusty and Henry's first gig. They start singing "Your Heating Chart" but the audience hate them so

203

much they hook the entire dance hall up to a tractor and tow it into the river, so that it floats off downstream.'

'You want some coffee, Mr Bell?' asked Daphne.

In their main office, Lizzie was sitting at her PC with a cigarette dangling out of her mouth, typing wildly. Today she was wearing a bright-green satin pants suit with a frilly scarlet blouse. 'Hi, Frank. How's things? How's the anonymous Astrid?'

'"Nameless here for evermore,"' said Mo, quoting Edgar Allan Poe.

'You told Mo about Astrid?' Frank asked Lizzie.

'Of course she told me,' said Mo. 'Lizzie and me, we're like brother and sister, except that we can't be, because my parents had excellent taste and they would have drowned her at birth. I mean, look at her. Green suit, red blouse. Kermit the Frog cuts his carotid artery.'

Frank sat down at his desk. 'Not that it's any of your business, but Astrid still refuses to tell me what her second name is, and when she leaves me in the morning she still won't tell me where she's going or how she's going to be spending her time.'

'You should thank the Lord,' said Mo. 'Every morning Naomi gives me a detailed breakdown of every store she's going to hit, and just how much she's going to hammer my credit cards.'

Frank sorted through his mail, but there was nothing particularly interesting, only promotional leaflets and bills. 'Lizzie . . . Mo tells me you've sketched out something for Dusty and Henry's first concert. Want to run it by me?'

Mo relit his cigar. 'Great idea. But when it comes to the singing bits, sweetheart, don't actually sing. Remember the last time you tried? The super thought we were gelding a warthog and called for the ASPCA.'

'Shut up, Mo.' Lizzie scrolled back on her PC screen, one eye closed against the smoke from her dangling cigarette. 'By the way, Frank, I did your cards last night, like I promised.'

'Oh, yes? When do I get my first Emmy?'

'Actually, your cards were very strange. I tried the Tarot, but they refused to tell me anything. The Tarot can behave like that – not often, but now and then. They're very huffy, as cards go. If they can't work out what your future's going to be, they come out all muddled and contradictory.'

Mo coughed and waved away a dense cloud of smoke. 'Did it occur to you that they might have come out muddled and contradictory because Frank has a muddled and contradictory life in store for him?'

'I know what *you* have in store for you, if you don't put a sock in it.'

'No,' said Frank, 'maybe Mo's right. Maybe I *am* muddled. Maybe it's time I made some clear decisions.'

'You're still grieving, Frank. Don't forget that. This isn't the right time to be making decisions. This is the time to be taking stock.'

'That's right,' said Mo. 'Go to Kansas and rustle some steers.'

Lizzie said, 'I used the Garga cards in the end. They're much more philosophical, not so grand guignol.'

'The Garga cards, what are they?'

'A deck of sixty-three cards devised by Garga, who was the father of Indian astrology. Each card is based on a different aspect of your star sign, so they can tell your fortune like a horoscope.'

'I never heard of them.'

'Well, they're quite rare. But you must have heard of the Eighteen Fates. The Garga deck has eighteen destiny cards; nine that tell you the *best* that you can expect, and nine that tell you the *worst*.'

'All right then, how did I make out? I know, I get a huge demand for unpaid tax and I win a date with Madonna.'

Mo shook his head. 'Nobody deserves a date with Madonna.'

'Actually,' said Lizzie, 'I brought your destiny cards into the office. I thought you might be interested to see them.' She bent down and rummaged in her large red woven bag. Eventually she produced two oversized playing cards and laid them face-down on her desk. On the reverse side they were decorated with purple lotus flowers entwined with serpents and stars.

'I didn't bring the whole deck, but the minor cards said

that you would be happy in your life and prosperous in your work, although you would have to go through many months of argument with somebody close to you – somebody you once loved but love no longer.'

'That sounds like Margot.'

'Well, it could be. But it could also mean the end of a business relationship.'

Mo clapped his hand to his head. 'You're going to fire me – I knew it! Well, don't think for a moment that I won't expect custody of your John Denver albums! Or weekend visitation rights, at least.'

'What about the destiny cards?' asked Frank.

Lizzie turned over the first one. 'This is the best that can happen to you.' It showed a walled garden, with rose bushes and a sundial. A smiling man was sitting on a bench, with a smiling woman sitting close to him. At their feet a child was kneeling, playing diabolo with two sticks and a top. The man was wearing an extraordinary hat with spiral horns, which made him look like a demon. His suit was embroidered with wide-open eyes. The woman was very calm and beautiful, draped in a sari that bared her right breast.

'So what does this mean?'

'This is the card of family reunion and forgiveness. Quite soon you are going to have all of your loved ones around you, and your life will be sheltered and sunny.'

'Your dress sense will border on the hysterical,' added Mo, 'but you will be well supplied with Oriental poontang.'

Lizzie turned over the second card. This showed two warriors struggling with each other, so closely entwined that it was difficult to tell whose arms belonged to whom. One was handsome and stern, with a winged helmet. The other was scowling, with demonic eyes and a helmet in the shape of a giant beetle. The men were surrounded by tongues of flame, and the sky was filled with jagged flashes of lightning. It was only on closer inspection that Frank could see that both men were skewered by the same spear.

'This is the worst that can happen to you,' said Lizzie. 'You will defeat the man you hate the most, but at a terrible cost to yourself.'

206

'Either that,' put in Mo, 'or you will have a nasty accident at a gay pride cook-out.'

'Mo,' said Lizzie, 'this is serious. The Garga cards are always very accurate. The only reason I don't use them very often is because they take such a long time to lay out.'

'Well, they may be accurate, but neither of these destiny cards means very much,' Frank said. 'I'm separated from Margot, Danny's dead, and *Pigs* is postponed. So much for having all my loved ones around me and a prosperous life.'

He picked up the second card. 'As for this one . . . well, I don't hate anybody – except Mo when he writes a scene funnier than me.'

Friday, October 8, 11:52 A.M.

Once the three of them had settled down, and drunk three cups of coffee each, and laid waste to a carton of cinnamon doughnuts, they started to write in earnest. By eight minutes of twelve they had reconstructed Lizzie's concert scene to the point where even Mo had to admit that it was 'almost humorous.' Having said that, he collapsed into uncontrollable laughter, punching his desk and stamping on the floor.

'I'm dying here,' he protested, gasping for air. 'You know what you did, Lizzie? You killed me.'

The phone rang. Frank picked it up and Daphne said, 'Mr Bell? I had a call for you but the caller hung up.'

'Do you know who it was?'

'A woman. She said that somebody needed to see you, down in the parking lot. She said it was urgent.'

'She didn't give a name?'

'No, that's all she said. "Tell Mr Bell that somebody needs to see him, down in the parking lot, urgent."'

Frowning, Frank slowly put down the phone and went to the window. He looked down into the parking lot, but at first he couldn't see anybody at all, except for a Pizza Hut delivery boy climbing out of his car. But then, close to the steps that led up to the commissary building, he saw a small figure standing in the shadows.

'Danny,' he breathed. And this time it could be the real Danny, not just another spirit pretending to be Danny. He tossed his script on to Lizzie's desk, crossed the office and opened the door.

Lizzie said, 'What? You're *that* jealous?'

'Sorry – back in a minute . . . There's somebody I have to see.'

Lizzie and Mo exchanged bewildered looks as he hurried out of the office. He ran along the echoing corridor until he reached the stairs. As he clattered down the first flight, he almost collided with the Pizza Hut delivery boy who was coming up. The delivery boy had spiky hair and dark glasses and was carrying a big insulated bag.

'Bell, Cohen & Fries Partnership?' he asked, peering at a grease-transparent delivery note.

'Fifth door on the right.'

Frank vaulted down the rest of the stairs, through the lobby and out of the front door. He ran across the parking lot, dodging out of the way of a wardrobe assistant who was pushing a rack of swaying ball gowns. By the time he reached the commissary building, however, Danny had gone. He stood on the steps, panting, looking around him.

An electrician in an *X-Files* T-shirt came past with pliers and screwdrivers hanging from his belt. 'You didn't see a young boy around here?' Frank asked him. 'Eight years old, brown hair, blue windbreaker.'

The electrician narrowed his eyes as if he were thinking extra hard. 'No, sir. Can't say that I have.'

Frank quickly walked the length of the commissary building but there was no sign of Danny anywhere. Either he had vanished, or else he was hiding someplace. So why had he appeared? And who had called the office to say that Frank was wanted so urgently? A woman. But who?

He was still circling around the parking lot when he saw the brown metallic Honda belonging to the Pizza Hut delivery boy. The Pizza Hut delivery boy who had asked where Frank's office was. Even though none of them had ordered pizza.

Dread gripped his chest like a heart attack. He turned around and stared up in horror at his office window, where he could see Mo placidly standing with his arms folded, puffing at his cigar.

'Mo! Mo! Get out of there! Mo!'

Mo must have heard him, because he took his cigar out of his mouth and lifted it up in salute. Frank frantically waved his arms and screamed, 'Get out of there! Get out of there! The pizza guy! For Christ's sake, Mo! It's the pizza guy!'

He sprinted back to the office building. As he ran across the lobby, he shouted to the receptionist, 'Police! Call the police! And the paramedics! It's a bomb!'

'A what?' said the girl, staring at him in bewilderment.

'*Bomb!*' he shouted, his voice distorted as he ran up the stairs.

Friday, October 7, 12:01 P.M.

Lizzie lit another cigarette. 'I'm not so sure about Dusty's grandma dying of cancer. What do you think? I mean, she could still be dying, but maybe she could be dying of something more amusing.'

'Oh, you mean like kwashiorkor? That would be a scream.'

'I don't know. I still don't think that tragedy is the right road for us to go down. OK, writing about death may help Frank to get over Danny, but *Pigs* is all about small humiliations, like having the holes in your shoes stuffed with newspaper and only having plain bread and butter for your packed lunch because that's all your mom can afford.'

'Whereas dying of cancer – that's *really* embarrassing, right?'

'Let's talk to Frank about it.'

Mo was staring out of the window. 'Frank's down there in the parking lot.'

'What?'

'Take a look at him – he's waving his arms.'

Lizzie stood up and looked out of the window, too. 'You're right. Maybe this is a new kind of script meeting by semaphore.'

'I've got it,' said Mo. 'He's thinking of writing an episode for deaf people. Great idea. We could call it *If Pigs Could Sign*.'

'He's coming back inside. Do you think he's OK?'

Mo sighed. 'I don't know, Lizzie. I think Frank's much more upset than he's showing us. When you lose somebody you love, it screws up your head. But when your kids die before you do – well, it screws up your entire reason for being here on earth.'

Daphne knocked at the door. 'Did either of you order pizza?'

'Not me,' said Lizzie. 'Mo?'

'Pizza? Are you kidding? I've just eaten four and a half doughnuts.'

Daphne turned around to the delivery boy, and said, 'Sorry,' but he pushed his way into the office behind her. 'Hey, this is the Bell, Cohen & Fries Partnership, right? Large Neopolitan with extra chilies.'

'Extra chilies?' said Mo. 'My proctologist would kill me.'

The delivery boy laid his insulated bag on Frank's desk and opened it up. 'Actually,' he said, sounding oddly breathless, 'you guys are only getting what you deserve.'

'What are you talking about?' said Lizzie. 'And for God's sake, don't open that thing in here. I *hate* the smell of pizza. Pizza smells like sweat.'

The delivery boy ignored her. He eased a large square package out of his bag, about the size of a pizza box, but wrapped in plain gray paper. As he put it down, Mo saw that two wires ran out of his sleeve into the side of it. He stared at the delivery boy and said, in a thick, congested voice, 'What the hell is that?' Then, more slowly, 'Is that what I think it is?'

The delivery boy took off his sunglasses. He couldn't have been older than twenty-three or twenty-four. His eyes were dark brown, with long feminine lashes, and there was an angry red spot by the side of his mouth. Any mother's son.

'That's right. We're taking you off the air, old man. You and all of your lies.'

'What is it?' said Lizzie. 'Mo? What's going on? What's he talking about?'

'Daphne,' said Mo, 'go dial nine-one-one. Tell them it's a bomb.'

'Don't fucking move!' screamed the delivery boy, holding up his right hand and displaying a small black electrical switch. Daphne stayed where she was, her eyes wide, biting her finger.

'That's a *bomb*?' Lizzie asked, adjusting her glasses so that she could see it better. 'So what are you planning to do, young man? Blow us all up? Why? What for? We're comedy writers. What did we ever do to you?'

'You mocked us, that's what you did,' said the delivery boy. He was beginning to hyperventilate.

'*Mocked* you? Who mocked you? Nobody ever mocked you.'

'Oh, you don't think so? We were going through hell and what did we see on TV? Happy families – and people laughing!'

'Come on, son,' said Mo. 'Nobody was laughing at *you*.'

'You don't think so? I had to hide behind the couch so that my father wouldn't find me and all I could hear was people laughing!'

'They were laughing at *jokes*, that's all. What makes you think they were laughing at you? Hey – you were hiding behind the couch, they couldn't even see you.'

'You're mocking me now! You're still doing it! Look at him! Look at this ridiculous little kid! He's so frightened he's wet his pants, and when his dad finds out that he's wet his pants, is he going to catch it then? Oh boy, is he ever!'

'Son,' said Mo, trying to sound calm, 'I think you're making a mistake here. We never mocked you, never. Shit, we don't even know who you are.'

The delivery boy had tears in his eyes and he was shaking as if he were running a temperature. 'Did your father ever pull down the pants of your pajamas and hold a cigarette lighter between your legs? Did your father ever hit you on the head with a hot steam iron?'

'No,' said Mo. 'But if your father did that to you, that's nothing to laugh at, and believe me, Lizzie and me, we'd be the last people laughing.'

'But you *did*! I heard you! I was hiding behind the couch

211

and I heard you! But you're never going to do that again! No other kid is ever going to suffer what I suffered!'

Mo said, 'We can work this out, son. Nobody has to get hurt. Tell me what your name is. Come on, at least let us know who's come here to blow us all to kingdom come.'

The delivery boy lowered his arm. 'Alexander Sutter.'

'OK. Do you mind if I call you Alex?'

'Why? Are you going to pretend that you're my friend or something, like all of those welfare workers and all of those shrinks?'

'I don't want to make friends with you, Alex. I'm sixty-two years old and I like golf and Tony Bennett records. I just want to persuade you that it wouldn't be a very constructive thing to do, killing us. You see, we can understand why you're feeling so angry. The world's a pretty unfair place, when it comes to happiness. Some people, they're born happy. They have loving parents and lots of money and whatever they do seems to turn out right. Other people, their whole life is unadulterated crap from start to finish. Imagine being born in some village in Africa where there's nothing to eat and no clean water and you're lucky if you don't go blind.'

'That doesn't excuse you!' Alex shouted at him, almost screaming. Lizzie and Mo could tell that he was terrified, as well as angry. 'If I was born in Africa, I never would have known any better, would I? But I was humiliated and punished all my life and what did you do? You showed me what it was like to be happy. You rubbed my nose in it. Well, that's never going to happen, ever again, to any other kid, ever!'

'Look,' said Mo, 'why don't you put down that detonator and we can talk it over? There has to be a much more sensible way to make things better.' He held out his hand. 'Come on, Alex. You don't want to be an ex-Alex, even more than I want to be an ex-Mo.'

'Dar Tariki Tariqat!' Alex yelled at him.

Friday, October 8, 12:04 P.M.

Frank had almost reached the office door when the bomb went off. Three feet nearer and he would have been hit full

212

in the face by a blizzard of flying glass. As it was, the door was blown across the corridor and the force of the blast knocked him backward so that he hit a framed poster for *The Grapes of Wrath* and cracked it right across.

Black smoke rolled out of the open doorway, filled with hundreds of fragments of burning paper. The stench of exploded Semtex and burned nylon carpet was overwhelming, and Frank found himself on his hands and knees, his ears ringing, his eyes streaming, whooping for breath.

The fire bell started ringing and he heard people shouting and screaming. He climbed on to his feet, leaning against the wall to support himself, and all he could think of was *no, not Lizzie, not Mo, not Daphne*. They were as much a part of his family as his father and mother, or Carol and Smitty. Closer, in a way, because he had spent every working day with them for three and a half years, laughing, arguing, writing and re-writing. He had probably known more about Lizzie and Mo than he had ever known about Margot.

Frank made his way to the office door, covering his mouth with his hand. Daphne's room was relatively untouched, although it was full of smoke and her computer was lying on the floor. Her yucca plant, too, had been stripped of its leaves and stood totally naked.

Daphne herself was lying in the open doorway to the main office. She didn't look as if she had been badly hurt. Frank crunched across the broken glass that littered the carpet, and knelt down beside her. 'Daphne?' he said gently, and shook her shoulder. She didn't reply, so he pulled her carefully on to her back. It was then that he saw the triangular metal arm of a chair had embedded itself into her chest. She was staring at him intently, as if she were about to say something important.

He looked across the devastated office. Mo was lying in the opposite corner, one hand raised as if he were trying to catch Frank's attention, except that the left half of his head had been blown away, and his left arm was a bloody, blackened tangle of bone and muscle and shredded skin. Lizzie was still sitting in her chair, surprisingly intact, her arms spread wide, her hair sticking up on end, and her mouth open in astonishment.

Frank circled the room, coughing. At first he couldn't understand what had happened to the pizza delivery boy, but then he saw something that looked like a wet red raincoat hanging over the back of his chair. He didn't want to look any closer.

He left the office just as three firefighters came bustling along the corridor. 'Sir? Are you OK?'

'Bombed us,' he choked, with a mouthful of grit. 'The bastards bombed us.'

Twenty-Two

'**B**ut why *us*?' he asked Astrid later that evening. He had hardly touched the Thai noodles she had ordered, and they lay congealing in their bowls. Why was it that, after a bereavement or a disaster, people always said, 'I know how you're feeling . . . but you mustn't forget to eat?'

Frank had no appetite for food. He didn't even feel like getting drunk. He was freshly bruised, and half deaf, and all he wanted to do was hunt down the man who had ordered Mo and Lizzie's murders and beat him to death with a baseball bat.

Astrid was wearing a tight black leather jerkin and tight black leather pants and spiky-heeled boots. Her hair was gelled back and there were huge silver hoops dangling in her ears. She looked as if she had just walked off the set of a low-budget horror movie.

'They said they were going to bomb the entertainment industry, didn't they?' she reminded him. 'They said they were going to set off a bomb a day, every day for eleven days. You were just unlucky.' Her voice sounded huskier than ever.

'I know that. But that pizza delivery boy *specifically* asked for Bell, Cohen and Fries. He hadn't come there to bomb Twentieth Century Fox. He came to bomb *us*.'

'All right, he came there to bomb you. But think about it.

If it's true what your psychic detective friend was telling you ... I mean, if Dar Tariki Tariqat are all abused people, trying to get their revenge ... well, you can see why they went for a program like *Pigs*.'

'*Pigs* is a comedy, for Christ's sake!'

'Yes, but it's folksy and warm and it's *happy*.'

'It's not *always* happy. Most of the time, Dusty and Henry are pretty miserable. And their dad is practically a manic depressive.'

'I know. But things always work out in the end, don't they? Every episode finishes up with that cheesy scene of the Dunger family gathered around the pigsty, laughing and hugging each other and scuffing the kids' hair.'

'Astrid, that's supposed to be a parody. Like, you know, "goodnight, John Boy."'

'Oh, yes? Tell that to some lonely kid who was beaten with a belt buckle and sent to bed without any supper.'

'So what are you saying? That TV families should always be dysfunctional, with dads who sodomize their daughters, and moms who drink, and kids who take crack and set fire to tramps, just so the viewing audience won't think we're being smug? For Christ's sake, Astrid, we've never tried to pretend that the world is perfect. But people *like* to feel folksy and warm and happy, and why not? What harm does it do?'

'You tell me. Look what happened to Lizzie and Mo and Daphne, and all of those other people. Look what happened to Danny.'

Frank covered his face with his hands, as if his hands were doors and he wanted them to remain closed for ever, so that he could stay in the dark. He was still shocked, and he still found it impossible to believe that Lizzie and Mo had been killed. He felt like crying, but he didn't seem to have any tears. He kept picturing Mo, frowning at the end of his cigar, trying to make up his mind if it was worth relighting; and Lizzie, toying with her Ethiopian food and telling him to enjoy life while he was still above ground.

Astrid sat close to him and stroked his hair. He could smell her perfume and her warm leather pants. 'I'm sorry,' she said.

215

'I can't even begin to imagine how bad you must feel.'

'Tell me it's still morning,' he said, his voice muffled behind his hands. 'Tell me I've just woken up and I haven't gone to the office yet.'

Astrid kissed him. 'When I was little, and something really bad happened, I used to pretend that it was only a movie, and that I was only playing a part. Somehow that made it easier to bear.'

Frank took his hands away from his face and looked at her. 'Do you know something . . . that's the first time you've ever told me anything personal.'

'I'm always telling you personal things, Frank. It's just that you don't always hear me.'

'All right. So what was so bad that you used to pretend it was only a movie?'

She smiled at him, still stroking his hair. 'I lost my innocence.'

'You lost your innocence? Who took it?'

'The world is full of thieves, Frank, and they don't only take wallets. They take everything and anything that's worth having. Beauty, joy, innocence. They don't really want it for themselves, they just don't want anybody else to have it.'

'Tell me,' said Frank.

'No. You're not in any fit state. You need a sedative and you need some sleep.'

'Sleep? No thanks. I'll only have nightmares.'

At that moment there was a knock at the door. Astrid went to answer it, and it was Nevile. He was immaculately dressed in a black shirt and black pants, as if he had been playing Well-Groomed Vampire #2 in the same movie as Astrid, and he smelled of Burberry aftershave.

'Oh,' he said in his tensile British accent. 'Not interrupting anything, am I?'

'Of course not,' said Frank. 'Come on in. This is Astrid, by the way. Astrid, this is Nevile – Nevile Strange, the world-famous psychic detective.'

'Well, well,' said Astrid. 'I'm so pleased to meet you at last. Frank and I were just talking about you.'

'I wondered why my ears were burning,' said Nevile. He

216

held out his hand but Astrid smiled and turned away as if she preferred not to make any physical contact.

Frank said, 'We've been trying to work out why Dar Tariki Tariqat would want to blow up *Pigs*. Listen, how about a drink? There's a bottle of dry white wine in the fridge.'

'No, I'm fine, thanks. The police told me all about the bombing and I just called by to make sure that you were all right.'

'I'm covered in so many bruises I look like a patchwork quilt, and a trolley car keeps ringing in my ears. But they took me to Mount Sinai for a check-up and otherwise I'm all in one piece.'

Nevile came over and peered into his bloodshot eyes. 'You were damned lucky you weren't in the office with the others. I'm so sorry about your friends; it's absolutely tragic.'

Frank lifted both hands. 'I feel, mentally, like I've had my arms torn off. Can you understand that?' He suddenly found it difficult to speak. 'I mean, we wrote that series together every working day for three and a half years and it was like we were . . .'

'I know. I don't know what to say.'

Frank cleared his throat. 'I need to talk to you, as a matter of fact.'

'I'm rather pushed for time, I'm afraid. Perhaps we can make it tomorrow.'

'The cops told you that it was a pizza delivery boy?'

Nevile nodded.

'Well, a couple of minutes before that pizza delivery boy showed up, Daphne took a phone message for me. She said it was a woman. Somebody wanted to meet me in the parking lot, urgently. I looked out of the window and I swear to you, I could see Danny standing out there. He was in shadow, I could only see a silhouette, but I swear it was him. That's why I left the office in such a hurry, thank God.'

Nevile raised one eyebrow. 'Was Danny still there when you got outside?'

'No, he wasn't, and nobody else had seen him, either. I was still looking for him when it suddenly hit me that none of us had ordered pizza. I mean, the delivery boy had asked

217

me which was our office – Bell, Cohen and Fries – but none of us had ordered pizza. I could see Mo up at the window, and I tried to warn him. You know, I waved, and I shouted . . .' Frank became silent for a moment at the memory of it. 'I guess he thought I was joking. Mo was incapable of taking anything seriously. Even a bomb warning.'

Nevile looked thoughtful. 'Seeing Danny in the parking lot could have been some kind of premonition, I suppose. Sometimes we see things that warn us of coming events. Birds, animals, certain vehicles like ambulances or hearses. But in this case, I'm not so sure. What makes this really unusual is that your secretary received an actual phone call, saying that you were needed outside.'

'Meaning what?'

'Either a real woman was ringing you, to warn you, or else you were receiving a warning from a very powerful psychic source – so powerful that it could make your phone ring. It's been known before, spirit voices being heard over the telephone. A woman in Wales used to hear her mother talking, even though she had died of cancer more than five years before. Electrical circuits are highly sensitive to spirit messages, like the automatic writing I picked up on my computer.'

'Any way of telling whether this was a real message or a spirit message?'

'We should meet tomorrow, and try another séance. Meanwhile, I really have to go. Lieutenant Chessman called me and I'm on my way to Century City right now. They want to see if I can pick up any vibrations from the bomber's shoes – although they're pretty sure that they know his name already.'

'Really?'

'He was carrying a photograph of his mother. His foster-mother, anyhow. There was a street sign in the background and they were able to trace her from that.'

'You know what really gets to me?' said Frank. 'He's blown himself up, too, and that means that I'll never get the chance to kill him myself.'

Nevile took out a leather-bound notebook. 'His remains haven't been formally identified yet, but he was a house painter from Culver City called Alexander Sutter, twenty-four years old. His foster parents were Mr and Mrs John Happel, of MacManus Park. Apparently he was put into foster care when he was eleven years old, after persistent sexual and physical abuse from his natural father.'

'*Another* abuse victim? It looks like your theory could be right.'

'After this, yes, I'm pretty sure of it.'

'All the same, it's hard to think of abuse victims getting themselves together and planning something like this. The only ones I've ever met – they're usually so *withdrawn*, you know? So *downtrodden*.'

'I agree with you,' said Nevile. 'But it looks as if somebody managed to get them together and inspire them to take some action. These bombings have taken some very careful organization. Dar Tariki Tariqat use a different type of explosive each time, and a different method of delivery, so it's very difficult to trace them back. Somebody's doing their planning for them, that's my opinion. Somebody clever, and very well financed.'

'What do the cops think?'

'They still believe that there's some kind of Arab influence at work here – even if they *have* used child-abuse victims to do their dirty work for them.'

'What's your opinion?'

'Well, I was talking to an FBI psychologist this afternoon and she agrees that child-abuse victims probably wouldn't have focused their resentment into a terrorist campaign unless somebody had focused it for them. And who wants to see Hollywood destroyed more than Islamic extremists?'

'You think she's right?'

'I don't know. She certainly has a point. But I think it's too easy to blame the Arabs. I have a very strong feeling that there's another dimension to this. I wish I could work out what it is.'

Frank showed him to the door. 'I'll give you a call around nine tomorrow, how's that?'

'Fine,' said Nevile. He was about to leave but then he looked over Frank's shoulder at Astrid and asked, 'Who *is* that?'

'She's the girl I was telling you about, the girl I met after the bombing at The Cedars.'

'She's very pretty, isn't she?'

'Yes, she is. And I must say that she's really helped me to get over Danny.'

Nevile continued to stare at her. 'She wouldn't take my hand, did you notice that?'

'Is that significant?'

'Not necessarily.' He sniffed. 'I think I can smell something, too. But I'm always oversensitive. Look . . . I'll see you tomorrow, all right?'

On the nine P.M. news, Commissioner Campbell read out a statement that he had received during the afternoon from Dar Tariki Tariqat. He looked very gray, and tired, and his voice trembled as he spoke.

'After today's act of retribution against Twentieth Century Fox, Dar Tariki Tariqat hopes that the entertainment industry will now realize that we mean what we say, and that they will immediately withdraw all of those television programs and motion pictures which revel in blasphemy and salacious behavior. If this is not done, a second explosion will take place tomorrow at noon at another location, and further explosions will take place at noon every day until the television and movie industries have been cleansed of the moral corruption that has already taken this planet to the very brink of damnation.

'In particular, we are proud to have punished the creators of a television show that made an open mockery of all moral and religious values. And let us say this: there are those who may think that they have escaped what destiny has in store for them, but anybody who has accused God of being cruel will be hunted down like the vermin they are, and made to pay for their slanders with their lives.'

Frank listened, frowning, and then sat up. 'Astrid, did you hear that?'

'Hear what?' said Astrid. She was lying with her back to him, naked, and she was almost asleep.

'Dar Tariki Tariqat made a statement about the bombing.

220

They said that anybody who escaped is going to be hunted down and killed.'

'So?'

'Anybody who escaped? Think about it! That means *me*!'

Astrid blinked at him, trying to focus. 'Are you sure?'

'Who else escaped from that explosion apart from me?'

'Well, nobody.'

Frank was excited now. 'There was something else. They said that anybody who accused God of being cruel is going to be hunted down like vermin.'

'I don't understand.'

'Who did I accuse of being cruel? Not God, maybe, but somebody who behaves like he's God. And who said almost those exact words: "If you repeat this slander, I'm going to have you hunted down like the vermin you are, and exterminated?"'

'You're not serious. You mean Charles Lasser?'

'Exactly.'

'I don't get it. What does Charles Lasser have to do with any of this?'

'You tell me. Who could organize a terrorist campaign better than him? He has money, he has influence. He has international contacts.'

'But why would he want to damage the entertainment industry? He's *part* of the entertainment industry.'

'No, when you think about it, he's not. He's always been an outsider. I don't know *anybody* in Hollywood who likes to work for Star-TV – not unless they have to. Star-TV isn't a television company. It's more like a bulldozer for Charles Lasser's ego. If you knew the contracts he's dishonored, and the producers he's ruined, and the number of bright young independents he's bought up, for the sole purpose of closing them down . . .'

'But he's offering ten million dollars, isn't he, for anybody who can catch these bombers? Why would he do that, if all the time it's been *him*?'

'Maybe it's a blind. Maybe he's trying to look like the knight in shining armor, when all the time he's wrecking the competition,' Frank said, picking up his pants from the floor.

221

Astrid said, 'What are you going to do?'

'I'm going to call the cops, what else?'

'But you don't know for sure that it's Charles Lasser, do you?'

'No, I don't. But it's still worth them looking into it. Think about it, Astrid, if it *is* Charles Lasser, he killed Danny, too.'

Frank could see himself reflected in the window, like a ghost. The ghost picked up the phone from the coffee table and waited while its call was connected.

'Lieutenant Chessman? It's Frank Bell, remember me? Listen, I've just heard the latest statement from Dar Tariki Tariqat. I may be wrong, but I think it contains a kind of a clue.'

'Oh, yes?' Lieutenant Chessman had his mouth full. 'What kind of a clue?'

'Well, first of all I think it's a warning, personally directed at me. They said they were proud of killing the people who wrote *Pigs*, but they were coming after anybody who survived.'

'I see. I haven't heard that statement yet.'

'I also think they might have given away the identity of the person who's behind all of these bombings.'

'They did *what*?'

'It's not easy to explain, but I think it could be Charles Lasser.'

There was a very long pause. 'I hope and pray that I didn't hear you say what I thought I heard you say.'

'If I can meet you, Lieutenant, I can explain.'

'Listen, don't say anything more over the phone. Where are you at?'

'Sunset Marquis.'

'OK . . . give me twenty minutes and I'll call around and see you.'

When he came back into the bedroom, he found that Astrid was tugging on her black leather pants.

'What are you doing?' he asked her. 'You're not going? It's almost midnight.'

'I know. But if the police are coming around, I think it's better if you see them on your own.'

'I *will* see them on my own. You don't have to leave.'

She brushed out her hair, and pouted at herself in the mirror. 'No, I'll see you tomorrow night, maybe. I'll call for a taxi, if that's OK.'

'Astrid, you really don't have to go. I can see the police downstairs in the lobby.'

Astrid stood on tiptoe and kissed him. 'You know what they say. If you find yourself on a runaway train, you should jump off while you still have the chance.'

'Astrid, two of my very best friends were murdered today. My son's dead. If Charles Lasser had anything to do with it, I want to see him arrested, and tried, and executed.'

'Of course you do. But what's your evidence? Something you heard on the television news?'

'Charles Lasser used the word "vermin." They said "vermin" too.'

'You can't really be sure that they were referring to you.'

'They bombed my fucking office! They killed my friends! They murdered Danny and he was only eight years old!'

Astrid buttoned up her jerkin. 'Even if you're right, and it *was* Charles Lasser, you don't think that you could possibly prove it, do you?'

Frank frowned at her. 'Is that a question, or is that something you know for a fact?'

'It's common sense. Charles Lasser has twenty-six lawyers.'

'Oh, you know that, do you? That exact number? Listen, I really think you owe me some kind of explanation about this. What is it between you and Charles Lasser? He says he doesn't know you, which I don't believe for one moment, and as for you – well, you won't say anything.'

Astrid reached out and touched his cheek. He took hold of her hand, tightly, and held it, so that she couldn't get free.

'I *can't* say anything,' she told him.

'Can't, or won't?'

'I don't love you, Frank, you realize that, don't you?'

'Who said anything about love?'

'You did.'

223

He released her hand. She collected her purse, then went through to the living area and picked up the phone. 'I need a taxi. Sunset Marquis, room 217. That's right. As soon as you can.'

Frank stayed in the bedroom. The television was showing pictures of his shattered office. Among the litter of scorched paper lay a broken statuette of three dancing pigs: one with its arms broken off, one without a head, and one without any legs. Embrace no more, think no more, dance no more.

Twenty-Three

Frank checked his watch. It was almost eleven twenty P.M. and he couldn't think why Lieutenant Chessman was taking so long. He tried calling him again but his cellphone was busy. The shock of the bombing was wearing off now and he was trembling all over, as if he were running a fever. He watched the news again and tried to make a verbatim note of Dar Tariki Tariqat's statement, but his hand was shaking so much that most of what he wrote was scribble.

He was about to give up and go to bed when there was a sharp rapping at the door.

'Just a minute, Lieutenant!' he called, and went to open the door.

He was about to draw back the security chain when a small hand reached up and stopped him. He looked down, and right beside him stood Danny, staring at him, his eyes very wide. He was wearing the coat and the shorts that they had buried him in.

Frank had thought that when he saw the real Danny – the real dead Danny – he would be overjoyed. But he was so frightened that he let out a kind of a whinny, and his knees gave way, so that he almost collapsed. Danny's hand was ice cold, and his fingernails were blue. It looked as if there was frost sparkling on his eyelashes, and his breath was fuming around his mouth.

'What . . . what are you . . .' Frank started, but he couldn't get the words out.

There was another knock, louder this time. 'Mr Bell! Police! You want to open this door?'

Frank didn't know what to say. Danny kept his hand on top of his, and gave him a solemn little shake of his head, as if warning him not to open up.

'I . . . ah . . . I just stepped out of the shower!'

'Come on, Mr Bell. We're busy men. We don't have all night.'

'OK, two seconds.'

He stared at Danny, almost willing him to vanish, but instead, in a creepy, elderly sounding croak, he said, 'Danger.'

'*Danger*? What danger? Those are the cops.'

'Danger,' Danny repeated. He was obviously having difficulty in enunciating his words, but this convinced Frank more than anything else that he was the real Danny. Unlike his previous manifestation, he sounded weak and distressed, as any child would if he had died only recently and was still struggling to come to terms with it.

Another knock, and this one was thunderous. 'Mr Bell! Open this goddamned door!'

'Just a minute, will you?'

Without another word, Danny fell backward. It was a strange, slow-motion fall. Frank could see his mouth gradually opening, and his eyes blinking like a time-delayed camera exposure. He lunged forward to catch him, and as he did so he heard more banging. Five distinct bangs, as if the police were beating on the door with a hammer.

As Danny fell to the carpet, he disappeared. Melted, like a snowflake on a hotplate. Frank fell face-first on to the floor, jarring his shoulder and hitting his nose. 'Shit,' he said, and rolled over. It was only then that he saw five large holes in the door, and smoke, and realized what had happened.

'Mr Bell!' the voice repeated. 'If you don't open up this door, Mr Bell . . .!'

There was a kick, and the door splintered, and then another kick, and another.

Frank rolled over again, and again, until he had rolled

himself across to the sliding door that led out on to the balcony. Thank God, he had left the catch unlocked. He dragged the door open and wriggled outside on his elbows. Below him, the British rock musicians were sitting around the pool, drinking and smoking. Three topless girls were splashing around in the water.

Frank crawled to the far end of the balcony, so that he was out of sight of his living area. He climbed up on to the railing, balanced for a moment, and then jumped. He hit the water with a loud clap, and his world went all bubbly and bright blue. When he broke the surface, the girls were shrieking and clapping, and the musicians were laughing at him.

'You're fucking mental, you are, do you know that?' one of them shouted. 'You're a certifiable nutter!'

Frank stayed low in the water, doggy-paddling to keep himself afloat. He looked up at his balcony and saw the two men behind the net curtains, like a shadow theater. They came to the open window and looked out, and he could see that neither of them was Lieutenant Chessman. They stayed there for a few seconds, and he could hear them cursing, but they obviously couldn't see him, so they left.

Frank climbed out of the pool, his pajamas clinging to his skin. One of the rock musicians tossed him a can of beer, but he tossed it back. 'No . . . no thanks. I think I've had enough refreshment for one night.'

'Mental,' the musician repeated, deeply impressed.

Frank padded cautiously back through the hotel lobby, leaving a trail of wet footprints across the marble-composition floor. The night porter was watching *Great Police Chases* on TV and didn't even look up. Outside, a car swerved away from the curb, and Frank assumed that the two men were making their getaway. All the same, he climbed the stairs with extreme caution, stopping and holding his breath at every turn. There was a party going on in room 221, with screaming and laughing and heavy-metal music that must have registered 8.5 on the Richter scale, so it wasn't surprising that nobody had heard the two men shooting through his door.

*   *   *

226

Back in his apartment, he toweled himself quickly and pulled on a pair of Ralph Lauren jeans and a pale-blue rollneck sweater. He was punching out Lieutenant Chessman's number on the telephone when – right on cue – Lieutenant Chessman appeared in person, followed closely by Detective Booker. Lieutenant Chessman looked hot and tired and his shirt was hanging out. He made a show of knocking on what was left of Frank's door.

'Mr Bell? What happened here? Forgot your key or something?'

'I was just about to call you,' Frank told him, holding up the receiver. 'Two guys came knocking at the door, pretending to be cops. When I wouldn't open up, they just went *blam!*'

Lieutenant Chessman pulled a face. 'They said they were cops?'

'That's right. It was lucky for me that I didn't let them in.'

'Certainly was. Why *didn't* you let them in?'

Frank shrugged. 'I don't know. Intuition, I guess.'

'Did anybody else know that I was coming around here?'

'No, nobody.'

'Seems like kind of a coincidence, doesn't it, that they should have pretended that they were cops, when you were expecting the real cops?'

'I don't know. Yes, maybe.'

Lieutenant Chessman came into the living area and looked around. 'How many shots did they fire?'

'Four or five, at least. I jumped off the balcony, into the pool.'

Lieutenant Chessman went outside and peered down at the rock musicians and the three topless girls. 'Well, at least you had some incentive.'

There were three bullet holes in the wall next to the couch. Lieutenant Chessman peered at them closely, and then he said, 'Booker, you want to call CSI?'

'Yes, sir.'

Lieutenant Chessman lifted his head and sniffed. 'You were alone here, Mr Bell, when this happened?'

Frank nodded.

'I can smell perfume, that's all.'

'A woman friend called by, earlier.'

'I see.' Lieutenant Chessman lifted the cushions on the couch, as if he expected to find some incriminating evidence underneath. 'So what's all this about Charles Lasser? You don't seriously think that he's involved in these bombings, do you?'

'I had a personal confrontation with Charles Lasser only a couple of days ago.'

'A personal confrontation?'

'An argument. He was beating up on . . . a woman I know. I went to his office and warned him to leave her alone.'

'Really? Can you tell me this woman's name?'

'I know it sounds bizarre, but I only know her first name – Astrid.'

'You know this woman but you don't know her name?'

'Look,' said Frank, 'do you think we could leave her out of this?'

'What's the problem?'

'Well, I think she may be married or something like that. She's never told me.'

'All right. Just for the moment, let's go back to you and Charles Lasser. You thought he was beating up on this woman, whose name you don't know, and so you went to his office and gave him a hard time?'

'That's right. He denied it, of course, and he said that if I ever repeated it, he would have me hunted down, "like the vermin you are, and exterminated." Those exact words. The next thing I know, my office is bombed, and Dar Tariki Tariqat puts out a statement that "anybody who accuses God of being cruel will be hunted down like vermin they are."'

Frank handed him the transcript. Lieutenant Chessman read it with his lips moving. Then he looked up and said, 'This is pretty tendentious evidence, Mr Bell. Maybe Dar Tariki Tariqat *are* referring to you, even if they don't actually name you. But they aren't necessarily referring to your accusations against Mr Lasser, are they? More likely they're talking about something that you've written in your TV program. For instance, did any of your *characters* ever say that God was cruel?'

'What? I don't think so.'

'All the same, it seems like a much more logical explanation, don't you think? It's what you're putting out on television that these terrorists are objecting to, Mr Bell, not you personally.'

'So what about "vermin?"'

'"Vermin" is a pretty common pejorative, Mr Bell. It doesn't really establish a connection.'

'But two guys came around tonight trying to kill me.'

'Dar Tariki Tariqat are fanatics, Mr Bell. You write a TV show that they think is blasphemous, and because of that they want to get rid of you. That's all.'

Frank said, 'Maybe you're right. But I still think Charles Lasser could be involved in this.'

'OK. I'll talk to Mr Lasser. I'm obliged to, since you've made a complaint. But I'll have to be honest with you and tell you that I don't think it's going to come to anything.'

'All right,' said Frank. He hesitated, and then he said, 'Ask him about Astrid.'

'Oh, I will, and I'll talk to her, too. Do you have some way that I can contact her?'

'I'm sorry. I don't know where she lives and I don't know her phone number. She always gets in touch with me. But I do know that she's been seeing Charles Lasser, both at home and at his office. And I do know that he's been hitting her, and worse. I've seen the bruises for myself.'

Detective Booker wrote that down. 'To your knowledge, sir, has she ever made any complaints to the police about the way that Mr Lasser was mistreating her?'

'Not that I know of. She didn't even complain to me.'

Lieutenant Chessman took out a tiny ball of Kleenex and blew his nose. 'Women . . . who can understand them, huh? The bigger the bastard, the harder they fall. Listen, I'll talk to Mr Lasser tomorrow and then I'll call you to put you in the picture, how's that?'

'What about protection? What do I do if those guys come back?'

'Well, I was going to suggest that you find someplace else to stay. Maybe another hotel.'

He was just about to leave when the night manager appeared – a young man with a wispy black moustache and a jazzy pink and orange shirt, and shorts.

'What's going on here? What the hell happened to this door? I mean, look at it! What the hell happened to this *door*?'

Lieutenant Chessman gave Frank a sympathetic slap on the back. 'Like I said, maybe another hotel.'

He stayed that night with Carol and Smitty. He told Carol that his room at the Sunset Marquis had been double booked, and that a late-arriving guest had shown up from Japan. He didn't want to frighten her. But when Carol had gone to bed and he and Smitty sat down to some late-night TV and a couple of beers, he explained to Smitty what had really happened.

'Shit,' said Smitty. 'Who did the cops think they were?'

'They think that they probably came from Dar Tariki Tariqat, and that they were trying to finish what they started.'

'They didn't see any connection with Charles Lasser?'

'They said that it was probably coincidence, him using the word "vermin." That's all.'

'And they didn't offer you any protection?'

'They suggested I change hotels, that's all.'

Smitty put down his can of beer, stood up, and went through to his study. After a short while he came back with a folded chamois leather. He cleared aside the ashtray and the empty beer cans, and then he laid it down on the coffee table.

'Here, I bought this in ninety-eight, when we had that burglary.' He unfolded the leather, and revealed a .38 nickel-plated revolver in a belt holster. 'Why don't you borrow it – you know, just till this is all over? It's loaded.'

'I don't think so,' said Frank. 'I'm not at all happy about guns.'

'I don't care if you're happy or not, so long as you're alive. Here – no argument, take it. You won't ever have to use it, now you've got it, but at least you've got it, in case you need it.'

Twenty-Four

The next morning he was on his way to Nevile's house when his cellphone rang.

'Frank. It's Margot.'

'Oh, yes? What do you want?'

She hesitated, deterred by his aggressive response. But then she said, 'I just wanted to tell you how sorry I was about Lizzie and Mo. You must be devastated.'

'Yes, well, thank you. It was a miracle they didn't get me, too.'

'If you want to meet me, Frank, and talk about it . . .'

'No, thanks. But thanks.'

'Frank . . . I don't want things to come to the point where we're not even speaking to each other.'

'No, me neither. I'll call you later, if I get the time, OK?'

'All right, then.'

He was still thinking about Margot as he overshot the entrance to Nevile's house. The truth was, he was beginning to miss her, in a way. She might have taken herself way too seriously, with her Eastern philosophy and her paintings and her macrobiotic diets, but that was one of the things that had first attracted him, because it had brought stability and order into his life, whereas he had always been susceptible to sudden enthusiasms, and to rush off and do things before he had thought them through – followed by deep depression because they hadn't worked out.

Even her paintings didn't seem so bad, in retrospect. They were calm; they were peaceful. And, as Mo had once remarked, they were no more objectionable than a blank wall, after all.

He U-turned outside the Earth Mother Juice Stand, his tires

231

squealing, and doubled back. Further up the road a hitch-hiker, his thumb already half lifted, frowned at him in annoyance, as if his future had suddenly changed in front of his eyes.

Nevile was sitting in his study, laying out picture cards on his polished black marble table.

'How are you feeling?' he asked. His black shirt was buttoned up to the neck but he wasn't wearing a necktie, so that he looked like an ascetic priest.

Frank eased himself down on the opposite side of the table. 'I feel like I've been over Niagara Falls in a barrel. Twice nightly, with an extra performance on Saturday afternoons.'

Nevile looked up. 'How about mentally?'

'Sad. And very angry. Revenge? Jesus . . . if I could lay my hands on those bastards . . .'

'When are the police going to talk to Charles Lasser?'

'Today sometime, they told me. It probably won't do any good.'

Nevile dealt more cards, then frowned.

'What's this?' asked Frank. 'Fortune-telling?'

'No, it's a game. Cats and Moons. It's like solitaire except that you play it with a spirit.'

Frank couldn't help looking around the room. 'You mean you're playing with somebody now?'

'A very old spirit. He was one of the first who ever came to me when I moved to California. His name's Erasmus and he used to own a fruit farm near Bakersfield. He died at the age of ninety-seven.'

Frank watched Nevile picking up cards and placing them one on top of the other. 'How does Erasmus, like, play his hand?'

'He gives me instructions,' said Nevile, tapping his forehead with his fingertip. 'And in no uncertain terms, too. "The Dog Star card next to the Siamese card, you moron!"'

Frank sat back. Now that he had seen spiritual manifestations for himself, he didn't find it at all unbelievable that Nevile was playing a game with a man who was long dead. In fact, he wished that he had known about spirits

232

years ago, especially how close they like to cluster to the living.

'Do you think it was Charles Lasser who sent those men to kill you?' asked Nevile.

'I don't have any proof apart from that news broadcast, but I'm pretty sure of it.'

'Three cats!' said Nevile, triumphantly. 'Beat that!'

'I'm just wondering how they knew that I was waiting for the cops to show up.'

Nevile began to gather up cards. 'I hate to say this, but your prime suspect seems to be Astrid. You told her, didn't you, that you suspected Charles Lasser of bombing your office, and you told her that you were going to call the police? Not only that, she made sure she left before they arrived.'

'I don't know. The police thing could have been a coincidence. I mean, if you want somebody to open up their hotel room door for you, then shouting "police!" is a pretty logical thing to do, isn't it? You're not going to say "hitmen!", are you?'

'There's something very unusual about Astrid,' Nevile mused. 'It's not just the fact that she won't tell you what her name is, or where she lives. Do you think she's still seeing Charles Lasser?'

'I don't have any idea. I can't follow her everywhere. I don't have the right.'

'You have the right to protect yourself.'

'What do you mean? You think she's dangerous?'

'If she called those two men last night, of course she is. But even if she *didn't* call them, it seems to me that she's getting you involved in something very complicated and very risky, although I can't think what.'

'Whatever you say, she's given me comfort, she's given me reassurance, she's kept me from falling to pieces.'

'Of course she has,' said Nevile. 'But at the same time, she could have been trying to win your trust, for the sake of her own agenda.'

'What agenda? I mean, I'm a comedy writer. What else could I possibly do for her, except make her laugh?'

'Maybe Danny knows.'

'Danny?'

'He's appeared to you twice this week, to save your life. The chances are that he knows who's trying to kill you. He may also know what Astrid wants from you, too.'

'So that's why you suggested another séance?'

Nevile lifted both hands. 'Not if you don't want to.'

At that moment, however, the Cats and Moons pack was suddenly knocked off the table and scattered across the floor. Nevile looked around the room and said, 'Temper, temper! If there's one thing I don't like, Erasmus, it's a sore loser!'

They sat in silence for more than twenty minutes while the sun crept stealthily across the study wall and illuminated a painting of a woman in lilac standing by an overgrown grave, her hair entwined with flowers and her hands covering her face, so that only her eyes looked out. For some reason, the painting was titled *The Gates*.

Nevile was staring out of the window. His breathing was very deep and slow, almost as if he were falling asleep. Frank's left nostril began to itch, and it was all he could do not to sneeze.

'I want to talk to Danny,' said Nevile at last. 'Danny, can you hear me? Your daddy's here.'

'You got through?' asked Frank.

Nevile said nothing, but continued to stare at the clouds in the sky outside. Another five minutes went past, and the sun edged even further across the painting. It had the strange effect of making the girl's hands melt away, so that Frank could see her face, serious and pale, and staring at him directly, as if she recognized him.

'Danny? Can you hear me?' said Nevile. He listened for a moment, and then he turned to Frank. 'He's here, but he doesn't think that he can speak to us.'

'Why not?'

Nevile listened some more, and then he nodded. 'He says that if he speaks to us, he could get into trouble.'

'Trouble? What kind of trouble?'

'He says that there's a lot of hurt, and that there's only one way to make it better.'

'Yes, but what trouble?'

'I'm not sure, but it feels to me like he's being threatened.'

'Threatened? In the spirit world? Who the hell can threaten him there?'

'Other spirits. He says they're looking for a way to get over their pain.'

'What the hell does he mean? Is there any way that I can talk to him direct?'

'He says he loves you. He says he doesn't want anything bad to happen to you, the same way it happened to him.'

'Yes, but can I talk to him myself? I want to know who's giving him such a hard time.'

'They're *spirits*, Frank. Even if he told you who they were, what could you do about it?'

Frank stood up. 'Danny! Can you hear me, Danny? Come on, Danny, you appeared last night, you saved my life! Let me see you, Danny, please! At least let me hear you!'

There was another silence, and then Nevile said, 'He says he can't talk to you, not now.'

'Danny, I need to know what's happening. I need to know who killed Lizzie and Mo. I need to know who killed *you*.'

An even longer silence. A fly settled on the Cats and Moons cards and began to walk across Ursa Major. Somewhere close by a dog started barking.

'He's gone,' said Nevile.

Frank looked at his watch. 'Five after eleven. Only fifty-five minutes before some other poor bastards get blown up. Dear God, Nevile, we have to find out who's doing this!'

'Danny couldn't have told you, even if he knows. As I told you before, spirits can never tell you who killed them. They can't break the laws of natural justice.'

'But for Christ's sake, so many innocent people are going to get killed! What kind of natural justice is that?'

Nevile collected up his playing cards. 'The world couldn't work without secrets, Frank. If we knew exactly was going to happen tomorrow, life wouldn't be worth living. All that keeps us going is hope, isn't it? That, and curiosity.'

Twenty-Five

A fter he left Nevile's house, Frank drove along Franklin Avenue, past The Cedars. Maybe he could make contact with Danny here, where he had breathed his last breath. He parked on the opposite side of the street and climbed out of his car. A demolition crew was bringing down the last of the school library, and the morning echoed with the heavy thumps of falling masonry. It was right here, only two weeks ago, that his life had changed forever.

'Danny,' he said, under his breath, and tried to think of Danny swinging his school bag, but he could only picture him lying in his casket, with that creepy center parting and those doll-red cheeks, like one of the kids from *Our Gang*.

He paced up and down outside the school for almost twenty minutes, checking his watch repeatedly. If Dar Tariki Tariqat were as good as their word, another bomb was due to go off in less than a quarter of an hour.

With a thunderous roar, another wall fell, and the air was filled with dust. A demolition worker appeared through the haze like a ghost, and Frank was reminded of the way that Astrid had emerged from the bomb smoke, limping. In some respects, Astrid had changed his life more than the bomb – more than Danny's death.

He thought of the feeling she had given him that morning – the feeling that he already knew her, or that he had met her before, and it occurred to him that the woman who had seen her walking down Gardner Street had said the same. Maybe Astrid had one of those faces that remind people of other people. It was a common enough hazard of living in Los Angeles. Frank had been approached in the street two or three times and asked if he was Johnny Depp. It happened.

He stood outside the school for a long time, thinking. Specks of glass still glittered in the gutters, and Mr Loma's security hut still leaned at an impossible angle, as if it were being blown by a long-forgotten hurricane.

He climbed back into his car and drove south toward Sunset. A few blocks west, he passed Orange Grove Avenue. He slowed. What had Danny said, up on that locomotive footplate in Travel Town? *Emeralds and orange groves.*

Frank stepped on the brakes, provoking an elephant blast from a Ralph's truck driver close behind him and an ostentatious fanfare of trumpets from a gold Mercedes convertible. He turned down Orange Grove Avenue and drove very slowly southward, hugging the right-hand lane. He had no idea what he was looking for, but he had the feeling that he was being guided here. He also had the feeling that he was very close to something important. *Emeralds and orange groves. Seven thousand and eleven orange groves.*

He reached the intersection with Melrose Avenue. The signal was red, so he had to stop and wait. Right opposite stood a derelict church with a flaking, turquoise-painted dome. It was surrounded by corrugated-iron fencing, which was plastered with faded and tattered fly posters for rock concerts and health clubs. But a signboard still stood outside, announcing that this was the Church of St John the Evangelist, 7011 Orange Grove Avenue.

Frank felt the same scalp-shrinking sensation that he had experienced when the image of Danny had first appeared on the patio. *Emeralds* – the stone of St John the Evangelist. *Orange Grove Avenue. Seven thousand and eleven.* When the signal turned to green, he crossed Melrose and managed to find a tight parking space right in front of the church, much to the annoyance of the woman driving the gold Mercedes convertible, who had been following close behind him.

'You couldn't drive a fucking shopping cart!' she screamed at him.

He climbed out of his car and walked around the hoardings. On the Orange Grove Avenue side there was a makeshift door, fastened with a padlock. He peered through a triangular

237

gap right beside it, but all he could see was half of the steps leading up to the church door, and a heap of rubbish, including an iron bedhead and several split-open bags of cement.

He took out his cellphone and punched in Nevile's number. Nevile was a long time in answering and when he did he sounded out of breath. 'Sorry, I was taking a swim.'

Frank said, 'You remember at Travel Town, when we were talking about Dar Tariki Tariqat, and where they might meet? And Danny said, "emeralds and orange groves and seven thousand and eleven?"'

'Of course.'

'I'll bet you didn't know that twelve biblical saints have their own stones – you know, like birthstones – and that emeralds are the stone of St John the Evangelist.'

'No, I didn't know that. What of it?'

'Guess where I'm standing now.'

Saturday, October 9, 11:59 A.M.

Frank was sitting in his car waiting for Nevile when he heard the explosion in the distance. A flat thud, over to the northeast. Within two minutes, KRCW reporter Kevin Jacobson had broken into the morning music program.

'Reports are coming in of a massive explosion on the Warner Brothers lot in Burbank. A number of people have been killed and seriously injured. So far we have no more details than that, but we will bring you more news as and when we receive it.'

By the time Nevile's shiny black Mercedes had turned the corner and parked on the opposite side of Orange Grove Avenue, Frank had heard that at least twenty-five people had died, and scores had been critically hurt. A furious Warner Brothers executive blamed the police and the FBI for their 'abject failure to protect the entertainment industry.'

Warner Brothers' French Street set had been almost totally demolished by 1,500 lbs of C4 explosive packed into a van. The director John Portman had been blinded and the actress Nina Ballantine had lost both legs. Five extras had been beheaded by the blast.

Nevile came across the street looking serious. 'You've heard the news, too?' Frank asked him.

'Yes,' said Nevile, 'and believe me, they're not going to stop. They'll go on bombing until they get what they want. It was the same with the IRA when I was working in Northern Ireland – same back-to-front thinking. They feel that they're totally justified in what they're doing, and they're blaming all of the casualties on the entertainment industry, for not giving in to them. It's a case of "now look what you made me do!" Even worse than that, they believe they have God on their side. I'll tell you something, Frank: a lot more people are going to die before this is over.'

Twenty-Six

They walked around the church of St John the Evangelist, occasionally shaking the corrugated-iron fencing to see if any of it was loose enough to pry free. In the end they concluded that they would have to force the padlock that was holding the gate closed.

'Tire iron?' suggested Nevile, and Frank unlocked the trunk of his car.

While Frank kept a lookout, Nevile inserted the tire iron into the padlock, and twisted. A police cruiser crept past, and one of the officers stared at Frank as if he suspected him of being a street-corner drug dealer, but Frank gave an exaggerated performance of checking his watch and frowning up and down the street, as if he were waiting for somebody who had let him down, and the cruiser kept on going. At last the padlock snapped like a pistol shot, and Nevile was able to scrape the door open.

They clambered over the rubbish until they reached the steps. Most of the stained-glass windows were broken, and there was graffiti on the doors. De Skul and Marmaduke had apparently been there, as well as Uncle Horrible and Señor Meat.

Together they climbed the steps. The doors were solid oak, and locked. Nevile laid his hands on them, his palms flat, and closed his eyes.

'Any vibes?' Frank asked him.

'A lot. This is quite overwhelming. There's so much *hatred* here, you wouldn't believe it. I've never felt anything like this in any building before, let alone a church.'

'You think that this is where they meet? Dar Tariki Tariqat?'

'I'd be very surprised if it isn't. My God . . . there's so much pain here, so much suffering. So much desperation.'

Frank took a few steps back down. 'The point is, how are we going to get in here?'

'Let's try around the back.'

They made their way down the narrow alley that separated the church from the tire-replacement workshop next door to it. They could hear drills and hammers and clanking jacks, and the banging of inflated tires. Halfway along the alley, Nevile said, 'Let's try this.' There was a basement window covered with a screen of fine mesh. Nevile slid the tire iron underneath the mesh and it took only four or five wrenches to pull it away. He climbed down into the space in front of the window, and gave it a hefty kick with his heel. The glass smashed and Frank heard it tinkling into the basement.

'You should have been a burglar.'

'There's not enough money in it.'

Nevile wriggled through the broken window and dropped out of sight. 'It's OK,' he called. 'It's only about six feet down to the floor.'

Frank looked left and right to make sure that nobody was watching, then squeezed himself through the window and jumped down on to the basement floor. 'Shit, I've cut myself.' He looked up and there was a single shark's tooth of glass left in the window frame, stained with his own blood.

'Here.' Nevile took a white linen handkerchief out of his pocket and deftly tied it around Frank's thumb. 'You can thank my mother. I was never allowed to walk out of the front door without a clean handkerchief and bus fare.'

As their eyes became accustomed to the darkness they could see that one side of the basement was stacked with folding chairs and other furniture, as well as painted panels draped in dust sheets. One of the dust sheets had slipped and the accusing face of Pontius Pilate was staring at Frank from behind the bars of a chair, as if he was imprisoned.

Nevile crossed the basement floor and opened the door. 'Brilliant. I was worried it was going to be locked.'

They climbed the narrow brick steps that led up to the main body of the church. The pews had gone, the altar had gone, and the font had gone. From high up above, rows of diagonal beams of dusty sunshine fell along the aisle, forming a shining archway. Underneath this archway were stacked dozens of khaki metal boxes, as well as ropes and truck wheels and sleeping bags and bottles of water and other paraphernalia, including a portable diesel generator and a capstan lathe.

They walked slowly down the aisle. The pungent smell of nitrates was eye watering.

'Look at this,' said Nevile. 'Cyclonite, IMI demolitions blocks, TNT, plasticized RDX. There's enough explosive here to flatten twenty square blocks.'

'I'm amazed there's nobody on guard here.'

'What for? Who's going to go looking for an arms dump in a derelict church? I saw the same kind of thing in Belfast – an old country chapel that was stacked floor to ceiling with AK47s and Semtex. There was only a rusty old lock on the door, but we would never have found it without a tip-off.'

Frank examined another stack of metal boxes, some of them with their lids hanging open. 'Detonators, fuses, switches, timers. And what are these?'

At the back of the stacks, there was a pile of at least a dozen navy-blue vests, with deep pockets sewn into them, back and front. Three of the vests had already had their pockets filled with large slabs of greasy, clay-colored material.

'Hey – don't go near those,' warned Nevile. 'They're tailor-made waistcoats for suicide bombers. Ten pounds of plastic explosive in each pocket, filled with ball bearings.'

'Jesus,' said Frank. 'They must be totally crazy, these people. Out of their heads.' But as he looked around he realized that these boxes of explosives had not been assembled

241

because of anybody's insanity, and somehow that made it much more frightening. This was nothing to do with madness; this was plain, unadulterated hatred. He began to understand what Nevile had felt when he laid his hands on the doors outside, and sensed that this was a place of evil.

'I think it's time we called the police,' he said. 'Don't you?'

'Not in here. Not with a cellular phone. Not unless you want to end up in eighteen million matching pieces.'

They started to walk back toward the basement. As they did so, they heard the rattling of keys. They turned around to see the main church doors opening and a tall young man step inside. He had long straggly hair and a beard, a hawk-like nose, and he was dressed in a loose linen shirt and worn-out jeans. He stopped when he saw them, and frowned.

There was a brief moment when none of them moved. But then the young man pushed his way back through the doors, and disappeared. Frank went after him. He ran down the length of the church, bounded down the steps outside, tripped, and crashed into the corrugated-iron fencing. He was just in time to see the young man escaping out into the street.

He followed, even though he had bruised his shoulder and twisted his knee. By now the young man was almost halfway along the block, loping toward Fairfax Avenue, his hair flying behind him. Frank had to run like Long John Silver – dot one, carry one – and his knee was so painful that he couldn't help himself from shouting out '*shit!*' with every step he took. But he had always kept up his tennis, and he was fit enough, and by the time the young man had reached Fairfax Frank was gaining on him.

The man ran into the street, holding up his hand to stop the traffic. But without warning a taxi came speeding across the intersection and struck him a glancing blow with its side mirror. There was a shout and a screech of tires. The young man tumbled back into a parked pickup, staggered, and then fell sideways on to the pavement. He was still trying to climb back on to his feet when Frank came bounding around the front of the pickup and seized his shirt.

'OK, Jesus. Got you!'

*   *   *

'His name's John Frederick Kellner,' said Lieutenant Chessman, finishing his chicken taco and smacking his hands together. 'Twenty-six years old, a web designer from Redondo Beach. He refuses to tell us anything, but we've been talking to his mother and his twin sister.'

'Did they have any idea of what he was mixed up in?' asked Frank.

'He was always involved with radical politics, ever since he was at high school. Animal rights, Stop the War, No More Nukes – that kind of malarkey. But his mother hasn't seen him for nearly a year.'

'What about his childhood?' Nevile asked.

'His father walked out when he was five, apparently, and he was sent to live with his uncle and his aunt from the age of seven. He was removed from their custody shortly after his thirteenth birthday because his uncle was suspected of abusing him. Until April of last year he was receiving regular treatment at the Westwood Center for clinical anxiety.'

'Another victim of abuse, then,' said Nevile. 'It looks as if my theory is correct.'

'He hasn't admitted to being a member of Dar Tariki Tariqat,' said Lieutenant Chessman. 'But he *is* an abuse victim, yes, and he did have access to explosives that we are ninety-nine percent certain belong to Dar Tariki Tariqat – so, yes, I guess your theory seems to be panning out, so far as it goes.'

They were sitting in Lieutenant Chessman's office at the Hollywood police station on North Wilcox Avenue. All around them was chaos. Phones rang incessantly, people were shouting and arguing, and the corridors were crowded with harassed police officers and jostling news reporters. Television vans were double parked in the street below, and all the doors were guarded by officers from the SWAT team. Kellner was being questioned under tight security by successions of police detectives, as well as special agents from the FBI and intelligence officers from the CIA.

Frank, Nevile and Lieutenant Chessman were still talking when Police Commissioner Marvin Campbell appeared on the six o'clock television news looking groomed and glossy and deeply relieved.

'Of course it's still too soon for us to be counting chickens, but today the forces of law'n'order struck a crushing counter blow against the terrorists who have been threatening our city, our freedom of expression and our very lives.

'Bomb experts have already removed large quantities of explosives from St John the Evangelist Church for forensic testing. However, we are in very little doubt that their chemical composition will match the residue from the recent bombings at The Cedars, Universal, Fox, Disney and Warner Brothers.'

Commissioner Campbell declined to disclose exactly how the store of explosives had been discovered. 'Let me simply say that the Los Angeles Police Department, in association with the FBI and other agencies, have contributed investigative work of the highest order – a unique combination of down-to-earth diligence and almost miraculous inspiration.'

'In other words,' Nevile said dryly, 'they had bugger all to do with it.'

During the course of the next few hours, Dar Tariki Tariqat unraveled at the seams. FBI computer experts went through John Kellner's PC and found that three years ago he had logged on to an online discussion society calling itself Whipping Horse. Ostensibly, Whipping Horse was a support group for the victims of any kind of abuse – child molestation, domestic violence, bullying, rape or sexual harassment. Unlike any other support group, though, it didn't offer comfort and friendly advice. It offered something far more exciting and liberating: the chance to get even.

Abuse victims were encouraged to strike back at the people who had made their lives a misery. They could do this in a small, irritating way by constantly ordering pizzas – or taxis, or mail-order goods – for their one-time tormentors, day after day, week after week. Or they could get more serious and infect their office computers with pictures of child pornography. Or they could jeopardize their careers by calling their companies and suggesting that they had been operating some kind of illegal kickback.

Trash Their Treasures! the website urged. 'Vandalize their houses, dig up their lawns, set fire to their cars. After everything they've done to you, it's nothing more than they deserve. And society should be punished, too, for turning a blind eye while you suffered.'

Members of Whipping Horse who had taken their revenge on their abusers were asked to report back to a secure email address, describing exactly what they had done, 'in full, grisly detail, please! So that we can all enjoy how you made the bastard(s) squirm!' Those who had carried out the most extreme acts of retribution would be invited to join an 'inner sanctum.'

'The inner sanctum will regularly meet to devise effective punishments for abusers of all kinds, and also for those who abuse by omission, by trying to pretend that abuse does not exist, and that life is all happiness and sunshine. For the first time, victims of abuse can show the world what it is like to have your life damaged beyond human repair, and your very soul taken away from you. For the first time, victims of abuse are being offered a path in the darkness.'

Dar Tariki Tariqat. In the darkness, a path.

At nine twenty-seven the following morning, Frank was woken by the phone ringing. It was Nevile.

'They've found a list of Dar Tariki's members. They include all the people who volunteered as suicide bombers. Richard Haze Abbott, Alexander Sutter, the man and the girl who blew up The Cedars – everybody. The police have been able to make two or three arrests, but at least seventeen of them must still be in hiding someplace. Presumably the ones who are going to carry out the next nine bombings.'

'Do they have any idea who's behind it?'

'Not so far. The FBI have been talking to John Kellner all night, apparently, but they don't think he *knows* who's behind it.'

'Maybe you should to talk to him, so that you can feel his aura.'

'I did suggest it. But the police are being more than a little cagey at the moment – not answering my calls, stuff like that. I don't think they're very happy that it was you and me who found that stash of explosives. They don't want the *Times* coming out with "Brit Mystic and TV Gag Writer Crack Terror Campaign." Wouldn't do much for their lustrous reputation, would it?'

Frank ran his hand through his sleep-tousled hair. 'So tell me, who bombed The Cedars?'

'An artist called Gerry Francovini, twenty-six years old, from West Hollywood. And a girl of twenty-four called Tori Fisher, from Palo Alto originally. She was a model or something.'

'Not much more than kids themselves.'

'True. But it still doesn't excuse what they did.'

'I don't really care about who they were, or why they did it. What I want to know is who put them up to it.'

The next call came ten minutes later, from Astrid. 'Do you want to meet me this afternoon?' she asked him.

'Why don't I buy you lunch? I've been staying with my sister but I'm moving into the Franklin Plaza, and the room won't be ready till three.'

'I'm sorry, Frank. I promised to have lunch with my friend.'

'Can't you put her off?'

'I'm sorry. I'll see you about three thirty, OK?'

'Astrid – before you hang up, I wanted to ask you something about your ring. You know, the one that your father gave you – the emerald. St John the Evangelist's birthstone. I mean, it was such a coincidence—'

Before he could say any more, she cut the connection. Frank stared at the receiver for a long time, almost as if he expected it to speak to him, and tell him the answer to everything he wanted to know. But then Carol called up the stairs that breakfast was ready, so he hung up and went to take a shower.

I may miss Margot, but it's Astrid that I really want, he thought as he soaped himself. The smell of her skin, the curve of her hip. The slight seductive droop of her eyelids, as if

246

she's dreaming. So Nevile thinks she's dangerous. That only makes her all the more exciting.

Twenty-Seven

Frank took Carol and Smitty for a Zen burger at Iyashinbou at Century City, by way of a thank you for putting him up. Carol had protested that he could stay with them for as long as he wanted, and it wouldn't cost him a bean, so long as he didn't mind babysitting now and again. But he didn't want to risk those phony cops turning up and shooting their way through her door, not with children around.

Iyashinbou was always preternaturally chilled out, with its raked-gravel garden and its pools full of lazily swimming carp, but this morning the atmosphere everywhere in Hollywood was palpably more relaxed. The bombing was over and the dreaded Dar Tariki Tariqat had turned out to be nothing more than a collection of vengeful geeks. People couldn't understand Islamic fundamentalists, but they could understand geeks – and they could understand why these particular geeks had gone the way of Timothy McVeigh. They could even empathize, although they couldn't forgive, especially those whose favorite soaps had been permanently canceled. All in all, it was a good movie-type ending. In fact, several screenwriters were busy working on bomb-outrage scripts, with Morgan Freeman already tipped for the role of Commissioner Campbell.

'You ask me, I blame the Web,' said Smitty. He was wearing a purple Rams sweatshirt and a baggy pair of Desert Storm combat pants. 'Before the Web, your average loser had no way of getting in touch with any of your other losers. All of your losers, right, they were *compartmentalized* – each loser stewing in his own bedroom. But as soon as the Web came along, that was it, they all connected up, and all that individual stewing combined to make one hell of a dangerous casserole.'

Carol said, 'I feel sorry for those young people. I know I don't have any reason to, but I do. They were beaten and sexually abused and God knows what else, and the world took no notice. I know it's been a terrible price to pay, but maybe it'll change some attitudes.'

'I'll have the teppanyaki burger with eggplant fries,' said Smitty. 'And a cold Sapporo to chase it down the old red lane.'

Frank and Carol both ordered yakitori chicken burgers and vinegared rice balls. Frank had chosen to have lunch at Iyashinbou because it had been Mo's favorite restaurant – apart, of course, from Shalom Pizza on West Pico. The idea of a Japanese burger restaurant had appealed to Mo's sense of total absurdity. He had liked it even better when he had found out that 'Iyashinbou' meant 'Greedy Guts.'

While they were waiting for their food, Carol took hold of Frank's hand across the table. 'You must feel you've gotten some kind of closure for Danny. Especially since you found those bombs yourself.'

'I don't know yet. We still need to know who organized all of this bombing, and who paid for it. I mean, how could a bunch of amateurs get themselves together to blow up half of Hollywood, Internet or not? Especially a bunch of emotionally damaged people like Dar Tariki Tariqat.'

'You know something?' said Smitty. 'We live in a different world these days. When we was young, what did we care about Islam? Nothing. Islam was what you said when somebody asked you what was for lunch. We didn't even know that Islam existed. Now we have to walk on fucking eggshells. Same with gays. Same with vegetarians. Same with pediatricians.'

'Don't you mean pedophiles?'

'Whatever.'

Smitty was still grumbling about political correctness when Frank saw a figure walking across the plaza in front of the restaurant. The windows of Iyashinbou were tinted dark metallic gray, so that it looked as if it were thundery outside. The figure was wearing a baseball cap with a long peak, and drooping maroon shorts, and he was dragging a dog on a very long string. As he came close to the restaurant, he stopped, and peered intently inside, even though he couldn't have seen anything but his own reflection.

'Will you get a load of that old geezer?' Smitty remarked. 'He must have X-ray vision.'

But without a word, Frank stood up, put down his napkin, and walked out through the restaurant door. Outside it was hot and glaring, not thundery at all, although a fresh breeze made the old man's shorts flap around his skinny, scabby knees.

'Hello, Frank,' the old man grinned. 'How's it going? I was real sorry to hear about your friends.'

'Tell me what I'm supposed to do now,' said Frank.

The old man shrugged his shoulders. 'Do what you damn well like, that's my suggestion.'

'No, no. You seem to be the expert when it comes to my destiny. You tell me.'

The old man shook his head. 'You've already decided, Frank. You crossed the street and here you are on the other side. There's no going back now, you know that. But watch your step. You never know what's going to hit you next.'

'Like what?'

'You ever see those cartoons, Frank? Like you're strutting along the street in your natty suit with a flower in your lapel, doing the double shuffle, when a safe drops off of the top of a building and flattens you? Or you're sitting at home with a six pack, watching the old TV, and there's a knock at the door, and when you open it, it's a Union Pacific locomotive, complete with cow catcher, coming toward you at full pelt?'

'I don't get you.'

'All's I'm saying is, take good care. Look *up*, as well as ahead, and look behind you, too. And always say "who is it?" before you open that door. Well, I think you learned that particular lesson already.'

'Is this a warning?'

'Let's just put it this way: somebody once told me that you can drop a toaster in the bath and that, contrary to expectations, it won't electrocute you. But I never took the chance by trying it.'

Frank was about to tell the old man that this was self-evident,

249

since he smelled as if he hadn't taken a bath since he was born, but at that moment there was a loud, dull explosion from the east, probably no more than three miles away. Everybody who was crossing the plaza stood stock still, their heads raised, their mouths open in shock. There were five seconds of utter silence, and then the explosion echoed from the mountains.

'At a guess, that sounds like CBS Television City,' said the old man, and sniffed.

Smitty came out of the restaurant, closely followed by Carol, and six or seven other diners, and three Japanese waiters.

'Jesus Christ!' said Smitty. 'That was another bomb, wasn't it? I thought you said this was over.'

Frank checked his watch. It was one minute after twelve. It looked as if Dar Tariki Tariqat were going to go on blowing themselves up until the last of them were dead.

Behind him a woman started to wail, as if she were a mourner at a Middle-Eastern funeral. There was nothing else that anybody could do. Frank looked around for the old man, but he had gone. All he could see was his dog, trotting off around the corner, and then it, too, disappeared from sight.

Frank dumped all his suitcases on to the bed at the Franklin Plaza and closed the door behind him. A message was already waiting for him on his answering machine. He pressed the *on* button then rummaged in the brown paper sack he had brought back from the supermarket, trying to find a beer.

'Mr Bell, this is Lieutenant Chessman. I tried your cell-phone but you were busy. I thought you'd like to know that I talked to Charles Lasser this morning. I have to tell you that he was very co-operative, but he totally denied any knowledge of any woman called Astrid. In fact he denied mistreating *any* woman of *any* name.' (Cough, shuffle of paper.) 'He's . . . ah . . . he's prepared to accept that he might have called you "vermin," but he says that he is constantly pestered by the media and by people attempting to extort money or favors from him, and that he was . . . er . . . under the impression that you were one of these. After all, you did push your way into his office uninvited, true?

250

'Mr Lasser has been unfailingly helpful in our efforts to put an end to this bombing. I told him of the valuable part you played in finding Dar Tariki Tariqat's cache of explosives and he seemed to be very gratified. If we succeed in getting convictions for the people we've arrested, you could be looking at a very substantial reward.

'I'll call you later, Mr Bell. But in the meantime, I wouldn't concern yourself with Mr Lasser any further. Believe me, he's one of the good guys.'

The call was timed at eleven forty-eight A.M., only thirteen minutes before the last bomb had exploded. The old man had been right: they had targeted CBS Television City. The death toll was seventeen adults and five children. Over thirty more had been critically injured.

Frank unlocked the sliding door and took his beer out on to the balcony. In the distance he could hear dozens of sirens warbling, and there was still a genie-like smudge of smoke hanging over Beverly Boulevard. Apart from the sirens, however, Hollywood was unnaturally quiet, as if people were afraid to go out, or even to speak. But then the phone rang.

'Mr Bell? It's Marcia, from reception. There's a woman down here, asking for you. She's in pretty bad shape.'

Frank hurried down to the lobby. A woman was sitting on one of the chairs by the front door, her head in her hands. The receptionist was bending over her, dabbing at her forehead with a bloodied tissue. A Mexican cab driver with a droopy moustache was standing close by, looking fretful.

'What's happened?' Frank asked.

The woman looked up. It was Astrid. Her hair was spiky with blood and it looked as if her nose had been broken. She was wearing a pale-green blouse that was drenched in blood, and her cream-colored Dockers were spattered, too.

'I picked her up outside Star-TV,' said the cabbie. 'I wanted to take her straight to a hospital but she said she had to come here to see you.'

Frank said, 'That's OK. That's fine. You did the right thing. Astrid, tell me what happened? For Christ's sake, Astrid, did Lasser do this?'

'I wanted to take her to the hospital,' the cabbie repeated.

251

'She just wouldn't let me. She said, "Franklin Plaza, take me to the Franklin Plaza."'

'That's OK,' Frank told him, and gave him two twenties and a ten.

'I'm not asking for no money,' said the cabbie. 'I was trying to act like the good Samaritan, that's all. None of the other cabs wanted to pick her up. She look like *Friday the Thirteenth*, you know what I mean?'

'Do you want me to call for an ambulance?' asked the receptionist.

'No, not yet,' Frank told her. 'Let me take her up to my room and get her cleaned up. Thanks for helping her out.'

'Looks like she picked a fight with Godzilla, and lost.'

'Something like that, yes.'

Astrid blinked up at him. 'Frank?' she said, thickly. 'Is that you?'

'Come on, sweetheart, let's get you upstairs. Do you think you can walk?'

Frank put his arm around her and helped her to her feet. She lost her balance, and almost fell, but the receptionist grabbed her sleeve. Frank coaxed her to walk two or three steps, but her knees gave way, and in the end he had to pick her up. She was surprisingly light, not much heavier than a child, and he had no trouble in carrying her into the elevator.

'Please call me if you need anything, sir,' said the receptionist.

'You bet. And thanks again.'

Astrid snuffled against his shirt. 'Never thought I'd find you,' she mumbled.

'Well, you've found me now. Everything's going to be fine.'

'He's such a bastard,' she said, and coughed, and couldn't stop coughing.

He carried her into his apartment and laid her down on the tree-patterned couch, propping her head up with cushions. Then he went into the bathroom and came back with a cold, wet facecloth. He cleaned the blood from her face, dabbing the facecloth very gently around her nostrils. Then he rinsed it out, folded it up, and laid it across the bridge of her nose.

252

She stared at him with those washed-out eyes, not blinking.

'Give me one good reason why you keep on going back to him,' he demanded. 'One.'

'I don't have to explain myself to anybody, Frank. Even you.'

'He's broken your fucking nose, Astrid.'

'I know. I think he's broken my ribs, too.'

'Why the hell did you go to see him? I just can't get my head around it. You're beautiful, you're intelligent, you've got everything in the whole world going for you. And yet you allow a middle-aged scumbag like Charles Lasser to beat you to a pulp. I mean, what are you, some kind of masochist?'

Astrid kept on staring at him. 'If I am, that's my own business, don't you think?'

'No, it isn't. You came back here because you needed my help. That makes it my business, too. I promised Charles Lasser that if he ever laid hands on you again, I'd make him pay for it, and I'm going to.'

She took the facecloth away from her nose. 'Frank . . . you don't know what you're getting yourself into.'

'Then tell me. Come on, tell me! What *am* I getting myself into? It seems like ever since we met you've been trying to get me involved in something or other, but I'm damned if I can work out what it is.'

Astrid said nothing, but he thought he detected something in her expression that could have been regret, or sorrow. For some reason he remembered a phrase he had read in *The Process*: 'One lifetime isn't enough. Give me more.'

'I'm taking you to the emergency room,' he said. 'You have to have your nose looked at. It just looks swollen at the moment, but it could need setting.'

'Frank, I'm OK. I just need to rest.'

'No way. I'm taking you to hospital and then I'm going to Star-TV and I'm personally going to rip Charles Lasser's head off.'

'Frank . . .'

'No arguments, OK? For once we're going to do things my way.'

*   *   *

253

He helped her into his car and then he drove her to the Sisters of Jerusalem Hospital. He guessed that Mount Sinai would probably be overwhelmed with casualties from the CBS bombing. Even at the Sisters of Jerusalem, the parking lot was chaotic and the ER waiting room was crowded with people suffering from minor injuries and shock. There were twenty or thirty dazed and blood-spattered people waiting to register and everybody was shouting at once.

Frank sat Astrid down in the corner and said, 'Listen, I'm going to leave you here. I won't be long.'

'Frank, I'm begging you. Don't go looking for Charles Lasser. This wasn't his fault.'

'Don't tell me. You tripped and fell. You broke your nose on a kitchen door.'

'I don't want you to get hurt, that's all.'

'Believe me, there's only one person who's going to be hurting.' He squeezed her hand to reassure her that everything was going to be all right. 'Give me twenty minutes, OK? I have to do this, Astrid, otherwise he's going to go on beating up on you until he kills you.'

'Frank, please . . .'

Frank went up to the nurse at the reception desk and said, 'Do me a favor, would you? Keep an eye on my friend. She's still in shock. I won't be longer than a half-hour . . . Here's my cellphone number in case you need me.'

He left the hospital without looking back. He had never felt like this before. He had lost his temper now and again, but he had never experienced this slow, burning rage. Normally, he would have stayed with Astrid and made sure that she was treated, but this was more important. This was more important than life itself.

He walked to the parking lot, unlocked his car, and leaned across the driver's seat so that he could take Smitty's gun out of the glovebox. Then he walked back to the front of the hospital and flagged down a taxi. He didn't want to drive because parking outside Star-TV was restricted, and he didn't want to start any trouble before he had even got into the building.

The taxi driver was Korean. He said, 'You know what I

254

would do with those suicide bombers? I would find all of their bits and put them back together again and then I would give them lethal injection. Just to show people, you know? You can kill yourself, my friend, but you can't escape justice.'

Frank thought about Charles Lasser. *You can't escape justice.* He didn't exactly know what he was going to do to him, but for the first time in his life he understood what it was like to be capable of killing a man.

Security was tight at Star-TV. He was stopped by two brown-uniformed guards as soon as he walked in through the revolving doors.

'You have an appointment, sir?'

'That's right. Four o'clock, with Mr Berenger.'

'And your name is?'

'Bell. Frank Bell.'

One of the guards checked his clipboard. 'No record of it here, sir.'

'What? He specifically told me four P.M., and don't be late.'

'OK, sir. Just wait a moment and I'll call his office.'

Frank waited while the guard punched out John Berenger's extension number. At the rear of the lobby, the elevator doors were opening. He wondered if by dodging around the guards and making a run for it, he could get inside the elevator before they could stop him. But he didn't know how long it would take the elevator doors to close, and in any case the lobby was crowded and he would probably be tackled by somebody else before he could escape.

At that moment, however, Rufus Newton walked past him. Rufus had been working in production at Fox when *Pigs* was first being developed, and they had immediately become friends. Rufus was hugely creative, but also wildly rebellious. Eighteen months ago he had been sacked by Kenneth Fassbinder for sending out a spoof promotion that mocked Fassbinder's passion for 'uplifting dramas involving man's best friend.' It had been titled *Raiders of the Lost Bark.*

'Rufus! Hey, it's Frank!'

'Frank, my man!' Rufus came up and shook his hand. He was looking thinner than before, and his hair was grayer. He

255

used to look like Eddie Murphy but now he looked like Eddie Murphy's uncle. 'What are you doing at Star, Frank? Don't tell me you've given up all of your principles and sold out to Charles Lasser?'

'*You* did.'

'No, I didn't, because I never had any principles to start with. Besides, I needed to pay my mortgage. Who are you here to see?'

'John Berenger . . . He and I were thrashing out this new comedy concept.'

Rufus shook his head. 'John's out of town right now, didn't you know that? They've sent him off on one of those reality TV shows. Get this: we book six celebrities into a fleabag motel in Mexico, and we take away all of their clothes and all of their money. The first one to make it back here to the studio wins fifty thousand dollars. It's called *Have Cojones, Will Travel.*'

'John's doing shit like that?'

'John's doing just what the rest of us are doing, *compadre*. He's doing like he's told. Especially now that all of the other networks are going down the toilet. This bombing – believe me, it's changed the face of TV forever.'

The security guard came over and said, 'I'm sorry, Mr Bell. It appears that Mr Berenger is out of town. Maybe he forgot to cancel your appointment.'

'Hey, why don't you come up and have a cup of coffee?' Rufus suggested. 'It's OK, officer. I'll vouch for this character. Come on over to the desk, Frank, you're going to need a security badge. You don't know how upset I was about your Danny. And then Mo and Lizzie. I cried all afternoon, man. I mean, Mo and Lizzie – they were the genuine article, you know? The last of the genuine articles.'

Rufus asked the receptionist for a security tag, and clipped it on to Frank's lapel.

'What are you working on now?' Frank asked him as they stepped into the elevator.

'*Where the Cheats Meet to Eat*. It's still in development. We interview couples in restaurants. We ask them what they think of the food, then we ask them if they're married to somebody else. The pilot was great. Fighting, screaming, pasta flying around. Like Jerry Springer with spaghetti sauce.'

'What's it all come to, Rufus?'

The elevator chimed its arrival at the seventh floor. 'The lowest common denominator,' said Rufus. 'You want art, go to the Getty.'

He led Frank into his office. At Fox, Rufus had been notorious for his untidiness, and his 'den' had been littered with scripts, photographs, unanswered letters, magazines, TV awards and half-eaten sandwiches. Here at Star, he had a large desk covered with gray leather on which stood nothing more than a telephone, a laptop, a digital clock, and a silver-framed photograph of his wife, Natasha. Outside the window there was a view of Century City, with the traffic crawling along the Avenue of the Stars.

Rufus picked up his phone and asked his secretary for two espresso. 'You still drink that horseshoe stuff, yes?' The clock on his desk showed it was four eleven. Frank could feel the gun weighing down the left side of his linen coat, and hoped that it wasn't too noticeable.

'You're really happy, then, working here?' he asked Rufus.

'You mean do I like Charles Lasser? What can I say? Charles Lasser gives people what they want, even if it isn't good for them. To be honest, I hardly ever see him, and I don't think he even knows who I am.'

'Do you think that he could have been behind this bombing campaign?'

Rufus stared at him, taken by surprise. '*What*?'

'Think about it. They bombed almost every TV network except HBO and Star.'

Rufus looked dubious. 'I don't know, man. The way I heard it, it's a group of psychos – child-abuse victims, trying to get their own back on society.'

'Somebody has to be financing them. Somebody has to be pulling the levers.'

'And you think that could be Charles Lasser?'

'I don't know. I'm asking you.'

Rufus stood up, went over to the door, looked up and down the corridor, and then closed it. 'It's a hell of a thought, isn't it? I mean, I see where you're coming from. Ever since the other networks canceled their soaps, our daytime Nielsen ratings have shot through the roof. Advertising revenues . . . I don't know . . . they've just about tripled. And we're picking up the talent, too. We've already had approaches from Bill Katzman and Gerry Santosky – people who swore that they wouldn't work for Charles Lasser even if you threatened to cut their dicks off.'

He sat down. 'Do you remember the TV Drama Awards, the year before last? When Lance Seelbach made that speech about Rats-TV? "Like Star-TV, only not so backward." Charles Lasser never forgave him for that, and he never forgave anybody at that ceremony who laughed at him – not Fox or Disney or NBC or CBS or UPN or *anybody*.'

Frank said nothing. After a while, Rufus leaned back in his swivel chair and there was a look on his face which Frank had never seen before. He looked troubled, but he looked beaten, too. 'I reckon you could say that Charles Lasser is a very vengeful man. But as for blowing up innocent people . . . I don't think so.' He paused, and then he said, 'I sure hope not, anyhow.'

There was a knock at the door and Rufus's secretary came in with two cups of espresso and some chocolate-chip cookies. Rufus said, 'You can leave the door open, Thelma.' When she had gone, he turned to Frank and added, 'Company rule, leaving the doors open. John calls it the Anti-Plotting Policy.'

The clock now said four seventeen. Frank sipped a little coffee and then said, 'Sorry – do you mind if I use the rest-room?'

He walked quickly along the corridor until he reached the elevators. He jabbed the call button and waited, glancing back toward Rufus's office in case Rufus came out and wondered why he had taken the wrong turning. But at last an elevator car arrived. He stepped inside and pressed the button for the penthouse.

The elevator stopped at the next floor and a man with Clark Kent glasses and an armful of folders stepped in. 'How's it going?' he asked, as if he had known Frank for years. 'Good,' said Frank. Three floors later the man stepped out again, and said, 'Take care of yourself.' Frank said, 'You, too.'

At last he reached the penthouse. The thickly carpeted corridor was silent. He waited until the elevator doors had closed behind him, and then walked quickly along to the receptionist's office and pushed his way through the double doors. There was a different girl sitting there today – a pretty Vietnamese girl in a shiny turquoise blouse.

'Excuse me, sir,' she protested, as Frank came in. 'Mr Lasser isn't seeing any more visitors today.'

'Oh, he's going to see me.'

'No, no. He give strict instruction.' The girl rose from her seat but Frank walked around her triangular glass desk and pushed her gently but firmly back down.

'Stay there. Don't say a word and don't call anybody, you got me?'

'You can't go into Mr Lasser's office! Mr Lasser will be so angry!'

'Look at me,' said Frank. 'You don't think *I'm* angry? I'm very *angry*. Compared to me, Mr Lasser is Mr Sunny Personality of the Year.'

'Please – if I let you in, I will lose my job here.'

'In that case, I'll be doing you a great favor, believe me.'

He reached across her desk and ripped the cord out of her phone. 'You don't call anybody and you stay right here, OK?'

Then he went to the doors of Charles Lasser's office and threw them wide open.

Twenty-Eight

Charles Lasser was standing in the middle of the room in his shirtsleeves, his shoulders hunched, grasping a golf club. His head was wreathed in cigar smoke, so that it appeared for a moment as if he didn't have a head at all. Then he looked up, and the smoke swirled away, and he was staring directly at Frank with eyes that glittered like nail heads.

'Who the hell let you in?' he demanded. 'Kim Cu'c!'

'Mr Lasser, please, I try to stop him.'

'It's not her fault,' said Frank. He took a few steps toward the window so that his back was covered.

Charles Lasser lowered his head again, hesitated, and then putted his golf ball under his desk. 'You're going to have to leave, Mr Bell. I have nothing to say to you. Besides, you're putting me off my stroke.'

'You may not have anything to say to me, but by God, I have plenty to say to you.'

'Oh, yes? I thought you would have been far too busy writing funeral speeches for your friends.'

'Jesus, you're twisted. If it hadn't been for you, my friends wouldn't be dead.'

'You're out of your mind, Mr Bell. You think *I* killed them? What on earth makes you think that?'

'Because you're a goddamned sadist and you know damn well who was financing Dar Tariki Tariqat – it was you. And you bombed my office right after I came here and warned you about Astrid. You didn't bomb any of the studios; you didn't bomb the executive cottages – no, you bombed *my* office, and if I hadn't stepped out for a minute you would have killed me, too.'

'You want me to go bring security, Mr Lasser?' asked his receptionist.

Charles Lasser shook his head. 'Don't worry, Kim Cu'c. I can deal with Mr Bell. Mr Bell is suffering from delusions, that's all.'

He walked back to his desk, which was a huge mahogany construction with carvings of satyrs' heads and bunches of grapes and fluted pillars. He parked one substantial buttock right on the edge of it, and sat there smiling at Frank, occasionally slapping the shaft of his golf club into the palm of his hand.

Frank said, 'Why don't you admit it? You bombed my office, didn't you? You organized *all* of these bombings. This was nothing to do with child-abuse victims getting their

260

revenge, not really. This was you getting your revenge on the entertainment business.'

Charles Lasser grinned. He seemed to have too many teeth, and even though they were perfect, they were yellowed by nicotine. 'That's a great theory, Mr Bell. I have to give you ten out of ten for creativity. I can't say that Star-TV hasn't profited from this terrorist campaign, and we've been very lucky so far that they haven't targeted us. But you're giving me far too much credit. I never would have had the brains to think of it, myself, and I certainly wouldn't have had the courage to carry it out.'

'You had the courage to break Astrid's nose.'

'What? Didn't I make this clear to you the first time? I don't know anybody called Astrid.'

'You beat up on her today. Don't try to deny it; it won't work. I just left her at the Sisters of Jerusalem, waiting for treatment.'

Charles Lasser sighed in exasperation. 'I've been in meetings all day. We're launching nine major new series next season. I don't have the *time* to break girls' noses.'

Frank approached him, so close that Charles Lasser could have struck him with his golf club if he had wanted to. 'I warned you,' said Frank. 'I warned you that if you touched Astrid one more time, I'd come back, and that I'd make sure that you never hurt her again.'

'So you did. But read my lips, Mr Bell. I didn't know any girl called Astrid when you first came here, and I haven't made the acquaintance of any girl called Astrid in the meantime. All right. So somebody's broken Astrid's nose. I sympathize, I really do, whoever Astrid may be. But you'll have to go looking for somebody else to threaten, because it wasn't me.'

Frank pulled the .38 out of his inside pocket. The hammer got caught on the lining, which tore. He pointed the gun at Charles Lasser's face and cocked it.

'Christ Almighty,' said Charles Lasser.

'Yes,' said Frank. 'Christ Almighty. May Christ Almighty forgive you for what you've done, for all of the innocent people you've killed, and for beating up on Astrid just for your own enjoyment. You're a sick man, Mr Lasser. You murdered

261

my son, you murdered my friends, you murdered women and children who hadn't even begun to live out their lives.'

'Kim Cu'c,' said Charles Lasser, without taking his eyes off the muzzle of Frank's revolver. 'Call security.'

'Police, too, Mr Lasser?'

'Are you deaf or something? I said call *security*. No police. Impress that on security, too – no police.'

'What, are you scared?' Frank asked him, even though his own hands were shaking and he found it difficult to keep it aimed at Charles Lasser's head.

'I'm not scared of anything, Mr Bell. Never have been, and never will be.'

'That's because you've never had to face up to someone your own size.'

'So what are you going to do? Shoot me? Then what? You'll spend fifteen years on death row and then they'll give you a lethal injection.'

'Not if I don't kill you. Not if I simply shoot your balls off.' With that, Frank slowly lowered the gun and pointed it between Charles Lasser's legs.

Charles Lasser took a deep breath. 'I'm telling you . . . I don't know a girl called Astrid. I haven't hurt *any* girl called *anything*.'

'Well, you're a pretty convincing liar, I'll give you that. Kim Cu'c, don't you go for that door! First of all we have to give your boss here a refresher course in "Girls I Have Busted the Noses of." Maybe you don't know Astrid by that name, Mr Lasser, but she came to see you today and you beat her very, very badly – the worst I've ever seen any woman beaten, not that I've seen very many. She's five feet four, brunette with pale blue eyes. She has a pattern of moles across her chest like Andromeda and she always wears an emerald ring. Now, does that jog any memories? It was only this afternoon when you busted her nose, after all.'

Charles Lasser's mouth opened, very slowly, and then closed again. 'You . . .' he began, but then he had to take two deep breaths to compose himself. 'Who the *fuck* have you been talking to?'

'I haven't been talking to anybody. I saw Astrid for myself.'

'Astrid? Is that what she says her name is?'

'Then you *do* know her?'

Charles Lasser didn't answer. His breathing was becoming increasingly labored, and he was almost chewing his breath with his perfect yellow teeth. Frank didn't really know what to do – whether to shoot him in the head or shoot him in the balls or whether to turn around and leave him gasping. He seemed to have struck him harder by describing what Astrid looked like than he could ever have done with a .38 bullet.

'I want your assurance,' said Frank, growing bolder.

'What?'

'Here and now, I want you to give me your assurance that you'll never see Astrid again.'

Charles Lasser shook his head in apparent disbelief. 'My *assurance*? How can I give my assurance?'

'It's simple. I count to five. If by the time I count to five you say "I promise that I'll never see Astrid again," I put the gun away and I leave. If you don't, I blow your balls off.'

'You're pathetic,' said Charles Lasser. 'Do you know that, Mr Bell? You're completely and utterly sad. You don't even know what the fuck you're asking me to do, do you?'

Frank was confused. 'I'm telling you to leave her alone, that's all! Is that so difficult to understand?'

Charles Lasser started to laugh – the loud, desperate laughter of somebody who finds the world so ridiculous that he can't think what else to do. 'I don't know where you belong, Mr Bell. I think you're too crazy even for a nuthouse.' Then abruptly he stopped laughing. 'You're not going to kill me, though, are you? You're not even going to shoot my balls off. Let me tell you this, Mr Bell: any man who walks into my office with a gun and threatens me with it, he'd better fucking use it or else he's going to pay.'

'I don't need a gun,' Frank retorted. 'All I have to do is tell the media about you and Astrid.'

'Tell them what? The cops have interviewed me already. I don't know any Astrid.'

'But you know a girl with an emerald ring and a pattern of moles like Andromeda.'

Without any warning at all, Charles Lasser got off the edge

of his desk, took two steps toward Frank, and whacked at his wrist with his golf club. The gun flew out of his hand and tumbled on to the carpet. Frank turned around, and as he did so, Charles Lasser whacked him again, right across the side of his head.

At first he couldn't open his eyes. He had a cracking headache, worse than any headache he had ever experienced before. He felt as if his skull was actually split open, just above the bridge of his nose.

Eventually he managed to open his left eye. He was lying in the back of a panel van, with a corrugated aluminum floor, between stacks of khaki boxes and cheap gray removers' blankets. The van's roof was made of amber-tinted fiberglass, through which he could make out a dark shadow and a narrow band of sunlight, as if it were parked in a garage, or under a bridge. He struggled to sit up and realized that his wrists were tightly tied up behind him, and his ankles, too. His right eyelid felt like it was glued together, and he could feel a map of sticky blood all over his face.

'Jesus,' he said. The pain in his head was almost unbearable. He thought of rolling over on to his side, but he was afraid that it would hurt too much. Instead he tried to concentrate on who he was and what he was doing here. 'Frank Bell,' he croaked, after a while. And when he said that, he remembered Charles Lasser hitting his wrist, but that was all.

He had no idea how long he had been lying here. It was obviously daylight, but it could have been the following morning. He felt stomach-empty sick, but he hadn't eaten anything before he had gone to see Charles Lasser, and the blow to his head could be making him feel nauseous. That, and the oily chemical smell that permeated the back of the van.

He managed to lift up his head a couple of inches. Not only was he tied up, hand and foot, but he was wearing a thick blue canvas vest. Raising his chin a little more, he could see that the vest had deep pockets in it, and that the pockets were filled with putty-colored blocks that looked like Play-Doh.

He let his head drop back. He was all dressed up like a suicide bomber.

About five minutes later, he lifted up his head again. It was gloomy in the back of the van, but there was enough light for him to be able to read the stenciled words on the side of the khaki boxes. IMI – Handle With Care. It didn't take an explosives expert to work out that there were enough demolition blocks in here to bring down a sizeable building.

'Hey!' he shouted.

He waited, but there was no answer. 'Hey!' he shouted again, and kicked his heels on the floor.

Still no answer. 'Get me out of here! Do you hear me? Get me the hell out of here! The cops are going to come looking for me! Do you hear me? I told the cops where I was going!'

He listened and listened. He could faintly hear traffic, and the sound of an airplane. He lowered his head again. He could only imagine what Charles Lasser had planned for him. This van was probably going to be used for Dar Tariki Tariqat's next attack on the entertainment industry, and when it blew up, he was going to be inside it, dressed like a martyr. If there was enough left of him for the crime scene team to identify, it was probably going to be assumed that he was a member of Dar Tariki Tariqat, too.

Why the hell hadn't he pulled the trigger when he'd had the chance? He had thought that he had been angry enough to kill Charles Lasser, after the way that he had beaten Astrid, but maybe the truth was that he would never be angry enough to kill anybody. He was a comedy writer. The worse things got, the funnier they were. He couldn't even stop himself from thinking what his friends would say, when he was blown to smithereens. 'That was Frank all over.'

He waited and waited and gradually the throbbing in his head began to subside, although his wrists and ankles were tied too tightly and they began to feel cold and numb. He wondered if Astrid had seen a doctor at the Sisters of Jerusalem. He wondered if she was wondering where he was. He wondered if *anybody* was wondering where he was.

He thought about Dusty and Henry, in *Pigs*, about writing

a story in which Dusty thought that Henry was kidnapped, except that he wasn't really kidnapped, he was hiding because Dusty had called him 'the stupidest thing since a single sock-suspender.'

He thought about *The Process*, and the susurration of the desert sand. You may never pass this way again in a lifetime. You have crossed the street, my friend, and you can never go back.

Maybe an hour later, he heard voices outside. He thought about shouting out but then decided against it. The voices went away.

He might have slept for another half-hour, although he wasn't sure. Suddenly he felt somebody shaking his shoulder.

'*Wake up!*'

He opened his eyes. It was Danny. He looked pale and worried and his hair was sticking up at the back, like it used to do when he first woke up in the morning. He was still wearing his funeral suit.

'Danny?'

'Wake up, we haven't got much time!'

'Am I dreaming this?' Frank asked him.

'No . . . turn over.'

'What?'

'Turn over, on to your front.'

Frank hesitated. He couldn't decide if he was dreaming this or not. But Danny had saved him back at the Sunset Marquis, hadn't he? And what had Nevile said, that spirits always stay close to the family they love? He rolled over, grunting with pain.

'Keep very, very still,' said Danny. 'I'm going to untie your knots, but it's very difficult.'

Frank's face was pressed against one of the corrugations in the floor, and he had an agonizing pain in the small of his back. He was trembling, but he managed to keep still while Danny tried to untie him.

Danny said, 'It's trying to *move* things, that's what I'm not very good at. I can touch things, but I can't really feel them.'

Over twenty minutes went past. Frank couldn't feel Danny's

fingers at all, only coldness, like a soft icy draft blowing through the crack in a window, in winter. But he could feel the cords that tied his wrists, and millimeter by millimeter they were working loose.

'Danny, even if you can't do this, I want to thank you for trying.'

'I can do it, Daddy. Just keep still.'

'You know how much I love you, don't you? You know that I never meant to hurt you?'

'I know.'

The cord jerked looser, and then suddenly the knot unraveled and Frank's hands were free. He rolled around again, on to his back, and managed to sit up. Danny was kneeling next to him, smiling.

'You're something, you know that? You're really something.'

'I'm always close by, Daddy. I can't let anybody hurt you.'

Frank shook his head. 'I was the one who was always supposed to look after *you*.'

'It doesn't matter,' said Danny. 'In proper families, everybody looks after everybody else.'

'Danny,' said Frank, and his eyes filled up with tears. He reached out to hold him close but Danny folded up and disappeared, as if he were as insubstantial as a silk scarf. Frank sat still for a few minutes, rubbing the circulation back into his wrists. Then he leaned forward and started untying his ankles.

Another two hours passed in silence. Then suddenly there was a loud bang and the back doors of the panel van were unlocked. Somebody said, 'Here you go, sir. Step up on this.' The van was shaken from side to side, and then the door was closed.

Frank looked up. Charles Lasser was standing amongst the boxes, looking down at him. He was wearing a baggy suit of natural-colored linen, with a large green handkerchief crammed into the breast pocket.

'You're awake, then, Mr Bell?' he said in a voice as rich as fruitcake.

Frank didn't answer.

267

'I guess you're interested to know how long you've been here. Well, I can tell you. Almost fifteen hours. The time is twenty minutes before noon.'

'The cops know that I came looking for you,' said Frank.

'No, they don't. Nobody knows that you came looking for me.'

'Astrid knows.'

'How many times? There *is* no Astrid.'

'Oh, really? So what was it that upset you so much when I described her?'

Charles Lasser smoothed his hand through his hair, again and again, as if to reassure himself that his head was still there. 'I wanted to ask you about that, Mr Bell. Where did you see this girl, and when?'

'I met her after you bombed The Cedars. My son was killed that day. She helped me to get through it.'

'You met her *after* The Cedars was bombed?'

'That's right. We've been meeting each other, on and off, ever since.'

'You never met her before?'

Frank gritted his teeth in exasperation. 'What do you care?'

'I care a great deal, Mr Bell. But I think you're telling me lies. Either that, or you're totally mad. Who told you I hurt her?'

'Nobody told me. I saw the bruises for myself, the cigarette burns. I followed her and she went to Star-TV and then she went to your house.'

Charles Lasser pressed his hands together as if he were praying. 'I don't understand this at all.'

'What's to understand?'

Charles Lasser was thoughtful for a moment. Then he looked around at all of the khaki boxes and said, 'I suppose you've guessed what's going to happen to you now. In fifteen minutes' time, this van will be driven through the gates of Culver Studios. Once it's well inside the studio complex, I'm going to take *this* out.'

He reached into his inside pocket and produced a black plastic box with a red button on it. 'A remote control, which is tuned to the detonator inside that very fashionable vest

268

you're wearing. Yes, Mr Bell – *you* are going to set off this particular bomb, or at least everybody will think that you did.

'There probably won't be very much left of you, but what there is will identify you as a suicide bomber from Dar Tariki Tariqat, which will make sure that yours is a name that Hollywood will speak of from this day forward with hatred and disgust. Oh – and more than likely, your father's name, too, because everybody will assume that you were abused when you were younger, like every other member of Dar Tariki Tariqat.'

'What the hell is *wrong* with you?' said Frank.

'Nothing at all. It's just that when I take my revenge, I like it to be very comprehensive, and wide ranging, and complete.'

'Revenge? Revenge for what?'

Charles Lasser looked at his Rolex. 'I have to be going, Mr Bell. I have a meeting at Spago's and you have a meeting in hell.'

'Just tell me why,' said Frank. 'If you're going to blow me to bits, I think I deserve that much.'

Charles Lasser hunkered down beside him. His linen pants were too tight between his legs, so that his testicles bulged. He smelled of stale cigars and a very heavy aftershave.

'I was born in Lithuania, Mr Bell, to a family so poor that I didn't have a pair of shoes until I was twelve years old. My father beat me and abused me every day. But one night, when I was fifteen, he climbed into my bed, drunk as usual, and I strangled him with my bare hands. I carried his body downstairs to the living room and sat him in his chair, and I poured lamp oil all over him. Then I set fire to him.'

There was a staccato knock at the van's rear door. 'Mr Lasser, sir? We're getting pushed for time.'

Charles Lasser called back, 'Coming, Michael!' Then he leaned closer to Frank's ear and said, 'On that night, when my father's body was blazing in front of me, I swore that I would never let anybody take advantage of me, ever again. I would never let anybody scorn me or laugh at me. I would always have my revenge, no matter how long it took, and I would always make sure that my revenge was a hundred times worse than what had been done to me.'

'And you call *me* mad?'

Charles Lasser gave him a slow, amused smile. 'I like you, Mr Bell. I'm sorry our acquaintance has to be so brief.'

'Me too,' said Frank, and as Charles Lasser turned to leave, he seized him around the neck and hit his head against the side of the van as hard as he could.

Charles Lasser gave an extraordinary high-pitched squeal, like an injured pig. Frank grabbed both of his ears and hit his head again, and again, and again. The van boomed like the inside of a kettle drum.

'Everything OK, Mr Lasser?' called the voice from outside.

'Everything's fine!' Frank shouted back, trying to sound gruff.

'Only a couple of minutes to go, Mr Lasser.'

Panting, Frank wrestled himself out of the suicide vest. Then he lifted up Charles Lasser's lolling arms, one after the other, and tugged it on to him. It was a tight fit, because he was so huge, but he managed to fasten two out of the three buckles at the front. Then he took the remote control box out of Charles Lasser's pocket and wedged it into his belt.

'Mr Lasser! Time to go!'

Frank slapped Charles Lasser's face. 'Wake up, you bastard! Come on, wake up!'

'That's it, Mr Lasser, else we're going to miss our twelve o'clock deadline!'

'Wake up, for Christ's sake!' Frank hissed at him. He hoped to God that he hadn't killed him. There was blood on his collar and his face was mottled and gray.

'Wake up, will you, for Christ's sake!'

Charles Lasser's eyelids quivered, and then he snorted and opened his eyes. He stared at Frank, trying to focus.

'Get up,' Frank ordered.

Charles Lasser looked around. He blinked once, and then he blinked again. Then he filled his lungs and roared, 'You piece of shit! I'll rip your fucking head off and piss down your neck!' He grabbed hold of one of the support bars along the side of the van, and heaved himself on to his feet.

Frank stumbled back. He hadn't expected him to wake up so volcanically. He took out the remote control box, yanked

270

out its antenna, and held it up in front of Charles Lasser's face.

'Stay there! Don't move!'

'You pathetic moron,' sneered Charles Lasser. 'Michael! Louis! Get in here!'

'Don't move,' Frank repeated. 'I don't think you understand what's happened here. You see what this is?'

Charles Lasser frowned at the remote control box, trying to get it into focus. Realization spread slowly across his face. Then he looked down at his chest and placed both his hands on his big, flat RDX breasts.

The rear doors were opened wide, and two men in brown coveralls climbed into the van. One was bald and wore earrings; the other had a shock of black hair like a young Columbo.

'Stay where you are!' Frank screamed at them. He sounded much shriller than he had meant to, like a panicking ballet dancer. The two men ignored him and started to push their way forward between the boxes.

'Do what he says!' Charles Lasser bellowed.

'Mr Lasser?' said the bald one.

'Don't you understand English? Do what he says! Or haven't you noticed that I'm wearing twenty-five pounds of plastic explosive and he's holding the remote?'

The man with the shock of black hair crossed himself twice. The bald one simply looked confused.

'Back off,' Frank ordered them. 'Get out of the van, and then walk away. When Mr Lasser and I climb out of here, I don't want to see you anywhere in sight, otherwise it's *boom*! You got it?'

'Boom, yes, OK, we got it,' said the man with the black hair. He pulled at the other man's arm and together they retreated to the rear of the van and scrambled out.

Frank turned to Charles Lasser. 'Now you.'

'And supposing I refuse? If you press that button in here, then that's both of us gone.'

'You know something?' said Frank. 'It would be worth it.'

Charles Lasser looked at him for a moment, and then he said, 'What do you want me to do? Apologize?'

'That's up to you. All I want you to do is confess.'

'There's still nothing to connect me with Dar Tariki Tariqat. Believe me, I was very careful about that. Nothing to connect me, except you.'

'Just get out of the van,' Frank told him.

Charles Lasser wiped the sweat from his forehead with the back of his hand. 'I could turn your life around for you, Mr Bell. You could write a show for Star-TV, and I'd give it the kind of promotion that most writers can only dream about. I could pay you three million dollars a year.'

'Get out of the van, please,' Frank repeated.

'Nobody's a saint, Mr Bell, not even you.'

'What kind of a man are you? You killed my only son, you killed my friends, you killed dozens of innocent men, women and children, and now you're offering me a TV show?'

'Life has to go on, Mr Bell.'

'Out.'

Twenty-Nine

Charles Lasser shrugged and began to shuffle toward the rear of the van. Frank followed him, keeping his thumb on the remote control box. When he reached the tailgate, Charles Lasser said, 'You're sure you won't reconsider?'

Frank said nothing. He was trembling all over and he felt as if his head were being repeatedly struck with a pein hammer. Charles Lasser climbed down to the ground and Frank said, 'Back away. That's it. Further.' He jumped down to the ground himself and looked around. The van was parked in a lock-up garage at the rear of a derelict warehouse. Outside, there was a wide concrete apron, glaring in the midday sun, where two rusty semis were parked. There was no sign of the bald man or the man with the shock of black hair.

'Where is this?' Frank demanded.

'Just off Hughes Airport. Fifteen minutes away from Culver

272

Studios. David O. Selznick burned down Atlanta at Culver Studios. Well, what he actually burned down was derelict sets from *King Kong*, *Last of the Mohicans* and *Little Lord Fauntleroy*. Me, I accept no substitutes. When I blow up Hollywood, I blow up Hollywood.'

They walked out across the concrete. After they had gone about seventy-five yards, Frank said, 'Stop. That's it. Stay there.' Charles Lasser stopped, and Frank backed well away from him.

'So, you're going to blow me up now, are you?' Charles Lasser asked him.

'Call nine-one-one,' said Frank. 'Tell them who you are, and where we are, and tell them you want to make a confession.'

'And what if I won't?'

'I think there's enough evidence here to prove that you were responsible for Dar Tariki Tariqat, don't you? The van, the explosives . . .'

'There's no evidence, Mr Bell. The police and the FBI can search till Doomsday, they won't find a single document or a single fingerprint or a single computer file that links Charles Lasser with Dar Tariki Tariqat.'

At that moment, however, Frank saw somebody approaching them. At first it was difficult to make out who it was, because of the rippling heat haze rising off the concrete, but as the figure came nearer he saw that it was a young woman in a white cotton dress. Charles Lasser realized that Frank was staring over his shoulder, so he turned around and saw the young woman for himself.

Almost half a minute went past. An aircraft screamed overhead, landing at LAX, and for a few seconds they were deafened. But as the screaming subsided, Frank heard Charles Lasser said, '*No.*'

The young woman came closer until she was standing only a few feet away from them. It was Astrid, her hair pinned back with white daisy barrettes. She was wearing mirror sunglasses so that it was impossible to see her eyes.

Charles Lasser stared at her and then he turned to Frank. He seemed incapable of speech.

273

'Here you are, then,' Frank challenged him. 'This is the Astrid who doesn't exist. This is the Astrid you've been beating up on. *Now* do you know who she is?'

'Her name's not Astrid,' said Charles Lasser. He sounded almost panicky.

'Whatever her name is, this is the woman.'

'*It's not possible!*' Charles Lasser screamed.

'Of course it's possible. Here she is.'

'*It's not possible because she's dead!*'

'Dead? What the hell are you talking about?'

'*She's dead! She's dead! She's dead!*'

Frank looked at Astrid in bewilderment. 'Do you know what he's talking about?'

'Oh, yes,' said Astrid, and took off her sunglasses. He saw now that she had no bruises on her face and that her nose wasn't swollen at all. In fact she looked exactly as she had on the morning that The Cedars had been bombed. And then it occurred to him – *how did she know where I was*? *And how did she get here*? There was no car in sight, and he hadn't seen a taxi.

Astrid started to walk toward Charles Lasser but he raised both hands as if he were trying to defend himself. 'Get away from me! Don't touch me! Get away!'

'Astrid!' called Frank. 'He's got explosives on him! Keep well back!'

Astrid stopped, and smiled at him. 'Do you think I care about that? He's right, Frank. Nothing can frighten me now.'

Charles Lasser dropped to his knees on the concrete. 'I didn't know you were going to join them, did I? How was I to know?'

'Didn't it occur to you that I was a prime candidate?'

'I didn't know where you were! I didn't know how to reach you!'

'You wouldn't have tried to, even if you had known. Look at you! Just look at you! You miserable, sweaty, cowardly bully!'

Charles Lasser squeezed his eyes tight shut and clenched his fists. His face was crimson and glistening with perspiration. Frank could almost feel the pressure rising inside of him,

274

like a steam boiler that was just about blow. Suddenly he popped open his eyes and roared, 'You're not here! You're dead and you deserve to be dead!' He climbed to his feet and staggered stiff-legged toward Astrid, his arms extended, as if he were walking through a shopping mall in a zombie movie.

'Astrid!' Frank yelled at her. 'Get away from him!'

But Astrid stayed where she was, still smiling, her eyes serenely half closed. Her white dress reflected the sunshine in a blurry dazzle, so that Frank felt as if he were looking at her through layers of muslin curtains.

Charles Lasser seized her by the throat and started to shake her head backward and forward. 'Lasser!' Frank shouted. 'Lasser, let her go!'

Charles Lasser was letting out that furious pig-like screech and pressing his thumbs so deeply into Astrid's throat that they almost disappeared. Astrid's face was strangely expressionless and her arms and legs were floppy, as if she were a life-size doll rather than a woman.

'Lasser!' Frank bellowed. But just then the remote control box flew out of his hand. He made a grab for it, missed, and made another grab for it.

There was a moment when the world seemed to disappear and there was nothing.

Somebody punched Frank square in the chest, and he found that he was flying backward. He tumbled helplessly over and over, and then he hit the concrete, jarring his shoulder, hitting his head, twisting his back. He lay there, winded, for five or ten seconds, and then he realized that he was wet. His face was wet, his hair was wet, his shirt was soaked through.

He sat up. He lifted both hands and saw that he was smothered in blood. He thought for one moment that he had been horribly injured, but then he looked around and realized that the blood had been sprayed in all directions, and that it had come from the spot where Charles Lasser had been standing.

A cloud of smoke hovered in the air like a huge gray vulture with outstretched wings. Beneath it, strewn all over the concrete, were pieces of Charles Lasser. His legs had been blown off at the hip and were lying at an angle, as if they were running. Not far away, his pelvis lay like a bloodstained

275

washbasin. His intestines had unraveled into yards of multi-colored gack. At first Frank couldn't see his head, but eventually he spotted it close to the garage doors, looking in the opposite direction, as if he was deliberately being stand-offish. There was no sign of Astrid anywhere. Not her body, not her white dress, nothing.

Frank climbed unsteadily to his feet. His ears were ringing but he could still hear the next 747 that went over, which blotted out everything. He didn't know what to do. It occurred to him that he ought to call the police, but he wouldn't be surprised if somebody hadn't heard the explosion and dialed 911 already.

He felt extraordinarily light-headed, almost *triumphant*. He kept turning around and around, wanting to tell somebody what he had done, but there was nobody there.

Thirty

Nevile opened the door himself. 'Come on in, Frank. Good to see you.'

He led Frank through to the living room, where a bottle of rosé wine was waiting in a frosty silver ice bucket. He was wearing flappy black Spanish-style pants and a satin shirt that flowed like quicksilver.

'How are you feeling?' he asked. 'You're looking a little worse for wear, to say the least.'

Stiffly, Frank eased himself into one of the white leather chairs and took off his sunglasses to reveal two purple-bruised eyes. 'Considering I was hit on the head with a golf club and blown up with plastic explosive, I think I'm in damn good shape.'

Nevile poured him a glass of wine. 'I was down at headquarters this morning, talking to Lieutenant Chessman. He says they're totally baffled by what happened, which doesn't surprise me. The police are always baffled. It's their natural state of mind. The crime scene people are still collecting up Charles Lasser with grapefruit spoons. Perhaps they'll know a little more when they've finished their lab work, but I doubt it.'

Frank said nothing for a long time. He wasn't quite sure how he was going to phrase his question. Eventually, however, he said, 'Did you have any idea?'

'What? About Astrid being dead?'

'You make it sound so . . . commonplace.'

'Being dead *is* commonplace. Let's face it, Frank, the dead outnumber the living by millions to one.'

'She seemed so *alive*. I could feel her, touch her, talk to her. Make love to her.'

Nevile nodded. 'I know. She was a very strong spirit, very determined.'

He went to the window and looked out. Frank could see his reflected face looking back in. He said, 'When you first introduced us, I had a very strong feeling that she wasn't quite what she appeared to be, although I didn't immediately realize why. And there was something else, too, for which I'm kicking myself. I smelled *vinegar*, which is the same smell I picked up at The Cedars. The acid aroma of extreme vengefulness. I'm just sorry that I didn't connect it.'

'She wanted me to kill Charles Lasser, didn't she?' said Frank. 'And she didn't care if I died doing it.'

Nevile nodded. 'I'm afraid so. She had such *hatred*, but she couldn't tell you who had killed her, not directly. Spirits can't do that, which is something of a pity, as far as we psychic detectives are concerned. It would make our lives so much easier. But . . . she gave you a motive for punishing Charles Lasser, didn't she? Jealousy, one of the most destructive motives of all.'

He sipped his wine, and then he said, 'The first time Danny appeared to us, that was Astrid, taking his shape. She was deliberately trying to break up your marriage, so that you would need to find somebody else to comfort you. The *last* time she appeared as Danny was when she met us at Travel Town. She must have been growing frustrated because she

277

gave us the clue about St John the Evangelist and Orange Grove Avenue – that was about as much information as the laws of natural justice would allow.

'Charles Lasser insisted that he didn't know any Astrid because it was true. He didn't. All of Astrid's bruises and cigarette burns were totally illusory. If she could appear as somebody else – as Danny – then she could certainly look as if somebody had beaten her up. She never went to see Charles Lasser, Frank, and Charles Lasser never hurt her. At least, not then.'

'What about the real Danny, when he appeared?'

'Well, you could certainly tell the difference *then*, couldn't you? The real Danny did everything he could to take care of you, and to stop you from being hurt. He untied you, even though that must have taken almost all of his strength.'

'I guess . . . I guess he must have forgiven me, then.'

Nevile laid a hand on his shoulder. 'Oh, yes. I'm sure of it. But look here, there's one more thing I want you to see.'

He sat down next to Frank and switched on the television. Then he started his video player. On to the screen came an episode of *Law & Order*, the fictional cop drama dealing with sex offenders in New York City.

'This was one of the early episodes,' Nevile explained. 'It took me quite a while to find it. But look, here you are. The two detectives go into this bar to talk to this hooker – and what do you know?'

Frank saw Christopher Meloni and Mariska Hargitay. But he also saw a striking young girl in a silvery sequined top and silver hoop earrings. Astrid.

'How did you find this?' he asked. 'Freeze it – let me take a look at her.'

Nevile froze the picture and there she was, shuddering slightly, with that dreamy look in her eyes and that smile that had tightened his scalp like a drumhead.

'I looked up Tori Fisher on the Internet,' said Nevile. 'You know, the girl suicide bomber at The Cedars. I kept thinking to myself, why did the security guard open the gates and allow that van into the schoolyard, without checking the driver's credentials? The only feasible answer was that he knew one of the people in the van. He knew Tori Fisher, and the reason he knew Tori Fisher was because she had once attended The Cedars herself, as a pupil. Tori Fisher was the stage name of Amanda Lasser, the only daughter of Charles Lasser and his second wife, Rebecca. Of course, he was on to his fourth wife by the time he popped his clogs.'

'"Daddy hurt me,"' Frank quoted. 'That was what she said when she was impersonating Danny. It wasn't Danny referring to me at all . . . it was Astrid talking about her father.'

'That's right,' said Nevile. 'And that's why she joined Dar Tariki Tariqat. She was the victim of serious sexual abuse and she wanted to get her revenge on society at large. What she didn't realize, until the instant she was killed, was that her own father had created Dar Tariki Tariqat as a bogus means to a very vindictive end.'

'How would she have realized that?'

Nevile switched off the television. 'When you die, Frank, you'll realize that everything is open to you. There are no secrets in heaven.'

Frank finished his wine. 'I feel exhausted,' he admitted. 'I think I need a good night's sleep.'

'You won't have another glass?'

'No, thanks.' He stood up. 'I just want to thank you for all of your help. If you hadn't agreed to do those séances . . .'

'Don't thank me, Frank. I could have had you killed.'

Frank took hold of both of his hands, and squeezed them. 'Let's get together in a couple of days. I'd like to talk some more about this. In fact, I think I need to.'

'You could always try Margot. I'm sure she'll listen.'

Frank left the house, climbed into his car, and drove up the steeply winding driveway to the main road. He was about to turn left, back to Hollywood, when he looked into his rear-view mirror and realized that he had left his sunglasses behind. He drove as far as the Earth Mother Juice Stand and did a U-turn. He steered slowly back down the driveway to Nevile's house, parked the car and climbed out.

To his bewilderment, all of the blinds had been drawn. He went up to the front door, pressed the door chimes, and waited. It was strange, but the front yard was strewn with dead leaves, as if it hadn't been swept in months. There were even dead leaves up against the front door. He pressed the chimes again.

He waited and waited but nobody answered. 'Nevile?' he shouted. 'Nevile, are you there?' He listened, but there was only the wind, sighing in the trees.

He pushed the front door and it opened. 'Nevile? Is everything OK?' He hesitated, and then he stepped inside.

The house was deserted. There was no furniture, no sculptures, no paintings hanging on the walls. Frank's footsteps echoed as he walked from room to room. Eventually he opened the door of Nevile's study, and found it empty. No books, no marble-topped table from Delphi, nothing. Not even marks on the wall where his photographs might have hung.

'Nevile,' he said under his breath. A few dry leaves rattled into the hallway, and circled around in a little dance. 'Nevile, you bastard.'

Frank saw a dark-blue rectangle on the floor. He bent down, picked it up and turned it over. It was a card from the Cats and Moons deck. It showed a star map of Andromeda, and underneath it were the words YOU WILL NEVER PASS THIS WAY AGAIN IN A LIFETIME.

He drove back down Laurel Canyon. As he drove, he started to hum, and then he started to sing. He was singing for Astrid, or Tori, or Amanda. He hoped that she could hear him, wherever she was.

'The girl I love is so beautiful
She makes the roses look ugly.
Her eyes they shine like a bald man's bean
And her sweaters fit oooh so snugly.

'The girl I love is a goddess on earth
But one day she fell from a blimp.
She hit a haystack at fifty-four and a half miles an hour
And she now has a left-footed limp.

280

'The girl I love is brilliant and bright,
"But I'm going noplace," she frowned.
"Every time that I try to walk straightly
I keep going round and around.

"'I go round, I go round, I go round, I go round
I try but I simply can't starpet.
I'm a gimp with a limp, a left-footed limp
And I've worn a round hole in the carpet."'

As he reached the intersection of Laurel Canyon and Hollywood Boulevard, he saw two odd figures standing beside the traffic signals. One was an old man in a duck-billed cap and baggy blue shorts, with legs that were gnarled with varicose veins. Next to him, holding his hand, his hair shining in the sunlight, was Danny. They didn't wave; they just stood there, watching him, and then they turned around and walked away.

A car horn hooted behind him. The signals had turned to green. Frank lifted his hand in apology and drove on. But he had only gone as far as Genesee Avenue when he had to pull into the side of the road, because he was blinded by tears.